T0116322

ALSO BY DAVID MORRELL

NOVELS

First Blood
Testament
Last Reveille
The Totem
Blood Oath
The Brotherhood of the Rose
The Fraternity of the Stone
Rambo (First Blood Part II)
The League of Night and Fog
Rambo III
The Fifth Profession
The Covenant of the Flame
Assumed Identity
Desperate Measures
The Totem (Complete and Unaltered)
Extreme Denial
Double Image
Burnt Sienna
Long Lost
The Protector
Creepers
Scavenger
The Spy Who Came for Christmas
The Shimmer
The Naked Edge
Murder as a Fine Art
Inspector of the Dead
Ruler of the Night

SHORT FICTION

The Hundred-Year Christmas
Black Evening
Nightscape
Before I Wake

ILLUSTRATED FICTION

Captain America: The Chosen
Spider-Man: Frost
Wolverine: Feral

NONFICTION

John Barth: An Introduction
Fireflies: A Father's Tale of Love and Loss
The Successful Novelist: A Lifetime of Lessons about Writing and Publishing
Stars in My Eyes: My Love Affair with Books, Movies, and Music

EDITED BY

American Fiction, American Myth: Essays by Philip Young
edited by David Morrell and Sandra Spanier
Tesseracts Thirteen: Chilling Tales of the Great White North
edited by Nancy Kilpatrick and David Morrell
Thrillers: 100 Must Reads
edited by David Morrell and Hank Wagner

THE FRATERNITY OF
THE STONE

BALLANTINE BOOKS TRADE PAPERBACKS

New York

THE
FRATERNITY OF
THE STONE

David Morrell

A   N O V E L

2009 Ballantine Books Trade Paperback Edition

Copyright © 1985 by David Morrell
Dossier copyright © 2009 by Random House, Inc.

All rights reserved.

Published in the United States by Ballantine Books,
an imprint of The Random House Publishing Group,
a division of Random House, Inc., New York.

BALLANTINE and colophon are registered trademarks of Random House, Inc.
MORTALIS and colophon are trademarks of Random House, Inc.

ISBN 978-0-345-51450-9

This edition published by arrangement with St. Martin's Press, Inc.

Book design by Mary A. Wirth

147028622

*With love
to my mother, Beatrice*

CONTENTS

PROLOGUE: WARRIORS OF GOD   xiii
The Desert Fathers
The Old Man of the Mountain
Holy Terror

PART ONE: ATONEMENT   1
The House of the Dead

PART TWO: PILGRIMAGE   67
Strange New World

PART THREE: GUARDIAN   119
Retreat House

PART FOUR: RESURRECTION   167
Satan's Horn

PART FIVE: VISITATION   215
The Sins of the Past

PART SIX: CHARTREUSE   259
Mirror Image, Double Exposure

PART SEVEN: JANUS   295
The Sins of the Present

PART EIGHT: JUDGMENT   351
The Fraternity of the Stone

EPILOGUE: "AND FOR YOUR PENANCE . . ."   429
The Wanderers
Exile

DOSSIER   441

In some respects, the intelligence profession resembles monastic life with the disciplines and personal sacrifices reminiscent of medieval orders.

—THE U.S. SENATE'S CHURCH COMMITTEE
REPORT ON INTELLIGENCE ACTIVITIES, 1976

WARRIORS
OF GOD

THE DESERT FATHERS

✤

Egypt, 381.

The Roman Empire, dangerously fragmented, made a desperate bid for unity by choosing Christianity as its sole official religion. A few Christian fanatics, disillusioned by this contamination of politics into their religion, retreated from society, venturing into the desert of Egypt, where they lived in caves to seek a mystical conjunction with their God. As word about these spiritual hermits spread, other disillusioned Christians soon joined them, establishing an austere religious community based on fasting, prayer, and physical mortification. By 529, the severe traditions of what some called these "holy madmen" had begun to drift northward through Europe.

And Christian monasticism was born.

THE OLD MAN OF THE MOUNTAIN

✠

Persia, 1090.

Hassan ibn al-Sabbah, leader of a fanatical sect of Muslims, adopted murder as a sacred duty in his fight to wrest control of his country from Turkish invaders and their ally, the Egyptian caliph. His secret organization of religious killers soon spread west to Syria, where his successors each acquired the title "The Old Man of the Mountain." In 1096, the European crusaders invaded the Mideast, commencing their papally authorized Holy War against the Muslims to regain the Holy Sepulchre. These intruders naturally attracted the attention of "The Old Man" and his followers, who were known as *hashishi* because of the hashish they allegedly smoked to achieve religious ecstasy and promote the frenzy with which they prepared themselves to face possible martyrdom.

But *hashishi* was mispronounced by the crusaders.

They carried a different name back to Europe—Assassins.

HOLY TERROR

✦

Palestine, 1192.

Though the sun had begun to set, the desert sand had not yet given up its heat. Surrounded by guards, the voluminous tent—made from heavy sailcloth—billowed slightly from a searing breeze. Exhausted horses, slick with sweat, raised dustclouds as the knights who rode them approached from opposite camps. Flagbearers preceded each column, their respective banners depicting three golden lions above each other upon a field of red—the English—and a golden fleur-de-lis upon a field of blue—the French. Though united in a holy cause, they nonetheless disagreed profoundly about politics between their countries, for the French contested land owned by the English in their territory. Due to these strained relations, neither column was willing to tolerate arriving first and thus being made to suffer the indignity of waiting for the other. Scouts on nearby dunes had signaled the progress of each group, ensuring that both delegations would converge on the tent simultaneously.

The columns met: four emissaries in each, along with their retainers. They peered toward a barren mountain in the distance where armies swarmed amid the smoking ruin of a minareted castle. The siege had been brutal, costly in lives, lasting for almost three months; but at last the Muslims here at Acre had been defeated.

For a moment, political differences between French and English were forgotten. Weary but resolute, they praised each other's valor, congratulating themselves on victory. First bodyguards dismounted, then valets who assisted their lords. In contrast with the pride that had made each group determined not to wait for the other, their courtly manners now required them to offer their rivals the privilege of being the first to enter the tent. Practicality solved the dilemma. Whichever lord was closest agreed to leave his servants behind and step ahead.

Inside, with the flap of the tent secured, the knights stripped off their weapons, helmets, and chain-mail armor. The air was stifling. After the blaze of the desert sun, their eyes adjusted slowly to the murky light. Shadows from the guards outside darkened the walls of the tent.

The knights assessed each other. On this, the Third Crusade to the Holy Land, the lessons of the earlier Crusades had taught them to wear long gowns to preserve their body moisture and prevent the deadly sun from burning their skin. The gowns were pale, attracting less heat than the brilliant colors that they favored in their homeland. The only concession to color was the large red image of a cross that adorned the front of their gowns—along with the coppery splotches of dried heathen blood.

The men had beards. Even so, their cheeks looked gaunt and dehydrated. Raising hoods to cover their matted hair, they drank wine from cups prepared for them. Given the purpose of this meeting, water would have been preferable. Clear heads, after all, were necessary. But the logistics of the Crusade, the massive territory involved, had resulted in insecure supply lines, and wine—which they had saved for a celebration—was the only liquid available. Though thirsty, they drank it sparingly. For now.

The tallest, most muscular man, an English lord known for

his skill with a battleax, spoke first, using the accepted diplomatic language, French. His name was Roger of Sussex. "I recommend that we complete our business first before . . ." He gestured toward the bread, olives, and dried spicy meat laid out for them.

"Agreed," said the leader of the French contingent, Jacques de Wisant. "Your King Richard will not be joining us?"

"We thought it prudent not to inform him about this meeting. And your King Philip?"

"There are certain matters best discussed in private. Should it prove necessary, he will be told what we decide."

Each knew what the other meant. Though they had guards, they themselves were guards as well, of a higher order. Their function was to arrange protection for their respective kings. Such protection required a network of informers who reported even the vaguest rumors about subversive plots. But seldom were these rumors passed on to Richard or Philip. What a king didn't know would not alarm him or make him suspect that his security staff was not what it should be. Dismissal might take the form of an ax to one's neck.

"Very well then," an Englishman, William of Gloucester, said. "I suggest we begin."

The nature of the group changed abruptly. Whereas before the knights had been conscious of their French or English allegiance, now their national rivalries disappeared. They shared a common bond, an exclusive code, comrades in the fraternity of the Greek god, Harpocrates.

Silence. Secrecy.

The Englishman, Roger of Sussex, held a Bible that the monks of his lands had copied for him, bound with leather and gilded with gold. He opened it. "The Book of Daniel," he explained. "The passage in which Daniel keeps control of his tongue despite the threat of being eaten by lions. It seemed appropriate."

The ritual began. The eight knights formed a circle. As one, they solemnly placed their right hand upon the Bible and swore themselves to secrecy.

In imitation of their enemies—and due to the difficulty of transporting furniture—they sat on an ornate rug that their armies had liberated from the defeated Muslim castle. They leaned back on pillows, swirled the wine in their cups, and listened to Pierre de l'Étang.

"As the man responsible for arranging the conditions of this meeting," he said, "I remind you that the guards outside stand well away from the walls of the tent. Provided that your voices remain at a normal level, you won't be heard."

"So my assistants informed me," an Englishman, Baldwin of Kent, replied.

The Frenchman nodded his compliments. "Yes, my own assistants apprised me that they were watched."

Baldwin nodded his compliments in return. "But *my* assistants informed me of something else. Your king intends to divorce his army from Richard's Crusade."

"Indeed?"

Baldwin narrowed his eyes. "Indeed."

"As Frenchmen, we weren't aware that this Crusade belonged to Richard."

"It does if Philip returns to France."

"Ah, yes, I grant the point." Pierre sipped his wine. "Your assistants have excellent sources. And did they tell you when our king intends to lead his army home?"

"Within a fortnight. Philip plans to take advantage of Richard's absence from court. In exchange for the territory that our country owns in France, your king has promised to support Richard's brother in his bid to take over the English throne."

The Frenchman shrugged. "And what do you propose to do with this information, assuming that it's true?"

Baldwin did not answer.

"I respect your tact." Pierre set down his cup. "It does seem that relations between our countries will soon worsen. Consider this, however. Without rivalry, our skills would not be of use."

"And life would not have interest. Which brings us to our reason for requesting this meeting," Jacques de Wisant interrupted.

The Englishmen sat straighter.

"Assuming that your sources are correct," Jacques said, "if indeed we leave the Crusade within a fortnight, we regret that we'll also leave a particularly fascinating unsolved problem. As a parting gesture of the fraternity we share, we'd like to assist you in finding an answer."

Baldwin studied him. "You're referring, of course—"

"To the recent murder of your countryman—Conrad of Montferrat."

"Forgive me for being surprised that an Englishman's death, no matter how shocking, distresses you."

"Almost as much as the previous identically shocking murder of our own countryman—Raymond de Chatillon."

No further explanation was necessary. Six years earlier, a truce between the crusaders and the forces of Saladin had been broken when Raymond de Chatillon attacked the caravan of Saladin's sister. For this violation, there was no peaceful redress, so the great Muslim counter-crusade, the *jihad*, had begun. One year later, during the siege of Jerusalem, Raymond's head had been found on the altar of the Shrine of the Holy Sepulchre. A curved knife lay beside it.

Since then, dozens of identical assassinations had taken place, achieving their intended purpose, teaching fear of the night to the crusading lords. Yesterday, after the fall of the Muslim castle here at Acre, Conrad of Montferrat's head had been found on the altar set up for the victory mass. A curved knife lay beside it, a knife that the crusaders had now learned to identify with The Old Man of the Mountain and his cult of fanatics.

"Assassins." Roger made a face as if intending to spit out his wine. "Cowards. Thieves plundering lives in the dark. The proper way for a lord to die is in daylight in battle, bravely matching his skills with those of his enemy, even if the enemy is heathen. These sneaks have no regard for honor, for dignity, for the pride of the warrior. They're despicable."

"But nonetheless they exist," Pierre de l'Étang pointed out. "More important, they're effective. I confess to morbid suspicions that my own head might be next on the altar."

The others nodded, admitting fears about themselves.

"Still there's nothing we can do, except to gather more bodyguards around us while we sleep," William of Gloucester said. "And even then, these assassins slip past our best defenses. It's as if they can make themselves invisible."

"Don't credit them with mystery," Jacques said. "They're human like ourselves. But highly trained."

"In barbarous tactics. There's no way to fight them," William said.

"I wonder."

The group regarded Jacques intensely.

"You have a suggestion?" Roger asked.

"Perhaps."

"What is it, then?"

"Fight fire with fire."

"I won't consider it," William fumed. "Use their obscene methods against them? Become as cowardly as they are, creeping upon their leaders while they sleep? It's unconscionable."

"But only because it's never been done."

William stood in distress. *Because it goes against the warrior's code.*

"But these sneaks are heathen. Uncivilized," Jacques said. "If they're too primitive to understand honor and dignity, we're not bound to respect them by adhering to the code."

His remark had force. The tent became silent as the group considered the implications.

William nodded. "I confess to wanting Conrad avenged."

"And Raymond," a Frenchman reminded him.

"I'd spear a mad dog regardless of whether he was or wasn't facing me," another Frenchman said, and made a fist.

"But the scheme isn't practical," Baldwin interrupted. "The Muslims would recognize any of us who tried to infiltrate among them. Even the night wouldn't hide the purity of our skin."

"And bear this in mind," Roger added. "No matter if we darkened our skin with substances, we don't understand their language or their ways. If one of them spoke to us while we went among them in disguise, or if we made a wrong gesture . . ."

"I wasn't proposing that we try to infiltrate," Jacques said.

"Then?"

"Not ourselves. We send in one of their own."

"Impossible. They hate us. Where would we find such a—?"

"One who saw the error of his heathen ways, who converted to the one true God, a Muslim who became a Christian."

The English were shocked.

"You're suggesting that you know of such a man?" Roger asked.

Jacques nodded. "In the Benedictine monastery at Monte Cassino in Italy."

The name was resonant. Monte Cassino had been founded

in 529, one of the earliest Christian monasteries, when the austere zeal of the desert fathers spread northward from Egypt through Europe.

"I accepted his order's hospitality for a night on my way here to the Holy Land," Jacques said. "I was given permission to spend an hour with him, and he was given permission to speak. His Christian zeal is remarkable. He'd do anything for the Lord."

"A monk?"

"Indeed."

"That's blasphemy," William said. "To ask a monk to kill?"

"For a sacred cause. The liberation of Christ's Holy Land. Remember that the Pope himself has absolved us of any sins we might commit in this divinely inspired Crusade. I've made inquiries among the priests who came here with us. They feel confident that the monk I have in mind would receive a papal dispensation. Indeed, by becoming a warrior of God, he'd be saving his soul. If it's true that my countrymen and I return to France within a fortnight, I could arrange to stop again at Monte Cassino. I'm sure that he'd be responsive. Rome—and papal encouragement—would not be far away."

The knights peered down at their wine cups.

Baldwin raised his eyes. "But he isn't trained."

"He's familiar with stories he heard about the assassins," Jacques said. "And rumors about their techniques. Mind you, I have technical suggestions of my own."

"How long to prepare him?"

"For what I have in mind? Three months."

"I needed a lifetime to learn my craft," William said. "We have to consider the strong chance that he'll be killed."

"In the attempt," Jacques said. "But don't you see? The attempt is what matters. Once the heathen understand that we—and even one who formerly was their own—are prepared to die for the one true God . . ."

"They'll sleep as restlessly as we do."

Baldwin squinted. "Fight terror with terror?"

"With a difference," Jacques said. "For our fight is holy."

PART ONE

ATONEMENT

THE HOUSE OF THE DEAD

1

It was north of Quentin, Vermont. You could see it partly hidden by fir trees a quarter mile off the two-lane blacktop, to the right on the crest of a hill. Beyond it loomed a higher hill, thick with maple trees, brilliant now in the autumn, vivid orange and yellow and red. A high wire fence ran parallel to the blacktop, the sides veering off at right angles, disappearing back into the forest. You'd have trouble calculating, since you couldn't see how far back the fences went, but you wouldn't be wrong to guess that the property covered at least a hundred acres. The nearest building—apart from the one on the hill—was a boarded-up service station quite a ways behind you, out of sight, on the other side of the corkscrew turn that led to this straightaway. And you wouldn't get to the maple syrup factory up ahead for more than a mile.

Remote. Secluded.

Peaceful.

Glancing toward the pine tree-studded hill, you might suspect that the partly hidden structure, with its gleaming wood, was a millionaire's retreat, a forest hideaway where the pressures of business could be relieved by who could imagine what distractions.

Or possibly the building was a ski resort, closed till the snow fell. Or . . .

But from just driving by, of course, you could never know. There was neither a mailbox nor a sign at the gate, and the gate itself had a thick chain holding it in place—an even thicker lock. The lane on the other side was weedgrown, squeezed by bushes and drooping pines. To be sure, you could always ask at the maple syrup factory if your curiosity lasted till then, but you'd only feel more frustrated as a result. The workers there, true New Englanders, were willing to talk to strangers about the weather but not about their own or their neighbor's business. It wouldn't have mattered, anyhow. They didn't know, either, though there were rumors.

2

From the air, the structure on the hill was larger than the view from the road suggested. Indeed, an elevated vantage point revealed that the building wasn't alone. Smaller buildings—otherwise hidden by pine trees—formed three sides of a square, the fourth of which was the lodge itself. Enclosed by the square was a lawn. Two white-stone walkways intersected at its middle, bordered by flower gardens, trees, and shrubs. The effect was one of balance and order, symmetry, proportion. Soothing. Even the smaller buildings, though joined like rows of townhouses, had small peaked roofs in imitation of the larger peaked roof on the lodge.

Despite the expanse of the estate, however, remarkably few people showed themselves down there. The tiny figure of a groundskeeper tended the lawn. Two miniature workmen harvested apples from an orchard outside one line of buildings. A wisp of smoke rose from a bonfire in a considerable vegetable garden flanking the opposite line of buildings. With so sizable a commitment to agriculture, the estate presumably had many residents, yet except for those few signs of life, the place seemed deserted. If there were guests, it hardly seemed natural for them to ignore the pleasure of this bright crisp autumn day. To remain indoors, they must surely have an important reason.

But then the seclusion of the inhabitants was part of the mystery about this place. Since 1951, when teams of construction workers had arrived from somewhere—not from the local town, though whoever was funding the project at least had the goodness to buy a decent amount of supplies from there—the citizens of Quentin had wondered what was happening on that hill. When the workers put up the gate and departed, the local busybodies noted a fascinating pattern. They recalled stories they'd recently read about the development of the atomic bomb in New Mexico at the end of the war. The government had built a small town on a mountain there, it was said. The local communities had therefore hoped for an increase in business; but they'd waited in vain, for the strange thing was that people went onto that mountain, but—as with the estate on this hill—they didn't come down.

3

The unit, one of twenty in the complex, each the same, consisted of two levels. On the bottom, a workroom contained whatever equipment its occupant had chosen to use to pass his leisure time. In other parts of the complex, some perhaps painted or sculpted or wove, possibly worked with wood and carpentry tools. Or, since each unit had a small private garden enclosed by a wall, adjacent to the workroom, some might practice horticulture, perhaps growing roses.

In the present case, the occupant had chosen exercise and composition. He knew that he couldn't concentrate if his body was not in condition. Indeed, in his former life he'd been intensely devoted to the principles of Zen, aware that exercise itself was spiritual. Each day for an hour he lifted weights, skipped rope, performed calisthenics, and rehearsed the *katas* or dance steps of the Oriental martial arts. He did all this with humility, taking no satisfaction in the perfection of his physique, for he realized that his body was but an instrument of his soul. In fact, the effect of his daily workouts had little obvious result. His torso was lean, ascetic, low on the protein his muscles required to replace the tissue his exercise wore down. He ate no meat. On Friday, he took only bread and water. Some days, he ate nothing. But his discipline gave him strength.

His compositions fulfilled another purpose. During his early months here, he'd been tempted to write about his motive for coming, to purge himself, to vent his anguish. But his need to forget was greater. To relieve the pressure of his urge for self-expression, he'd written haikus first, an understandable choice given his sympathy with Zen. He selected topics with no relevance to what disturbed him—the song of a bird, the breath of the wind. But the nature of a haiku, its complicated tension based on purity and brevity, led him to greater attempts at compression and refinement until no statement at all seemed the perfect haiku, and he stared past his pen toward the vacuum of a barren page. Compulsively, he'd switched to the sonnet form, alternating between Shakespearean and Petrarchan, each with a different rhyme scheme, both demanding a perfect organization of fourteen lines. The problem of that intricate puzzle was enough to occupy him. More interested in how he wrote than what he wrote, he expressed himself about minuscule matters and was able to forget the troubling great ones. He wrote as best he could, not out of pride, but out of respect for the puzzle. Even so, he knew that eloquence eluded him. Perhaps in another unit of this complex, an occupant had—like himself—become engaged with poetry. Perhaps that other occupant had produced such perfectly beautiful sonnets that they rivaled those of Shakespeare and Petrarch themselves.

It wouldn't have mattered. Nothing any occupant devised—paintings, statues, tapestries, or furniture—had any value. All were insignificant. When the men who fashioned them died, they were placed on a board and buried in an unmarked grave, and the objects they left behind, their clothes, their few belongings, their sonnets, even a skipping rope, were destroyed. It would be as if they had never existed.

4

The psychiatrist, as expected, had been a priest. He'd worn the traditional black suit and white collar, his face somewhat wrinkled, bullet-gray, as he lit a cigarette and peered at Drew from across his desk.

"You understand the gravity of your request."

"I've considered it carefully."

"You made your decision—when?"

"Three months ago."

"And you waited . . . ?"

"Till now. To analyze the implications. Naturally I had to be sure."

The priest inhaled from his cigarette, thoughtful, studying Drew. His name was Father Hafer. He was in his late forties, his short hair the same bullet-gray color as his face. Exhaling smoke, he made an offhanded gesture with the cigarette. "Naturally. The other side of the issue is, how can we be sure? Of your commitment? Of your determination and resolve?"

"You can't."

"Well, there it is then."

"But *I* can, and that's what matters. This is what I need. I've resigned myself."

"To what?"

"Not 'to.' "

"I beg your pardon?"

"From." Drew nodded toward the clamorous Boston street beyond the first-floor window of this rectory office.

"Everything? The world?"

Drew didn't respond.

"Of course, that's what the eremitical life is all about. Withdrawal," Father Hafer said and shrugged. "Still, a negative attitude isn't sufficient. Your motive has to be positive as well. Seeking, not merely fleeing."

"Oh, I'm seeking all right."

"Indeed?" The priest raised his eyebrows. "For what?"

"Salvation."

Father Hafer considered him, exhaling smoke. "An admirable answer." He brushed an ash from his cigarette into a metal tray. "So quick to the lips, so readily given. Have you been religious long?"

"For the past three months."

"And before?"

Again Drew didn't respond.

"You *are* a Roman Catholic?"

"I was baptized into the faith. My parents were quite religious." Suddenly remembering how they'd died, he felt his throat ache. "We went to church often. Mass. The Stations of the Cross. I received the sacraments up through confirmation, and you know what they say about confirmation. It made me a soldier of Christ." Drew bitterly smiled. "Oh, I believed."

"And after that?"

"The term is 'lapsed.' "

"Have you made your Easter duty?' "

"Not in thirteen years."

"You understand what that means?"

"By not going to confession and communion before Easter,

I in effect resigned from the faith. I've been unofficially ex-communicated."

"And put your soul in immortal peril."

"That's why I've come to you. To save myself."

"You mean your soul," Father Hafer said.

"That's right. That's what I meant."

They studied each other. The priest leaned forward, placing his elbows on the desk, his eyes somewhat brighter with interest. "Of course . . . Let's review the information you provided on this form. You say that your name is Andrew MacLane."

"It's sometimes shortened to 'Drew.' "

"But if we agree to accept your application, that name will be taken from you. Like everything else you own—a car, for example, or a house—your identity will need to be abandoned. In effect, you'll be no one. You're aware of that?"

Drew raised his shoulders. "So what's in a name?" He allowed the bitter smile to appear now. "A rose by any other name . . ."

"Or by none," the priest said, "would smell as sweet. But to the nose of God . . ."

"We don't exactly smell like roses. I don't, anyhow. That's why I applied. To purify myself."

"You're thirty-one?"

"Correct." Drew hadn't lied. All the information he'd provided on the form was verifiable, as he knew the priest would take pains to discover. What mattered was what he hadn't put down on the form.

"The prime of life," Father Hafer said. "Indeed, even a few years before it if we use thirty-three as the appropriate age for coming into one's own. You're dismissing the possibilities of the road ahead of you. Throwing away your potential, as it were."

"No, I don't think of it that way."

"Then . . . ?"

"I've already discovered my potential."

"And?"

"I didn't like it."

"I don't suppose you'd care to elaborate."

Drew glanced at the floor.

"Eventually you'll have to." Father Hafer seemed troubled. "But never mind. For now, we have other matters to discuss. Our applicants are usually past their maturity, to use a delicate phrase, when they make their request." He shrugged. "Of course, very few request, and even fewer . . ."

"Are chosen. Less than five hundred worldwide. And here in the United States, only twenty, I believe."

"Good, I see that you've done your homework. The point is—to use a less delicate term—most of those men are old." Father Hafer stubbed out his cigarette. "They've pursued their ambitions. They've accomplished, and sometimes haven't, their worldly aims. Now they're ready to spend their dwindling years in retirement. Their decision, though extreme, can be viewed as natural. But you—so young, so robust. Women no doubt find you attractive. Have you considered the implications of giving up female companionship?"

With a stab of longing, he remembered Arlene. "*You* gave it up."

"I gave up sexual relations." Father Hafer sat straighter. "Not female companionship. I encounter women many times a day. A waitress in a restaurant. A clerk at the medical library. A secretary of one of my lay colleagues. All perfectly innocent. The sight of women, rather than tempting me, makes my vow of chastity seem less severe. But if we accede to your request, you'll never see a woman again, and very few men, and even then rarely. I emphasize. For the rest of your life, what you're asking to be is a hermit."

5

The unit's second level, reached by crude pine stairs, consisted of three sections. First the oratory, otherwise known as the "Ave Maria" room, where a simple wooden pew, its kneeler an unpadded board, faced an austere altar with a crucifix on the wall. Beyond it was the study—sacred texts, a table and chair—and then the sleeping quarters—a wood stove, but no bed, just an inch-thick woven-hemp pallet.

The pallet was six feet long and three feet wide. It could easily have been rolled up and placed downstairs in a corner of the workroom, spread out when he needed to rest. But the point was to segregate his various activities. To go from his workroom up to his sleeping quarters, or from his sleeping quarters down to his workroom, he had to pass through the oratory, and the rule required him to stop there each time and pray.

6

"If it's simply a life of devotion that appeals to you," Father Hafer said, "consider a less strict order. The missionary fathers, perhaps?"

Drew shook his head.

"Or possibly the Congregation of the Resurrectionists. They do good work—teaching, for example."

Drew told him, "No."

"Then what about this suggestion? Earlier you mentioned how the sacrament of confirmation had made you a soldier of Christ. I'm sure you're aware that the Jesuits have intensified that concept. They're much more rigorous than the Resurrectionists. Their training takes fifteen years, ample reason for their nickname—the commandos of the Church."

"It's not what I had in mind."

"Because they confront the world?" Father Hafer hurried on. "But during a considerable part of the training period, you'd be cloistered. It's only toward the end that you'd be nudged from the nest, and perhaps by then you'd appreciate the push. And even earlier, at various stages, you'd have a chance to reconsider your priorities, to change your direction if you cared to."

"I don't think so."

Father Hafer sounded more distressed. "There's even another option. The Cistercians. The second most demanding order in the Church. You live in a monastery cut off from the world. Your days are filled with exhausting work, farming, for instance, something that contributes to the order. You never speak. But at least you labor—and pray—in a group. And if you find the life too difficult, you can leave and reapply at a later time, though not beyond the age of thirty-six. The advantage is that there's a system of checks and balances that allows you to change your mind."

Drew waited.

"Good heavens, man, why must you be so determined?" Father Hafer lit another cigarette, flicking his butane lighter. "I'm trying to make you understand. In the fullness of your youth, you're asking to be admitted into the most severe form of worship in the Church. The Carthusians. There's nothing more extreme. It's the total denial of a human being as a social animal. The eremitic way. For the rest of your life, you'd live alone in a cell. Except for an hour of leisure, you'd do nothing but pray. It's complete deprivation. Solitude."

7

He wore a coarse hair shirt, designed to irritate his skin. At times, its aggravating sensation became a pleasure since at least it was an experience, something intense. When that temptation aroused him, he fought to distract himself, praying harder, sometimes flagellating himself with his skipping rope, stifling his groans.

You're not here to enjoy yourself. You came to do penance. To be left alone.

Over the hair shirt, he wore a white robe, and above that a white biblike scapular, and then a white hood. On the limited occasions when he was forced to endure communal rituals such as choir, perverse requirements designed to test his fortitude, he wore a drooping white cowl that hid his face and allowed him to feel invisible.

8

"There's no need for us to be this intense," Father Hafer said, forcing a smile. "Why don't we relax for a moment? Debate may be good for the mind, after all, but not for the constitution. May I offer refreshment?" Stabbing his cigarette into the ashtray, he approached a cabinet, opened it, and removed a carafe of glinting emerald liquid. "A glass of Chartreuse, perhaps?"

"No, thanks."

"Its taste does not appeal to you?"

"I've never . . ."

"Now you have the opportunity."

"No, I don't drink."

Father Hafer narrowed his eyes. "Indeed? A weakness that you guard against?"

"I've never indulged. In my line of work, I couldn't afford poor judgment."

"And what was that? Your line of work?"

Drew didn't answer.

Father Hafer considered him, swirling the emerald liquid.

"Yet another topic for later discussion. I wonder if you realize how appropriate this substance is."

"Chartreuse." Drew spread his hands. "The liqueur is reputed to be the finest. Its distinctive flavor—something I wouldn't know about—is due to angelica root. And, of course, one hundred and fifteen different herbs. It's the principal source of income for the Carthusians. Manufactured at the fatherhouse at La Grande Chartreuse in the Alps of France. The name of the liqueur comes from the place where it's made. Chartreuse. The green type you're holding has an alcohol content of fifty-five percent while the yellow type has forty-three percent. Its recipe was concocted in the early sixteen hundreds, I believe, by a layman who donated its formula to the Carthusians. A century later, a chemical genius in the order perfected it. A bogus version appeared on the market, but those who discriminate know which label to look for."

Father Hafer blinked. "Remarkable."

"In more ways than one. An order of hermits maintains its independence because of the income generated from a liquid designed to produce conviviality. Of course, the liqueur is manufactured by a lay fraternity. Even so, I ignore the contradiction."

9

His needs were attended to by non-eremitic brothers, whose quarters were in the lodge, which also contained the chapel, the refectory, the kitchen, and a guest room. His spartan meals were given to him through a serving hatch beside a door in his workroom. On Sundays and major feasts, however, the rule required him to leave his cell, which was never locked, and eat with the other hermits in the refectory at the lodge. On those occasions, subdued conversation was permitted, but he never indulged. He was also required to leave his cell and join the other monks in the lodge's chapel at midnight for matins, at 8 A.M. for mass, and at 6 P.M. for vespers. He disliked these interruptions, preferring to worship in the isolation of his cell.

His only distraction was the mouse.

10

"*The vows,*" Father Hafer said, distressed. "Have you truly considered their gravity? Not only those of poverty, chastity, and obedience, arduous enough on their own. But add to them the oath of fealty to the principles of the Carthusians. I need to be brutally direct. When the committee meets to judge applicants, we customarily reject young men as a matter of course. Their immaturity makes us question their ability to keep their vow of solitude. The consequence of disobedience is unthinkable."

"If I broke my vows, I'd be damning myself."

"That's right. And even confession could not return your soul to a state of grace. Your only alternative would be to request a dispensation. So serious a request takes months to be considered. In the meantime, if you should die . . ."

"It wouldn't matter."

"I don't . . ."

"I'm already damned."

Father Hafer flinched and raised his voice. "Because you failed to make your Easter duty for thirteen years? By comparison with violating sacred vows, that other sin is minor. I could reinstate you now by hearing your confession and giving you communion. But even confession could not return your soul to a state of grace if you had no dispensation and you continued to violate the vows. You surely understand why the committee would turn down your request to join the order. If we accepted you but doubted your ability to endure the

Carthusian way of life, we ourselves would be scorning the vows you would take. To a great degree, we'd be helping you to damn yourself, and that would make us culpable. We'd be threatening the state of our *own* souls."

"But if . . ."

"Yes? Go on."

"If you don't admit me, you'd be culpable anyhow."

"For what?"

"For what I'd be driven to do. I said I felt damned. I didn't mean because of my failure to make my Easter duty."

"Then what?"

"I want to kill myself."

11

During his fifth year at the monastery, after the first chill of autumn had colored the maples, he sensed a movement to his right as he knelt on the hardwood floor of his workroom, praying for his soul. The movement was minuscule, a subtle blur that might have been due to eye strain, the result of his anguished concentration. Sweat beaded his brow. Ashamed that he'd allowed himself to be distracted, he meditated with greater fervor, desperate to shut out the horrid images from his past.

But the movement continued, barely perceptible, nonetheless there. For a moment, he wondered if he'd reached the stage of experiencing hallucinations—other monks, after intense devotion, were rumored to have witnessed presences—but skepticism as well as humility discouraged him, and besides, the movement was on the floor at the base of a wall. What sort of religious vision would be appropriate there?

Deciding that his fortitude was being tested, he resolved not to look; but again the blur caught the corner of his gaze, and in a moment of weakness that eventually saved his life, he turned his head to the right, toward the floor at the base of the wall, and saw a small gray mouse.

It froze.

Drew was taken by surprise.

But so, apparently, was the mouse. Each watched the other for quite a while. As if losing patience, the mouse twitched its whiskers. Unconsciously, Drew scratched the side of his nose. Alarmed, with amazing abruptness, the mouse sped toward a hole in the wall.

Drew astonished himself by almost laughing. As the mouse disappeared, however, he frowned at the implications. The hole had not been in his workroom wall when he went to the vespers service last night. He focused on the freshly gnawed wood and wondered what to do. Tonight, while he was again away at the vespers service, he could ask a custodian brother to obtain a trap or possibly poison. After slipping one or the other into the hole, the brother could use his carpentry tools to plug up the hole.

But why? Drew asked himself. In the chill of autumn, the mouse had come to the monastery for refuge, as he himself had wanted refuge. In a sense, they were two of a kind.

The thought was comical to him. Sure, me and the mouse. He did consider the danger of chewed electrical wires, of mice reproducing behind the wall till the monastery was vermin-ridden. Common sense suggested that to tolerate the mouse would be impractical.

But the mouse intrigued him. Something about its daring. And yet its . . .

Helplessness, he thought. I could easily kill it.

But not anymore. Not even a mouse.

He decided to let it stay. On probation. As long as you don't raise hell. As long as you're celibate, he allowed himself to joke.

12

Father Hafer turned pale. "You admit . . . ?"

"I truly believe," Drew said, "that retreat from the world is my only chance to be saved. Otherwise . . ."

"If I deny your application, I'd be responsible for your suicide? For your unforgivable sin of despair? For your going to Hell? Absurd."

"It's the logic you used a moment ago. You said that you'd be culpable if you let me in despite your misgivings and I later damned myself by breaking my vows."

"So now I'd be culpable if I *didn't* let you in and you later damned yourself by committing suicide? Ridiculous," Father Hafer said. "What's going on here? Who do you think you're talking to? I'm a man of God. I've tried to treat your extreme request with respect, and now you want to blame me for . . . It's all I can do to keep from telling you to get out of here."

"But you *are* a man of God. So you won't turn your back on me."

Father Hafer seemed not to have heard. "And this application." He pointed angrily at his desk. "I suspected there was something wrong. You claim that your parents died when you were ten."

"That's true." Drew felt his throat swell shut.

"But there's little indication of what happened to you after that. You do say you were educated in an industrial school in Colorado, but you've obviously had training in the arts—logic, history, literature. Next to 'occupation,' you say you're unemployed. As what? The natural inclination is to state your occupation, whether you're unemployed or not. I asked you a while ago, but you wouldn't tell me. Unmarried. Never have been. No children. Thirty-one years old"—the priest rapped the form on his desk—"and you're a shadow."

Drew bitterly smiled. "Then it ought to be easy for me to erase the evidence of my former life."

"Since it seems to have been erased already." Father Hafer glared. "Are you in trouble with the law, is that your motive? You think the Carthusians would make a good hideout? Perverting the Church to—"

"No. In fact, what I used to do was encouraged by the law. At the highest level."

"That's it. I've lost my patience. This interview is finished right now if you don't—"

"In confession."

"What?"

"I'll tell you in confession."

13

The mouse turned out to be as reclusive as himself. He didn't see it for the next few days and began to think that it had gone away. But on a cold drizzly afternoon when the clouds hung low and the sodden maple leaves fell dismally to the ground, he sensed the blur of movement again as he knelt in meditation, and peering across his workroom, he saw just a nose and some whiskers poking from the hole.

He remained as still as possible and watched. The mouse strained its head from the hole, its nostrils twitching, testing for danger. Determined not to scare it, curious about what it planned to do, Drew tried not even to blink.

The mouse took a tentative step, its shoulders appearing. Another step, and now Drew saw its side, its tiny chest heaving, its eyes darting this way and that. Another step, and it left the hole.

But it didn't seem the same. Though gray as before, its fur looked duller, its body thinner, making Drew wonder if this was a different mouse. His previous concern about not just one mouse but a nest of them made him question his refusal to tell a custodian brother to deal with the problem. Instead of amusement, he now watched the mouse with uneasiness.

It inched along the baseboard, sniffing. But it seemed off-balance, listing as if it had injured a leg or was dizzy. Or sick? Drew wondered. No way of telling what diseases it carried or if they could be communicated to humans. Perhaps even rabies, he realized with alarm.

He almost stood to scare the mouse back into its hole, but as it reached a corner and veered from one baseboard to another, continuing to sniff, he guessed what it might be doing—searching for food. That would explain its apparent dizziness. It could be trembling from hunger.

But shouldn't there be plenty of food around? he wondered. Then he realized that the rain outside had almost turned to sleet. The mouse would have to risk freezing to death and overcome difficult obstacles to travel what for it would be a considerable distance to the few ungathered apples in the orchard or the remnants of vegetables in the garden outside the cloister. There was food, of course, in the monastery's kitchen and cellar, but the mouse had made the mistake of choosing this cell in a wing that was far from the lodge. Obviously it hadn't figured out where the kitchen was; otherwise it would have nested there.

You really screwed up, mouse. Your survival instincts are pathetic.

As the mouse reached another corner, wobbling along the next baseboard, it faced in Drew's direction. Its eyes abruptly widened—its nose jerked. It suddenly bolted, streaking across the workroom, shooting out of sight inside the hole.

Drew exhaled what was nearly a laugh. He watched the hole for a moment longer, then turned as he heard the rattle of a latch being lifted. In the hallway outside, unseen hands swung open the serving hatch beside his door. With a scrape and thump, his evening meal was placed on a shelf. The hatch was closed.

He stood and went over, removing a cup and bowl from the shelf. He didn't have a watch or a calendar. His only ways of measuring time were the monastery's bell, the passage of the seasons, and the types of meals he was served. Thus today must be Friday, he concluded, glancing at the contents of his cup and bowl, for that was when he received only bread and water.

He set the spartan meal on his workbench and glanced toward the dreary rain beyond his window. Possibly because of the chill and the damp, he felt uncommonly tempted by hunger today, and as a consequence, for added discipline, he forced himself not to eat all the bread.

He later wondered if all along he'd had another motive for partially fasting, but it nonetheless surprised him when on impulse, as the chapel bell beckoned him to leave his cell for the vespers service, he set a small chunk of bread in front of the mouse's hole.

When he returned, the bread was gone, and he allowed himself to smile.

14

"Abuse the sacrament?" Father Hafer was shocked. "If you're worried about guaranteeing my silence, there's no need for confession. Don't forget, I'm also a psychiatrist. My professional ethics force me to keep this conversation strictly private. I'd never discuss it in a court or with the police."

"But I prefer to depend on your ethics as a priest. You put great emphasis on sacred vows. You'd damn yourself if you revealed what you heard in confession."

"I told you I won't abuse the sacrament! I don't know what trick you're trying to get away with, but—"

"*For God's sake, I'm begging you!*"

The priest blinked, startled.

Drew swallowed, his voice pained. "Then you'll know why I have to be allowed to join the order."

15

It became a ritual. Every evening, he left a portion of his meal—a piece of carrot, a leaf of lettuce, a section of apple—in front of the hole. His offering was never refused. But as if suspicious of Drew's generosity, the mouse stayed in its hole.

Of course, Drew thought, why bother coming out when your meals are delivered?

The motive that he attributed to the mouse amused him, though he didn't allow his amusement to interfere with his resolve. His purpose was worship, his days taken up with prayer and penance, for the honor and glory of God and the atonement of his heinous sins.

The gusting snow of his fifth winter here piled huge drifts outside his window. He persisted, purging his awful emotions, subduing the guilt that tortured his soul. But sometimes during his prayers, the mouse now ventured out. It looked fatter, its eyes more alert. It went no farther than a yard from its hole, but its pace was steady. Its fur had a healthy sheen.

Then spring came, and the mouse had sufficient confidence to show itself when Drew was exercising. It sat outside its hole, its front feet raised, contemplating what must have seemed odd behavior.

Each balmy day, Drew expected that the mouse would leave. It's time for you to play, he thought. Taste the sweet new buds, and meet some pals. I'll even absolve you of chastity. Go on, kiddo. Raise a family. The world needs fieldmice, too.

But the mouse appeared more often. It came farther from its hole.

When the season grew so hot that sweat rippled down Drew's chest beneath his coarse hair shirt and his heavy robe, he felt a tiny movement against his leg as he sat at his work-bench, eating. Glancing down, he saw the mouse sniffing at his robe, and he realized that the animal was here to stay.

A fellow hermit. He didn't know its sex. But given their cloistered circumstances, he preferred to think that it was male, and recalling a mouse that he'd read about long ago in a book by E. B. White, he gave it a name.

Stuart Little.

When I was innocent, he thought.

16

"I don't have my vestments with me."

"Where?" Drew asked.

"In my room here at the rectory."

"Then I'll go with you while you get them. We'll have to leave, anyhow—to use a confessional in the church across the street."

"It isn't necessary," Father Hafer said. "The rules have been relaxed. We can perform the sacrament here in the open, in my office, face to face. It's known as 'public confession.'"

Drew shook his head.

"What's wrong?"

"Let's say I'm old-fashioned."

They crossed the congested street toward the church. Inside the cool dim loftiness, their footsteps echoed as they each went into a bleak compartment of a confessional. Drew knelt in its musty darkness. Behind a partition, the priest slid a panel to one side. Drew whispered to the shadow behind the grill.

"Bless me, Father, for I have sinned. My last confession was thirteen years ago. These are my sins." He told.

And told, not even stopping when he described the photographs in his pocket and the priest began to gasp.

17

It was autumn again, October, his sixth year in the monastery. The ruddy glow of sunset tinted the brilliant maples on the hill. He heard the rattle of the serving hatch, then the familiar scrape and thump of a cup and bowl being set on the shelf beside his door.

He lowered his ax, the blunt end of which he'd been striking against a metal wedge to split logs for his wood stove, and glanced toward the tiny hole at the base of the workroom wall where Stuart Little suddenly appeared. The mouse sat on his haunches, raising its forearms to brush its whiskers.

All you need is a knife, fork, and bib, Drew silently joked, amused at how the rattle of the serving hatch had become Stuart Little's dinner bell.

The mouse scurried over as Drew brought the meal to the workbench. Bread and water; another fast-day. His stomach rumbling, he noticed Stuart trying to climb up his robe, and with a sigh of feigned disgust, he tore off a piece of bread, tossing it down to the mouse. He sat at the bench and bowed his head, pressing his hands together, praying.

You know, Stuart, he thought as he finished, you're getting greedy. I ought to make you wait to eat till grace is finished. A little religion wouldn't hurt you. How would you feel about that, huh?

He glanced toward the mouse on the floor.

And frowned. The mouse lay on its side, unmoving.

Drew stared in surprise, not moving either. His chest tensed. Shocked, he held his breath, then blinked and, inhaling slowly, bent down to touch Stuart's side.

It remained inert.

Drew gently nudged it, feeling the soft sleek fur, but got no response. His throat seemed lined with sand. As he swallowed painfully, he picked Stuart up. The mouse lay still in his palm. It weighed almost nothing, but the weight was dead.

Drew's stomach felt cold. In dismay, he shook his head, baffled. A minute ago, the mouse had practically been dancing for its supper.

Was it old age, he wondered. A heart attack or a stroke? He didn't know much about mice, but he vaguely recalled having read somewhere that they didn't live long. A year or two.

But that was in the wild, exposed to predators, diseases, and cold. What about here in the cell? He strained to think, telling himself that even with warmth and good care, Stuart Little had been bound to die. There wasn't any way to know how old it had been when it showed up last autumn, but in human terms, by now it might have been ninety.

I shouldn't be surprised. By feeding it, I merely postponed. . . . If it hadn't died today . . .

Tomorrow.

He bit his lip, grieving as he set the small corpse back on the floor. And felt guilty because he grieved. A Carthusian was supposed to shut out all worldly distractions. God alone mattered. The mouse had been a temptation that he should have resisted. Now God was punishing him, teaching him why he shouldn't become infatuated with transitory creatures.

Death.

Drew shuddered. No. I wouldn't change anything. The mouse was fun to have around. I'm glad I took care of it.

His eyes stung, making him blink repeatedly as he stared

down at his lifeless friend. Terrible thoughts occurred to him. What should he do with the body? For sure, he wasn't going to have a custodian brother dispose of it, perhaps even dump it in the trash. The mouse deserved better. The dignity of burial.

But where? Through misted vision, he glanced toward his workroom window. Sunset had turned to dusk, casting his garden wall into shadow.

A cedar bush grew in a corner of the wall. Yes, Drew thought. He'd bury Stuart Little beneath the shrub. An evergreen, it lived all year. Even in winter, its color would be a reminder.

His throat felt swollen, aching each time he swallowed. Thirsty, he reached for his cup of water, raised it toward his lips, glanced past it toward the thick slab of bread in his bowl.

And paused.

His spine began to tingle.

He peered down at the bread on the floor, the chunk he'd thrown to Stuart Little. He stared at the water in the cup he held. And slowly, cautiously, making sure that no liquid spilled over the top, he eased the container back down on the table. Reflexively he wiped his hands on the front of his robe.

No, he thought. It couldn't be.

But what if you're not imagining?

His suspicion filled him with shame. In his sixth stern year of penance, did he still retain the habit of thinking as he had in his former life? Had his training been that effective? Were his instincts that resistant to change?

But just supposing. You know, for the sake of argument. What kind might it be? Did it kill on contact?

Tensing, he stared at his hands. No, he'd touched the mouse. And the bread. Just a minute ago. But the mouse had died quickly. In the time Drew had taken to close his eyes and say grace. If it's poison and it kills on contact, even with my greater size, I ought to be dead now, too.

He breathed.

All right, then, it has to be ingested.

(You've got to stop thinking this way.)

And it's powerful. Almost instantaneous.

Assuming it's poison.

Of course, just assuming. After all, it's still quite possible that Stuart Little died from natural causes.

(But what would you have thought six years ago?)

He struggled to repress his terrible memories. No. God's testing me again. He's using this death to learn if I've truly purged myself. A man of detachment would never think like this.

(But in the old days . . .

Yes?

You thought this way all the time.)

He narrowed his vision till all he saw was the unmoving mouse on the floor. Slowly, frowning so hard he felt the beginnings of a headache, he raised his eyes toward the serving hatch beside his door.

The hatch was closed. But beyond it was a corridor.

(No. It makes no sense. Not *here*, not *now*! Who? Why?)

Besides, he was merely guessing. The only way to know for sure if the bread had been poisoned was to . . .

Taste it? Hardly.

Have it tested? That would take too long.

But there *was* another way. He could investigate the monastery. He stiffened with doubt. The notion repelled him.

But under the circumstances . . .

He stared at the door. In the six years he'd been here, he'd left his quarters seldom, only to convene with the other monks for mandatory communal rituals. Those ventures outside had been keenly disturbing to him, nerve-racking intrusions on his peace of mind.

But under the circumstances . . .

He wiped his sweaty lip. His years of disciplined regimen told him to wait a short while longer until he normally left for vespers. Yes. The decision calmed him. Avoiding extremes, it appealed to his common sense.

Dusk deepened, shifting to dark. A misty drizzle beaded on his window. He shivered, grieving, too preoccupied to force himself to turn on a light.

The vespers bell stayed silent, but in rhythm with his daily cycle, he knew that it should have struck by now. He told himself that the mouse's death had disturbed his judgment. Time was passing with exaggerated slowness, that was all. He didn't have a clock in the cell, so how could he be sure when vespers was supposed to occur?

He counted to one hundred. Waited. Started to count again. And stopped.

With a painful sigh, he repressed his inhibitions, broke six years of habit, and opened the door.

18

A light glowed overhead. The hallway was bare, no paintings, no carpeting. Soundless, deserted.

That wasn't unusual. True, when the bell tolled, he on occasion met other monks leaving their cells to go to the chapel. But equally often, he went earlier or later than the others and walked alone down the corridor.

He did so now. Still determined to obey the ritual, he reached the end, turned left, and passed beneath another light to enter the lodge. In shadow, the chapel door was fifty paces ahead of him, to the right.

His misgivings increased, his instincts alarming him. Instead of continuing toward the chapel, he made an abrupt decision and turned sharply right, descending the stairs to the monastery's refectory. As he expected, at this time of night (and except on Sunday) it wasn't occupied. But thinking of the bread he'd been given, he stared toward a light in the rear where the kitchen was. Passing empty tables with barren tops, he took a deep breath, pushed through the swinging door, and studied the massive stove, the vaultlike door to the freezer, the extensive counters and cupboards. And the two dead men on the floor.

Though custodian brothers, not hermits, they nonetheless wore the white gown, scapular, and hood of the true Carthusian. The chest of each gown was soaked with blood, each hood stained red at the temple.

Drew surprised himself. Perhaps because he'd unconsciously expected something like this, or because his instincts had not been as neutralized as he'd hoped, his heart stayed perfectly calm.

But his stomach felt scorched.

The shots would have been silenced to keep the monastery from being alerted, he thought. Two assassins at least. Each brother had fallen in roughly the same position, suggesting that they'd been caught by surprise. No sign of panic, of either brother trying to escape, which meant that they'd been shot in the chest simultaneously. Drew nodded. Yes, two assassins at least.

And experienced. A wound in the chest was sometimes not fatal. The protocol required a follow-up—just to be sure. And to minimize suffering. The required coup de grâce. A shot to each temple. Professional. Indeed.

Drew controlled the pressure swelling in him, turned, and left the kitchen. Outside the refectory, he nodded in anguish, knowing what he had to do now, what he'd considered doing when he left his room. But he'd put it off as long as possible, until he had no other choice. It would be the absolute violation of the Carthusian rule. As severe as leaving his room at any other time except for the required rituals.

The thought was repulsive to him. But it had to be acted upon.

Going up the stairs, he went back the way he'd come. He reached the end of the corridor in the lodge and angled right to enter his wing of cells. There he paused at the first door he came to. Studied the knob.

And opened the door. An overhead light glowed in the workroom. The monk who occupied it must have switched it on as sunset deepened. The man lay sprawled on the floor. The chair before his workbench was overturned. A wedge of bread was clutched in his hand. A pool of urine spread from his gown.

Drew hardened his jaw and shut the door. Repressing the bile that rose to his mouth, he went down to the next door and opened it. In this case the workroom light had not been turned on. But the light from the hallway was sufficient for Drew to see the monk slumped across his table, the bowl of bread pinned beneath one arm.

He went on like that, opening and closing each door, proceeding to the next one, and the next. A light was sometimes on and sometimes not. The body was sometimes on the table, sometimes on the floor. Sometimes the monk in dying had brushed against his cup of water, spilling it, so that water and urine were indistinguishable.

All of them—the nineteen other monks who'd secluded themselves in this refuge—had been poisoned by the bread. Or by the water, Drew thought. It was logical that the water had been poisoned as well. No sense in not being thorough. Professional.

Too many questions intruded. But the foremost of all was why.

He now understood his motive when, as dusk had thickened, he hadn't turned on his light. He'd assumed that his grief over Stuart Little had robbed him of even the resolve to cross his workroom and flick on the light switch. But now he knew better, his subconscious having warned him. Whoever had poisoned the food would have posted someone outside, probably in the courtyard, to watch the monastery for signs of life. A light that came on when it shouldn't have would have drawn the assassins to his cell.

More questions. Why use poison? Why not shoot each monk as the kitchen staff had been shot? Why wait this long to come in and verify the kill?

Why kill everyone? And where was the death team?

With each door that he opened, with each corpse that he found, he increasingly reverted to his former state of mind. Six years ago, on the run from Scalpel, he'd have naturally assumed that he was the target. But he'd been careful. Scalpel didn't know he'd entered the monastery. Scalpel thought he was dead.

Then who else could be hunting him? Possibly he wasn't the target at all. Maybe one of the other monks had been the target. But why? No, it wasn't likely. And why had *every* monk been killed? The tactic didn't make sense.

In a moment it did, however, and the back of his neck felt cold. The death team couldn't have known which cell was whose. The monks were all anonymous, the doors unmarked. There wasn't any way to determine who secluded himself in which unit. The team couldn't very well have checked each room—so complicated an operation would have been too risky, leaving too many chances for mistakes. It was one thing to confront the kitchen staff on the lower level where no one was likely to hear a commotion. That risk was acceptable. But on the main floor where the monks lived close together—that was quite another matter. Entering each cell, even with silencers to muffle the shots, the team would still have been concerned about an unpredictable scream from a startled monk, a shout that might have alerted the other monks and—if I'm

right, Drew thought—one monk in particular, the man the
team had come for.

Me.

His forehead knotted in torment. Because of my sins? Is
that why everybody had to die? Dear God, what have I done
by coming here?

The logic of using poison was clear to him now. A way of
taking out the entire monastery (with the exception of the already executed kitchen staff) at once. Equally important, it
was death from a distance. By remote control.

Because the team respected the skills of the man they'd
come to assassinate, because they didn't know if six years of
seclusion had been enough to blunt his talents, they'd chosen
not to come at him directly. An added precaution. To make
extra sure.

But everyone else had to die.

Drew's throat made a terrible choking sound.

He suddenly realized that wherever the assassins were hiding, they'd soon come out. When sufficient time had passed
for them to feel confident, they'd inspect the monastery.
They'd search each cell. They'd want to verify the kill, *to guarantee that one man in particular had been killed.*

His shoulders tensed as he glanced in both directions along
the corridor.

The vespers bell began to toll.

19

I t sounded unnatural in the otherwise deathly silence, echoing down the hallway, through the courtyard. Mournful, as
if announcing a funeral.

His sinews compacted. He crouched, strong habits insisting, making him understand how a moth must feel when attracted to a flame. Every day for the past six years, that bell

had beckoned him, so much a part of his daily schedule that even now as he recognized the threat, he still felt compelled to obey its call. As would any surviving monk who by virtue of extra discipline had decided to refuse even the minimum meal of bread and water. Drawn to the chapel for vespers, the monk would open the door.

And be shot by a silenced handgun that accomplished what the poisoned food had failed to do. No witnesses, no interruptions, refinement upon refinement.

It made Drew quiver with rage.

But this was obvious. When the bell had rung sufficiently, when the team was satisfied that no fasting monk could have possibly refused its call, the search would begin. He had to hide.

But where? He couldn't risk leaving the monastery. He had to assume that its perimeter was being watched. All right then, he had to stay inside.

Again the question, *where*? When the team didn't find his body, they'd check every room and cranny in the cloister. Even if he hadn't been the specific target, their intention had clearly been to kill everyone. He had to assume that they wouldn't be satisfied until they accounted for every corpse. True, he had the advantage of knowing the layout better than they did. Even so, they'd be methodical, determined. The odds were against him.

Unless. Desperation primed his thoughts. If he could manage to convince them that . . .

Each stroke of the bell seemed louder, stronger. He hurried to return to his cell. From custom, he'd closed its door as he left his workroom to go to vespers. But that had been a mistake, he concluded, and now left the door open after stepping back inside. The dead mouse beside the chunk of bread on the floor would show the team that he'd learned about the poison. The absence of his body, the significance of his door—and only his door—being open, would make the team think he'd fled. They'd focus their search in other parts of the monastery, more likely outside, alerting the guards on the perimeter that he was trying to get through the woods. They'd feel urgent, impatient.

He hoped. Rushing soundlessly up his dark stairs, he reached his oratory, and for once in six years, he didn't stop to pray. He darted through it to the blackness of his study, and then to his sleeping quarters, where he veered toward the small, murky bathroom.

In the ceiling above the sink, a trapdoor led to the insulation beneath the roof. He removed his shoes so he wouldn't leave marks on the porcelain and, holding them, climbed upon the sink, hearing it creak beneath his weight. He groped above him, exhaled when he felt the rim of the trapdoor, pushed it up, and lifted himself into the musty, cold, yet sweat-producing closeness. After sliding the trapdoor back into place, he crawled across the irritating glass wool insulation toward a far corner, where he lay as flat as he could, hiding behind joists and upright support beams. He tried to keep his mind still but couldn't.

Breathing dust, he brooded. About his fellow monks.

And Stuart Little.

20

The bell stopped tolling, its muteness eerie. He became rigid, straining to listen, knowing that his hunters would be leaving the chapel now. The drizzle that had earlier beaded on his window increased to a steady rain that drummed on the slanted roof above him. Shivering from the chill and the damp, he pressed himself harder against the insulation. Despite its bulk, he felt the sharp-edged two-by-sixes that formed the skeleton of the floor beneath him. He waited.

And waited.

On occasion, he thought that he heard far-off muffled sounds. No voices, of course—the team would follow established procedures and communicate with gestures. But other noises were unavoidable, doors being opened, footsteps on hard bare floors. Indeed, with an ear against the insulation, he suspected that several indistinct creaks he heard below him were due to someone creeping through his oratory, study, and sleeping quarters. These sounds could easily have been imagined. Nonetheless he concentrated his attention across the dark attic toward the unseen trapdoor, listening apprehensively for the scrape that it would make if someone pushed it up. He licked his dry lips.

And waited.

The night passed slowly. Despite his tension, the stifling air made him groggy. He blinked at the dark through heavy eyelids, woke with a jerk, and fought not to drowse again. The next time he woke, disoriented, quickly on guard, he noticed a hint of light through the cracks in a ceiling vent that allowed the build-up of heat to escape during summer. Morning. He no longer heard the drumming of the rain on the roof. Indeed, except for the dry controlled hiss of his breath, he heard nothing.

All the same, he waited. In his former life, he'd once been hunted for five days through a jungle. He'd eaten almost nothing, only non-toxic leaves that gave his brain the potassium and lithium it needed to remain alert. Unable to trust the bacteria-ridden water, he'd depended on rainfall to give him moisture. By comparison with that jungle, this attic presented few problems. He was sedentary, after all, and accustomed to fasting. If the month had been August instead of October, the swelter up here (even with the heat vents) would have been unendurable. But given his circumstances, chilly but not dangerously cold, he could remain here for three full days. That was the limit for surviving without water. Perhaps he could last even longer, but he'd be delirious.

He brooded throughout the morning, feeling death below him. The corpses would have passed beyond rigor mortis now, entering the stage of livor mortis, beginning to swell from body gases, stinking. The same would be happening to Stuart Little.

His forehead ached from frowning. In 1979, he recalled, he'd been in such despair that he'd wanted to kill himself. The monastery had provided his only alternative, a way to punish himself and try to save his soul.

Then why now was he so desperate to avoid whoever was hunting him? Why did he feel compelled to stop them from doing what he'd almost done to himself? If the assassins killed him, it wouldn't be suicide, after all. He wouldn't be damning himself.

Wrong. It was one thing to be martyred, quite another to invite being martyred. Presumption was as damning a sin as despair. He couldn't dare count on God to save him merely because he'd been killed for his sins. He had to fight for salvation. He had to use every device in his power, every trick he could think of, to avoid his executioners.

I want to be punished. Yes. For my former life. For the monks who died because of me.

But . . .

Yes?

I'm also under an obligation.

Oh? To do what?

To punish others, those who killed them.

But you didn't even know those monks. They were hermits like yourself. Personally, they meant nothing to you.

It doesn't matter. They were human beings, and they were cheated. They deserved the chance to pursue their holiness.

Maybe they're in Heaven now.

There's no guarantee. That's presumption again.

So in its place, you prefer revenge? Is that a proper Carthusian motive? An eye for an eye as opposed to turning one's cheek?

He didn't have an answer. Unfamiliar disturbing emotions, dormant for six years, welled up in him. The world had intruded, corrupting him.

21

The next night, late, it stormed again. Lightning flashed, dimly visible through the slots in the air vents. Thunder shook the roof. He decided to take advantage of the weather and crawled toward the trapdoor, shifting it as silently as possible, easing down to the darkness that hid the sink. As the storm raged outside, he crept to his murky sleeping quarters, pausing, sensing. An assassin would have to be terribly determined, not to mention patient, to wait here two nights in a row on the slim chance that Drew was hiding in the attic. More likely, the team would have sent someone up there after him or at least have used tear gas to force Drew down. Besides, once the team had suspected that Drew was out of the building, they'd have felt compromised, afraid that if he escaped he'd alert the police. When their harried search had failed to reveal him, they'd have been forced to pull out.

Or so Drew hoped. Nothing was sure. But here in the night he had an advantage. One of his principal skills, the result of concentrated special training, was hand-to-hand combat in total darkness. Even after six years of inactivity, he hadn't forgotten how it was done. For an instant, he felt transported back to that oppressive black room in the abandoned airplane hangar in Colorado. Now motionless, breathing slowly, listening intently, he neither smelled nor heard a lurking assailant.

Of course the drumming of the rain would obscure other sounds. At a certain point, he had to act on faith, crossing his sleeping quarters, on guard against a brush of cloth, a sudden rush in his direction. It didn't occur. He glanced back. As rain lashed his window, lightning streaked beyond it, illuminating the room, giving him a hurried chance to reassure himself that no one was there.

Darkness returned as thunder rumbled, and he realized that staring at the lightning had been a mistake. His pupils had contracted to protect themselves against the sudden brilliance; now in the dark they were slow to dilate again. His night vision had been impaired. He had to wait, unsettled, temporarily blind. With agonizing slowness, he began to see murky outlines in the dark. He bit his lip. All right, he'd made a mistake. He admitted it. But the mistake had been a useful one. He'd learned from it. His skills were returning. Already he was calculating a way to turn the lightning to his advantage.

Keeping his back to the window, he left his sleeping quarters, then passed through the deeper blackness of the study and the oratory, again still feeling and ignoring the tug of habit to stop there and pray. On the stairs that led down to his workroom, he saw his open door, the light that glowed from the hall. He smelled a too-familiar, stomach-turning stench. When he reached the bottom, he cautiously surveyed the room. His cup and bowl remained on the workbench. Stuart Little was in the same position on the floor. But as he'd anticipated, the mouse was now bloated, filled with gas.

Drew swallowed, not in disgust but pity. Because he needed the body, he lovingly picked up the corpse by the tail and gently wrapped it in a handkerchief that he'd left on his woodpile. He tied the handkerchief to his skipping rope and tied the rope around the waist of his habit.

From a drawer in his workroom bench, he removed four

photographs, the only items he'd brought with him from his former life. Six years ago, he'd shown these photographs to Father Hafer after the priest, gasping, had heard his confession. The photographs had verified what Drew had said, convincing the priest to relent, to recommend Drew's acceptance by the Carthusians. The photographs showed a man and woman consumed by flames, a young boy screaming in horror. In the monastery, Drew had studied these images every day, reminding himself of what he'd been, of his need for penance. He couldn't bring himself to leave now without them.

Shoving them into a pocket in his robe, he glanced around. What else? He needed a weapon. The ax from his woodpile.

The storm became more violent. Even with his back to the window, he saw another blaze of lightning fill the room. He approached his open door, peered both ways along the empty corridor, glanced back with longing toward the place that had been his home for the past six years, then hefted his ax and crept down the hall toward the rear of the monastery.

He made one stop—to examine another cell. The sharp, nauseating stench as he budged the door open told him everything. But he pushed the door farther and stared at the grotesquely misshapen body of a monk.

So the team had left the monastery as they'd found it, closing each door on the ultimate secret, not bothering to dispose of the dead—no time to do so—but at least perversely respectful of their victims.

That too didn't matter. Regardless of their peculiar ethics—Drew himself had once been faithful to such ethics—there would be hell to pay.

22

At the rear of the monastery, he faced the exit that led to the vegetable garden. Thunder shuddered through the thick wooden door.

He reconsidered his decisions. The obvious way to leave the monastery was out the front of the lodge, then down the dirt road through the forest to the paved country road at the bottom of this hill. Granted, he'd seen the approach to the monastery only for a brief time six years ago when he'd been driven here. But he remembered that country road and the town—what had its name been? Quentin?—ten miles or so to the south. Still, if leaving through the front toward the road was the obvious route, precisely for that reason he had to take a different direction. Because, although the team had apparently fled from the area, there was a chance—a strong one—that a man had been left behind to watch the monastery from a distance, in case Drew was still on the premises. Their suspicion would be that Drew had escaped and alerted the police. But what if the police didn't arrive? The death team would have to conclude that Drew had *not* escaped. They'd risk returning for one more search. All the more reason for Drew to get out of here.

But not out the front, not by a route that a spotter would pay close attention to. Okay, out the back. Even so, given the quality of the team's professional conduct, Drew had to make other assumptions.

First, the spotter would not ignore the other exits from the cloister. He'd stay a careful distance away, choosing a location that gave him a confident view of the entire complex. Only one location allowed for such a vantage point: in back of the cloister, on the wooded hill that rose above this one.

Second assumption. The spotter would be equipped for

night surveillance, using either an infrared scope, which projected an invisible beam, or a Starlite scope, which magnified whatever minuscule light was available. Because this storm would obscure the stars, an infrared scope was the better choice.

Drew studied his robe. Usually white, it was now a dingy gray from the cobwebs, dust, and insulation in the attic. But even if the robe were caked with coal dust, he knew that it could still be seen through a night scope. *Unless,* Drew thought, and remembered the lightning.

He glanced above him, toward the bulb that glowed in the corridor's ceiling. The moment he opened the door, the spotter would be attracted by the new illumination. There wasn't any light switch in the hallway—Drew assumed that the switch was on a master panel in a custodial room he'd never been shown—so he reached up, tall enough to wrap his scapular around the bulb and unscrew it. As an added precaution, he went farther along the corridor and unscrewed two other bulbs, surrounding himself in darkness. Because the hallway had no windows, a spotter couldn't know what had happened.

He returned to the door, took a long breath, exhaled, and twisted the latch. He pulled the door open slowly, trying to avoid an obvious change in this section of the cloister. As he pulled, he stood out of sight behind it.

At last it was fully open. He waited, flexing his shoulders. Timing was everything now, because both infrared and Starlite scopes had a common weakness: sudden illumination blinded the observer. The temporary sightlessness that Drew had experienced in his sleeping quarters when he used the lightning to help him scan the room would be drastically intensified through a night scope. The normal instinct would have been for Drew to run from the cloister during the intervals of blackness between glaring flashes of lightning. Drew realized, however, that his only chance to get out unseen was to do the opposite—to prime himself, to alert every reflex, to race outside for cover as soon as a new fork of lightning blazed.

In darkness, he shifted from behind the door, studying the garden. With breath-held caution, he peered toward the rain-enshrouded night. He closed his eyes and glanced away as lightning struck a tree beyond the garden. A branch crashed. Night resumed abruptly. But he knew where he had to go now. Thunder. Soon the streaks of lightning came closer together. Drew imagined the agony that a spotter would be enduring.

Well, what are you waiting for? he asked himself. You want to hang around, go to mass?

The instant the next bolt flashed, Drew charged from the open doorway. At once rain lashed his face. Keeping his ax away from him, he dove to the oozing mud behind a sculpted cedar bush. The frigid rain drenched his robe, soaking through to his skin. Almost instantaneous thunder shook the sodden earth beneath him. Despite the assault on his senses, a portion of his consciousness registered the unfamiliar sweetness of the air, the forgotten sting of the wind—feelings formerly ordinary to him, now powerfully sensual after long seclusion. But he didn't have time to savor them or to realize how much he'd missed them. He pawed at his mud-splattered eyes, studying his next destination. When lightning flashed once more, he'd already braced himself, skittering through slippery puddles, thudding behind a compost heap. Its fetid odor made him gag, yet it too was unexpectedly welcome.

Though the rain was cold, he started to sweat. Where next? His ultimate destination was the brooding forest beyond the garden, but he had to approach it in a zigzag fashion—to a narrow equipment shed, then a watery furrow between rows of harvested corn, their wilted stubble helping to shield him. His heart pounded sickeningly. But he couldn't sprint more than ten feet during any blaze of lightning. He didn't dare remain in motion when the spotter was able to see through the night scope again. Another flash. He darted from the corn rows, sprawling in mud behind a straw-covered mound where potatoes had been grown. He quickly scrunched his eyes shut, protecting them against a fierce new blaze of lightning. When thunder roared, he opened them again. The interval between lightning and thunder was lessening, only two seconds apart, the center of the storm coming closer. Good. He needed all the distraction that it could possibly give to the spotter.

He studied the dark. Blinking through the cold heavy rain, he chose his next cover, a waist-high stretch of raspberry bushes. Lightning gleamed, and he lunged, but slipped on ooze and lost his balance, landing on his face, water spewing up his nostrils, cramming his mouth. He coughed, unable to breathe, rolling toward the raspberry bushes. Darkness enveloped him. He snorted, desperate to clear his nose and mouth.

Had he reached the bushes in time? Had the spotter seen him? Adrenaline spurted into his stomach; his lungs heaved. He shook, exhausted, as if he'd been sprinting for several miles. With his face to the sky, he let the rain wash his eyes, his nose, his lips. He swirled water around in his mouth, released it, then let the rain fill his mouth again and swallowed, tasting its sweetness, luxuriating in the relief to his swollen throat.

He had to keep moving! First to a row of grapevines along a wooden frame.

And after that . . .

At last he burst through the undergrowth, gaining the protection of the forest. Gobs of mud sagged from his scalp, his face, and his robe. Chunks slid down his arms, collecting on his fingers, plopping onto the dead leaves at his feet.

But he'd been successful. He hadn't been seen by the spotter.

By definition. If the spotter had seen him, he'd be dead by now.

He struggled to catch his breath. *I'm out. I'm free.* Now all that remained was to push through the forest, to use its cover and get away.

Where to? For a moment, the question stunned him. In his former life, he'd have automatically sought refuge with his network, Scalpel. But Scalpel in the end had become his enemy. To survive, he'd made Scalpel believe he was dead.

Then where else could he turn? A sudden spark of long and forcefully subdued affection told him to get to Arlene. She would help him, he knew. They'd once been lovers. Despite the separation of years, he was willing to risk that, because of what they'd shared, he could count on her. And reaching her, he'd also reach Jake, her brother. Jake, his friend.

Yet reluctantly he had to dismiss them. If in the old days his obligation would have been to contact his network, that obligation still existed, but not to Scalpel; instead, to his present network, the Catholic Church. He had to warn the Church about the hit on the monastery. He had to let the Church decide how to deal with the crisis. The Church would protect him.

But with a goal now in mind, he still didn't use the cover of the forest to get away. Instead, he faced the hill behind the monastery, its looming wooded shape made visible by another blaze of lightning. While darkness cloaked him again, he didn't understand his hesitation. Escape was before him—his chance to get away and warn the Church. Then why did he feel compelled . . . ?

He stared with greater fierceness toward the hill, realizing what he had to do, a strenuous priority insisting. The spotter. Yes, he had to get his hands on the spotter, to make him talk. The man would logically have chosen a vantage point where the trees would not impede his view. That suggested he'd hide with a clearing before him. But after years of living in its shadow, Drew was quite familiar with the contour of that hill. Even in the darkness and the storm, he could pinpoint the three major clearings at the top of the slope, the three most likely vantage points.

If indeed there was a spotter. He had no proof; he was still assuming.

But there was one way to know for sure.

And one way to learn why the death team had been sent here—to find out who was to blame.

23

The storm intensified. Ignoring the stunning impact of the rain, he stalked through the forest, veering past stumps and deadfalls, aiming toward the greater blackness of that hill.

He clutched his ax so hard that his knuckles ached, reached the base of the hill, and walked in a semicircle around it. At its back, he climbed. Trees thrashed him, their branches bent by the wind. He grabbed at saplings, branches, bushes, anything to pull himself up through the mire.

At the summit, he didn't worry about making noise; the din of the storm was louder than any sound he could have made, even an angry scream. He began to creep, using the shelter of bushes and dangling limbs.

From a careful vantage point, he decided that the trees behind the first clearing weren't being used as a hiding place. He stepped back into the woods and approached the second clearing. Below the hill, despite the shroud of rain, specks of light were visible from the monastery. It probably looked the same as on any other night. Except that it wasn't a monastery any longer. Someone had made it a house of death.

He studied the cover behind the second clearing, decided

that it too wasn't occupied, and turned to approach the third, when an unnatural ripple among the trees attracted his attention back toward the second clearing. His nerve ends quickened. Squinting from a flash of lightning, he saw a dark nylon sheet supported at head level like a makeshift tent, its sides and back tilted halfway to the ground to prevent rain from slanting under it. Its four ends were tied to the base of trees, the ropes tugged viciously by the wind. A tall upright stick held up its flapping middle. Of course. A spotter wouldn't have wanted the trouble of carrying even a compact tent up here. But in case of bad weather, a nylon sheet would have taken little room in a knapsack. Not as comfortable as a tent, but comfort wasn't the point.

He had to wait for the next bolt of lightning. The effect was like glimpsing sporadic images caught by a strobe light. Under the nylon sheet, through the space between the low sides and the ground, he saw a man's legs and hips—hiking boots, jeans, a sheathed knife on a belt.

Darkness. Drew crouched to peer up beneath the back of the sheet at the rest of him.

Lightning, and he saw the man's upper torso. Tall and muscular, wearing a knitted watchman's cap, a padded nylon vest, and a heavy outdoor shirt, the colors dull to blend in with the forest. The man peered down the slope toward the monastery. He used an infrared scope—its long, wide outline easily recognizable—mounted upon a bolt-action sniper's rifle attached to a swiveling tripod. With the next flash of lightning, the man turned away from the scope, rubbed his eyes, and drank from a Thermos that he'd propped along with a knapsack in the crook of a tree.

Drew backed off, rain streaking across his face. He glanced at the ax in his hand and decided that he couldn't attack by rushing beneath the tilted back of the nylon sheet. That posture would be too awkward. There was too much risk of his slipping in the mud or nudging the sheet and warning the man.

No, Drew thought, there had to be a better way.

He watched the nylon sheet being buffeted by the wind and nodded, creeping toward the right, toward the rope that attached one corner of the sheet to a tree. He felt the knot and recognized its shape. A slip knot. Strong and dependable, it could nonetheless be easily released by a quick tug on the free end of the rope.

He did so now. His plan was to trap the man inside the sheet and knock him unconscious with a blow from the blunt end of the ax. But instead of collapsing, the sheet was caught by the wind and driven upward, exposing the man to the storm. As lightning shattered a nearby tree, the man whirled in surprise and noticed Drew.

The ax was useless now. Too heavy, too slow. Drew dropped it, lunging, but surprise was still in his favor, for the man seemed startled not only by the upraised sheet but as well by what confronted him—the righteous eyes of a raging monk, his ascetic face an image of terror, his robe so dripping with mud that he might have been a nightmare sprung from the earth.

The hit on the monastery had shown that the team was professional, but even so, the spotter screamed reflexively, and at that moment, Drew screamed as well, the traditional Zen outcry, intended to distract his opponent while helping Drew to focus the strength he released along with the air from his lungs. He hadn't engaged in hand-to-hand combat for years, but his daily exercises, in part involving the dance steps of martial arts, had kept his reflexes tuned. Those dance steps had been practiced for spiritual reasons. But some things apparently could never be forgotten. His prior instincts returned with alarming precision.

To an untrained observer, what happened next would have

seemed even quicker than the thirteen seconds it took to occur. Blurred movements would have been confusing, almost impossible to distinguish from each other.

But to Drew—and no doubt to his opponent—the passage of time became amazingly extended. As a champion tennis player paradoxically sees the ball approach across the net with the bulk and lethargy of a beach ball, so these men confronted each other as if they were giants in slow motion.

Drew struck the heel of his palm against his opponent's chest, directly above the heart. The blow should have shattered his enemy's ribcage, thrusting bone splinters inward to impale both the heart and lungs.

It didn't happen. Through the heel of his palm, Drew felt at once what was wrong. His opponent's padded nylon vest was so filled with down, or more likely quick-drying Thinsulate, that it had absorbed the force of the blow. A grunt from the man indicated that damage had been done, but not enough to incapacitate him.

Drew's opponent had already braced himself, bending his knees, supporting his back against a tree. Drew had to thrust with the heel of his other palm, this time toward the throat. But his opponent responded. As lightning blinded Drew (but presumably his opponent as well), he sightlessly tried to deflect the blow that he knew would be aimed at his heart.

He'd used his right hand first. So now he thrust his left palm upward, tilting it slightly inward, anticipating that his opponent—having been struck at the heart—would have to respond from the opposite half of his body.

Drew's left palm struck his opponent's lunging right arm at the elbow, dislocating it. The force of the impact caused them both to reel off-balance in the mud. Drew heard the man's groan. His enemy slipped, colliding with him, entangling his dislocated arm in the bib of Drew's muddy robe. The bib was large enough that it could have been used as a sling.

As darkness returned, they found themselves locked together, chest to chest. Drew smelled the garlicky sausage that the man had eaten. The unfamiliar stench of meat was nauseating.

He pushed, then braced himself, his enemy pushing back. They skittered one way, then another, sliding across the mud, their breathing strident.

Drew felt his opponent reaching backward, groping for something on his hip.

He remembered.

The knife sheathed on his opponent's belt.

Prepared to grab for the hand that would hold the knife, Drew frantically changed his mind. He had to strike sooner. He needed a weapon.

The weapon was close at hand. Oblivious to the significance, he grabbed the crucifix that dangled on a chain around his neck. He clutched Christ's head and rammed the long slender base of the crucifix up his opponent's widened right nostril.

The storm unleashed its full fury. As if condemning what Drew had done, the sky blazed with so many jagged bolts of lightning that Heaven itself seemed fractured.

The man wasn't dead. Drew hadn't expected him to be. But such an invasion to a bodily orifice would produce shock. Predictably, the man straightened in agony, wailing, beginning to shake. Amazingly, his survival mechanisms continued to function, his free hand lunging with the knife.

Still locked against the shuddering body, Drew parried the knife, its blade slicing through the sleeve of his robe, and jabbed the web of skin between his thumb and first finger up hard against the man's throat, hearing the windpipe crack.

Lightning struck beside him, disintegrating the nearest tree. The roaring brilliance stunned him, lifting him off his feet. While splinters lanced him, he and the man were thrown from the forest. They tumbled into the clearing, rolling down the slope, twisting over each other, now Drew on top, now the man, thumping to a stop against a boulder. Drew gasped from the impact. Straining to disengage the man's arm from his robe, he peered down at the gloom-obscured face, touched the vein on the side of the neck, and realized that the man was dead.

Drew gagged. The crack of the lightning still reverberated in his ears. Dizzy, he shook his head and squinted through double vision toward the top of the clearing, toward the glowing smoke that rose from the shattered base of a tree ten feet from the now shredded nylon sheet. The smell of ozone drifted heavily around him. Lightning formed a rictus in the sky.

He shuddered, again peering down toward the man he'd killed. When he'd entered the monastery, he'd sworn that the killing had come to an end. And now?

He could have justified killing the man in anger—for the monks, if not for Stuart Little. Anger was a natural human fault, an innate weakness. The legacy of Cain. But he hadn't killed in anger. He'd passed far from anger, descending into an even more basic motive, survival. And the years had made no difference. He still retained the instinct, and his training had been so effective that even now he was capable of unleashing death automatically—as a knee will jerk when the hammer taps.

If I'd killed him by chance, I wouldn't care. But I did it reflexively. Because I was better at it.

Oh, Jesus. He prayed, recalling with horror what he'd done with the crucifix. Have mercy on this sinner. I didn't want to become what I am. It was forced upon me. But I should have had more control.

While rain streaked down his face, mingling with tears, he

bowed his head toward the man he'd killed and struck his breast. *Through my fault. Through my most grievous fault.*

He wanted to vomit.

Still, he had no choice. He had to keep himself in control. Bitterly he stood and took off his robe and hair shirt. His naked body shivered in the icy rain. He stripped the dead man, putting on his clothes. If he was compelled to reenter the world, he couldn't expect to survive by attracting attention in a habit. He had to take precautions. This man had not been alone; others were out there, waiting to kill him. Why? He didn't know. But a new understanding had come to him. His motive had passed beyond the need to avenge his fellow monks. A base emotion, necessarily dismissed. For now that he'd killed again, he'd put his immortal soul in jeopardy, and whoever was responsible had better have a damned good reason.

24

His enemy's clothes fit Drew badly, everything too loose. He had to pull his own socks over the dead man's in order for the hiking boots to feel firm. The jeans sagged as if he'd been on a diet, which in fact he had. If not for the padded vest on top of the heavy outdoor shirt, Drew might have looked as if his chest had caved in. He put the handkerchief that contained Stuart Little into a pocket of the vest and tied the skipping rope around his waist. He retrieved the photographs from his robe and slipped them into the other pocket of the vest. Then he stalked up the slope toward the tripod, rifle, and infrared scope.

Rain drenched him. Glancing around, he focused on the knapsack that his opponent had wedged in the crook of a tree. He opened it . . .

A Mauser pistol. He checked it, making sure that it was fully loaded, and shoved it behind his jacket, beneath the belt at the base of his spine.

Two magazines filled with ammunition. He put these in the pocket with Stuart Little.

A large plastic bag containing chocolate bars, peanuts, and dehydrated fruit. Starting with the peanuts, wanting their salt, he chewed them slowly, hungrily.

No time. What else could he scavenge before he left? He forced himself to think. What else would he need to confront the world? What had he formerly taken for granted but learned to live without?

One item occurred to him, and he reached for the hip on the jeans he wore, removing the dead man's wallet. He opened it, squinting to protect his eyes as lightning flashed, and saw several twenties and fives. All right, then, he had what amounted to another weapon. In a compartment of the wallet, he felt several plastic cards, which he assumed would be a driver's license and credit cards. All the statistics on them would be fake, of course. A professional would never go into an operation with bona fide I.D., the purpose of the documents merely to avert suspicion if the man were inadvertently involved in a traffic incident or forced to spend a night in a motel. But the fake identity would survive offhanded scrutiny, and Drew could temporarily use it.

What else? As he glanced around, debating, he suddenly heard a voice behind him. He crouched, spinning, his palms raised to defend himself. Despite the shrieking wind, he heard the voice again—ahead, to his left, strangely muffled, loud yet distant.

"George?"

Drew frowned, suspicious, scanning the woods.

"George, where are you?" The voice sounded amplified, vaguely metallic. Static crackled. "George, what the hell are you doing, taking a leak? You're supposed to check in." More static.

Drew relaxed, feeling the urgency drain from his muscles. He approached the sound of the voice. The walkie-talkie hung near the knapsack on the tree, formerly sheltered by the nylon sheet but now exposed to the rain.

"For Christ's sake, George. Check in."

Drew almost pressed the send button, strongly tempted to answer—not to pretend to be George, however, for Drew had no idea of whether George's voice was high or low, whether George had a distinctive accent or even a cold. It was highly unlikely that the man on the other end would be deceived. But Drew nonetheless wanted to answer, to imagine the shock that the man would feel if an unfamiliar voice came over the walkie-talkie and suddenly announced, "I'm sorry. George can't come to the phone right now. He's dead. But can I take a message?"

Get control, Drew thought. When you start imagining jokes like that, you're close to the edge.

He restrained the impulse. But already he knew more than he had a minute ago. The spotter had not been out here alone. Somewhere close, the spotter had a partner.

He assessed the possibilities. This hill above the monastery was the best place from which to study all the exits from the compound. But was it practical to put two men up here? Did it make more sense for the men to work in shifts, taking turns so that they each had a chance to get out of the cold and sleep?

Sleep where? Did the surveillance team have a vehicle in the area? As much as Drew wanted answers, he also needed transportation, but he didn't have much time to look for it.

"George, what the hell's going on?" the crackling voice demanded from the walkie-talkie. "Quit fooling around! Are you okay?"

Before the man on the other end became sufficiently disturbed to search for his partner or else drive away from the area, Drew had to find him. And if Drew's logic was valid, he had a good chance by searching along the road.

He left the trees, pushed by the rain, descending the gloomy slope. But coming to the dead man, he stopped abruptly. He'd asked himself what else he would need to survive in the world. An object on the naked corpse, the only thing that Drew hadn't thought to remove, attracted his attention. Totally artificial, completely unnecessary for the past six years, it suddenly seemed essential.

He knelt in the rain and took the wristwatch from the body.

Buckling it on, he felt a change come over him. Yes, he thought with immense sorrow, tears again flowing. He'd rejoined the world now.

Time had begun again.

25

At the bottom of the slope, Drew angled right, shifting quickly through another stretch of forest till he came to a section of the high chain-link fence that enclosed the land around the monastery. The noise of the storm persisted, hiding the jangle that the fence made as he climbed it. The moment he dropped to the mud on the other side, he assumed an instinctive defensive crouch. He'd crossed yet another threshhold. Like the watch on his wrist, the fence was one more shift from the peace of the monastery toward the turmoil of the world.

But he couldn't allow his regrets to disturb him. He had to reach the Church, specifically Father Hafer, his contact, his protector. He had to accept the conditions that had been forced upon him, to go where necessity took him. The answers, the dead monks in the monastery, *they* were what mattered. Not his reluctance.

He proceeded through the storm down the next wooded slope until he reached the road. A flash of lightning revealed that, as he'd remembered, it was paved. Rain glistened off it. After the difficult landscape through which he'd struggled, the smooth, unobstructed surface invited him. But he didn't dare show himself; he'd have to creep through the undergrowth along its border.

He paused to assess his location. The monastery was now to his left. Farther to his left, several miles away along corkscrew winding turns, was the nearest town, Quentin. He tried to imagine the strategy of the death team. If he was one of two men they'd left behind to check the monastery—just in case their quarry had remained in the area—he wouldn't want to be camping in the woods. Too damp and cold. He'd want a dry, warm place in which to sleep and change clothes and get something to eat while his partner took his turn on the hill. But he'd also want mobility, the chance to leave the area in a hurry if he had to. That combination of requirements suggested a vehicle large enough to hold equipment and a bed— a camper-truck, for example, or a van. And he certainly wouldn't park it where the authorities might drive by. Its probable hiding place would not be along the portion of the road that led toward Quentin. Instead, it would be on the opposite side of the monastery. On Drew's right. Where the road led toward the maple syrup factory, and after that, scenery, little else.

He found a van fifteen minutes later. On the far shoulder of the road, just before a curve would have made it impossible for an occupant to see the entrance to the lane up to the monastery. The position was logical, Drew thought. The only sure sign that I escaped would be a lot of vehicles arriving at the monastery—ambulances, cops, the coroner. Who else could have warned the authorities except a survivor of the killings? As soon as the team felt confident that I wasn't in the area, their back-up pair could pull out. Conversely, the longer the authorities failed to arrive, the more suspicious the team would be that I hadn't escaped.

But he had to verify that the van wasn't parked here simply because of a breakdown or an innocent sleepy driver. He crawled farther through the undergrowth along the road until he faced the rear of the van—no windows along the side but a bubblelike window in back. Ducking to keep from being spotted through that window, he sprinted across the pavement to crouch beside the rear right tire. The convex back window could have been designed to deflect the heat of the sun; on the other hand, it could have been designed to keep an outsider from getting an undistorted view of the interior. Perhaps the window worked only from inside to out; or perhaps it had a pull-down blind. The glass might even be bullet-proof, the van's body reinforced against attack also. These possibilities were hypothetical, of course, unverifiable except by assault.

Nonetheless, there was one easy test to find out if a seemingly ordinary vehicle had been designed to go into combat. All Drew needed to do was sink to the pavement and peer beneath the chassis. In the dark, he had to wait for lightning to reflect its gleam off the asphalt, but even with the brief illumination, he saw what he needed. The van had no visible gas tank.

The conclusion was obvious. Mounted inside the back compartment of the van, the fuel tank would be as protected as the vehicle's occupants. There wasn't any question now. He had to believe that the van was armored. To get into it, he'd need a weapon considerably more powerful than a Mauser pistol.

But even Goliath could be defeated. A reinforced vehicle was designed to survive an attack while it was moving. Stopped, it became more vulnerable, especially if the enemy got close to it. He knelt to feel the right rear tire, concluding without surprise that the rubber was extra thick and no doubt layered with metal. A bullet from the Mauser would do little damage, not enough to prevent the driver from speeding away.

The trick was to convince the occupant—already distressed because he couldn't raise his partner on the walkie-talkie—that he had another and more immediate problem: the rain's long-term effect on the gravel shoulder of the road. Even a bullet-resistant tire had to be inflated, or to use that logic in the reverse, it could also be deflated. True, by letting air from the tire, Drew wouldn't be able to drive the van away, but this well-equipped vehicle would surely have a spare.

Feeling along the gravel shoulder, he found what he needed. The van's designer had not anticipated that an attacker could get this close. The caps on the air valves didn't have a lock. Drew hurriedly unscrewed the one on the right rear tire, jammed a chunk of wood inside it, and heard a hiss of air.

The van began to list in Drew's direction, slowly sinking onto the rain-soaked gravel shoulder. He yanked the Mauser from behind his belt at his spine and scurried back to position himself with a good view of the rear door and both doors in front. His tactic was based on the assumption that as the occupant felt the van tilt beneath him, he'd conclude the rain had weakened the road's shoulder to such an extent that the van was sinking into the mud, listing toward the forest.

Would the driver come out to check?

A door banged open.

Drew rolled to the ditch and lay in frigid muddy water, waiting for the driver to check the listing side of the van.

But the driver did something else. Already nervous because he couldn't contact his partner, he bolted. Drew heard footsteps charge across the pavement toward the forest on the other side, and lunged to the top of the ditch. On his stomach, unable to reach the man, he fired the Mauser through the space between the van and the road, shifting his aim toward the sound of the rushing footsteps, clustering his bullets.

He heard a groan, a body toppling onto the asphalt. He scrambled to his feet and veered past the van toward the road. He hadn't shot to kill; instead, he'd chosen the legs as a target, needing to subdue the man and get some answers. Who'd ordered the hit? Why had they tried to kill him?

The man crawled awkwardly ahead of him.

A cracking flash from a handgun made Drew dart left. A second shot missed even farther. The man stopped shooting, pivoted forward again, and scuttled farther toward the trees beyond the road. He reached the edge of the pavement. In a moment, he'd be into the ditch and gain the cover of bushes from which to defend himself. Drew had to stop him now.

He sprinted at the man from the side. With no other choice, he kicked the man's forehead and stomped the hand that held the weapon. The man wailed, slumping off the pavement onto gravel, landing hard on his battered forehead. Drew yanked the weapon from his hand and kicked him again. The man groaned, rolling onto the leg that he'd been dragging, where a liquid darker than rain soaked the calf of his jeans. The resulting shriek was louder than that of the wind. The shriek broke, losing its pitch, descending to a moan, then silence.

The man lay still. As much as Drew could tell, he'd passed out from pain and shock. Even so, the next step was risky, for now Drew had to stoop to touch him. If the man was faking unconsciousness, if he had a knife . . .

Drew bound the arms with the skipping rope from around his waist. Next, he searched the man, not finding any other weapons. Then he grabbed his collar and dragged him across the pavement toward the van, tilting him slightly so that the wounded leg took a lot of stress. He needed to keep applying pain, to make sure the man stayed unconscious. He paused at the driver's door, which the wind had shut (or had it?), and studied the darkness beyond the window. Suppose he was wrong? His calculations had been based on the assumption that two men—and only two—had been left behind by the death team. After all, the fewer the members of the surveillance team, the less chance of drawing attention if the authorities arrived, and two was the minimum for the job. But suppose there *was* a third man who'd stayed inside, ready to shoot as Drew opened the door.

Standing out of the line of fire, pressed against the side of the van, Drew pointed his Mauser and slowly pulled the driver's door open. As he expected, the interior light did not come on. In the old days, he himself had always unscrewed the interior light of any vehicle he drove, anticipating a night when he might not want to show himself as he got out. But the corollary was that he'd always left a flashlight under the seat where he could get to it in a hurry if he needed it. So many habits of his former profession (*former?* he asked himself; what do you think you're doing *now?*) were common practice for everyone in it. That was one advantage when dealing with experts. You worked within a set of rules. The anxiety of the unpredictable came only when you dealt with amateurs.

The flashlight was under the seat where he himself would have left it, rubber-coated, a long, high-powered, four-battery model. Drew pressed the switch and sent its beam toward the back of the van.

No one.

The air inside smelled stale. He saw two sleeping bags on top of two mattresses. One wall held a bank of sophisticated two-way radio equipment. Against the other wall were two open knapsacks with clothes poking out of them, a partly empty pack of Cokes, a naphtha-fueled Primus stove, several cans of Hormel chili, Heinz spaghetti and meatballs, and Armour corned-beef hash. Drew's mouth tasted rancid. Didn't

these guys eat anything that didn't contain meat? Beneath the
edge of one sleeping bag, the tips of two rifles protruded.
There's no place like home.

He leaned back from the van and glanced down through
the rain toward the man at his feet. Nudging the wounded leg
and getting no response, he confirmed that the man was still
unconscious. Only then did he stoop and grab the man's
armpits from behind, lifting him to shove him into the back.

He froze when he saw headlights in the distance, two
specks getting larger, approaching from the direction of
Quentin, passing the lane up to the monastery, continuing this
way.

Take it easy, he thought. The lights might pose no danger.
Just a late-night motorist trying to stay on the road in this
storm.

But what would the motorist think when he or she passed
and saw one man pushing the motionless body of another
into the van?

Drew shut off his flashlight. Breathing quickly, he tilted the
driver's seat forward, shoving the body through the gap between the seat and the door frame. As soon as the man lay in
back, he covered him with a sleeping bag, even his head, then
leaned in to shift the knapsacks on top, anything to increase
the impression of clutter, to disguise the fact that a body lay
underneath.

Pivoting, he glanced along the road. The headlights magnified, growing brighter, closer. There wasn't time to scramble
inside without looking furtive and arousing suspicion. He
didn't want the driver to stop or, worse, become concerned
enough to stop in the next town and call the police.

Or what if the car belonged to the people who were after
him? If he climbed inside the van, he'd be trapped. He
couldn't even drive away since he hadn't changed the deflated
tire and he didn't know yet where the key was.

You'd better watch yourself, he thought. It's just a car. Six years out of action have made you paranoid. All the same, in the old days, he remembered, he'd respected the small details.

Needing an acceptable reason to be standing out here, he shut the van door and walked around the hood to face the ditch, then pulled down the fly on his pants. Glancing toward the headlights that were now blinding him, so large they seemed like searchlights, he turned with apparent indifference toward the forest and pretended to urinate. If this car did belong to the death team, he'd have a chance to reach the trees.

The approaching vehicle began to reduce its speed, its headlights gleaming. Drew watched in dismay. It slowed even more. He squinted through the rain and shivered when he saw a rack on the roof of the car. On the rack were two domes.

Oh, swell, he thought. Wonderful.

The police. It was hardly a reprieve. Drew couldn't risk telling them what had happened at the monastery. The first thing a cop would do would be to take him to the station, and after that, the police band on the C.B. radio would be filled with talk. He had to assume that the death team was monitoring transmissions from the area. They'd learn where he was, come for him, and sooner or later they'd get past the cops.

The cruiser stopped beside the van. A spotlight came on, aimed at Drew.

Okay, Drew thought. I've just spent six years in the strictest order of the Catholic Church. I've just survived a multiple hit. I stalked and killed a man. I wounded another man. I tied him up and managed to throw him in the back of this van before the cop arrived. Now let's see if I can do something really hard.

Like urinate.

Increasing pressure on his bladder, he squinted behind his shoulder toward the spotlight, vaguely able to read the words along the cruiser's door: VERMONT STATE POLICE. He contracted his muscles and sighed with mental relief as the liquid flowed.

"You couldn't wait?" a gruff male voice said behind the spotlight.

Drew shook himself and pulled up his fly. Turning, he grinned with feigned embarrassment toward the unseen presence behind the spotlight.

He opened his mouth to speak, but no words came. Except for mandatory choir and required responses at daily mass, he hadn't spoken to another human being for the past six years. His only conversation, one-sided, had been with a mouse.

"Couldn't wait? I asked you." The policeman was impatient.

Drew continued to grin with feigned embarrassment. Words formed in his mind, but his vocal cords resisted. Come on, you know you can talk. Pretend you're responding at mass. His lips and tongue felt thick. "Well—sure—I—hey, when you've got to go, you've got to go."

Amen. His voice sounded hoarse and gravelly.

"Something wrong with your throat?"

Drew shook his head but pretended to cough. "It's just a cold." The words came easier.

"You sound like you'd better see a doctor. Where you headed, into Quentin?"

Drew pretended to be puzzled. "Where?"

"Next town. Twelve miles south. The direction I came from."

"If I'd known a town was that close, I'd have tried to wait to take a leak. This isn't exactly cozy." Drew held out the palm of his hand, collecting rain.

"It's damp all right." The policeman was silent for a moment, unseen behind the spotlight. "You'd better get inside."

Drew coughed again. "Right." But as he turned toward the

driver's door on the van, he suddenly wondered if the cop had meant for him to get inside the cruiser. He reached for the latch on the driver's door.

"You didn't tell me where you were headed," the cop said.

"Massachusetts. Down to Boston." Drew waited tensely.

"You're driving late."

Apparently he'd answered acceptably. "They need me back at the office. I took a fall vacation, hunting up in Canada."

"You get anything?"

"Yeah. This cold."

The policeman laughed. "Well, next time don't stop with your lights off. In this storm, somebody might have come around this bend behind you and—"

"Whacked into me. It's true. I wasn't thinking." Drew coughed. "I guess I just didn't want to advertise what I was doing."

The policeman shut off the spotlight. Drew's eyes relaxed. From the lights on the cruiser's dashboard, he could make out the face—younger and thinner than the husky voice had suggested. "Stay awake, huh?" the cop said. "Keep your eyes on the road."

"You can count on it."

Raising his thumb, the policeman drove away. Drew watched the red specks of his taillights disappear around the bend in the road. He exhaled, leaning against the van. If the man in back had woken up and started making noises . . .

But what if he'd woken up anyhow and used the time to slip out of the rope, and now he's waiting for me? Drew yanked the door open. Turning on the flashlight, he saw that the heap beneath the sleeping bags wasn't moving. *Dead? Had he suffocated?*

Drew scrambled in, tugged off the sleeping bags, and relaxed when he heard faint breathing. But the wounded leg was pumping blood. The sleeping bag was soaked with it. He had to hurry. After making sure that the rope still bound the man's arms, he used the man's belt to apply a tourniquet above the bullet wound in the calf of the leg. The blood slowed.

Drew pulled him forward, easing him into the passenger seat, where he propped him into what appeared to be a comfortable position, then secured him across the waist and chest with the safety belt. He didn't want his enemy out of sight behind him, and this way, to a casual observer, the man seemed just a passenger fallen asleep.

Drew searched him, found a ring of keys, and got out in the rain to open the back of the van, looking for a spare tire. In an under-the-floor compartment, he did find a tire, but even better, he found an emergency air pump with a foot pedal and a pressure gauge. Five minutes later, he'd reinflated the back right tire. Then, getting behind the steering wheel, he tested several keys until one at last fit the ignition slot. He turned it; the engine started smoothly. But he frowned at the unfamiliar dashboard, the confusing levers and knobs on the steering column, many more than he was used to. The last time he'd driven was in 1979. He had no way of knowing what design changes had been introduced since then. Had the technology altered so much that he might not be able to control the van?

At least the transmission was automatic; he shouldn't have any trouble merely pressing the throttle and steering. But as he put the floor-shift into drive, he realized that he couldn't see through the rain on the windshield, and it took him thirty seconds to figure out that one of the knobs on the turn-signal lever controlled the wipers. A knob on another lever worked the headlights.

Get moving, he thought. That cop might come back this way. He had to head into Quentin. He didn't want to; there was still a risk that other members of the team were watching for him there. But he couldn't afford to go in the opposite direction, where he might run into the cop again.

At least Quentin lay south, and south was where he needed to go, to Boston, to his contact in his new network. To his confessor, Father Hafer. The Church would protect him.

But as he proceeded along the road through the storm, obeying the speed limit—was it still fifty-five?—he was filled with misgivings. He glanced to his left toward the murky gate and the narrow lane that wound up through the concealing forest toward the monastery. He imagined the peak of the lodge poking up above the fir trees at the top of the hill. He imagined the silence of the dead in their cells. His jaw muscles hardened.

Then the lane was behind him, and when he glanced toward his rearview mirror, all he saw was darkness. His heart sank, heavy with sorrow, hating to leave.

What strange new world lay ahead of him? he wondered. What answers? For six years, he'd lived in suspended time. But the world had moved on. About to confront what for him was an alien future, he knew that what he also would have to confront was his past, for the answers lay somewhere behind him. Who had attacked the monastery? Why? Was it Scalpel, his previous network? But Scalpel believed that he was dead. Again he thought about Arlene, his former lover, and about her brother, Jake, his friend. Jake, the only person, apart from Father Hafer, who knew that Drew wasn't dead. All right then, he thought. First I'll talk to Father Hafer; then I'll go to Jake. Despite his confusion, this much was sure. During his former life, he'd made many enemies, not just Scalpel. In stalking the sins of his past, he'd also be stalking himself.

PART TWO

PILGRIMAGE

STRANGE NEW WORLD

※

1

Ahead, Drew saw streetlights muted by the rain. He entered the outskirts of Quentin and veered from the main road, using side streets, avoiding the straight route through town where a hostile observer would be most likely to expect him to pass. At the far end of Quentin, he returned to the main road and continued south.

The clock on the dashboard was different from the type he'd been used to in cars in 1979. Instead of a circular face with arrows, this had a row of green glowing digits and letters, which made him feel as if he faced the cockpit of an aircraft. Another change he'd have to adjust to. 5:09 A.M. Dawn would come soon, he thought, anxious to get as far from Quentin as he could before it was light.

The man secured in the passenger seat began to groan. Drew glanced at him with concern, not yet prepared for him to wake up. Then the reason for the groan became obvious— the tourniquet had been on too long. He had to stop at the side of the road and loosen the belt, allowing the leg to get some circulation. Blood flowed from the wound and trickled onto the floor. The van was filled with a sick-sweet coppery odor.

He opened his window and drove ten minutes longer, peering through the rain on the windshield, then stopped again to refasten the tourniquet and once more proceeded. It occurred to him that this road was as likely a place for the team to be watching for him as the central route through Quentin, so as a further precaution, he turned left at the next intersection. A narrower road took him through several mountain valleys, winding past storm-shrouded peaks, climbing, dipping. He passed a few small towns, seeing their once familiar New England quaintness as if through the freshness of foreign eyes. A white peaked church aroused associations with the great New England preachers, Cotton Mather, Edward Taylor, Jonathan Edwards, though they of course had not achieved their greatness in Vermont. Edwards reminded him of the famous sermon "Sinners in the Hands of an Angry God," and he discovered that he'd begun to pray out loud.

"Forgive us our trespasses as we forgive those who trespass against us, and lead us not into temptation, but deliver us from evil."

Forgiveness, though, was not the issue. Survival was. Atonement was. Temptation? Yes. And evil.

At dawn, the road he was on intersected with another, and turning right, he proceeded south again, always south, toward Boston and Father Hafer. As the storm eased off, becoming a mist, a road sign told him that his route had taken him across a river into New Hampshire. That was all right. To get to Boston, it was quicker to cut through the bottom of New Hampshire anyhow. But now as he entered towns, he began to see sporadic traffic, occasional people on the streets, the world waking up to go about its business. He'd have to perform his errands before too many witnesses had a look at him. Though he hadn't slept since the previous night, the sensory bombardment of seeing the world again kept him fully awake. Soon the sun was high enough to burn off the mist that remained from the storm, and he noticed a sign for a picnic area up ahead. This early—8:14, the clock said—the place wouldn't be occupied, and he needed to stop again to loosen the wounded man's tourniquet.

The picnic area was small but attractive. A dense line of woods concealed it from the road. Five redwood tables were dispersed amid a grove of chestnut trees, their leaves turned autumn brown. A white stone path led to a narrow log bridge that went across a stream toward a seesaw and swing.

He stopped beside the first table and admired the glinting stream—no doubt unexceptional to jaded eyes, but to Drew, it was sensational—and then got to work. This time, he sensed a change in his prisoner.

Drew's defensive instincts took charge. He aimed the Mauser, staring at his prisoner's face. The man's eyelids came open; not completely, somewhat listlessly, but nonetheless open.

"Don't move," Drew said. "I'm not sure how awake you are, but in case you feel lucky, you ought to know we're alone here. I'll shoot if you force me to."

The warning got no response.

"You hear me?" Drew asked.

No answer.

"Do you understand?"

No reply.

There was one way to find out how groggy the man truly was. Drew waved his free hand in front of his prisoner's face, then abruptly touched his index finger against the tip of the prisoner's nose. This technique was favored by referees in boxing matches. If a boxer was fully conscious, his eyes would automatically follow the movement of the finger.

That happened now.

"You're awake all right," Drew said. Words came easier the more he talked. "Pay attention. I have to loosen the belt on your leg. It's in your best interest not to try kicking me while I do it. I'd only have to give your wound a punch to calm you down."

The prisoner studied him harshly. "Go ahead. Loosen the belt."

Drew did.

The prisoner squinted out the window toward the picnic tables. "Where's this? We still in Vermont?"

"New Hampshire."

"Ah." The man licked his cracked lips.

"What's wrong?"

"If we're all the way to New Hampshire, I guess I can't expect . . ."

"Your friends to find you? No, I wouldn't count on it."

The man stared down at his leg. "How bad?"

Drew shrugged. "The bullet went straight through. It missed the bone."

"That's something to be thankful for, isn't it? I've got a first-aid kit in the back. If you wouldn't mind."

Drew thought about it. "Sure. Why not?"

The man seemed surprised.

"And you'll be thirsty from loss of blood. I'll open one of those Cokes. Too bad they're not cold."

Drew cleaned the wound, disinfected and bandaged it. He swabbed crusted blood off the man's forehead, then tilted an opened Coke can against his lips. "Don't swallow too much at once. I don't want you sick."

The man blinked, incredulous.

Thirsty, Drew opened a Coke for himself. After six years of nothing to drink but water, milk, and fruit juice, the carbonated beverage was cloyingly sweet. "How bad's your pain?"

"I've had it worse."

"No doubt."

"If I need to"—he sounded indignant—"believe me, I can take more."

"Of course, but even so . . ." Drew opened two small sealed packs of aspirin from the medical kit and pushed four pills between the man's lips.

"Why all the help?"

"Let's just say I'm a good samaritan."

"Tell me another one. You wouldn't have brought me along unless you wanted to question me. You think you've invented some new technique? I'm supposed to crack up from all this kindness?"

Drew sighed. "Okay, if you insist, let's get down to it. What you're thinking now is that as long as I need information, I'll keep you alive. So you're weighing your life against the pain I'd give you to make you talk. Under those conditions, you're prepared to suffer the maximum. Or maybe you're planning to tell me whatever lies you think I might be dumb enough to accept. But then again, maybe the lies aren't such a good idea. After all, if I believed them and decided that I didn't have any further use for you, I might just finish you off. Are you with me so far?"

The man stayed silent.

Drew spread his hands. "If I had chemicals—sodium amytal, for instance—I could make you tell me whatever I wanted. But when it comes to torture, your survival depends on keeping your mouth shut. So here's the point. I don't intend to torture you, and I don't intend to kill you."

"What kind of—?"

"As far as I'm concerned, you're a hired hand. You were just doing your job. The person who hired you is the one responsible, not you."

"I don't know what the hell—"

"All right, I'll make it simple. When you hit the monastery, did you know who I was? Were you told about my background?"

"I get it." The man scowled. "This whole thing's a trick to get me to tell you who—"

Drew shook his head. "I did my best to explain. Then settle for this. In case you haven't guessed, I'm not just a monk. I'm not an amateur. Whatever I do with you, I want you to know it'll be professional. And I expect your standards to be the same. No panic, no stupid moves, no sloppiness. All right?"

The man looked baffled.

"For instance," Drew said, "I'm going to fasten the tourniquet again. Then I'm going to cover you with a sleeping bag up to your shoulders. You'll pretend to be asleep. We're going to drive till we find a service station. I won't leave the van. I'll talk to the attendant from my window. I need to buy something from him. And you'll keep pretending to be asleep. Otherwise, if you make a commotion, in all good conscience I'll have to stop you."

"Aside from that? You said no killing, no torture."

"You've got my word."

"But you still figure you can make me talk?"

"That's right."

"This I have to see."

Drew smiled.

As he drove from the picnic area, he felt assaulted by the noise and commotion of increased traffic. The cars seemed even smaller than he remembered them, a legacy from the gas crisis in the mid-seventies. But then two enormous motorhomes went by, and he recalled predictions from 1979 that fuel-squandering vehicles would be a thing of the past.

Apparently not. The motorhomes were followed by a luxury car, the style and name of which he didn't recognize (had the gas crisis ended? Had a new cheap plentiful fuel been de-

veloped?), and then by a big convertible. He didn't understand—convertibles had been discontinued before he entered
the monastery. What had happened to cause the turnaround?

He reached a series of fast-food drive-ins. Offensive to him
in the seventies, he'd nonetheless been used to them, familiar-
ity rendering them invisible. But now, to his unaccustomed
perspective, their ugliness was overwhelming. A sign adver-
tised a special on something called a taco pizza. And what on
earth were Chicken McNuggets?

He found a service station. Gas was a dollar twenty per gal-
lon, fifty cents higher than the outrageous price he remembered from 1979, and yet cars still crowded the road.

"I feel like I've come here from Mars."

The man beside him said, "What?"

Or maybe this *was* Mars.

Drew parked the van near the service station pumps.
"Close your eyes and keep quiet. Someone's coming."

Drew bought a radiator hose from a young attendant, using
cash from the wallet that he'd taken from the man on the hill.
As he drove past the pumps toward the street, he tossed the
hose onto his prisoner's lap. "Here. Got a present for you."

Despite the restraining safety belts, the man almost
jumped. "What the hell is this for?"

"Why are you upset? Don't you like surprises?"

"I said, what's it *for*?"

"Take a guess."

"It's used to beat somebody and not leave marks! But you
said you wouldn't—"

"Right. No beating. Wrong guess. But keep on trying. It'll
help pass the time."

"And aren't we going back the way we just came?"

"To that picnic area."

"I get it now."

"Get what?"

The man squirmed. "Holy God, you're crazy!"

Drew stared at him. "I wish you wouldn't take the name of the Lord in vain."

2

They reached the deserted picnic grounds. Concealed from traffic by the wooded stretch along the road, Drew backed the van until it was almost against a chestnut tree. He shut off the engine and stepped out, smiling. "Be right back," he promised, and cheerfully waved the radiator hose.

He shoved one end of the hose on top of the van's exhaust pipe, opened the rear door, and bent the hose until its opposite end was inside the van. Restarting the engine, he backed toward the chestnut tree so the rear door was secure against the hose. He left the engine running. The van began to fill with dense blue acrid exhaust.

The man became hysterical. "Christ, I was right! You are, you're fucking nuts!"

"Get too excited," Drew said coldly, "and you won't be able to hold your breath."

The man's eyes widened. Surrounded by haze, he started coughing.

Drew used the sleeping bags to seal the cracks around the back door. He made sure the windows were rolled up tightly. As a parting thought, he switched on the radio. "How would you like some music?"

He'd expected something more strident than heavy-metal rock. But what he heard instead was: "Linda Ronstadt and the Nelson Riddle Orchestra," an announcer said.

Against a lush arrangement typical of Frank Sinatra's Capitol recordings from the Fifties, Ronstadt (whose raw-throated versions of "When Will I Be Loved?" and "Back in the U.S.A." Drew vividly remembered) began to sing a standard from the Forties. He felt his sanity tilt.

His prisoner's coughing snapped him back to normal. The exhaust was thicker inside the van.

"Can't breathe," the man said. "Don't . . ."

Drew closed the door. He walked in front of the van, along the white stone path to the log bridge spanning a stream, where he dropped a few pebbles into the water. The air smelled cool and sweet.

With apparent indifference, he glanced back toward the van. The interior was obscured by haze, but he could nonetheless see the man writhing in the passenger seat. More important, the man could see him. Drew stretched his arms and leaned against the railing on the bridge. From the van, he heard screaming.

Shortly, when the screams began to subside, Drew left the bridge to stroll back along the white stone path. He opened the driver's door and shut off the engine. "How are you doing?"

The man's face was faintly blue. His eyelids were three-quarters closed. As a breeze helped the exhaust to drift from the van, Drew gently tapped his cheeks. "Don't go to sleep on me. I'd hate to think I was boring you. I asked you, how are you doing?"

The man retched, dry-heaving. "You son of a bitch."

"That well, huh?"

The man coughed again, hacking desperately to clear his lungs. "You bastard, you gave me your word."

"About what?"

"You promised. No killing, no torture."

"I'm keeping my promise. You're the one to blame if it's torture. Asphyxiation's supposed to be peaceful. Like going to sleep. Relax and drift with the flow. Make it easy on yourself."

The man wheezed, his eyes red, watering. "And this is what you call not trying to kill me?"

Drew looked insulted. "I meant it. I haven't the slightest intention of letting you die."

The man squinted. "Then?"

"I've got questions. If you don't answer them, I'll give you another dose of exhaust. And *another* if I have to. The monoxide's bound to have an effect. Only you can judge to what extent, though there's always the risk that your mind will become too weak for you to realize when you shouldn't stay quiet any longer."

"You think I'm afraid of dying?"

"I keep telling you, death's not at issue here. You'll survive."

"Then why the hell should I talk?"

"Because you're facing something worse than death. What's in your future, if you don't talk"—Drew scratched his beard stubble—"is brain damage. Permanent."

The man turned pale.

"You'll be a vegetable."

"They should have told me."

"Told you what?"

"How good you are. Since the moment I woke up, you haven't stopped screwing with my mind. You've played a half-dozen personalities. You've kept me off-balance all the time. Crazy? Hell, you're as sane as they come."

Drew turned on the engine again and shut the door.

3

Two sessions later, the man started answering questions. It took a while. He was semicoherent by then, and his statements were frequently garbled. But though forced to be patient, Drew at least felt confident that the man was telling the truth, for the carbon monoxide made him so groggy that it destroyed his inhibitions and in that respect was somewhat like sodium amytal. Two hours later, Drew had learned about as much as he figured he could expect.

But he wasn't encouraged. The hit had been purchased in as professional a manner as it had been carried out. For obvious reasons, the rule was that the client was never directly involved with the operation. If something went wrong, if a member of the team was captured or decided to try to blackmail his employer, there wasn't any direct trail back to whoever had paid the bill. Instead, the client got in touch with a broker, who contacted a sub-broker, who hired the necessary talent and made sure that the job was done. Except for the team itself, none of the principals met face to face. Arrangements among the client, broker, and sub-broker were conducted by intermediaries, using neutral phones. Nothing was ever communicated on paper. Fees were transferred through anonymous Swiss or Bahamian bank accounts.

As much as Drew could determine from what his prisoner told him, that procedure had been followed in this instance. The man convinced Drew that he'd been hired by what amounted to his agent, whose name he'd never learned. The agent knew where to get in touch with his talent, though his talent didn't know how to get in touch with him, and of course, the agent hadn't told his talent who was paying for the hit or why. A job was a job. Bizarre in this case, granted. However, the down payment had been generous.

Drew had frequently needed to rouse the man from his stupor, using smelling salts from the medical kit. Now he let him drift off to sleep, making sure that he had ventilation.

He brooded, discouraged. He'd desperately hoped to find the answers easily, but God had determined otherwise. His ordeal was to be prolonged. Yet another penance.

All right, he'd tried but failed here. Still, the failure wasn't his fault; if he hadn't tried, he'd have been foolish. But now he'd stayed too long. He had to get moving. Boston. His contact, Father Hafer. He had to tell his sponsor what had happened. To warn the Church and be given sanctuary.

He took the radiator hose off the end of the exhaust pipe, removed the sleeping bags from the back door, and closed it. As the man slept sickly beside him, Drew steered the van from the picnic grounds and continued through New Hampshire, heading southeast now, toward Massachusetts.

4

It was twilight when he came to Boston. He took his prisoner's wallet, then left the van and its unconscious occupant on the nearly empty top level of a parking ramp at Logan Airport. He had to do something with his prisoner, after all, and he had made promises. But that didn't mean he couldn't cause trouble.

Dusk had turned to dark when he found a pay phone near a bus stop in front of the airport, and called airport security, telling them where the van was parked (he'd taken care to wipe off his fingerprints) and what they'd find inside.

"He's a terrorist. I'm telling you, it's twisted, sick, perverted. You just ask him. He's got all these guns and—hey, he bragged about how he planned to hijack an overseas plane, make it fly to Florida, and crash on Disney World. Sick. So what could I do? Just put yourself in my place. I had to shoot him."

Drew hung up. Smiling inwardly, he got on a downtown bus, paid the driver, and took a seat to himself in back. The other passengers stared with disapproval at his stubble and grimy clothes. They'd remember him, he thought, and imagined the activity back at Logan.

Airport security's equipment would be sophisticated

enough to trace even his twenty-second call, because a jam-ming device would keep the line open as if he'd never hung up. By now, a security team would have found the van, and an-other would be rushing toward that pay phone in front of the airport. They'd question people near it. Someone was bound to remember a disheveled, grungy-looking man in jeans and a padded outdoor vest coming out of the phone booth—and possibly even remember that the unshaven man had boarded a bus.

He was leaving a trail. If he intended to disappear, he'd have to get off the bus and do something about his appear-ance, change it, improve it. Soon. Only then could he go to Fa-ther Hafer.

He glanced out the back toward traffic in the Boston night. No flashing lights of pursuit cars sped this way. Not yet at least. But how long . . . ?

The stores were closed; he'd have to wait till morning to get unobtrusive clothes. Meanwhile? Assessing his options, he rejected a hotel, even a sleazy one. Not the way he looked. All hotel clerks had memories. Right now, he needed camouflage.

He amused himself by imagining the questions that his prisoner would have to answer when the security officials found him. What kind of story would the man invent to ex-plain the bulletproof van, the weapons, the radio equipment? Whatever the story, Drew thought, the one thing the man didn't dare refer to was the monastery.

He recalled the exhilaration he'd felt when talking to his prisoner, when making his speech to airport security. After six years of relative silence, talking had made him feel strangely good. His mood changed abruptly as he asked himself why he'd bothered to leave his prisoner in the van.

Well, I couldn't very well have taken him with me.

No, of course not. But . . .

I had an option.

Yes, but you didn't take it.

In the old days . . .

True. When you fought for your life on the hill, you killed your opponent. (*Mea culpa.*) But here you had a choice.

At once the implication struck him. In the old days, he wouldn't have allowed the man to live.

5

Despite the changes in the world while he'd been away, one aspect at least remained the same. Or possibly it too was worse. Boston's Combat Zone.

After leaving the bus, he headed toward downtown Boston, walking through streetlight-haloed darkness along the city's weirdly angled streets (the legacy of the haphazard 1600s, a city planner's nightmare), passing chrome-and-glass structures next to historic brick-and-board facades, their interiors no doubt stripped and varnished, filled with hanging plants and Oriental rugs.

But as he ventured farther into the city's labyrinth, the buildings became oppressive. Pride gave way to neglect. He reached the jungle of the predators. The scavengers. The Combat Zone.

Prostitutes, twenty feet apart, lined both sides of the streets. Despite the cold October night, some wore tight skirts, often leather, hitched above their knees, or slashed long dresses that bared the skin up to a buttock.

As Drew walked past, they squinted at him, assessing.

"Hey, sweet thing."

"How'd you like your string pulled, love?"

Drew studied them as they studied him, scanning their faces, searching for a faint suggestion that this or that woman could be of use to him.

A garish yellow car screeched to a stop beside him. Drew pivoted on guard, gripping the Mauser beneath his padded vest. He blinked, startled, as a woman in the passenger seat exposed her breasts, the nipples encircled by lipstick, and raised her eyebrows in question.

Drew felt an unfamiliar tingle in his groin. He shook his head fiercely. She laughed and turned to the man beside her, who raised a beer can to his mouth and stomped on the gas pedal, roaring away.

He struggled to subdue the perverse swelling. His sex drive had disappeared effortlessly in the monastery; now, within hours of returning to the world, it was back. He forced himself to continue walking, searching, but Arlene's face came vividly to his memory.

A young black woman attracted his attention. Her thick dark hair was cropped close, like a boy's. Her breasts swelled beneath a Celtics sweatshirt; above it, she wore an open plastic coat. But what attracted him was that she kept pinching in distress at what appeared to be a rip in the calf of her panty hose. The gesture evoked his sympathy.

As he approached, her eyes flickered. She straightened, jutting out her breasts.

"Have you got a place?" Drew asked.

"What for?"

"It has to have a bed."

"*What for?*"

Drew frowned. He couldn't believe that he'd made a mistake about her.

"Be specific," she added. "What are you asking me?"

He understood. "Entrapment? You're afraid I might be a cop?"

She blinked her long eyelashes. "Now why would a cop want to bother me?"

"It's been so long I forgot. I'm supposed to ask how much.

If I'm the one who mentions the money, you can't be charged
for soliciting."

"How much for what?"

"To spend the night."

"And what do you want to *do* for the night?"

She wouldn't believe the truth, he realized, so he made a
proposition.

"Oh." She relaxed. "Is that all? For a minute, I thought you
looked kinky. All I can say is you must have a high opinion of
yourself if you think you can do *that* all night. Fifty bucks."

Even six years ago, that price would have been low. "For all
night?"

"Hon, one thing at a time. Maybe. We'll see." She tapped
him gently on his stubbled cheek. "But we'll have to do something about that sandpaper."

"That's part of the idea."

The glint returned to her eyes. "Just follow me."

6

She led him two blocks over, to a dingy apartment building
with grime on the bricks and dust on the windows. The
concrete front steps were spotted white with bird droppings.

At the door, she paused. "Now, love, what you have to
know is my boyfriend lives in the apartment next door. So in
case you're the kind who enjoys the rough stuff . . ."

"He and two pals with baseball bats pay us a visit."

"There you go. I knew you'd understand."

They entered a musty vestibule and went up two creaky
flights of stairs, the bannister wobbly. She unlocked a door to
a small apartment and spread out her arm in a gesture of welcome. "Home is where the heart is. The den of inequity."

Noticing the pun, Drew suddenly realized that she was

intelligent beyond being street smart. "You've been to college?"

"Yeah, the school of hard knocks. But if it's loving you want to learn about, I'll teach you tonight." She grinned and shut the door. The room was small but neat and attractive. "You'll notice I didn't lock us in, just in case my boyfriend has to pay us a visit. There's booze in the cabinet. Scotch, rye, bourbon. Beer in the fridge. It all costs extra. I've even got a place to send out for sandwiches, but that costs extra too."

"I bet," Drew said. "No booze. But I'm starving. Anything that doesn't have meat. Tomato and lettuce sandwiches. Three, no make it four. Milk." He scanned the room, his stomach rumbling, as she used the phone to order the food. A small Zenith television, a Sony stereo, a sofa, a director's chair.

"Is that the bedroom?" he asked, pointing toward a door.

She laughed. "You think you're in the Ritz? That's the closet. Over there's the john. Excuse the expression. The sofa's the bed. Just lift the cushions and pull that sucker out."

He did so. At once he heard the rustle of cloth behind him. Alarmed, he turned. Too late. With practiced efficiency, she'd dropped her plastic raincoat, tugged off her Celtics sweatshirt, and was now yanking down her leather skirt.

He raised a hand. "No. What I said I wanted to do—I lied."

She froze in an awkward crouch, her skirt down around her knees, wearing only panty hose, her pubic hair showing darkly through them. Her eyes blazed. Stooped as she was, her breasts dangled, making her look vulnerable. "What?" Furious, she straightened. "*What?*"

Her breasts and hips showed creamy stretchmarks against the smooth chocolate skin, evidence that she'd once had a child.

"It's not what I had in mind. I wanted to explain on the street, but I didn't think you'd—"

"Hey, I told you. Any rough stuff, anything kinky and—"
She raised a fist to slam it against the wall of the room.

"No! Stop!" Drew held up his arms. He knew that the walls
were so thin that shouts would be as disastrous as her pounding. He strained to speak softly. "Please, don't do it. Look, I'm
backing away. I'm nowhere close. You've got nothing to be
afraid of."

"What the hell?"

"I meant exactly what I said on the street. I want to spend
the night. That's all. To have a bath. To use your razor and
make myself presentable. And go to bed. And sleep."

Her eyebrows arched. "You're into baths? I'm supposed to
wash you, is that it?"

"Not at all." Though he tried not to look at her pubic hair,
his body betrayed him. After all, he hadn't seen a woman, let
alone a naked woman, since 1979, and he couldn't help feeling
attracted to her. But he *had* to resist, and struggled to focus on
her dark boyish face, ignoring her breasts. "Please, I wish
you'd put some clothes on."

"Now that," she said, but her voice was no longer angry, "is
kinky for sure. You mean to tell me"—she posed suggestively,
her eyes amused, sticking out one hip—"you don't like what
you see?"

"If it helps you to understand, I'm . . . or almost was . . . a
priest."

She narrowed her eyes. "So what? A friend of mine, she
does two priests a week. I believe in equal opportunity. I don't
discriminate."

Drew laughed.

"There, that's the idea. Loosen up, huh?"

"Really, how much for the night? But no sex."

"You're serious?"

He nodded.

"Would I have to leave?"

He shook his head. "In fact, I'd prefer it if you stayed."

"If that isn't weird." She calculated. "Okay, then, two hundred bucks." The furtive movement in her eyes suggested that she expected him to argue.

"That's just about what I have." He pulled out the wallets he'd taken from the man on the hill and the one in the van, tossing money on the pulled-out bed.

"You never heard of a hotel?"

He gestured toward his dirty clothes. "Like this? I'd be remembered."

"And you don't want to be remembered?"

"Let's just say I'm shy."

Her smile became a sober reassessment of him. "And love, you're also cool. Okay, I read you now. No need to fret. You're safe here. Have your bath."

"But if it's all the same to you," Drew said.

She opened the closet, pulling out a housecoat.

"I'd feel better if . . ."

She turned to him.

"You were in there with me."

"Oh?"

"Yeah, I've got some questions for you."

7

And, he didn't add, he wanted to keep her in sight.

In the bathroom, he took off his grimy vest. She sat on a chair in the corner and lit a joint.

"You sure you don't want a drag?" she asked.

"It goes against my religion."

"What does, relaxing?"

"Dulling my senses."

She chuckled. "We wouldn't want to do that."

Hot water from the faucet cascaded into the bathtub, raising steam that coated the mirror above the sink.

Drew put his clothes on the shelf behind him, unobtrusively shoving his Mauser beneath the padded vest. The act of stripping in front of her wasn't difficult. Physical shame had never been one of his—what was the slang from the old days?—hang-ups.

"Not bad," she said, judging his physique, then inhaling sharply, retaining the smoke. "A little gaunt in the haunches." She gestured with the joint. "A little skinny in the ass. If I had your rear end, I'd have to go on welfare. All the same, not bad."

Drew laughed. "I owe it all to diet and exercise."

"Exercise? Hell, you look like one of those guys that runs."

Drew's chest warmed; he'd been a passionate runner. "Yeah." He smiled. "Jim Fixx, Bill Rodgers."

"God, I hope not. Fixx is dead."

Drew felt a jolt. "You're kidding."

She sucked on the joint and shook her head. "Nope. He went out happy. Died on his jog." She looked at him. "Where have you been? If you're into that stuff, you'd know Fixx is dead. He had an inherited heart condition. All that jogging and—"

Drew tried to recover from his shock. "I guess there aren't any guarantees." He turned to step into the bathtub.

Abruptly she leaned forward from her chair. "Holy shit!"

He swung back, ready to grasp for the gun beneath his pile of clothes. "What's wrong?"

"What's *wrong*? Good Christ, your back! What happened to you?"

"Keep your voice down."

"Sorry, I forgot. My boyfriend."

"What about my back?"

"The scars."

"The *what*?"

"It looks like somebody whipped you."

Drew felt cold. He'd never realized. The years of penance he'd inflicted upon himself. The skipping rope with which he'd lashed his back. "Yeah, I was in Nam. Tortured."

"It must have been awful."

"I don't like to talk about it. I don't want to think about it anymore."

Drew kept his back turned away from her and stepped over the side of the bathtub. He shut off the water and slowly sank down, feeling it rise past his groin, then above his waist, the heat relaxing his aching muscles. Indeed, he hadn't had a hot bath since he'd entered the monastery, and the unaccustomed luxury made him feel vaguely guilty. He inhaled the lilac fragrance of the soap. As if he'd never seen one before, he studied a huge sponge that she'd given him to use as a washcloth, then soaked it and squeezed soapy water over his head.

She'd taken another drag off the joint and now exhaled the smoke she'd been holding as long as she could in her lungs. "Well, I was wrong. About your being shy."

"It's only a body."

"Yeah, I learned that quite a while ago. The shampoo's on that plastic shelf near your head. Talk about dirty. Look at the water. You'll have to drain the tub and start all over. What were you doing, rolling in mud?"

The irony amused him. "You don't know how right you are." He scratched his stubble. "We both agreed that I need a shave."

"The razor's next to the shampoo on that shelf."

She didn't have shaving cream, and he had to use hand soap. "I'm sure this'll sound odd," he said. "Who's President?"

She choked on the smoke she'd inhaled. "You're kidding me."

"I wish I was."

"But that's the second time you've . . . When I mentioned Fixx. Don't you watch television, read the papers?"

"Not where I've been."

"Even in jail, they've got television and newspapers."

"Then that should tell you something."

"You weren't in jail? But I had the impression . . ."

"Believe me, don't ask. The less I tell you . . ."

"The better off I am. All right, you claim you're a priest."

"Almost. What they call a brother."

"If that's your story, I'll pretend to believe you were in a monastery. Reagan's President."

Surprised, Drew stopped shaving for a moment. "So Carter didn't get reelected."

"Not the way he let those Iranians make fools of us."

"Iranians?"

"The hostage crisis. Don't you know anything?"

"I guess that's becoming obvious. Tell me."

Class was in session, and it distressed him. He learned about the Iranian assault on the American Embassy in Teheran in 1979. He learned that in 1980 the Soviets, claiming to be nervous about the violence in Iran, had invaded Afghanistan to make that country a protective buffer. Both of these crises, he realized with a shudder, had occurred because of him, because of something he'd done, or rather *hadn't* done. Ripples. Causes and consequences. If he'd completed his last assignment, if he'd killed the man his network had ordered him to, the sequence would probably never have started. Instead, he'd entered the monastery, and his target had risen to power in Iran.

Was I wrong? Drew thought. How many people have suffered because of me? But how can the decision not to kill be wrong?

The woman continued. Because of Afghanistan, President Carter had refused to allow American athletes to attend the 1980 Moscow Olympics. The Soviets in turn had refused to allow their athletes to attend the 1984 Olympics in Los Angeles.

"The Russians claimed they didn't go to the Olympics because they were worried about terrorists," the woman said. "But everybody knew they were just getting even for what Carter did."

Terrorists. Inwardly, Drew groaned. He'd hoped never to hear that word again.

But there was more, much more. As she smoked another joint, free-associating about the major events of the past six years, the sickness in his soul became worse. He learned that Reagan had nearly been assassinated by a love-struck maniac who wanted to attract the attention of a teenage movie star who'd just begun classes at Yale. The Pope had been wounded during a procession in St. Peter's Square by a Turkish religious fanatic supposedly working for the Bulgarian secret police. A South Korean commercial airliner filled with passengers, some American, had intruded on Soviet airspace and been shot down with no survivors, but nothing really had been done about it.

"Why not?" she asked indignantly. "How come we let them push us around?"

Drew couldn't bring himself to tell her that nothing in such matters was ever what it seemed, that commercial airliners didn't just happen to stray into hostile airspace.

The gist was clear. These disasters seemed commonplace to her, but after his six peaceful years in the monastery, the effect of her list was devastating to him. He tried to avoid concluding that the unacceptable had become ordinary, that the world had gone insane.

"Détente?" he asked.

"What's that?"

"The arms talks. Nuclear treaties."

"Oh, they keep trying. But do you know what some ass-holes—they call themselves experts—are claiming? That we can actually win, *survive,* a nuclear war. They say it's pre-dicted in the Bible. That Christians will defeat the Commu-nists."

Drew moaned. "Don't tell me any more." He stood, drip-ping water, preparing to step from the tub.

She threw him a towel. "Better cover yourself up, love. Oth-erwise"—she raised an eyebrow—"you never know. I might get interested."

He'd made the right choice, he decided. She was good for him; she made him laugh. He wrapped the towel around his waist, then glanced at his clothes. "I guess I'd better wash them."

"I might as well do *something* for what you paid me. Let me help."

He wasn't able to stop her in time. With a look of disgust, she picked up his grimy clothes. And stared at the Mauser be-neath them.

She was motionless. "You're full of surprises."

He regarded her intensely. "So what do we do about this one?"

"I scream. Then my boyfriend comes running."

"I hope not."

She studied his eyes.

He didn't want to hurt her. What would he do if she did start to scream?

"All right, I won't."

He exhaled.

"Half the people I know pack guns, but they don't mind their manners like you do. I'll grant you this. You sure give a girl an interesting time for two hundred dollars." Still holding the clothes, she wrinkled her nose. "But what's this bundle in your vest pocket? It smells kind of off."

"I told you, you'd better not ask."

He took the vest and set it on top of the shelf. Then he drained the tub and washed the socks, underwear, jeans, and wool shirt in fresh water. He asked her for a plastic bag, and while she phoned to find out what was taking their food so long to be delivered, he put the bloated body of Stuart Little into the plastic bag and tied the end in an airtight knot. Next, he set the bag and the Mauser beneath a towel, along with the photographs he'd brought with him from the monastery, and finally washed the vest.

Later, when she gave him a brown corduroy housecoat to wear, he waited until she wasn't looking and transferred the mouse, the photographs, and the gun to its pockets. She noticed the bulges, but by now she'd learned.

"I know," she said. "Don't ask."

8

The knock made him nervous. Holding the gun in the pocket of the housecoat, he stood on the blind side of the door while she asked, "Who is it?"

"Speedy's Take-Out. Gina, it's Al."

She nodded to Drew and opened the door just wide enough to pay with the money Drew had given her and take the food. She closed the door.

"Gina? Is that your name?"

"Sort of. My mother called me Regina. I had to shorten it. In my line of work, I didn't need jokes about being a queen."

He grinned. "If you wouldn't mind, Gina, could we lock the door?"

"My boyfriend wants to be able to get in here fast if he has to."

"But we both know he won't have to."

She studied him. "I'm not sure why I'm taking these chances with you."

But she did what he asked, and at once, he felt easier. Famished, he sat at the table and ate his sandwiches quickly. The bread was stale, the lettuce and tomatoes soggy, but after his recent diet of peanuts, chocolate bars, and freeze-dried fruit, he didn't care. Even the lukewarm milk tasted delicious.

The food hit him right away, the sugar making him tired. He hadn't slept in thirty-six hours. His eyes felt raw from the effort of driving all day. He glanced at the bed. "I hate to do this, but I have to ask one more favor."

She dipped a French fry into ketchup. "I haven't turned you down so far."

"I'd like to go to sleep now."

"So?" She chewed the French fry, licking a drop of ketchup off her lip. "Then go to sleep."

"But I want you with me."

"What?" Her eyes flashed. "I wish you'd make up your mind. First you make a big deal about giving me the night off, and now . . ."

"Next to me in bed. That's all. Nothing else."

"Just lie there?" She frowned. "Come on. You must want me to do *something*."

"Go to sleep. The same as me."

She looked baffled.

He wasn't sure how to explain that he wouldn't be able to sleep if he didn't know where she was and what she was doing. If he told her the truth—that he couldn't trust her with his life while he slept—she might not cooperate. He fidgeted, pretending to be embarrassed. "It's hard to . . . See . . . Let me put it this way. I . . ."

She tapped her long fingernails on the table.

". . . need someone to hold."

Her rigid face relaxed. "That's got to be the saddest thing I've ever—" She took his hand.

He walked with her to the pulled-out sofa and helped her to put a sheet across it and to cover two pillows that she took from a cupboard.

"It's cold tonight." She shivered and spread two blankets out, but despite her remark about the cold, she started to take off her housecoat.

"No," he whispered.

"Force of habit. Sorry." She grinned and refastened the robe, then turned off the lights.

He crawled beneath the blankets with her. In darkness, holding her, feeling her softness, he ignored the temptation of her breasts, her mound, her hips. He hadn't been in bed with a woman since 1979, and the memory of Arlene aroused him again. In his former profession, he hadn't been close to many women, unable to risk a commitment. Only Arlene had been important to him, a member of his former network, the one woman he'd permitted himself to love. His throat ached. Gina squirmed beside him, getting comfortable, and he distracted himself with the practical matter of making sure that the Mauser was under his leg where she couldn't reach it without waking him.

He snuggled against the mattress—the first he'd lain on since he entered the monastery—and tried to relax.

"Sweet dreams," she murmured against his ear.

He hoped. And amazingly, it was so.

Or rather he had *no* dreams. Terribly, he slept like the dead. A flicker of light woke him. He realized that Gina wasn't next to him any longer. Startled, he sat up in the dark, on guard, realizing that the light came from the television set. The images made him think he was still asleep and having a nightmare. He saw wild-eyed young men, their faces as pasty as corpses, dressed as Nazi storm troopers, and—he had to be hallucinating—purple Mohawk hair with rings through their earlobes. Women wearing black leather motorcycle jackets aimed fire hoses at billboards depicting hydrogen bomb-blast mushrooms.

A shadow stirred in front of the television.

He groped for his Mauser. But stopped.

The shadow was Gina. Turning, she took something out of her ear. The insane images persisted in silence.

"Sorry," she said. "I didn't think the television would wake you. I figured if I used this earphone . . ."

He pointed toward the screen. "What is *that*?"

"MTV. It stands for Music Television. These are punkers."

"What?"

"Hey, I said I'm sorry. I know you wanted me to sleep, but you've got to understand, my hours aren't the same as yours. I'm used to the night shift. Right now, I'm wide awake. Unless it's eight o'clock in the morning, after I get a doughnut and coffee with some friends down at the . . ."

"What time is it?"

She squinted at her watch. "Almost five-thirty."

"That late?" In the monastery, he'd have been awake and ready for mass by now. He pulled the blankets off and stepped from the bed. Even in Gina's robe, he felt cold. After using the bathroom, he touched the clothes he'd washed where they hung on towel racks. They were still wet. "Have you got a hair dryer?"

She laughed. "Now I *know* you weren't in a monastery."

"For my clothes."

She laughed again. "You'd better hope it doesn't make them shrink."

It didn't, and at breakfast—"Fruit," he said. "Give me any kind of fruit you've got"—he surprised himself by leaning over and kissing her on the cheek.

She too was surprised. "What was that for?"

"Just saying thanks."

"You mean half a thanks."

He didn't resist when she returned his kiss. Not long, not sensual, but intimate. On his lips.

In another life, he thought, his nostrils filling with her sweetness. Again he thought about Arlene. But that other life was denied to him.

Because of my sins.

9

At half-past nine, he used a phone booth in a drug store two blocks west of Boston Common. Despite his tattered outdoor clothes, he was shaved and clean and didn't seem to attract attention from the pharmacist typing a prescription at the counter next to the phone booth.

"Good morning. Holy Eucharist Parish," an old man's brittle voice said, as dusty as the better sherry sometimes used for mass wine.

"Yes. Father Hafer, please."

"I'm terribly sorry, but Father Hafer won't be available this morning."

Drew's heart fell. At the airport last night and several times later at Gina's, he'd called the rectory, but no one had answered, or rather a machine had answered, this same dusty brittle voice, prerecorded, explaining that the priests weren't near the phone right now, requesting the caller to leave a name and message. In Drew's case, that wasn't likely. Not the message *he* was bringing.

Dear God. Clutching the phone, he debated his options.

"Hello?" the brittle voice asked uncertainly on the phone. "Are you still—?"

Drew swallowed. "Yes, I'm here. Do you know . . . ? Wait. You said he won't be available this morning? Does that mean you expect him this afternoon?"

"It's difficult to be sure. Perhaps. But he might not want to be available after his treatment."

"Treatment?" Drew clutched the phone harder.

"If it's a priest you need, I can help you. Or any of the other priests here. Is this an emergency? You sound distressed."

"It's personal. I have to talk to *him*. I don't understand. What treatment?"

"I'm sorry. I don't feel at liberty to discuss it. But since you know him, no doubt he'd be willing to explain it to you. Why don't you leave your name and number?"

"I'll call back."

Drew hung up, opened the door, and stepped from the booth. The pharmacist glanced toward him. Trying to hide his distress, Drew looked at his watch, then walked past shelves and counters, exiting onto the noisy street.

This afternoon? And maybe not even then?

Someone had to be told. At Gina's apartment, he'd seen yesterday's *Boston Globe*. There'd been no mention of what had happened at the monastery. Unless the authorities were keeping the story a secret, the bodies had not yet been found. But it was hard to believe that such a story could be contained. As he proceeded along the crowded sidewalk, heading back toward Boston Common, his imagination conjured up the bloated corpses sprawled across the table or on the floor of their cells. Dead. All dead.

Again, reluctantly, he thought about the police. Perhaps if he simply called them. But they wouldn't believe him. They'd ask him to identify himself, to meet with them, and he wasn't prepared to do that, not until he was guaranteed safety. In the meantime, if he managed to convince them that he wasn't a crank, they'd alert the authorities in Vermont, where someone would check the monastery. When the bodies were found, it would soon be clear that one monk had escaped. The Boston police would make the connection with the man who'd called them. Who else could have known about the bodies, except a survivor or someone who'd killed them?

Drew shook his head. At worst, the police would suspect he was implicated in the deaths. At best, even if they believed he was innocent, they'd send out an APB for him, in effect helping the hit team to narrow their own search. And he hadn't even considered what would happen when the police looked into his background, first puzzled, then alarmed by the smokescreen of his past. It would be disastrous if their questions led them in that direction.

No. The route he'd first selected remained the best, the safest. Father Hafer. His confessor. Bring me in. As soon as possible. And help me find out who my enemies are!

Alien, he wandered the haphazard maze of Boston's streets. He roamed through shopping centers, introduced to glaring noisy video arcades and the incredible technology that taught adolescents to develop the deadly reflexes of fighter pilots. At every game he examined, the purpose was to attack and destroy. The winner obliterated the enemy. And sometimes nuclear clouds announced survival or defeat.

Adolescent males strode through the shopping centers in fashionable camouflage combat fatigues, while style-conscious older men wore imitation World War II bomber-pilot leather jackets.

Madness. Dear God, he asked himself, what had happened in the six years that he'd been away?

He fought to subdue his concern. Something was more important. Salvation. If the world was determined to destroy itself, very well. But what he needed was peace and seclusion.

To die was inevitable. To do so during prayer made death acceptable.

He phoned the rectory several times that afternoon, feeling more lost and impatient when he learned that Father Hafer had still not returned. Time became torturous. The newest edition of *The Boston Globe* still contained nothing about the monastery, though that in itself was not significant. Several explanations for the absence of the story were possible. But he couldn't bear the thought that the corpses had not yet been discovered, a blasphemous secret. At almost half-past four, as he walked through another shopping center, he suddenly faltered, blinking at what confronted him. A crowd shuffled toward him, their eyes red, wiping tears away.

Something horrible must have happened, he thought. He remembered 1963, America's reaction to President Kennedy's assassination, and braced himself for the worst.

He went over to them, alarmed by their grief. "What's happened? Why are you crying?"

A heavy middle-aged woman sniffled into her handkerchief, shaking her head. "So sad."

"What?"

"Seen it eight times. It still makes me cry. She looks so beautiful, dying from cancer."

"Cancer?"

"Debra Winger."

"*Who?*"

The woman looked shocked. "*Terms of Endearment.* Where have you been?"

The woman pointed beyond the crowd behind her. A movie theater. The show had just ended, the audience coming out.

In confusion, he found a row of phones next to a Lady Godiva lingerie store, its window filled with panties. A man wearing earrings walked past, then a woman with a heart tattooed on her hand. Drew shoved coins in the phone and hurriedly dialed the number he'd memorized.

"Holy Eucharist Parish."

"Please, is Father Hafer in yet?"

"Ah, it's you again. I told him about your calls. Just a moment. I'll see if he can be disturbed."

Drew slumped against the wall and waited. When at last he heard a rattle as the phone was picked up, he didn't recognize the strained, out-of-breath voice. "Yes, hello. This is Father Hafer."

Drew frowned. He hadn't spoken to Father Hafer in six years. How could he be sure? "I have to meet with you, Father. Now. Believe me, it's urgent."

"What? Who *is* this?"

Drew stared at the phone, suspicious. Suppose in their search the hit team had guessed the logical man to whom Drew would go for sanctuary? Suppose this voice, which sounded too hoarse and breathless to be Father Hafer's, belonged to one of the men who was after him? No, Drew had no choice. He had to follow the safeguards of his former profession. He couldn't afford to be careless.

"I asked, who *is* this?" the raspy voice insisted.

Drew's thoughts became frantic. Despite his misgivings, he nonetheless hoped. He needed to believe. A recognition code, some information that only the two of them shared. "Six years ago, we met in your office. We had an argument. But then we went to the church across the street, and you heard my confession."

"I've heard a lot of . . . six years ago? There's only one confession I can think of that anyone could be certain I'd remember."

"We had a discussion about a liqueur."

"Good God, it can't be! *You?*"

"No, listen. The liqueur. Do you remember its name?"

"Of course."

Drew scowled. "It comes to mind so quickly?"

"The Carthusians make it. I chose it deliberately. It's named for the fatherhouse. Chartreuse."

Drew relaxed. Good. Or at least, it would have to do.

Father Hafer kept talking. "What in heaven's name is all this mystery about? Where on earth *are* you? Why are you calling me?" The priest was even more out of breath. "You're obviously not at—"

"No, there's been an emergency. I had to leave. We've got to talk."

"Emergency? What kind?"

"I can't say on the phone. I have to meet with you. *Now.*"

"Why are you being so evasive? Meet where? And what's wrong with telling me over the phone?" The voice paused abruptly. "Surely you're not suggesting . . . ?"

"It might be tapped."

"But that's absurd."

"Absurd is what it is out here, Father. I'm telling you I don't have time. An emergency. Please listen to me."

The phone was silent except for the priest's strained breathing.

"Father?"

"Yes, all right. We'll meet."

Drew glanced around the shopping center, keeping his voice low but urgent. "Get a pad and pencil. I'll tell you the way to do this. You've got to help me, Father. You have to bring me in."

10

A classic intercept operation. A version of the dead drop. Theoretically. But this time Drew had to make allowance for more than one variable.

His primary fear, after all, was that the hit team had assumed where he'd need to go for help. By definition, not to the police, not with Drew's background. And not with his predictable need to avoid being held in their custody.

The logical alternative? The priest who'd sponsored him as a candidate for the Carthusians. After all, who else would be understanding? But by the same logic, the hit team would maintain surveillance on the priest. And when Father Hafer suddenly left the rectory during supper hour, an alert would be issued. He'd be followed.

The extra factor? Suppose the police had become involved, either because the bodies had been discovered or because Father Hafer was sufficiently disturbed by Drew's call to ask them for protection? It was possible that not only the hit team or the police but both would follow the priest. That complication changed an otherwise textbook operation from the equivalent of algebra into calculus. Regardless of how sophisticated the plan became, Drew had to begin with the basics.

Several times during the day, he'd passed Boston Common, scouting it from every angle, calculating its advantages. A large park filled with trees and paths, gardens, ponds, and playground equipment, it was flanked by rows of adjoining buildings, commercial and residential, on every side. He'd chosen a likely vantage point and, by seven o'clock that night, had positioned himself on an apartment building's roof. He crouched behind the cover of a chimney, concealing his silhouette, and peered down toward the Com-

mon. In mid-October, the sun had already set; the park was
in darkness except for streetlights along the borders and
lamps beside the paths.

The advantage of this rooftop location was that Drew
could study three of the four streets flanking the Common.
The far side was cloaked by the black intersecting branches of
leafless trees. But the far side didn't matter; it was too remote
for the hit team or the police to rush to this side without exposing themselves and giving Drew a chance to get away. And
it was on this side that Drew intended to approach Father
Hafer.

But not in person.

He'd been cautious about what he told the priest. If he'd
merely instructed Father Hafer to go to the Common and wait
for further developments, he'd have risked being found on this
roof by either the hit team or the police when they predictably
checked the buildings along the Common's perimeter. That
way of thinking assumed that the rectory's phone had been
tapped or that the priest was cooperating with the authorities.
But Drew's survival depended upon assumptions. Even now,
after many years, he vividly recalled the Rocky Mountain Industrial College in Colorado, Hank Dalton, and his lectures:
"Paranoia will save your life. In *your* world, boyos, it's crazy
not to be paranoid. Assume the bastards are against you. All
the time. Everywhere."

So Drew's instructions had been so complicated that he'd
told Father Hafer to write them down. No hit team or police
force could possibly have so many men that they could cover
the complete itinerary with only a few hours' notice. They'd
have no specific target area. From their perspective, contact
might be established anywhere.

But needing an extra margin of safety, Drew had decided
not to make that contact in person. As he scanned the three
shadowy but visible streets—below him, and to his right and

left—he saw no evidence of surveillance, no loiterers or vehicles that stopped with no one getting out. The streets looked normally occupied, innocent, ordinary.

He'd soon find out. At ten past seven, he saw the priest. Father Hafer wore a long dark overcoat, its top buttons open as instructed, the white of his collar clearly visible in the partly illuminated night. But the way Father Hafer moved caused Drew to frown. The priest didn't walk so much as he shuffled, slightly stooped, with evident fatigue. He came from the corner on Drew's right, beginning to cross the Common. Something was wrong. Drew shifted his gaze toward the street that the priest had left. No one seemed to be following.

Drew darted his eyes back toward the priest, and abruptly his alarm increased. Not because he'd discovered a trap, but because of something far more unexpected, though now that Drew thought about it he'd been given all the clues. He should have realized. Father Hafer was bent over, coughing so hard that fifty yards away Drew was able to hear it. The priest seemed in pain. And thinner than Drew recalled. Even at night, his pallor was evident.

The priest was dying.

"Treatment," the sherry-dusted voice had said from the rectory phone. "He might not want to be available after his treatment."

Chemotherapy. Radiation. Father Hafer was dying from cancer. The hoarseness, the lack of breath, how else to account for them? The cancer was in his throat, more likely in his lungs. And with terrible sorrow, Drew recalled the cigarette after cigarette that Father Hafer had smoked six years ago during the interview. The priest once more bent over, coughing, in evident pain. He used a handkerchief to wipe his mouth and straightened slowly, proceeding with difficulty toward the Common. Drew concentrated on the third bench along the path that the priest had been instructed to walk along.

The first. The second.

As Father Hafer reached the third, a shadow darted from bushes, rushing toward him.

Now, Drew thought. If he's under surveillance, *now*. Instead of watching the lean, jackal-like figure that seemed to be attacking the priest, Drew focused all his attention on the neighboring streets.

But nothing happened, no shouts, no sirens, no sudden eruptions of shadows or gunfire. Nothing. Eerie, the night remained still and, except for nearby traffic, silent.

Drew jerked his attention back toward the third bench along the path. His instructions to the lunging shadow had been explicit, based on the location of lamps in the park, allowing Drew an unimpeded view of what would happen. If the priest had been given a microphone and battery pack to hide beneath his clothes, the shadow's hasty frisk would reveal it. The figure would raise his right hand, warning Drew to run.

Of course, the shadow needed incentive to perform the frisk, and earlier Drew had looked for an evident but functional junky in the Combat Zone. He'd given the addict some, but promised him more, of a glassine bag of heroin that Drew had spent part of the afternoon relieving from a second-rate pusher. The bribe had been sufficient to motivate the junky but not enough to moderate his desperation, and not enough for Drew's purpose—or the possible danger—to be questioned.

Drew watched as the darting shadow collided with the priest, frisked him without seeming to, and delivered a note to the palm of Father Hafer's hand. At once, the shadow lunged away, retreating through a dark space between two path lamps, visible again when he scrambled through illuminated playground equipment, rushing as instructed toward the corner of the Common on Drew's left.

My, my, Drew thought. Well, what do you know? Not bad. Really not too shabby. It just goes to show—in a pinch, don't underestimate a junky, as long as he's properly motivated. Drew was delighted not only by the junky's performance but by his survival. The junky had not been killed.

Conclusion: If the hit team was in the area, they'd realized that the shadow down there wasn't Drew but instead a courier. They'd devote their attention to the courier as much as to the priest, in the hope that the courier would lead them back to Drew or at least give them information about what was in the note. The courier would lead them all right—to a cul-de-sac alley three blocks away where Drew had promised to pay the junky the rest of the heroin in the glassine bag.

Drew had left the bag on a window sill, and now, as he watched the junky disappear safely, he began to believe that neither the hit team nor the police had followed Father Hafer. But he still wasn't totally sure. He'd planned yet another diversion, and that was the purpose of the note that the priest now held in his hand.

Drew switched his attention back to the park. Father Hafer stood next to the third bench on the path, clutching one hand to his chest as if to control the startled pounding of his heart. Recovering from the assault, he peered down mystified at the note he held in his other hand, but before he could read it, he suddenly burst into another fit of coughing, pulling out his handkerchief, retching into it.

May God have mercy, Drew thought.

The priest wearily approached a nearby lamp and hunched his shoulders, straining to read the note. Drew knew what he would see.

My apologies for the surprise. I have to be sure that
you're not being followed. If there'd been another way . . .
But we're almost there. Go back the way you came. Return to the rectory.

The priest jerked his head up from the note, glancing
around with what, even at this distance, was evident annoy-
ance. He crammed the note into his overcoat pocket, bent forward again, and coughed painfully into his handkerchief.
With energy born from impatience, he turned to shuffle angrily from the Common, back the way he'd come.

If I'd known you were sick, I wouldn't have done it this
way, Drew thought. I'd have chosen a shorter, less difficult
route. Forgive me, Father, for the suffering I've caused you. I
had no choice. I had to make the enemy feel as impatient as
you are.

He watched the priest walk with effort away from the Common, then trudge out of sight down the street to Drew's right.
He saw no evidence of hastily reorganized surveillance. No
vehicle turned to head in the priest's new direction. No figure
pivoted, hurrying to keep the priest in sight.

Drew waited twenty seconds longer, and when he still saw
nothing unusual, he became as convinced as he was going to
be that neither the police nor a hit team were involved.

Still, from his rooftop position, Drew couldn't see the street
that the priest had entered. Unless he hurried from this roof
and rushed to peer around the corner, he couldn't know if that
street was safe. To approach the priest there might be a risk.

He did have another option. If he couldn't go to the priest,
the priest could come to him.

11

From the darkness of bushes beside the church, Drew peered across the street toward the rectory. Above him, light from within the church cast a glow through stained-glass windows depicting the Stations of the Cross. Though the windows were closed, Drew heard the prayers of an evening mass, a priest's muffled voice intoning, "Lamb of God, who take away the sins of the world, have mercy on us. Lamb of God . . ."

The congregation joined in, "Give us peace."

Drew's note had told Father Hafer to retrace the meandering directions he'd been given, returning to the rectory. But Drew had used a direct route to get here sooner. He needed to study various vantages on the rectory, to determine if anyone was watching it. A final precaution. After all, if a hit team had followed Father Hafer, one of its members might nonetheless have been left behind, a final precaution of their own. Only when Drew felt satisfied that the rectory was safe would he risk going forward with the rest of his plan.

But after six years in the monastery, he'd forgotten that during the seventies the Church had relaxed its rules on obligating Catholics to attend Sunday mass—a Saturday-evening mass could take its place.

And this was Saturday evening. With mass in progress, with parishioners' cars parked along the street of this well-to-do neighborhood, others pulling to a stop in front of the rectory, their motors running, their drivers apparently waiting to pick up worshippers when mass was completed, Drew found himself confronted with too many possible trouble spots. A match flared in a car down the street, a silhouette lighting a cigarette. Would a professional reveal his position that blatantly? Perhaps—if he wanted to seem like just another driver waiting for a passenger.

And what about the woman on the steps leading up to the church? She hugged an infant in a pink knitted cap and soft-looking blanket, patting its back as she paced. Had she left mass early because the infant had begun to cry, disturbing the parishioners, and now she waited for her husband? Then why was the infant no longer crying? And given the frost that escaped from the woman's mouth, why didn't she wait in the vestibule of the church, where she and the infant could be warm?

Too much to worry about.

Worse, he knew that his suspicions would increase when mass ended and the parishioners came out. In the swarm of activity, he'd never be able to determine if the area was safe. His plan had depended upon his being able to reach the rectory before Father Hafer returned. The priest would be coming back any time, and Drew couldn't risk crossing the street.

Unless. The mass, he decided. Instead of ruining his scheme, it might be a blessing. He turned and crept back through the bushes toward the side door of the church. In shadow, the door was thirty feet from the rear, adjacent to a sidewalk that allowed parishioners convenient access from the street behind it. He turned the iron latch, then tugged at the large oak door.

It resisted, and for a moment, his heart pounding, he worried that the door was locked. He tugged it harder; it opened, creaking.

His shoulders became rigid as he peered inside. He faced a concrete landing, its smooth plaster walls painted gleaming white. To his left, seven steps led up to a door behind which the service was being said—the main part of the church. Straight ahead, other steps led down to the church's darkened basement. And to his right, a third set of steps led up to another door.

He climbed the steps to his right, gently trying that door. It wasn't locked; he hadn't expected it to be. The priest who not long ago had gone through here to prepare himself for mass would hardly have expected an intruder while he and his servers were at the altar. Even so, Drew had to be silent.

Behind him, shuffling footsteps beyond the door to the main part of the church suggested that communion was now in progress, the congregation approaching the altar rail to receive the host. At once, from the church he heard the muffled strumming of guitars, a soprano singing the John Lennon-Yoko Ono tune "Give Peace a Chance," on occasion substituting "God" for "peace." Remembering the liturgical hymns that he and his fellow monks had sung at daily mass, Drew winced at the contrast. But at least the congregation was occupied, though now that he thought about it there were always a few impatient worshippers who left mass early, as soon as communion was nearly finished. Any moment, someone might come through that other door from the church and see Drew sneaking into here. He had to hurry.

He stepped through the opening, closed the door behind him, and studied the chamber that curved around behind the wall in back of the altar. This area was the sacristy, and it was here that the priest put on his vestments—the alb and cincture, chasuble and stole—before saying mass. Closets, cupboards, and shelves contained not only these vestments and others, but also altar cloths, candles, linen towels, incense, bottles of mass wine, and various other objects necessary for the many Catholic rituals.

He'd been concerned that one of the priest's assistants might have come back here in search of some forgotten item, but the sacristy was empty. To his left, he saw the archway that led out to the altar, the twinkling candles that flanked the golden tabernacle into which unused consecrated hosts, contained by a chalice, would be locked. The space in front of the altar was deserted, the priest and his assistants still down at the rail, giving communion to the parishioners. The guitars kept strumming. The soprano must have had the Beatles on her mind—she'd switched to the verse of George Harrison's "Here Comes the Sun," but now the "sun" meant "Son" and was sometimes changed to "Lord."

The sacristy was designed so that the congregation could not see into it through the archway. Confident of concealment, Drew opened several cupboards, at last discovering what he needed—a black, ankle-long cassock. He quickly put it on and secured the numerous buttons. Next, he chose a white, linen, hip-long surplice, pulling it over his head and down on top of the cassock. This combination of vestments was commonly used by priests who took the place of altar boys, assisting the celebrant of the mass.

On a counter beside the sink, he found a formal head covering known as a biretta—a black square hat with three symmetrical ridges at the top and a pompom in the middle. On impulse, he also took a prayer book from a stack beside an incense burner. The fragrance of the incense, even unlit, suffused his nostrils.

He stared toward the archway, hearing muffled footsteps cross the carpet toward the altar. He had to get out of here. Quickly returning to the door, closing it behind him, his chest tight, he caught a blurred glimpse of the priest and his servers arriving at the tabernacle now that communion was over. The guitars and the soprano mercifully stopped.

He gently slipped the latch into place, turned to dart down the stairs to the landing, and froze when the door that led to the main part of the church creaked open.

A red-haired man and a freckled woman backed out of the

church, glancing inward—to the right, toward the altar—each dipping their right hand in a marble holy-water basin, making the sign of the Cross. They were too preoccupied leaving mass early to notice him, but the instant they closed the door and turned to start down the stairs, they straightened, seeing his vestments, and fidgeted with embarrassment.

Drew lowered the hat to his side, holding the prayer book against the front of his surplice.

"Oh, uh . . . Hello there, Father," the man whispered.

Drew nodded soberly, his voice low. "My son. Escaping the benediction, are we?"

"Well, yes, that is, you see, Father, we . . ."

"Quite all right. No need to explain to me."

The man and woman glanced at each other, relieved.

"But you might explain to the Lord. I'm sure you've heard the parable about the guests who left the banquet early."

They blushed until the woman's freckles were hidden and the man's face matched the color of his hair. "I'm sorry, Father." The man bowed his head.

Beyond the door, Drew heard the priest intoning, "The mass is ended. Go in peace."

He gave the man and woman a paternal smile. "But I'm sure you had what you thought was a valid reason. At least you came to mass in the first place."

"As often as we're able to, Father."

The door to the main part of the church came open, the congregation leaving.

Drew raised his right hand in blessing. "The Lord be with you," he told the man and woman, then opened the door that led outside and motioned for the couple to go ahead of him.

On the shadowy sidewalk next to the church, he exhaled frost in the chill October night and put on the hat. He started to say good night, but seeing that the man and woman were headed toward the front of the church instead of toward the street in back, he walked with them. Behind him, parishioners left the church, many of them heading in his direction. That was fine with him. The bigger the crowd, the better. He heard them talking about the sermon, about the weather, about Michael Jackson (whoever *he* was).

"You must be new in the parish, Father," the woman said. "I haven't seen you before."

"I'm here for just a few days, visiting."

They reached the front of the church, where the bulk of the congregation streamed out the main doors, dispersing both ways along the street. Several cars started; traffic became congested. People clustered, talking. Perfect, Drew thought. If anyone was watching the rectory, so much commotion would be a distraction, and the one person who'd most blend with the scene would be a priest.

"Well, good night, Father," the man said. "See you in church." He seemed to think he'd made a grand joke.

When the man took the woman's hand, Drew assumed the proud look of a priest who'd just had the satisfaction of meeting a good church-going Catholic couple.

He didn't change expression when, beyond the crowd and the procession of departing cars, he noticed Father Hafer approaching the rectory on the opposite side. The priest had his handkerchief to his mouth, coughing. With all the activity, Drew couldn't tell if the priest was being followed, but in a way, it no longer mattered. He'd done as much as he could, had taken as many precautions as he could invent. From now on, everything was out of his control, in the hands of God.

No, you don't dare think that way, Drew warned himself. You can't presume to depend on God. The Lord helps those who help themselves.

He crossed the street toward the rectory. For a moment, he had a desperate misgiving about having put on the white surplice over the cassock. In the lamp above the door to the rectory, the surplice would make a perfect target. His spine itched. He clutched the doorknob, turned it, pushed the door open, and stepped inside.

But he wasn't in the rectory. Having been here before, he remembered that the rectory had a vestibule, a short narrow hallway that led to another door, the top half made of frosted glass beyond which pale light outlined the shadows of bulky furniture. A tiny lever projected from the middle of the door, just below the opaque glass, and Drew recalled from the last time that, if he turned the lever, a bell would be set off on the other side, a housekeeper soon arriving to let him in. If he decided not to ring the bell, he could simply open the door and enter, his assumption being that the door wasn't locked.

But he did neither. Instead, he turned and watched the outside door and waited. In winter, this vestibule would prevent wind from penetrating the rectory's interior, though Drew couldn't help concluding that those drafts would be insignificant when compared with the bone-cold winters he'd spent in the monastery, where his only source of heat had been the logs the custodian brothers had brought to his cell for his wood stove. The custodian brothers. The hermits. Dead! All dead! A groan escaped from him. He suddenly realized that Father Hafer was taking too long, that the priest who'd celebrated the mass would soon be coming from the church and discover him here, a stranger pretending to be a priest, and raise an outcry when he recognized the vestments that Drew had stolen from the sacristy.

Drew's pulse quickened as he heard the outside latch. He lunged behind the door as it swung open. A shadow appeared. Drew squeezed himself against the wall, feeling the pressure of the door against his chest. The shadow entered. And as Father Hafer shut the door, coughing, he found himself face to face with Drew.

12

"Father, I can explain."

Father Hafer's eyes widened, dark, yet bright with anger. "*You.*"

Drew raised his hands. "I'm sorry. Honestly. If I'd realized you were sick, I wouldn't have—I'd have found another way—"

"*You!*"

"There isn't time. We have to leave. It isn't safe to talk here." Drew spoke in a rush, trying to calm the priest, to keep him from such an outburst of indignation that he'd attract concern in the rectory. "Believe me, I wish I hadn't made you walk so—"

"Isn't time? We have to leave? It isn't safe?" Father Hafer glared. "What in God's name are you talking about? You've left the monastery. You've forced me to suffer through that charade with the note. Look at the way you're dressed. Have you lost your . . ." At once he halted, his role as a psychiatrist taking precedence over his other role as a priest. He seemed to recognize the mistake he'd made.

"No, Father, not my mind. My soul perhaps." Drew gestured toward the traffic noises outside the door. "And if I'm not careful, my life. The monastery was attacked. All the monks are dead. I'm being hunted."

Father Hafer's gray face turned shockingly pale. He stepped back, either revolted by what Drew had said or afraid to be within Drew's reach. "Dead? But that's impossible! Do you realize what you're saying?"

"I told you there isn't time. We're both in danger. Whoever killed the others might be coming here. They might be here already."

Father Hafer stared toward the door. "But this is madness. I don't . . ."

"Later. I'll explain. But first we've got to leave. Do you know a place where we can talk? A place that's secure."

Hearing a sudden noise, Drew whirled toward the inside door to the rectory. It opened, a tall, thin priest squinting out with concern.

"Yes, I thought I heard voices." The priest studied the two of them, focusing on Drew's surplice and cassock, frowning as he became aware of the agitation on their faces. "Father Hafer? Is everything all right?"

Drew's chest pounded. He kept his eyes on Father Hafer.

Father Hafer seemed to hold his breath. He returned Drew's gaze, intense, debating, then swung toward the priest in the open doorway. "All right? No, not at all. I've just received bad news about someone I've been counseling. I'm afraid I'll have to go back out again."

Drew felt his stomach muscles relax.

The priest at the door considered what he'd heard. "If you have to. Remember, Father, you're supposed to rest."

"In time. But this matter can't wait."

The priest at the door brought his attention back to Drew. "You must have come in a hurry that you didn't change your vestments after mass. What parish are you . . . ?"

Father Hafer interrupted. "No, it's better if he doesn't violate a confidence. You wouldn't want to be burdened with troublesome information."

"Yes, that's true. I understand."

"But"—distressed, Father Hafer turned to Drew— "perhaps the vestments *can* be taken off now."

They stared at each other.

PART THREE

GUARDIAN

RETREAT HOUSE

✠

1

"No. Surely not. *All* of them?" Father Hafer's voice cracked. Drew sat across from him, assessing. The priest appeared to believe, and yet to fight against believing, as if having first suspected that Drew had lost his sanity, he now was frantic to protect his own by questioning the unacceptable, the unendurable.

"*None*—God help us—survived?"

"I didn't check every cell. There wasn't time. It wasn't safe. But in the ones I did check . . . and in the kitchen where I found the two custodians who'd been shot. See, at first the vespers bell didn't ring. Then it did, but later than it should have. That's how I know that the others are dead."

"I'm not sure I—"

"Habit. If any monk survived, he couldn't have known that the others were dead. When he felt the summons of the bell, he'd have automatically gone to the chapel."

"And?" Father Hafer seemed to want to add "escaped."

"Been executed. I didn't hear any shots, but the guns would have been equipped with silencers. Then, too, I have to assume that the team had garottes."

Father Hafer stared at Drew as if the word "garottes" came from an unintelligible language. With the shock of sudden comprehension, his face contorted. He leaned forward in his chair, buried his face in his hands, and moaned. "May God have mercy on their souls."

2

They were in an apartment on the fifteenth floor of a glass-and-chrome building. Father Hafer had parked the rectory's station wagon in an underground garage, then taken Drew in an elevator to the private entrance of this unit.

But after the priest had locked the door and turned on the lights, Drew had glanced around in confusion. The living room was well appointed, yet strangely impersonal, reminding him of an expensive hotel room.

"What *is* this place? Are you sure it's . . . ?"

" 'Secure' is the word you used earlier. You needn't worry. No one, or at least very few, have any knowledge of it."

"But why?" The apartment made Drew nervous. It looked unlived in. "What's it used for?"

Father Hafer seemed reluctant to answer. "For matters of discretion. My duties as a psychiatrist aren't limited to advising the Carthusians. I'm often called upon to counsel priests from various orders who—let us say—have special problems. A crisis of faith. An overfondness for a young woman in the parish choir. A preference for alcohol, or drugs, or even another man. I trust I'm not saying anything that shocks you."

"Temptation's the key to human nature. In my former life, I took for granted that everyone had a weakness. I just had to look till I found it. If people weren't sinners, every intelligence network would be out of business."

Father Hafer nodded sadly. "The threat of embarrassment, of scandal. In that respect, perhaps our worlds aren't far apart. A priest who finds himself in moral conflict with his sacred vows sometimes becomes so distressed that he—"

"Cracks up?"

"I'd prefer to say has a nervous breakdown. Or perhaps he drinks so much that he jeopardizes the reputation of the Church."

"So you use this place to calm them down or dry them out."

"For rest and counseling. Or in an emergency, it's a temporary cloister while arrangements are made to take them to their order's rest home. Then, too, the separation of Church and State isn't always as clear as the constitution demands. Politicians offering incentives to the Church in exchange for the Catholic vote often prefer to meet here rather than be seen arriving at the office of the bishop or the cardinal."

"In other words, a safe house for priests," Drew said grimly. "No, Father, our worlds aren't different at all."

3

"May God have mercy on their souls."

Drew wasn't sure whose souls Father Hafer meant—those of the monks who'd been killed or the men who'd murdered them.

The moan produced another coughing fit.

Drew watched him, helpless. As sick as Father Hafer had appeared when Drew first saw him from the distant roof at Boston Common, the priest looked even worse up close. His skin, which had always been gray, was now even darker, drabber, making Drew think of lead poisoning.

Or another kind of poisoning. Chemotherapy. The flesh had shrunk on his cheeks and chin, emphasizing his facial bones. At the same time, the flesh seemed unconnected to those bones, about to peel away. His eyes seemed to bulge. His hair—once salt-and-pepper—was now a lusterless white, thin and brittle, sparse.

His body as well had begun to shrink; the black suit and white collar hung on him as if they'd been borrowed from a larger man. Drew couldn't help comparing their oversize fit with the way his own borrowed jeans, shirt, and vest were slightly too large for him. But there was a difference. Drew's lean, lithe body had the healthy glow of asceticism, whereas the priest's seemed to absorb light instead of giving it off—a collapsing black hole.

Of death.

"*Garottes?*" Father Hafer swallowed sickly. "But you don't know for sure. As far as you can tell, only the two custodian brothers in the kitchen were shot. You saw no evidence of strangulation."

"That's right. Except for the kitchen staff, the bodies I saw had been poisoned."

"Then—God help them—there's a chance that they didn't suffer."

"Oh, more than a chance. They never knew what hit them."

"*But how can you be sure?*"

"Because of the mouse."

The priest stared with utter incomprehension.

"That's something I've been waiting to tell you about." Sighing, Drew showed him the plastic bag containing the body of Stuart Little. "The poison killed him instantly. If I hadn't tossed him a chunk of bread and paused to say grace, I'd be dead myself."

Father Hafer reacted with horror. "You've been carrying that *thing* with you all this time?"

"I had to."

"*Why?*"

"When I came down from the attic, I didn't know if the corpses had been removed. Later I saw that they were still in their cells. But what if, after I escaped, the team came back and disposed of them? I still had to take the mouse's body with me to find out what poison was used. Some specialists have trademarks. They're fond of particular types. I'm hoping that an autopsy will tell me—"

"Specialists? Trademarks? Autopsy on a mouse? And you've been carrying it in your pocket? I was wrong. May God have mercy on them? No, not on them. May God have mercy on us *all*."

Father Hafer stood angrily. "You say that the monastery was attacked four nights ago?"

"That's right."

"And you escaped two nights later?" The priest's voice became strident.

"Yes."

"*But instead of going to the police, you wasted all that time coming to me.*"

"I couldn't take the risk that they'd keep me in jail. I'd have been a target."

"But for Heaven's sake, couldn't you at least have phoned them? Now the trail's gotten colder. It'll be harder for them to investigate."

"No. There was another reason that I didn't call them. *Couldn't.*"

"I can't imagine why."

"It wasn't my choice to make. The Church authorities had to know first. They had to decide what to do."

"Decide? You honestly think they'd have had an option and not have called the police?"

"They probably would have, but not right away."

"You're not making sense."

"Perfect sense. Remember who I am. Who I was. *Where* I was."

As the implications struck him, Father Hafer groaned. "How I wish that you'd never come to my office." He paled. "You say that our worlds aren't different? That's certainly how the Church's enemies will interpret this. Because of *you*.

And *me*. Because of my weakness in believing that you wanted salvation despite your shocking sins."

"But I do!"

Father Hafer dug his fingernails into his palms. "Because I recommended that the Carthusians accept you. Because your crimes caught up with you and now those holy monks have suffered the punishment intended for you"—he coughed—"I've jeopardized the reputation not just of the Carthusians, but of the Holy Mother Church herself. I can see the headlines now. Catholic Church Protects an Assassin, Gives Refuge to an International Killer."

"But I was on the side of . . ."

"Good? Is that what you wanted to say? Good? Killing?"

"I did it for my country. I thought I was right."

"But then you decided you were wrong?" Father Hafer's voice was filled with scorn. "And you wanted to be forgiven? Ah. Now those monks are dead. *And you've put the Church in danger.*"

"You'd better get control."

"*Control?*" He walked to the sofa, grabbed the phone on the table beside it, and pressed a sequence of numbers.

"Wait a minute. Who are you calling? If that's the police . . ." Drew reached for the phone.

With unexpected strength, Father Hafer shoved Drew's hand away.

"This is Father Hafer. Is he in? Well, wake him. I said wake him. It's an emergency."

With his ear to the phone, Father Hafer cupped a hand across the mouthpiece. "I'll be dead by the end of the year." He held up his hand, asking for silence. "What does it have to do with this? Do you recall our interview six years ago?"

"Of course."

"We talked about vows. I said I was fearful that if I recommended admitting so young a man as yourself to the rigors of the Carthusians, I'd be responsible for your soul if you found the order's sacred vows too harsh and broke them."

"I remember."

"And your response? You said that I'd be responsible anyhow, in a different way, if I refused your application. Because you felt such despair that you were tempted otherwise to kill yourself. If I turned you away, I'd be responsible for your damnation."

"Yes."

"It was specious reasoning. Every man's soul is his own responsibility. Your suicide would have been self-willed damnation. But I heard your confession. I thought, a man with your past, what hope did you have for salvation? What possible penance could compensate for your terrible sins?"

"So you recommended that the order accept me."

"And now, if not for me, those monks would still be striving to save their souls. Because of me, they're dead. This isn't just a scandal. It's not just a controversy about the Church protecting a killer. God damn you. You're responsible. To them, to me. And I to them. Because of you, I've jeopardized my soul. I told you I'm going to die. By Christmas. *I think you've put me in Hell.*"

Drew stared, absorbing the accusation, and now it was his turn to lean forward, to bury his face in his hands. He glanced up abruptly, hearing Father Hafer speak into the phone.

"Your Excellency? I deeply regret disturbing you this late, but something terrible has happened. Catastrophic. It's imperative that I meet with you at once."

4

The bishop, His Excellency the Most Reverent Peter B. Hanrahan had a lean, rectangular face. He was in his late forties, and though he'd been wakened less than an hour ago, his short, sandy hair looked freshly washed and blow-dried. It was combed impeccably. His green eyes reminded Drew of porcelain, but their glint, he noted, was that of steel.

The bishop sat behind a large oak desk in a paneled office decorated with testimonial plaques from various charitable organizations—Protestant and Jewish as well as Catholic—along with framed glossy photographs of him in a grinning handshake with various mayors of Boston, governors of Massachusetts, and presidents of the United States. But the pictures of him with several popes took the place of honor on the wall behind his desk.

Perhaps because he'd sensed that this meeting would be both disturbing and lengthy, he'd arrived at his office wearing clothes that looked considerably more comfortable than his bishop's robes or his priest's black suit and white collar. He'd chosen gray loafers, navy corduroy slacks, a light-blue Oxford button-down, and on top of it a burgundy sweater, the sleeves of which were pushed up slightly, revealing a Rolex watch. Steel, though, not gold.

To Drew, he looked like a politician, an appropriate comparison since at this level a Church official had to be a politician. The smoothness in the voice, the carefully effective choice of words, were probably less the result of Sunday sermonizing than negotiating with local Catholic businessmen for donations to construction projects in the diocese.

His Excellency sat behind his desk, tilting his chair back, eyes firm with concentration, as first Father Hafer and then Drew explained.

Four times, the bishop asked Drew for clarification. He considered the mouse in the plastic bag, nodded, and gestured for Drew to continue.

At last Drew concluded what he automatically thought of as his debriefing, indeed his second of the night. He glanced at his watch. It was seven minutes after one. Though thick beige draperies covered the windows, the muffled roar of a car rushing past outside intruded. Otherwise the room was silent.

The bishop shifted his gaze impassively from Drew to Father Hafer, then back to Drew. He blinked but otherwise stayed motionless. The silence persisted. At once his chair creaked as he leaned forward, placing his elbows on the desk.

His eyes glinted sharply. "You've certainly endured a most remarkable series of events." His voice remained resonant, smooth. "And of course most disturbing." He debated, then pressed a button on his intercom. "Paul?"

An equally smooth male voice responded. "Your Excellency?"

"Ah, good, you haven't gone back to your room."

"I thought you might need me."

"I don't know how I'd get along without you. Do you remember Pat Kelley?"

"Vaguely. But I can check his file."

"No need. He owns a construction equipment business. Last summer he and his wife took a trip to Rome. He asked if I could arrange for His Holiness to give them a blessing."

"Ah yes, I remember now." The voice chuckled. "He framed the certificate of the blessing and hung it on a wall in his office."

"If memory serves, his firm owns a helicopter. He claims it's for lifting heavy equipment onto high-rises, but I've always suspected that it's merely a toy that he writes off on his income tax. Would you phone him, please? Tell him that his Church needs a favor from him, the loan of his helicopter. Explain that I'll be in touch to thank him as soon as I can."

"Of course, your Excellency. I'll make sure I talk to him before he leaves his home for the office."

"No, now."

"You mean wake him?"

"I want that helicopter available by dawn. If he hesitates,

hint that the Knights of Columbus might hold a banquet in his honor. Next, check our computer for priests in the diocese who've had experience in hospitals or been in combat. Three will be sufficient, but one of them has to be able to fly the helicopter."

"Very good, your Excellency. Anything else?"

"Yes, bring us some coffee, maybe some doughnuts. I'm going to be busy for quite a while."

Bishop Hanrahan took his finger off the intercom and seemed to organize his thoughts. "Let me ask you something, Brother MacLane. I want to make sure that I understand the situation. After you escaped, your concern—apart for your safety—was for the well-being of the Church? That was your reason for not alerting the authorities but instead coming to your confessor and then to me?"

"That's right."

"Then may I assume you have some practical suggestions about how I should deal with this information?"

Drew nodded.

"What precisely?"

"Three possibilities." Drew touched his index fingers together. "First, as Carthusians those monks had removed themselves from the world. They'd sold whatever property they owned, closed out their bank accounts, quit their jobs. They'd said their final goodbyes to friends and relatives and made clear that no one from their former life could ever be in touch with them again. No visits, no phone calls, no letters. They even notified the government that they'd stop filing tax returns."

"I'm aware of that. Please make your suggestion."

"As far as the world is concerned, those men might as well have been dead already. They'd made themselves invisible, and in the normal course of events, when they did die, they should have been equally invisible. As I'm sure you know, the Carthusians don't use a coffin. The fully clothed body is placed on a board, the face covered with a cowl. The robe is nailed to the board. Then the corpse is buried in a private cemetery, marked only with a simple white cross. To emphasize humility, there's no inscription."

"I'm aware of that, too. Just what are you getting at?"

"Follow the procedure."

"What?"

"Go ahead and bury them."

"And not tell anyone?"

"Who otherwise would know? If they'd died from an epidemic or from accidental food poisoning, would the Church have publicized it? The Church would merely have laid them to rest. They'd have still been invisible. The Church's secret."

"In other words, you're suggesting that the Church cover up a mass murder?"

"It's one possibility."

Bishop Hanrahan stared. "But if the authorities can't investigate, if they can't track down the men responsible, who may I ask is supposed to punish . . . ?"

"God."

The bishop jerked his head back. "I seem to have forgotten that you too were a Carthusian. Your faith is remarkable."

"No, please don't say that. Faith? I believe in Hell."

"Indeed." The bishop frowned. "So to protect the Church's reputation, we consign the murderers to their ultimate judgment and in the meantime pretend that the killings never occurred?"

"I said it's one option. It has to be considered."

"But would you act upon it?"

"No."

"Why not?"

"Because there's too great a risk of the story getting out. That kind of operation—the cleanup, the burial—requires a lot of personnel, the probability of gossip. If this were an intelligence assignment, if professionals did the cleanup, I wouldn't be worried. But priests would be doing the work, and what they'd have to deal with would be so shocking that they might not be able to keep their mouths shut afterward."

The bishop considered. "Perhaps. But don't forget that priests are used to the vow of secrecy. I could make them swear discretion."

"Even so, what's the point of doing it the hard way? Why involve a lot of people? The problem isn't that those monks were killed. The problem is . . ."

"You," Father Hafer said, the first time he'd spoken in quite a while.

Drew nodded somberly. "Me."

"And you as well," the bishop told Father Hafer. "If not for you, there would have been no massacre."

"I'm well aware, your Excellency. *Mea culpa*. I'll soon have to make a case for my soul." Father Hafer tried unsuccessfully to stifle a cough.

The bishop's hard gaze softened. "Forgive me. I shouldn't speak harshly." He turned to Drew. "Your second suggestion?"

"Don't erase the evidence of the murders. Instead, erase the evidence of my presence in the monastery. Take everything out of my cell. Make it look unlived in. Remove my file from the order's records. Then alert the authorities, and when they ask about the empty cell, explain that the order's been having difficulty attracting recruits, that the monastery wasn't fully occupied. Because there'll be no way for the police to find out that a former assassin was given refuge there, the Church avoids the scandal."

"And do you recommend that second option?"

"It has the merit of being simple. The police can investigate. There's almost no chance that someone'll talk. The only people who'd know are the three of us and whoever cleans out my cell." He paused. "There is a third option, of course."

"Indeed?"

"The simplest of all."

"And that is?"

"To tell the police the truth."

The bishop narrowed his eyes.

The intercom buzzed. He pressed a button on it. "Yes?"

"Your Excellency, I've made arrangements for the helicopter."

"And the crew?"

"Jesuits. Before they joined the order, they served in Vietnam. One of them flew a gunship."

"Appropriate. The commandos of the Church. A few other things," the bishop said. "I'd like you to make an appointment for me with the cardinal as soon as possible this morning."

"Do you want me to wake him?"

"Good gracious, no. Wait until seven. Before he says his private daily mass. And, Paul, I'm a little confused about who has jurisdiction over the Carthusians in Vermont. Find out."

"At once, your Excellency."

The bishop released the button on the intercom. He settled back. "You must be wondering what I'm doing."

"Not at all," Drew said. "You're planning to send those Jesuits up to the monastery. To make sure I'm telling the truth."

The bishop blinked.

"And you plan to meet with the cardinal in time to send a message to stop them if he disagrees with you. But you doubt that the cardinal will. The chances are that he'll commend you for acting so quickly. But the hard part, the final decision, you'll leave to him."

"You have to admit that your story makes one skeptical. A monastery filled with corpses? Really, I'd be foolish to make decisions before I had all the facts."

"But why would I lie?"

"Perhaps not lie. Perhaps after six years as a hermit, you're mistaken. Confused."

"Deranged?" Drew felt angry.

"Of course not. *Confused*. At this point, who can say? All I know is that you've been carrying a dead mouse in your pocket for several days. In my place, would you feel that inspires confidence?"

The bishop glanced at the plastic bag on his desk. Too casually, he reached for it.

In a blur, Drew intercepted his hand. The bishop flinched. Drew put the bag back into his pocket.

"Attached to your little friend?"

"Let's say I'm sentimental."

The bishop's expression hardened. "Very well. If His Eminence, the cardinal, agrees, the helicopter should arrive at the monastery by midday. And if what you claim is true, we'll decide which of the options you suggest seems wisest."

"And in the meantime?"

"You'll need a place to stay. Whatever the truth of what you've been through, you're clearly exhausted. And I might suggest that a change of clothing would be appropriate."

Drew peered down, self-conscious, at his battered woodsman's clothes. "Then where are you sending me?"

"I don't quite know yet. I'll have to consult with Paul."

Father Hafer coughed. "And what about myself? Should I plan to go with him?"

The bishop pursed his lips. "I think not. We don't want to draw attention to ourselves. Until we know exactly how the situation stands, it's better if we go about our regular routine. There is one thing I suggest, however. Did you hear this man's confession?"

"Of course. Before I recommended that the Carthusians accept him. His life as a hermit was his penance."

"No, I mean recently. Tonight."

"Well, no. That is . . ." Father Hafer frowned. "I never thought . . ."

"Because he claims he killed a man two nights ago. If true, his soul is in danger. He has to be absolved."

Drew remembered the crucifix that he'd used as a weapon and wondered if absolution was possible.

5

"Wake up. We're there," the voice said.

Drew lay on the rear seat of the black Cadillac that the bishop had sent for. The driver—a young, trim, athletic-looking man with blue eyes and a brushcut, wearing deck shoes, jeans, and a U. of Mass. sweatshirt—had been introduced to him as Father Logan. "But you can just call me Hal." The priest looked as if he belonged on a varsity track team. It took Drew a moment to recognize the double significance of "Mass" on his sweatshirt.

They'd left the bishop's residence shortly before dawn, and as the Cadillac headed west on Interstate 90 through the sparse lights of traffic out of Boston, Hal had said, "We'll be driving awhile. You might as well get some sleep."

But there'd been too much to think about. Drew hadn't felt tired. Still, after they'd stopped for breakfast, he'd fallen asleep as soon as he got back in the car. He later wondered if he'd been sedated. But Hal had never been close to Drew's food. Except, Drew thought, when I went to the men's room. But why would the bishop want me sedated?

He thought about it as he lay in the back of the Cadillac, pretending to waken slowly after Hal had spoken to him. Sitting up, he rubbed his eyes and squinted at the brilliant morning sunlight, the gorgeous hues of maples on the hills along the road. At once he realized that, even if he hadn't been sedated, the effect was the same. He didn't know where he was.

"We left the Interstate?"

"Quite a while ago. How did you sleep?"

"Like a baby."

Drew noticed Hal's smile.

The road was a two-lane blacktop with mountains on either side. Drew didn't see any traffic or buildings. The digital clock on the dashboard showed 10:31. "Are we still in Massachusetts?"

"Yep."

"What part?"

"Far west."

"But where exactly?"

"It's a complicated route. It'd take too long to explain."

"And you said we'd arrived—wherever it is that you're taking me."

"It isn't far ahead. I wanted to give you the chance to wake up before we got there."

Dissatisfied, Drew studied the terrain, still wondering where he was. They entered a gentle wooded valley and turned down another road. A quarter mile along it, they reached a high stone wall on the right and drove through an open iron fence. In the distance, Drew saw a looming white crucifix, haloed by sunlight, on top of a large rectangular building. Smaller buildings flanked it. The grounds were spacious. The lawn, though brown in October, looked recently cut. Shrubs bordered gardens whose flowers had died. As Drew came closer, he noticed a deserted basketball court.

"What *is* this place?" Its apparent peacefulness did not reassure him. He wondered if it might be a sanitarium.

"A couple of things," Hal said. "It started as a seminary. But candidates for the priesthood haven't exactly been lining up these past few years. So the Church decided that the empty rooms ought to be put to use. That building to the right is a dormitory. Once a month for a weekend, various Catholic men's clubs come here to have a retreat."

Drew nodded, sympathetic with the concept. The Church believed that the faithful needed to escape the pressures of the world from time to time. So for forty-eight hours, usually from a Friday to a Sunday night, parishioners had the chance for a nominal fee to go to a "retreat house," often a seminary, where they immersed themselves in Catholic rituals. A retreat master, usually an eminent priest, gave lectures on matters of dogma and spirituality. Except during discussion groups, conversation was not permitted. Abundant religious literature was available in each dormitory room as an aid to meditation.

"But that's just once a month," Hal said. "That building on the left gets the most use. It's a rest home. At the bishop's, I saw you talking to Father Hafer. I guess you know he's a psychiatrist. I wouldn't want his job for anything. He has to counsel priests who can't bear the strain of their vows."

"Well, people get weak sometimes."

"Don't I know. It's sad. You'd be surprised how many burned-out cases I've driven out here. From what I'm told, there are three or four other places like this in the country. But this is the only one I've seen. That building to the left of the seminary is where they sleep. They don't have any duties, except of course to say their daily mass. Otherwise, they get medication and therapy from the local staff."

"How long do they stay?"

"A month or two for most of them. Till they're off the booze or they realize that even saints don't have to work twenty-five hours a day. But a few of them—well, I took an old pastor out here four years ago, and he still swears that the Virgin Mary sings to him every night."

6

They stopped at the large middle building, the one with the crucifix on top. The angle of the sun was such that the cross's shadow fell across the Cadillac, and as Drew got out, he noted that despite the clear bright sky, the air was crisp.

He faced the building, scanning its windows. The bricks looked dingy. The concrete steps were cracked.

"The place seems deserted."

Hal shrugged. "It's almost eleven. The seminarians must be in class."

As if on cue, the voices of young men drifted out from somewhere deep in the building. "Lord have mercy. Christ have mercy. Lord have mercy. Glory to God in the highest . . ."

"It sounds like the Kyrie and the Gloria," Hal said. "They must be practicing the liturgy."

Drew shook his head. "Classes on Sunday? I don't think so. And mass would have been first thing this morning. No, something isn't right."

He started up the cracked concrete steps.

Hal stopped him. "Sure, but this Sunday was special. Mass was postponed till now."

Puzzled, Drew turned to him.

"We're supposed to stay away from the seminarians. The bishop told the housemaster you'd be here. But it's understood that you're not to attract attention. You'll be sleeping over there." Hal pointed toward the building on the right. "Where they hold the retreats."

Drew felt uneasy. "But if they're holding a retreat, what's the difference, if *they* see me or the seminarians do?"

"There's no retreat this weekend. We've got that building all to ourselves."

How much has Hal been told about me? Drew wondered.

Why do I feel I've met his type before? The way he stands at attention. The way he kept checking the Cadillac's rear-view mirror.

In another line of work.

"Yeah, it'll be nice and quiet. Restful," Hal said.

A slight wind touched Drew's face. Unsettled, he came back down the steps and walked with Hal across the lawn toward the building on the right. Something else bothered him. "If we're not supposed to be noticed, don't you think you'd better move the car?"

"I will in a couple of minutes. I've got to come back anyway."

"Oh?"

"To get you some clothes. I don't have much to choose from. These seminarians don't exactly dress for style. Black shoes, black socks, black pants. Depressing. But they like to play sports, so I think I can get you a sweatshirt. Maybe a workshirt. Could be even a windbreaker. Are you hungry?"

"Vegetables. Fresh. A lot."

Hal laughed. "Yeah, carrots, huh? What's up, Doc? You want anything to read?"

Drew shook his head. "I figured I'd exercise."

"Great! You like basketball? You feel like a little one-on-one? No, wait a minute, that's no good. The court's outside. You're not supposed to show yourself."

Drew stopped abruptly.

"Something wrong?"

"A question. I'm bursting to ask it."

"Be my guest."

"Are you really a priest?"

"Does the Pope hate Polish jokes? Was John a Baptist? You better believe I'm a priest."

"What else?"

"Beg pardon?"

"What else are—were—you? You've got military intelligence written all over you." Drew watched him soberly.

"Okay. Yeah, I used to be in military intelligence. The Navy. Like *Magnum, P.I.*"

Drew didn't understand the reference. "What made you join the priesthood?"

Hal started walking again. "You've got your choice of rooms. Which one?"

Drew answered quickly, not wanting to change the subject. "Anything near the stairs on the second floor."

"Yeah, that's what I'd choose, too. No chance of somebody coming through your window. And the high ground's easier to defend. But it's not like on the third floor, where it takes too long to get outside."

"I asked you, why did you join the priesthood?"

"And you can keep asking."

"Then let me ask you this."

Hal stopped, impatient.

"I'm used to a pattern. Five days ago, I was forced to give it up. And now it's Sunday."

"So?"

"At the bishop's, Father Hafer heard my confession. Five days are too long. I want to receive communion."

"Hey, now you're talking. Never mind basketball. I haven't said my mass for today. But I don't have a server."

"Sure, you do. Just show me the way to an altar."

"There's a chapel in the retreat house."

"I'll fill the cruets for your water and wine. I'll serve the best mass you ever said."

"Pal, you've got a deal. What's funny?"

"We sound like two kids getting ready to play."

7

A board creaked. Drew knelt, praying, in the front pew of
the chapel. He raised his head to look past his shoulder
toward the shadows behind him.

No one. He turned to the altar and resumed his prayers.

It was after midnight. Though the mass he'd served for Hal
had been almost twelve hours earlier, he still remembered the
touch of the thin stiff host on his tongue. His spirit had
swelled.

The rest of the day had depressed him. He'd tried to keep
busy—washed and shaved and put on the clothes that Hal had
brought him. He'd paced his room, done push-ups and sit-
ups, rehearsed the dance steps of martial arts, and wondered
where Hal had gone.

By mid-afternoon, he knew that the helicopter would long
ago have reached the monastery. The Jesuits would have found
the bodies and told the bishop. The bishop would have talked
to the cardinal. The cardinal would have talked to Rome. So
why hasn't someone talked to me? What decisions were made?
What's happening?

The irony of his nervous boredom struck him forcibly. For
six years, living in solitude, he'd never felt the burden of time.
And now, after five days' absence from the monastery, he
couldn't keep from looking at his watch, a watch that he'd
taken from a man he'd killed. Moaning, he sank to his knees
and begged for this burden to be lifted from him. I know that
nothing happens without a reason. I'm only an instrument.
But please, Lord, pass this cup from my lips. All I want is
peace.

All? He touched the bulge in the jacket pocket, remembering the urge he'd felt to seek revenge for the death of the
monks. He felt the photographs in another pocket—the man

and woman in flames, the young boy screaming—and prayed for his soul.

Near six, Hal entered his room. "I brought you some milk and vegetables. Raw cauliflower you said you wanted? I can't even stand the stuff cooked."

"How long am I supposed to stay here?"

"Till they tell us different, I suppose. Hey, if you're bored, they've got just one television here, and that's in the seminary building, but I can get you a radio."

"What about a phone?"

"Just relax, why don't you? Smell the country air."

"Indoors?"

"You've got a point. But not to worry. Everything's taken care of."

"Oh?"

"It's going down to thirty tonight. But I figured out how to get the heat turned on in the building."

Hal left.

Drew glanced impatiently at his watch again. Its hands were aimed precisely at six—when for years the vespers bell had rung.

He craved the satisfaction that he'd felt today during mass. He wanted to reestablish the blissful pattern of the monastery. Six o'clock. As if he heard the vespers bell start tolling, he obeyed its summons and left his room.

8

The retreat house was silent. A light glowed at the end of the hall, beckoning him to the stairwell. With his hand on the pitted metal railing, he descended, reached the first floor, ignored the half-lit lobby, and continued to the basement. He brushed his hand against a clammy plaster wall and proceeded through darkness toward a door to the right. The chapel where earlier he'd served at mass, where the vespers service ought to occur.

He pushed the door open and entered. Blackness. Recalling a light switch to his left, he felt for it and flicked it on. But the power for the basement must have been on a different circuit from the one for his room on the second floor, because the blackness continued to face him. Earlier, sunlight gleaming through windows high on one wall had been sufficient for him to help at mass. But now . . .

He imagined the hands on his watch moving farther past six. His compulsion increased.

As he groped along the wall to his left, he bumped against a chair. Then he reached another wall and felt his way past the bulky compartment of a confessional. The odor of mildew widened his nostrils. But beneath the mildew was the redolence of incense from years of services. When his waist touched the altar railing, he knew that he was almost home.

Now if only there were matches. He remembered the rows of votive candles that flanked the inside right and left stretch of the altar railing. Yes, when he straddled the altar railing, stepping forward, he felt matches in a metal cup, struck one against the cup, and smiled at the gleam. His smile persisted as one by one he lit the numerous candles, filling the front of the chapel with a shimmering radiance. He knelt in the first pew, silently reciting the vespers prayers.

At midnight, with still no word from the bishop, he again felt compelled by the ritual, coming back to recite the matins prayers.

And heard the creak behind him.

9

The first time he heard it, he told himself that the sound was only wood contracting because of cold.

The second time, he told himself that the tired old building was sagging.

The third time, he pulled his Mauser from beneath his jacket and sank to the floor.

"Okay, pal, relax," a voice said in back. "I didn't mean to make you nervous."

Hal.

Drew stayed out of sight on the floor beneath the pew.

"Come on," Hal said, concealed by the dark at the rear of the chapel. "I know where you are. I saw you duck down. But first I saw you pull a gun from under your jacket. So let's be calm, all right? I'm supposed to keep an eye on you, not let you use me for target practice."

Drew didn't intend to take chances. He glanced ahead of him toward a door on his left beyond the altar railing, remembering from the mass he'd served at noon that it led to the sacristy behind the altar. Beyond it, another door opened on a stairwell. If I have to, I can jump the altar railing and get away.

Another creak, coming closer.

Drew's forehead felt slick with sweat. But the chapel was terribly cold.

"Just loosen up, okay," Hal asked, "while I explain? See, I know you came down here at six. I figured you were following the routine you had in the monastery. Vespers service. The next service is matins, at midnight. So I got here earlier. I thought I'd watch you from out of sight so I wouldn't disturb your prayers. I'm only doing my job. How was I to know that the floor back here creaks every time I breathe?"

Drew debated. Hal could be telling the truth. But why

didn't he just come down here with me? I wouldn't have cared if he was in the chapel while I prayed. No, something's wrong.

Another creak. Closer.

Drew eased from the pew and began to squirm toward the candlelit altar railing. His chest felt chilled by the floor.

"We're in a bind," Hal said, a little closer. "You don't want to show yourself till I do. But I don't want to do it first, not with that gun in your hand. Hey, I made a mistake by not letting you know I was here. I admit that. But we've got to end this stand-off. I'm on your side."

Another creak.

Drew squirmed a half-foot closer to the altar rail. The candles shimmered.

"Think," Hal said. "If I wanted to move against you, I could have done it while you slept in the car."

Good point.

"Or I could have . . ."

Creak. Drew squirmed another half-foot closer to the altar railing.

" . . . shot you while you were praying just now."

A second good point.

"So, let's call a truce. I'm a victim of circumstance."

All right, Drew thought. I like to believe I'm open-minded. Instead of crawling the rest of the way to the altar railing, he rolled in the opposite direction, toward the pews on the right side of the chapel.

He aimed, and for the first time, spoke. "Then all you have to do is tell me why you joined the priesthood."

At the sound of Drew's voice, the door to the chapel burst open. A man in a priest's black suit and white collar lunged forward, aiming an M-16.

"No!" Hal screamed. He stood, much closer than Drew had expected, raising an arm. It was hard to tell in the shadows. He might have been holding a pistol.

But the priest swung in Hal's direction, squeezing the trigger on the M-16. The muzzle flash lit the shadows in back as the weapon—on automatic—rattled, ejecting empty casings which clinked on the floor. The force of the volley lifted Hal off his feet and threw him back against a wall. Blood spattered. Hal rebounded, shuddering, toppling to the floor.

As Drew rose, kneeling, aiming his Mauser, a second priest appeared in the doorway, flanking the first, clutching an Uzi, strafing the chapel. The noise, magnified by the echoing walls, struck Drew's ears. In agony, they started to ring.

He crouched back down below the pew. *Priests? Killers?* His sanity tilted. *Religion? Violence?* The contradiction shocked him.

The priest-assassins had the advantage of darkness back there. He didn't dare show himself in the candlelight to aim and shoot. A Mauser against an M-16 and an Uzi? The odds were against him. As the acrid stench of gunpowder wafted toward him, he turned, thrust upward from his knees, and vaulted the altar railing. His body arched. He landed hard on the carpeted floor beyond, gasping from the impact against his shoulder, and lunged up, scrambling toward the sacristy door. Bullets tore apart the altar behind him.

At once the staccato reports of a handgun interrupted the rattling gunfire. The unmistakable wallop of a .45 semiautomatic pistol. Again. And again.

Drew grabbed the knob on the sacristy door, twisting it, shoving inward, falling to conceal his body. He glanced back and caught a furtive glimpse of someone else in the chapel. Enough to make him pause where he crouched.

Another priest. But this man was older. Early fifties, average height, but large in the chest. Muscular shoulders. Dark hair, Slavic features, mustache.

In the dark of the sacristy, Drew forced himself to keep

staring. The priest had appeared from—Drew shuddered, suddenly realizing—the confessional on the right.

Had he been there all along? When I groped through the dark and bumped against that confessional earlier?

He had stepped out, shooting, when Hal had been killed. Drew still aimed his pistol toward the priests in back, his caution needless. The men lay motionless in the aisle, a pool of blood spreading around them at the edge of the candlelight.

The pistol was in the priest's left hand. Drew's perspective gave him a good view of the outside of that hand. A glint of reflected illumination attracted his attention. Off the middle finger.

A ring, and even at this distance, it was compelling. Eerie. It seemed to glow.

A ring with a large red brilliant stone.

The priest, his pistol still raised, swung toward the open door to the sacristy. Though he couldn't possibly see Drew in the darkness back there, Drew had the terrible sense that their gazes met. His jaw set grimly, the priest stalked toward the altar railing.

Drew tightened his finger on the Mauser's trigger. He didn't know whether to shoot the man or to question him. After all, the man had saved his life.

Or had he? Two priests just tried to kill me. Hal's dead. And this guy looks like he'd kick your teeth in for penance if he didn't like what you told him in confession. Why was he hiding in the chapel? What in God's name is going on?

The priest lunged out of sight, ducking for cover beneath the altar railing.

Drew held his breath.

The voice from out there was full-throated, husky, tinged with a Slavic accent. "I know you're in the sacristy. Listen to what I tell you. Yanus."

With difficulty, Drew controlled his breathing.

"Yanus," the Slavic voice repeated. "We have to talk about Yanus."

Drew's delicately balanced choices tipped. Hearing sudden footsteps rushing along the corridor outside, louder as they neared the chapel, he bolted.

10

He wasn't the only one. As voices entered the chapel, the priest ran too, leaping the altar railing, charging toward the sacristy.

Drew reached the door that led to another hallway and yanked it open. At noon, when he'd helped Hal prepare for mass, he'd glanced beyond the door and seen a stairwell angling up. But now, at night, without the sun streaming through a window, he couldn't see the stairs.

Not that it mattered. He didn't intend to use them. Instead he sprinted straight ahead, toward a tunnel's entrance. He didn't know where it led, but he did know this—the two priests who'd tried to kill him had acted with such professional detachment that they would surely have followed other professional standards and not have moved alone. In case Drew had managed to escape, there'd be other assassins watching the stairs up from this basement. As soon as they heard him approaching, they'd prepare themselves for the kill. If there'd been time, he could have tried to mount the stairs silently. But behind him, the pursuing footsteps of the priest who'd hidden in the confessional forced Drew to take the route he hoped was least expected and one that the hit team possibly didn't even know about. In that case, all he had to deal with was the priest chasing after him.

The footsteps came closer.

Far back, other footsteps charged into the chapel.

Drew hurried through blackness. He walloped against a table, battering his thighs, wincing as the impact scraped the bottom of the table's legs across the concrete floor.

He turned. Though he saw nothing, he heard the subtle crunch of carefully lowered shoes, the brush of stealthy footsteps coming toward him. Drew resisted the urge to shoot. The Mauser's muzzle flash would reveal his position. And what would be the use if he couldn't see his target? True, he could try to judge his opponent's location from the sounds he made. But suppose his opponent made deceptive noises to trick him? If Drew fired, the muzzle flash would doom him. Of course, he could stay where he was, crouching to one side. After all, the dark was his specialty. Hand-to-hand combat with total sightlessness. But that type of combat was painstaking, time-consuming. To do it properly, which meant to survive, required the care of a specialist defusing a bomb.

Drew didn't have the time for care. He had to get out of here. Voices echoed from the sacristy. He thought about the likelihood that other assassins were waiting in the retreat house and listened to the solitary footsteps shifting toward him.

"You don't understand," the Slavic voice whispered. "I don't want to hurt you. Yanus. We need to talk about Yanus. I'm here to protect you."

Disoriented, Drew couldn't afford to believe him. He hurried forward again. His pursuer followed. When Drew stopped, his pursuer stopped.

"You must let me explain," the Slavic voice insisted.

No way, Drew thought, plunging forward again. I don't know who you are or if you're even a priest. I don't know who the hell tried to kill me in there or why. But I do know this. I tried to do this by the rules. I got in touch with my confessor, my control. I trusted my superiors in the Church (Drew almost substituted "network"). But someone else isn't playing by the rules. There's been an informer. A leak. Someone's told them where I was.

So now I'll play by my own rules. I'll do this my way.

He charged through spiderwebs, feeling them stick to his face. Water dripped. He smelled fetid dankness and mold. Behind, the footsteps continued after him. As he splashed through a pool of water, feeling it soak his shoes and pants, he heard the echo of voices far back in the tunnel. The group that had entered the chapel now came this way. He hurried on. Too soon, the man behind him splashed through the water. The voices seemed louder behind him. Turning to listen, he slammed the side of his head against a pipe that stretched from one wall to the other. He reeled back, seeing crimson behind his eyes, clutching the lump that began to swell. Feeling moisture in his hair, he lowered his fingers to his mouth, relieved when he tasted the salt of sweat, not the copper of blood. He scurried forward again.

What was the tunnel used for? Where did it go? He stooped as he rushed, protecting his head from other pipes. But as he bumped past a row of insulated ducts against the left wall, he guessed that it must be a maintenance tunnel. Sure. The water and heating systems must be routed through here, he thought, making it easy for the seminary's work crew to make repairs. If so, the tunnel must lead to the seminary building. With a goal at last in mind, he felt better. But something was wrong. The sounds behind him had stopped.

Why?

Ahead of him, he struck a wall. His nose stung.

He'd been wrong—the tunnel was a trap! And now his pursuer waited back there.

Drew clutched the Mauser, turned, and squinted uselessly toward the pitch-black gauntlet through which he'd have to return. He felt along the wall to his left, inching back the way

he'd come. But as his shoes touched a chunk of broken concrete on the floor, the sound of his own footsteps changed. He
stopped and frowned. Easing forward again, he heard the
scuff of his shoes return to the narrow echo he'd been used to.
He tried an experiment, took three steps back, and the echo
became more full again.

Understanding, he groped toward the wall across from him,
and as he expected, where the wall should have been, his hand
touched nothing. His foot struck concrete, though. He raised
the foot, and now it, like his hand, touched nothing. A little
higher, concrete again. A stairwell! He scurried up.

The stairway turned. He reached a wooden door, turned
the knob, and pulled it. Nothing happened. He had a sudden
intuition, pushed instead of pulled, and exhaled as the door
swung open. In case someone was hiding behind it, he shoved
it against a wall, then peered out, facing a dimly lit hall. The
tunnel had led him to the seminary building.

Seeing no one, he lunged to the left. He reached a large
room: sofas, chairs, tables, a television. Moonlight gleamed
through windows, revealing the lawn in front of the building.
Beyond the lawn would be the forest and the mountains.
Safety.

But he had to leave before a seminarian found him or his
pursuers intercepted him. Passing the room, he entered a
lobby, seeing a door on his left that led outside. But as he
moved in that direction, he heard the rustle of cloth behind
him. Pivoting, he aimed the Mauser and froze.

"Oh, Jesus, thank you."

Drew's scalp tingled.

"I knew you'd come." From the dark, the voice sounded
desperate, ancient, brittle. "Deliver me. You know how much
I've suffered." The voice began to sob. "They won't believe
that your mother sings to me each night."

From a shadowy corner, an apparition appeared. An old stooped man. His hair and beard were white. He wore a white nightgown.

Drew's stomach felt chilled. The old man clutched a staff. His feet were bare. His eyes gleamed insanely.

Dear God, Drew thought, I'm not in the seminary building. I passed that staircase. I went farther. I'm in the rest home. This is the old priest that Hal said he'd brought here. This is where they keep—

The old man knelt, pressing his hands together, peering up in rapture. "But thank you, Jesus." The old man wept. "You'll make them understand. You'll tell them I wasn't lying about your blessed mother. I've waited so long for you to deliver me."

Drew stumbled back in horror. The old man gasped, and Drew thought that he might be having a heart attack. But he was only inhaling, beginning to sing.

"No, please," Drew said.

The brittle voice cracked in its frenzy. "Holy Go-od, we praise Thy name. Lord almighty, we wor-ship, ad-ore Thee."

Drew rushed toward the door that led outside.

Upstairs, a man's voice scolded. "Father Lawrence, have you snuck out of your room again? You know you're not supposed to sing at night. You'll wake—"

"A miracle!" the old man yelled. "A miracle!" He burst into song again. "In-fi-nite, Thy va-aaa-st do-main."

11

Drew charged outside, breathing the cold air, feeling it sting his nostrils. He raced down concrete steps, sprinting across the lawn through the dark, the frost-hardened grass crunching under his shoes.

To his left, he saw that all the lights were on in the seminary building. The seminarians crowded outside, staring toward the retreat house farther to the left. Some ran toward it; others had already reached it, scrambling inside.

The retreat house itself was dark. But abruptly it began to brighten, first floor, second floor, third floor, every window gleaming in rapid succession.

Why? Drew wondered as he ran. Do they think I'm still in the building, or are they looking for somebody else? The priest who chased me, the rest of the death team?

Shouts filled the night. He sprinted harder as other lights came on, directly behind him, from the rest home. Their sudden blaze stretched far enough for him to see the shadow he cast ahead of him and the thick gasps of frost exploding from his mouth.

Someone yelled, so near that Drew turned. A tall man in a bathrobe stood at the rest home's open door, pointing in Drew's direction. He scrambled down the steps, but his stride was awkward. He lost a slipper, stumbled, and fell.

Still, his shouts had attracted attention. A group of seminarians sprinted toward the fallen man in front of the rest home. Another group raced after Drew.

He thought he was seeing things. A chunk of grass erupted ahead of him, but he didn't hear the shot. It might have been muffled by his hoarse rapid breathing and the frantic yells behind him. Or the weapon might have had a silencer. All he knew was that, as he reached the edge of the light coming from the rest home, another chunk flew up ahead of him. He veered, beginning to zigzag.

Now he heard, not the next shot itself, but the *whump*! as another bullet tore up grass. The angle was such that the sniper had to be ahead of him. On the wooded slope.

And I'm in the middle, Drew thought, hearing the seminarians rushing after him. Did they know about the sniper? Would they stop when they realized?

But instead the sniper stopped, and with a final burst of speed, Drew lunged through bushes into the greater darkness of the forest.

His chest felt tight. Bent low, he shifted past trees, through undergrowth, over a fallen trunk. With a disconcerting sense of déjà vu, he recalled his escape from the monastery. But the parallel wasn't exact. Six nights ago, the marksman on the hill hadn't known that Drew was out of the building, stalking him. And Drew had not been chased. Now he couldn't take the time to stalk the sniper without his pursuers catching him; and if he concentrated on eluding his pursuers, he might head into the sniper's sights.

"It's going down to thirty tonight," Hal had said.

Drew wasn't dressed for that. The lightweight black pants, cotton sweatshirt, and unlined jacket that Hal had brought him were useless against the cold. Already, despite the burning in his lungs, Drew shivered, his sweat absorbing the forest's chill. He could have easily survived in the insulating wool of the robe that he'd worn in the monastery. But what he now wore retained the cold instead of protecting him against it. If he spent all night in the woods, he would risk being overcome by hypothermia. And that took only three hours before it killed.

The Mauser's cold metal numbed his hand. He snuck past a deadfall, creeping deeper into the forest. Behind him, bodies charged through bushes. Branches snapped.

Would the sniper decide that the situation was out of control and back away? But even then, Drew realized, the seminarians won't stop chasing me.

What I need is a car.

The Cadillac that Hal had used to bring him here. It was parked somewhere. From his second-floor retreat house window, Drew had watched Hal drive it around to the back of the seminary building. There had to be a garage in back. Hadn't Hal insisted that the seminarians weren't supposed to see it?

Avoiding the threats behind and ahead, Drew veered to the right. He'd been angling in that direction already, but his eventual plan had been to head deeper into the woods. Until now, however, it hadn't occurred to him to move in a semicircle, doubling back toward the seminary. After all, what would have been the point? Crossing the open lawn, he'd again have been a target. And what would have been his goal? He wanted to get away from here, not hide as he'd done at the monastery. But now?

12

He stepped from the trees to the edge of the lawn. Behind, he heard his pursuers thrashing deeper into the forest. Before him, lights continued to gleam in the rest home, seminary, and retreat house. Figures still milled in front of the buildings.

Those figures would see him, of course, if he crossed the lawn from here, so he decided to follow the edge of the forest. The grass was silent, and the dark of the woods behind him hid his silhouette. He moved toward the area behind the buildings, risked exposing himself, and sprinted toward the rear of the seminary.

No one raised an alarm.

His suspicion proved correct. In a section behind the seminary—the lights were much less bright back here—he found a cinderblock structure with five garage doors. The first two he tested were locked. But the third budged when he tugged up on the handle.

He raised it slowly, trying to make as little sound as possible. The glimmer of moonlight showed him the bishop's black

Cadillac. Drew assumed that Hal had left this garage door unlocked in case he had to leave quickly. He opened the driver's
door, and the inside lights came on. Normally he would have
turned them off, afraid of making himself a target. But now
he so appreciated the lights that he propped the door open,
lying on his back, peering beneath the dashboard, finding the
wires he needed. He pressed two together. They bypassed the
Cadillac's ignition and started the engine.

It purred. He scrambled behind the steering wheel and
slammed the door. Again, as in the van that he'd driven from
Vermont, the dashboard confused him. He wasn't sure how to
turn on the headlights. Not that it mattered. The last thing he
wanted now was headlights. He pressed his foot on the accelerator and rocketed the Cadillac from the garage.

The car gained speed so rapidly that, before he could turn,
he left the driveway and jounced over a concrete curb, his head
snapping back. He swung the steering wheel and skidded sideways across the grass. A clatter behind him suggested that the
impact against the curb had dislodged a hubcap. He kept
turning sharply left and felt the Cadillac's wheels gouging fur-
rows in the lawn. Then he straightened the car, came back
down off the grass and the curb to the driveway, and drove
along the side wall of the seminary. The lane would curve to
the left in front of the seminary, he anticipated, take him past
the retreat house, and finally curve again, this time to the
right, leading him through the woods beyond the lawn,
toward the metal gate and the public road.

But he wasn't about to try to pass the figures in front of
those buildings. Instead, as he left the side of the seminary, he
aimed straight ahead, struck yet another curb, and fishtailed
across the grass until the tires gripped, gaining traction, tear-
ing up more lawn.

He sped across it. His window was down. He heard shouts.
Figures bolted toward him from the buildings. Ahead, he saw

utter blackness. With his headlights off, he didn't know where to steer to reach the continuation of the lane. For all he knew, he'd soon crash into the forest. He tapped his brakes, then realized that his taillights would flash, so that even without headlights, he'd be making himself a target.

Damned if he did, and damned if he didn't.

Why not, then?

He pawed at knobs and levers and, with seconds to spare, turned on the headlights as the forest's black wall loomed before him. Wrenching the steering wheel to the left, he scraped past a tree and heard the Cadillac's right rear fender crunch. Then he saw the road and aimed down its wooden tunnel. For a moment, he felt relieved. But at once his scalp froze—ahead he saw the priest from the chapel, the one with the dark hair, mustache, and Slavic features. The one with the .45 semiautomatic pistol.

The priest stood with his legs apart, facing Drew's onrushing car, blocking the road. The Cadillac's headlights glinted off the priest's white collar. They flashed off the disturbing red ring on his left hand, the hand he used to raise the pistol.

Drew pressed the accelerator, feeling his stomach surge against his spine, aiming the Cadillac toward the priest. The trees pressed narrowly on each side.

Instead of shooting, the priest frantically waved his hands, signaling Drew to stop.

No way, Drew thought. He steadied the steering wheel and pressed even harder on the accelerator.

The priest kept waving his hands, his gestures urgent, his body larger and larger through the windshield.

Two seconds would have made the difference.

But the priest turned sideways, darting back to the left, aiming. Drew's ears were stunned by the .45's roar. However the priest hadn't shot toward the Cadillac. He had shot above it, beyond the car's roof.

An automatic rifle rattled fiercely from the forest on Drew's right. Bullets smashed against the Cadillac. Windows ruptured, chunks of glass showering Drew.

Desperate, he tried to steer at the same time he shielded his eyes from the flying glass. He sensed the priest falling back toward the woods. The road curved, narrowing. Trees scraped the car. A sudden jolt in the rear suggested that the bumper had snagged on something. As his headlights gleamed down a straightaway, the Cadillac like a rocket again, Drew saw the high stone wall on either side. The metal gate was before him.

But the gate was shut. Another automatic weapon rattled behind him. He strengthened his grip on the steering wheel.

Thirty feet.

Twenty.

Ten.

13

The impact threw him forward against the steering wheel. Groaning from the pain in his ribs, he heard a sharp blat from the horn and rebounded against the seat.

The front of the Cadillac buckled. A headlight shattered. Glass arched, glinting in the glare from the other headlight. The chrome rim around the headlight frisbeed through the air. A chunk of metal starred the Cadillac's windshield. Drew fought to control the broken steering wheel. To his right and left, the metal gate separated. Bent, the sections walloped against the stone wall on either side.

Though he stomped the brakes, the Cadillac shot across the road. A ditch opened up before him, and the car flew across the gap. Dipping, it hit a stretch of grass, skidded ahead, veered sideways, and jerked to a stop. Drew stared. Another ten feet, and the Cadillac would have struck a jumble of trees and rocks. His chest ached, making him wince when he breathed.

He shook his head to clear it. Have to get away. The headlight on the left still gleamed, though the force of hitting the gate had deflected its aim toward the right. Steam hissed from the radiator. The engine still worked, though its purr had become a clatter.

He tried the accelerator. The car responded sluggishly, crossing the stretch of grass. The suspension had been destroyed, jostling him every time he hit a bump. He reached a stream, turned left to avoid it, and found a shallow part of the ditch. A little encouragement, and the car went down, then up to the road. He increased speed.

But the right front wheel had a wobble now. The speedometer—digital like the clock—showed zero. The engine wheezed, and the radiator hissed. He didn't know how far or fast he could go. If the engine overheated, it might be ruined.

That struck him as funny. Ruined? The bishop's Cadillac was a total wreck as it was. He couldn't cause it much more damage.

But the car amazed him. It kept going. And that too struck him as funny. Takes a licking, keeps on ticking.

He glanced toward his rear-view mirror, wanting to check for pursuing headlights. But he couldn't find the mirror. Squinting down, he saw it on the floor.

Nothing was funny after that.

He turned left at the first intersection, then right at the next, five miles farther on, anxious to lose his pursuers in a maze of mountain roads.

His chest tightened, pinching him. The broken steering wheel felt awkward in his hand. When he next turned right, sensing the looming mountains around him, he made out a road sign that told him a town called Lenox was twelve miles in the opposite direction.

Lenox? The name nudged his memory. The little red house. He'd never been there, but he knew that the town and that house were famous.

Hawthorne once had lived there. Hal hadn't lied when he'd said that they'd driven to western Massachusetts. I'm in the Berkshire Hills.

And Pittsfield ought to be close, where Melville had lived. Melville, who'd often ridden down to visit Hawthorne, wanting so much to be Hawthorne's friend that he'd written *Moby Dick* for him.

There were ghosts around him. Drew's reverie ended as the pain in his chest made him cough. The engine was overheating. He heard it straining. The radiator no longer hissed.

Because it was empty.

The car began to slow. A piece of grill fell off, clanging on the road. He chugged past a dark country store, lurched into a sleepy town, and as the engine coughed, dying, he glided to a stop in front of a dingy house whose lawn was badly in need of mowing.

Though the house was dark, a corner streetlight showed motorcycles propped against the side and front of the listing porch. He left the Cadillac and soon discovered that none of the motorcycles was chained to anything.

How trustful. They probably figure that no one would dare to fool with them. Well, I'm in the mood.

He chose the biggest Harley-Davidson and pushed it down the street. Among trees, he emptied the chopper's saddlebags, which were stuffed with tools and an old leather jacket. He exposed the electrical system and hot-wired the bike as he had the Cadillac. To start the engine, he had to straddle the seat and stomp down on the ignition lever. The engine rumbled to life.

He hadn't ridden a motorcycle in almost ten years, since the time he'd used one in an operation that required him to—

No. He shook his head. He didn't want to remember.

The cold October air stung his face as he twisted the throttle lever and roared through the night. He wondered how the bikers would react in the morning. Would they feel so angered by the stolen bike that they'd strip what was left of the Cadillac and sell the parts for revenge? He wiped away the tears that the wind forced from his eyes. The bishop's Cadillac. Four wheels and a board. He knew he shouldn't find that thought amusing. All the same he did, just as he felt exhilarated by the powerful roaring thrust of the Harley under him, taking him back to Boston.

And some answers.

14

"Father Hafer, please." Drew kept his voice flat, standing in a phone booth next to a service station, just after 8 A.M., struggling to hide his anger. His hands were numb. He shivered from the cold wind that had buffeted him all night. The morning sun, bringing a hint of Indian summer, blessedly warmed the booth.

The male voice who'd answered the phone at Holy Eucharist Rectory didn't reply.

"Can't you hear me?" Despite Drew's effort, he couldn't keep rage from his voice. He wanted explanations. Who screwed up? Why had he been attacked at the seminary? By priests! "I said I want to speak to Father Hafer."

He glanced angrily through the dusty glass of the booth toward the road out front, checking for motorcyclists, cops, anybody who showed an interest in him. His plan had been to go all the way into Boston, but he'd gotten too cold and had to stop in Concord, nineteen miles to the west.

The voice on the phone still didn't reply.

Stalling for time? Drew thought. Was the call being traced?

Abruptly the man said, "Just a moment."

Drew heard a thump as the phone was set down. Voices murmured in the background.

I'll give him twenty more seconds, Drew thought. Then I'm hanging up.

"Hello?" A different male voice. "Did you say you wanted to speak with—?"

"*Father Hafer.* What's the problem?"

"Who is this, please?"

Drew became apprehensive. "A friend of his."

"Then you obviously haven't heard."

"Heard *what*?"

"I'm sorry to have to tell you like this. It seems so impersonal over the phone . . . I'm afraid he's dead."

The booth seemed to tilt.

"But that's . . ." The word "impossible" stuck in Drew's throat. "I saw him early yesterday morning."

"It happened last night."

"*But how?*" Drew's voice was hoarse with shock. "He was dying. I know that. But he told me the doctors had given him till the end of the year."

"Yes, but it wasn't his illness that killed him."

15

Stunned, Drew hung up. He forced himself to move, knowing he had to get out of Concord as soon as possible—in case his call had indeed been traced. He needed a place where he'd feel secure.

To allow himself the luxury of grief.

To try to understand.

The trip to Lexington farther east, eleven miles from

Boston, did not register on his brain. He remembered none of it, his eyes—his consciousness—misted with pain. He left the motorcycle on a quiet side street, doubting that the report of its theft would have reached the Lexington police this soon.

In brilliant sunshine that mocked his gloom, he wandered through the village green, pretending interest in the spot where America's War for Independence had begun.

His fists clenched, he barely noticed the golden autumn trees, or the smell of woodsmoke, or the rustle of fallen leaves beneath his feet. His mind was too full of sorrow and rage.

Last night, Father Hafer had received a phone call at the rectory. He'd told the other priests that he had to go out. He'd crossed the street to the sidewalk in front of the church, where a car had struck him. On the sidewalk. The force of the impact had thrown him all the way up the steps and against the church's front door.

("He couldn't have suffered."

"But . . . how do you know?"

"There was so much blood. The driver didn't stop. He must have been drunk. To lose control like that, to veer off the street. The police haven't found him yet, but when they do . . . The law isn't strict enough. The poor man had so little time left. To have it stupidly wasted by an irresponsible drunk!")

Drew clenched his fists harder as he walked, oblivious to the crunch of leaves.

Received a phone call? Hit by a car while he stood on the sidewalk? The principal link between my former life and the monastery killed by a drunk?

Like hell.

Drew felt the bulge in his jacket pocket. The plastic bag. The body of Stuart Little. He thought of the dead monks. Now he had something else to make someone pay for.

16

"**P**ut me through to the bishop." Drew's voice was hoarse as he stood in another phone booth, glancing toward his motorcycle on the side street, then toward the tourists on the green.

"I'm terribly sorry . . ."

Drew recognized the resonant voice. It belonged to Paul, the man the bishop had spoken to on his office intercom two nights ago.

". . . but his Excellency isn't available now. If you'd care to leave your name and number."

"That's all right. He'll talk to me."

"And who . . . ?"

"Just tell him the man with the mouse."

"Yes, that's correct. He wants to talk with you."

Drew heard a sudden click. He glanced at his watch and made a bet with himself: fifteen seconds. But the bishop came on the phone even sooner, in twelve.

"Where *are* you? I've been waiting for your call. What happened at the—"

"Seminary? Funny thing. I was hoping you'd tell me."

"Make sense. My phone's been ringing since five A.M. about this. I asked you what—"

"Two priests tried to kill me, that's what!" Drew felt like slamming a fist through the glass of the booth. "They did kill Hal. And someone else, another priest, was hiding in the confessional!"

"Have you gone insane?"

Drew froze.

"Two priests tried to kill you? What are you talking about? Hal's dead? I just received a note from him. What I want to know is why you shot at those seminarians. Why did you break into the rest home, scare those priests half to death, and steal my car?"

Drew's heart felt squeezed by ice.

"And something else—this fantasy of yours," the bishop said.

"Fantasy?"

"About the monastery. Thank God, I took the precaution of sending those Jesuits to investigate. If the cardinal and I had decided to alert the police, it would have been a disaster. There aren't any bodies in that monastery."

"What?"

"There aren't any monks at all. The place is deserted. I don't understand where they went, but until I learn a *lot* more about this situation, I don't intend to make a fool of the Church."

Drew's voice shook with rage. "So you chose the first option, the cover-up. And you're leaving me out here alone."

"I don't intend to leave you out there. Believe me, I want some answers. Listen carefully. It isn't wise for you to come to my office. I'll tell you where to report."

"Forget it."

"Don't speak to me that way. You'll report to the address I'm about to give you."

"No."

"I'm warning you. Don't compound the trouble you're in. You vowed obedience. Your bishop is giving you an order."

"I won't obey it. I tried things your way. They didn't work."

"I'm very displeased by your attitude."

"Wait till you see your car." Drew slammed down the phone.

17

Impatient, he straddled the motorcycle. His chest, already in pain from the impact of the steering wheel against it, ached more sharply from grief and rage. He kicked down on the ignition lever. The engine rumbling, he grabbed the throttle.

But where could he go? What should he do?

The Church, it was now clear, could not be considered a refuge. Someone somewhere in the chain of command could not be trusted. The bishop perhaps, though not necessarily—he might very well be sincere, as confused as Drew himself.

Then what about Paul, the bishop's assistant? But the bishop had treated Paul with absolute trust.

Then who? And more important, why?

And what about the Slavic priest with the strange red gleaming ring and the .45, who'd hidden in the chapel's confessional?

All right. Drew bit his lip. The Church no longer mattered. God did. Drew's own survival. To save his soul.

He had to forget that he'd joined the monastery. He had to ignore his retreat from his former life.

Pretend that you're still in the network, he told himself. What would you have done if you couldn't trust it, if you feared an enemy within it?

The answer was obvious. Instinctive. But tainted with pride, for which he begged God's forgiveness. He'd once been the best. He could still be the best. Six years meant nothing.

Yes. He twisted the throttle, roaring away, determined. But not toward Boston now. Not east, but south.

New York. To the only people he could depend on. To his former lover and his former friend, Arlene and Jake.

PART FOUR

RESURRECTION

SATAN'S HORN

※

1

The brownstone on Twelfth Street, near Washington Square, was familiar to him from the old days. Of course a stranger might now be living there, Drew thought, so before he began his surveillance, he took the precaution of finding a phone booth whose residential directory had miraculously not been stolen by vandals. His pulse sped as he flipped through the pages for H, moved his finger down one list, and exhaled, finding Hardesty, Arlene and Jake.

The same address.

That didn't mean Arlene and Jake were in town. For sure, Drew wasn't about to put in the effort of watching the house unless he knew it was occupied. The problem was that he couldn't simply call to find out—the phone might be tapped, and he didn't want to let his enemies know he was in the neighborhood. They might have figured he'd try to contact Arlene and Jake.

He chained the motorcycle to a metal fence near Washington Square and strolled through the large square park, ignoring the junkies and dealers who slumped on benches. He passed the playground equipment, gravitating toward the huge graffiti-covered arch that marked the beginning of Fifth Avenue, the wide majestic thoroughfare stretching north as far as he could see. The sky was gray, but the temperature was warm, upper fifties, and the customary crowd of park musicians gathered beneath the arch, playing mournfully, as if the omen of the dismal sky was sufficient warning that they wouldn't be using the park much longer.

"You want to earn five dollars?"

The young man he'd chosen sat to the side of the arch, beneath a leafless tree, replacing a broken string on his guitar. Long blond hair, a beard, CCNY jacket, a rip in the knee of his jeans, and a toe coming out of one sneaker. Glancing up, the young man said—his voice surprisingly guttural—"Get lost."

"Don't get me wrong. This isn't an obscene proposition. And it isn't illegal. All you have to do is make a phone call for me. I tell you what. I'll even raise the price to ten."

"Just to make a phone call?"

"I'm feeling generous."

"It isn't obscene or illegal?"

"I guarantee it."

"Twenty."

"Done. I'm pressed for time."

He could have paid the young man even more. Last night, he'd gone hunting, walking dark streets, making himself a target for predators. Three times he'd attracted attention, confronted respectively by a pistol, a knife, and a club. He'd left each mugger with broken kneecaps and elbows ("For your penance. Go in peace and sin no more") and taken whatever money they had. The mugging business was lucrative. His total take was two hundred and twenty-three dollars, enough to buy an earth-tone Thinsulate-padded coat and a pair of wool gloves this morning. But though he could afford to be generous with what was left over, he didn't want to give this young man so much money that common sense would suggest something was terribly wrong.

As it was, the young man seemed unable to believe his good fortune. He stood, suspicious. "So where's the money?"

"Half now, half later. The way this works, we find a phone booth. I touch the numbers for you. I give you the phone. If a man answers, ask if he's Jake. Tell him you live down the street, and you're angry about the noise from last night's party. It kept you awake."

"Did he have a party?"

"Doubt it. Who knows? But stick to your story. Slam the phone back on the hook. If a woman answers, use the same story, but ask if she's Arlene."

"What's this supposed to prove?"

"Isn't it obvious? That either Jake or Arlene is home."

Five minutes later, the young man stepped from a nearby phone booth. "A woman," he said. "Arlene."

2

As usual, Drew started three blocks away from his target, walking with apparent leisure along Twelfth Street, seemingly indifferent to the neighborhood while studying every detail ahead of him. In keeping with so many other skills he'd reactivated, his instinct for surveillance had not been blunted by his years of inactivity. Nor had the pleasure he'd always taken from it. He let his mind luxuriate in the memory of how he'd first learned.

Hong Kong, 1962. When he was twelve. His "Uncle" Ray had been distressed because Drew was playing hooky from the private school in which most parents at the embassy enrolled their children. Ray's distress had been even greater when he learned what Drew was doing—roaming with Chinese street kids, hanging around the slums and the docks.

"But why?" Ray asked. "An unattended American boy in

some parts of this city—*those* parts—can get himself killed. One morning, the police'll find you floating dead in the harbor."

"But I'm not alone."

"You mean those kids you hang around with? They're used to surviving in the streets. And they're Chinese, they fit in."

"That's what I want to learn. To fit in on the streets here, even though I'm American."

"It's a wonder those kids don't just beat you up instead of accepting you."

"No. You see, I give them my allowance, food from home, clothes I've grown out of."

"Good God, why is it so important?" Ray's usually ruddy face had lost its color. "Because of your parents? Because of what happened to them? Even after two years?"

Drew's tortured eyes said everything.

The next time he played hooky, prowling the streets with the Chinese gang, Ray offered a compromise.

"You can't keep doing this. I mean it, Drew. It's too dangerous. What you think you're learning isn't worth the risk. Don't take me wrong. The way you feel about what happened to your parents, that's your business. Who am I to say you're wrong? But at least do it properly."

Drew squinted, intrigued.

"To start with, don't settle for fifth-rate teachers. And for heaven's sake, don't ignore the things you can learn at school. They're just as important. Believe me, someone who doesn't understand history, logic, mathematics, and the arts is just as defenseless as someone who doesn't understand the streets."

Drew's expression changed to puzzlement.

"Oh, I don't expect you to understand what I mean right away. But I think you respect me enough to know that I'm not a fool."

"Fifth-rate teachers?"

"Promise that you won't miss any more school, that your grades won't be less than Bs. In return . . ." Ray debated with himself.

"In return?"

"I'll arrange for you to have a proper teacher. Someone who really knows the streets, who can give you the discipline that your friends in the gang can't."

"Who?"

"Remember our bargain."

"But *who*?"

Thus began one of the most exciting times of Drew's life. After school the next day, Ray escorted him to a restaurant in downtown Hong Kong where the food, though Oriental, was not Chinese. And where the owner—amazingly short, round-faced, always grinning, old but with gleaming black hair—was introduced to him as Tommy Limbu.

"Tommy's a Gurkha," Ray explained. "Of course, he's retired now."

"Gurkha? What's a . . . ?"

Tommy and Ray laughed.

"See, you're learning something already. A Gurkha"—Ray turned with deference to Tommy, almost bowing—"is the finest mercenary soldier in the world. They come from a town by that name in Nepal, a mountainous state north of India. The region's principal business is export. Soldiers. Mostly for the British and Indian armies. When the job's too tough for any other soldier, they send in the Gurkhas. And the job gets done. You see that curved knife in a scabbard mounted on the wall behind the bar?"

Drew nodded.

"It's called a *kukri*. It's the Gurkhas' trademark. The sight of it will make most otherwise tough men afraid."

Drew glanced with skepticism toward the short, grinning, seemingly ineffectual Nepalese, then back toward the knife. "Can I hold it? Can I touch the blade?"

"You wouldn't like the consequences," Ray said. "The Gurkhas have a rule. If you draw the knife from its sheath, you also have to draw blood. If not your enemy's, then your own."

Drew's mouth hung open.

Tommy laughed, his eyes glinting. "Good gracious me." He surprised Drew not only by his genteel English but by his British accent. "We mustn't scare the boy. My heavens, no. He'll think I'm an awful terror."

"Tommy lives in Hong Kong because many Gurkhas are stationed at the British barracks here," Ray explained. "Off-duty, they like to come here for a meal. And of course, they remember him from when he belonged to the regiment."

"You'll be my teacher?" Drew asked, still skeptical about this eager-to-please, jolly man.

"My, my, no." Tommy's voice was mellifluous, almost as if he were singing. "Dear me, my bones are too old. I'd never have the energy to keep up with a dervish such as yourself. And I have my business to manage."

"Then?"

"Another boy, of course." With gleeful pride, Tommy turned to a child who, unnoticed by Drew, had silently come up beside him. A miniature image of Tommy, even shorter than Drew, though Drew would later learn that the boy was fourteen.

"Ah, there you are," Tommy proclaimed. "My grandson." He chuckled and turned to Drew. "His father belongs to the local battalion and prefers to have the child stay with me instead of in Nepal. They visit when he's on leave, though in truth that seldom happens. At the moment, he's helping to settle an unsavory but no doubt minor altercation in South Africa."

As Drew later learned, Tommy Two's last name was the consequence of the British attempt to deal with the confusing similarity of names among a people who referred to themselves by the tribes they belonged to (hence the elder Tommy's last name, Limbu). Because the bureaucracy couldn't distinguish one Tommy Limbu from the other, at least on paper, Two had been chosen instead of Junior.

But Tommy Two was essentially different from his grandfather. He didn't smile. He didn't even say hello. Drew sensed his disinterest and, overcome with misgivings, couldn't help wondering how they would ever get along—or what this sullen boy could possibly teach him.

His misgivings waned within half an hour. Left alone by the adults, they went out onto the narrow busy street, where Tommy Two informed him in perfect English that Drew was going to be taught to pick pockets.

Drew couldn't restrain his surprise. "But Uncle Ray brought me here because the gang I hung around with was doing that stuff. He doesn't want me . . ."

"No." Tommy Two held up a finger, like a magician. "Not just any pocket. Mine."

Drew's surprise increased.

"But first"—Tommy Two moved his finger back and forth—"you have to understand how it feels to have someone do it to *you*."

The sight of this little kid assuming command was startling. "And you're the one who's going to do it?" Drew asked, raising his eyebrows in disbelief.

Tommy Two didn't answer. Instead, he gestured for Drew to follow him. They turned a corner and went out of sight from the restaurant. Less confident now, Drew found himself facing a still narrower street, cluttered with shoppers, bicyclists, pushcart vendors, and awninged stalls. The babble of voices, the mixture of smells, mostly rancid, were awesome.

"Count to ten," Tommy Two announced. "Then walk down this street. By the end of three blocks"—he pointed toward Drew's back pocket—"I'll have your wallet."

Drew's confusion changed to fascination. "Three blocks, huh?" He peered down the chaotic street. Inspired, he removed his wallet from his back pocket and shoved it into a tighter pocket in front, then subdued a smirk. "Okay, you're on. But it doesn't seem fair. I mean, while I'm counting, don't you want me to hide my eyes? To give you a chance to hide?"

"Why bother?" As glum as ever, Tommy Two walked down the street.

Drew mentally counted. One, two . . . Watched Tommy pass between a moped and a rickshaw. Three, four, five . . .

All at once, he frowned. Tommy Two had vanished. Drew straightened, staring. How had he done that? Like a stone dropped into water, Tommy Two had become absorbed within the swirling mob. By the time Drew adjusted to the trick he'd just witnessed, he realized that the remaining count of five should long ago have been over.

Trick? Sure, that was all it had been, Drew decided. A trick. Bracing his shoulders, mustering confidence, he started down the street. But as he himself became immersed in the crowd, he realized that this was more complicated than he'd first anticipated. There were too many choices. For one thing, should he walk slow or fast, be cautious or hurry? For another, should he keep glancing around, on guard against Tommy Two, or should he look straight ahead, so he'd be able to avoid—

A bicyclist sped by so close that Drew was forced to jump to the right, jarring an elderly Chinese woman carrying a basket of laundry. She barked what must have been unfriendly things at him in Chinese, which he didn't understand. All the kids in the street gang had been better at his language than he was at theirs. Maybe Uncle Ray was right about school having its advantages. Hearing a shout behind him, Drew turned in reflexive alarm, but never did learn its source. He stumbled on a crack in the cobbled road and banged against a pushcart filled with fruit. The elbow of his shirt came away wet with juice. As the vendor shrilled at him, Drew almost stopped to pay the man, but then he realized that if he took out his wallet . . .

Tommy Two. Drew swung around, suspicious, feeling his stomach flutter, rushing forward through the crowd. The vendor kept yelling at him. But soon the yells were swallowed by inviting cries from hucksters in stalls that flanked the street. The smells worsened—stale cooking oil, charred meat, rotten vegetables. Drew began to feel sick.

Nonetheless, he hurried. He had to keep his mind on his wallet. Pressing his hand against the satisfying bulge in his front pants pocket, he reached the second block. Now he noticed the attention he attracted, a Caucasian among an even denser throng of Orientals. He darted his eyes in every direction before him, searching for a hint of Tommy Two, and entered the final block.

Walking fast, he felt relieved when he saw the end of the swarming gauntlet before him and a prominent sign, HARRY'S HONG KONG BAR AND GRILL. He used the sign as a beacon, dodged a man without legs who pushed himself on a platform equipped with rollers, and swelled in triumph as he noticed Tommy Two lounging against the wall on the corner beneath the sign. With a grin, he crossed the teeming intersection and stopped.

"So what's so hard about it?" Drew shrugged with disdain. "I should have made a bet that I could do it."

"How would you have paid?"

Troubled, Drew reached for the wallet in his front pocket. "With this, of course." But even as he touched the wallet, he knew that something was wrong. Pulling it out, he blushed. The wallet was dirty, made of cloth. His had been brand-new polished leather. And this one, when he looked inside, was empty. He opened his mouth, but no words came out.

"Would this be what you're looking for?" Tommy Two pulled a hand from behind his back and held up the trophy. "I agree with you. We should have made a wager." But this round-faced boy with gleaming black hair, three inches shorter than Drew though older, showed no satisfaction in his triumph—no grin, no swagger, no ridicule.

"How did you do it?"

"Distraction is always the key. I kept pace with you, out of sight in the crowd. When you mashed the vendor man's fruit, you were too confused to notice that I'd switched wallets with you. All you cared about was that you still felt something in your pocket."

Drew scowled, angry that he'd been made a fool of. "So that's all there is to it? It's easy. Now that I know what's up, I'd never get caught that way again."

Tommy Two shrugged. "We shall see. You still have thirty minutes remaining in your lesson. Shall we try again?"

Drew was taken aback. Thirty minutes left in the lesson? Briefly he'd assumed that they were playing together. But now he realized that Tommy Two was teaching him for money.

"Try again?" Drew asked, his feelings hurt but responding again to the challenge. "You're darn right."

"And this time, would you care to make a wager?"

Drew almost said yes, but suspicion muted his determination. "Not just yet."

"As you wish." Tommy Two straightened. "I suggest that we use the same three blocks, but this time in the reverse, moving back to our starting point."

Drew's hands were sweaty. Putting his own wallet back into his pocket, he watched Tommy Two again disappear like magic within the crowd.

And two blocks later when, just to be sure, Drew reached

inside his pocket, he knew right away that the wallet he carried was not his own. He cursed.

As before, Tommy Two lounged against a wall at the end of the third block, showing Drew his wallet.

The next afternoon after school, Drew tried it again. The results were the same.

The next afternoon. And the next.

But each time, Tommy Two gave Drew an added piece of advice. "To avoid an attack, you must not invite one. You have to become invisible."

"Easy for you to say. You're Oriental. You fit in."

"Not true. To you, an American, no doubt all Orientals seem alike. But to a Chinese, a Nepalese such as myself attracts as much attention as you. Or should."

Drew was bewildered. "Or should? You mean you don't?"

"I move with the rhythm of the street. I don't look at anyone's eyes. I'm never in any spot long enough to be noticed. And I draw myself in."

"Like this?" Drew tried to squeeze his body tighter, assuming such a grotesque position that Tommy Two permitted himself a rare laugh.

"No. Good gracious me, of course not. What strange ideas you have. I mean that I draw my thoughts in. Mentally I make myself"—he grasped for the words—"not here."

Drew shook his head.

"In time, you will learn. But something else. You must never—never—become distracted. Allow nothing to confuse you or to disturb your concentration. Not just here while we practice. Any time. Everywhere."

This kid's supposed to be fourteen, Drew thought. No way. Just because he's short, he thinks he can lie about his age. He has to be twenty at least. Become invisible. Move with the crowd. Don't let anything distract you. Drew tried again.

And again. Until one afternoon after school, as Drew came

through another gauntlet, approaching Tommy Two, who lounged as usual against a wall, he reached in his pocket, disgusted at another failure, only to blink at the wallet he pulled out. His own. "You let me win."

Tommy Two soberly shook his head. "I never let anyone win. You did what I taught you. You didn't react to the beggar who wanted money. You never glanced at the parrots on sale at that stall. Above all, you showed no interest in the cart of vegetables that overturned, but merely stepped around it, not even glancing at the peppers beneath your feet. You made it impossible for me to trick you."

Drew's heart beat faster with pride. "Then, I—"

"Did it once. Once is not a pattern. Are you ready to try again?"

The next time, Drew again produced his own wallet.

But Tommy Two did not congratulate him. The young yet ancient Nepalese seemed to take for granted that success was its own reward. "Now we begin the hard part."

"Hard?" Drew's spirits sank.

"You've proven that I can't steal your wallet. Is it possible for you to steal mine?"

Drew shifted his feet. "Let's give it a try."

Drew snuck through the crowd, coming from behind, seeing his chance, darting forward, reaching. Tommy grabbed his hand. "I knew where you were every second. You didn't become invisible. Try it again."

And, "Let the crowd absorb you."

And, "Anticipate what might distract me."

"*Nothing* distracts you."

"Then that's a problem for you to solve."

Three days later, Drew lounged against the wall at the end of the gauntlet. When Tommy Two saw the posture, his eyes flashed with understanding. Reaching into his pocket, he pulled out the wrong wallet.

"When the orange struck my shoulder?" Tommy Two asked.

"I paid a kid to throw it at you."

"Foolishly, I turned in that direction. Because I was sure you'd thrown it."

"But I was behind you."

"Excellent!" Tommy Two laughed. "Good gracious me, what a joke!"

"But aren't you forgetting something?"

Tommy Two looked puzzled. At once, he understood and shrugged. "Of course." Without a hint of disappointment, he gave Drew an American dollar.

Because this time Drew had decided to bet.

3

Proceeding down Twelfth Street, beginning his surveillance of the brownstone from three blocks away, Drew realized he'd begun to think of Tommy Two. He had never seen him after the lessons were over, but Tommy and his lessons had remained vivid in his memory. He knew that Tommy would look glummer than usual—and be more sternly rebuking—if he were somehow here and knew that Drew had allowed himself to be distracted, even for an instant.

Blend with the pattern of the street. Compact your spirit. Make yourself invisible. Concentrate. Drew obeyed the silent genteel British voice and knew that everything would be okay. Composed, he stepped from the first block, crossing the noisy intersection, approaching the other two blocks.

But he didn't intend to pass the midpoint of this second block. The tactic he employed required patience, circumnavigating the neighborhood, using several approaches from different directions, always narrowing the area. Confident that he attracted no attention, he crossed the street halfway down the second block and returned the way he'd come. At the intersection he headed south, walked down to Tenth Street, proceeded along it in a direction parallel to the brownstone, and eventually headed north, coming back to Twelfth. Now he was three blocks away from the brownstone again, but this time coming from the opposite direction. As before, blending with the rhythms of the street, studying every detail before him, he began his reconnaissance. When he reached the middle of the second block, he crossed the street again, returning.

All right, he thought, I've narrowed the perimeter, and so far everything looks fine. By definition—because I haven't been attacked. If the house is being watched, the spotters are within a block and a half on either side.

He knew exactly what to look for. First, a car. You had to assume that if your target left the surveillance area, he or she would get in a taxi. And that meant you needed a car to keep up. But the city's parking problem was so severe that once you found a spot, you didn't dare give it up. What's more, you had to stay near the car in case your target left quickly. Two men in a parked car would attract attention, so one man usually stayed in the car while the other man found a vantage point in a nearby building.

There were variations on these tactics, and Drew had been watching for all of them: the car whose hood was up while someone made repairs, the van with too many antennas, the man setting up an umbrella stand on the corner.

But already he'd seen what he wanted to know. At the west end of the brownstone's block, a man sat in a dark blue (the rule was never to use a bright-colored) car, more interested in the brownstone than in a platinum blonde in a tight leather suit who passed him, walking a Malamute.

Blend with the rhythm of the street, pal, Drew thought. If the occasion demands, look distracted even though you're not.

Drew wasn't sure where the other spotter was. In fact, he assumed there'd be two more in the area, one to remain near the brownstone, the third to get in the car with the driver and be let out wherever the target decided to go.

But their primary purpose, Drew reminded himself, was not to watch the Hardestys. The brownstone was just the bait. I'm the reason the spotters are here, and they'll follow Arlene and Jake only on the chance that I might try making contact somewhere other than the brownstone.

Fine, he thought. No problem. Having determined the closest safe distance from the brownstone, he hurried back to where he'd left the motorcycle near Washington Square. He unlocked the chain with which he'd secured it to a metal fence and kicked down on the starter lever, heading back to Twelfth Street. He parked between two cars three-quarters of a block behind the spotter in the car, pushed down the kickstand, leaned against the padded seat, and, shielded by the vehicle in front of him, began to wait.

4

Three hours.

Shortly after 4 P.M., as it began to drizzle, he saw a woman step out of the brownstone two blocks down. Even at this distance, her outline so small that Drew felt he was watching her through the reverse end of a telescope, he recognized her.

Arlene. His throat swelled tight till he had trouble breathing. He'd thought he'd prepared himself for the shock of seeing her again, but his pent-up emotions, denied for six years, assaulted him. His love for her rushed back with a jolt. Her training as an athlete, specifically as a mountain climber, had given her a distinctive sensuous walk, energetic but with no movement wasted, her footsteps springy yet firmly placed.

Disciplined gracefulness. He remembered the feel of her body and the sound of her voice, and he longed to touch her and to hear that voice again.

Her clothes revealed her background. She almost never dressed formally; instead, she preferred jogging shoes or hiking boots, jeans, a heavy sweater, a denim jacket. In place of a purse, she carried a small nylon pack slung over a shoulder, walking in the opposite direction down the street, oblivious to the drizzle that fell on her auburn hair.

His throat still swollen, tears suddenly in his eyes, he started the motorcycle but didn't move from between the cars that shielded him. When Arlene had almost reached the far corner of her block, a wino moved from the steps down to a basement door across the street from the brownstone. Skirting an iron railing, he veered toward Drew, crossing the street toward the surveillance car on the corner. The wino scrambled into the back of the car and hadn't closed his door before the driver pulled out onto the street and sped toward the corner where Arlene now turned right.

Drew grinned, his predictions proved accurate. Somewhere in that block, another spotter would have been left behind. In the meantime, the surveillance car would reach that other corner in time to learn if Arlene stayed on the avenue or went inside a store or hailed a taxi.

Drew started driving, but he couldn't continue down Twelfth Street where the remaining spotter might notice him. Instead, he avoided the block by turning right at the intersection before it and heading north, parallel to Arlene. He turned left onto Thirteenth Street and sped toward the next corner of the avenue that Arlene had taken, hoping to catch up to her.

He didn't see her. What he did see was the dark blue surveillance car. Inside, the two men stared forward as they drove past the corner. Who are they working for? Drew wondered. Scalpel?

When he reached the intersection, Drew glanced up and down the avenue. No Arlene. He restrained his impatience long enough to let several cars go by before he roared out into traffic to follow the surveillance car, which presumably had her in sight.

His assumption was that when she'd reached the avenue, she'd hailed a taxi. If so, her choice surprised him because she almost always walked where she was going, even if her destination was at some distance.

At least he had the surveillance car ahead of him, and that was as good as seeing Arlene. The several cars between the spotters and himself made it improbable that they would notice him if they happened to look back. The drizzle, which had now become a full-fledged rain, provided a shield as well, though the cold drops streaking down his face made it difficult for him to stop blinking.

To control the blinks, he mustered the discipline he'd learned in fencing classes at the Rocky Mountain Industrial School. The object had been to make him so accustomed to the lethal tip of a rapier being jabbed at his unprotected eyes that he learned to subdue the reflexive action of his eyelids. Some students never did develop that skill; they weren't at school much longer.

Through the stronger rain that now had soaked his wool gloves and collected beneath his coat collar, he followed the dark blue car. He entered midtown Manhattan and turned onto Fiftieth Street.

He slowed as the surveillance car did. In a moment, he understood why. Ahead, near enough to distinguish the sheen in her auburn hair, the glow on her healthy skin, he saw Arlene getting out of a taxi stopped at the curb.

He felt his heart race. She'd never needed makeup; the sun and wind had always given her sufficient color. Her forehead, cheekbones, and chin were perfectly proportioned, her features exquisite. But she was hardly a porcelain doll. Though she had an angular figure, her hips, waist, and breasts equal to those of any actress, she was sinewy, not at all soft.

The surveillance car stopped. The man in the grimy clothes of a wino crawled from the back seat into the front, sliding behind the steering wheel. The well-dressed driver got out to follow Arlene. As horns blared, the replacement driver responded, moving the surveillance car ahead. Drew sympathized with his problem. Where could this new driver find a parking space in midtown Manhattan? Unless he double-parked and risked a challenge from a policeman, he'd have to drive around the block, again and again, until his partner reappeared. At once, though, Drew noticed that the executive who followed Arlene had put a set of small earphones over his head. A wire dangled from them to an inside pocket of his suit.

Back in Boston, while walking through the mall, Drew had been puzzled when he saw teenagers and even adults wearing similar earphones. On occasion, he'd heard dim music drifting from them. He'd gone to a stereo store and learned that the earphones belonged to compact radios and tape players, known as Walkmans. The well-dressed man wasn't using a Walkman, though the earphones looked like they belonged to one and didn't attract attention. No, he was maintaining contact with the driver of the surveillance car by means of a small hidden two-way radio. The wino could drive the car around the block for the rest of the afternoon and still know exactly when and where to pick up his partner.

Though the time was now four-thirty, the gloom made the afternoon seem like dusk. Drew straddled his motorcycle at the curb, deciding to risk a ticket. Passing vehicles ignored him. He in turn ignored the chill of the rain and looked fifty yards ahead, past the well-dressed man with the earphones, watching Arlene go into a store.

Drew had already guessed where she was going when he saw her leave the taxi. The store she entered had its windows filled with sporting equipment, most of it for mountain climbers. Coiled, lightweight, twisted-nylon ropes, one hundred and fifty feet long, capable, he knew, of sustaining four thousand pounds of stress; carabiners, pitons and piton hammers, nylon slings, mountain packs, ice axes, climbing boots.

The store sold ordinary sporting goods as well, but because of its specialty, climbers from all over the northeast knew about it. Drew himself had been here with Arlene and Jake several times.

The swinging glass door closed behind her. The well-dressed man with the earphones moved casually along the sidewalk close to the buildings, then found a break in traffic and crossed the street to a spot beneath an awning where he could watch her through the windows in the store without being noticed.

But if he glances this way, Drew thought, he might notice me.

The dark blue car would soon be coming around the block. Drew raised his motorcycle to the sidewalk, turned, and walked it back to the intersection. He crossed the avenue and moved the bike far enough back on the sidewalk to ensure that the wino driving the dark blue car wouldn't see him when the car came around the other block. Despite the rain and the distance, he could still see the man who watched the store and be able to notice Arlene when she came out.

Twenty minutes later, she did, carrying three packages.

Her luck was amazing. She hailed a cab right away. But the surveillance team's luck was equal to her own—the dark blue car came around the corner just as her taxi was pulling away. While the executive scrambled into the back, the wino kept moving, continuing their pursuit.

Then Drew's luck failed him.

He pushed the motorcycle across the sidewalk onto the street, kicked down on the starter lever, gripped the throttle, and found himself blocked by traffic, the light against him. By the time red had turned to green, they were out of sight.

5

The man behind the counter looked Swiss—tall, robust, blue-eyed, blond. In his early thirties, Drew guessed, and in excellent shape, broad back, muscular arms and chest. With an energetic smile, he turned from placing coiled ropes on a shelf as the swinging glass door hissed shut behind Drew.

His accent was closer to the Bronx than Switzerland. "Hell of a day, huh? Glad I'm not on a slope in this." He gestured toward the downpour outside. "You want a cup of coffee? Your coat's so wet, you look like you'll catch hypothermia."

Drew returned his smile. "Coffee? I'm tempted. But it makes me feel like I'm on speed."

"Decaffeinated?"

Drew wondered what on earth he was talking about. Decaffeinated coffee? What was that? "No. But thanks just the same. I was in a store across the street, and I happened to notice a woman come in here. Good-looking athletic type, auburn hair, carried an equipment pack instead of a purse? She looked like a friend of mine. Arlene Hardesty."

"That was her, all right. She and her brother buy a lot of stuff from us."

"Good old Jake. I figured I'd step in and say hello. But one thing led to another. I see I missed her."

"Ten minutes ago."

Drew feigned disappointment. "That's the way the pitch angles, I guess. I haven't seen her in so long I ought to make sure I call her."

"Pitch angles?" The clerk's eyes twinkled. "You're a climber?"

"Lately I don't have much time, but I used to climb a lot. With Jake and Arlene, in fact. Maybe I should ask them if they'd like to go out again soon."

"Sooner than you think. You'd better get in touch with Arlene right away. That's why she was in here. Replacing worn-out equipment. She's going up tomorrow. The truth is, you'd be doing her a favor if you asked to go along."

"Why a favor?"

"Because she told me she was going up by herself. I don't know how strict you are about the rules, but even with expert climbers, we discourage them from climbing alone. It just isn't right. Oh, sure, she knows what she's doing, but what if there's an accident? And the rock she's climbing isn't any practice slope."

"Where?"

"Satan's Horn. Over in Pennsylvania."

"The Poconos."

"You know it?"

"I've been there with Jake and Arlene a couple of times. Arlene used to say Satan's Horn worked better than aspirin to cure a headache. Whenever she was troubled, she used to climb it as therapy."

"Well, I've climbed it too, and believe me, what it did was give me a headache. You've been there, so you know it isn't something you try alone. That damned shale. Every time I got a grip on an overhang, I started believing in God again for fear the rock would come loose in my hand."

Drew grinned. "In God? I know the feeling."

"Then talk her out of it, okay? Or failing that, invite yourself along."

"I'd hate to have her get hurt." Drew pretended to think

about it. "But what the heck, lately I've been working too hard. Okay, you've convinced me. But if I'm going climbing tomorrow, I'd better get some equipment. The stuff I use is at my summer place."

The clerk's eyes twinkled even brighter. This near to closing time, he apparently hadn't expected another sale. "Let's start with boots."

6

Surrounded by early-morning mist, Drew walked down a damp wooded slope. The saturated leaves and earth were spongy beneath him. Rounding two boulders, he reached a stream. The sun eased above the slope behind him, burning off some of the mist, allowing him a better view of the fallen trunks and boughs around him. He selected one—ten feet long and ten inches thick, less rotten than the others—and carried it to the stream, dropping it across the bank. With his coiled rope and nylon sling around one shoulder, he walked over it, his arms slightly outstretched for balance, hearing the log beneath him groan.

On the other side, he climbed a slope, his nostrils spreading from the musky odor of pungent loam, and paused at the top. He'd taken a half hour to walk the quarter mile of dense forest to get here. His motorcycle was hidden in bushes off the two-lane road that led to the gravel parking area where hikers and climbers usually began their expeditions. In New York, he'd slept at a shelter, telling the priest in charge that he'd wash dishes in exchange for a meal and a cot. And now, after two hours of driving, he enjoyed the exercise, the relief to his stiff cramped muscles, the stillness in contrast with the vibrating roar of the chopper.

Ahead, through scraggly undergrowth, the mist disappearing as the sun rose higher, he saw his destination, peering up and up toward the gray cone called Satan's Horn. On the far side, it was thirty feet from a neighboring cliff, once linked to it by a natural bridge of rock that had crumbled back in the fifties. The fact that the Horn had separated from the cliff was dramatic evidence of how brittle the rocks here were. And judging from the pile of fallen fragments at its circular base, Drew knew that the Horn would one day crumble as the bridge had.

For now, though, it loomed, imposing—inviting?—protected from the erosion of wind at least by the bluffs of this semicircular basin.

He pushed through the undergrowth, crossed a stretch of dead brown ferns and knee-high grass, their tassels having given up their seeds, feeling moisture from them chill his skin through his pantlegs. He carefully placed his boots on the rock shards that angled up toward the Horn, concerned that the shards might shift beneath him and cause him to sprain an ankle.

The stillness of the basin was eerie, the bluffs around him amplifying, emphasizing, the intrusive crunch of his footsteps. Indeed, as he took another cautious step, he heard branches scrape behind him.

He spun alarmed, his Mauser drawn in a blur, aiming . . . Where? The scraping continued, coming closer.

The nearest cover was thirty yards away, back in the forest, and what guarantee did he have that the bushes he chose would not already be occupied?

To his right.

There. Branches parted. Bushes moved.

He aimed.

Three white-tailed deer, two does and a buck, stepped into the stretch of ferns and grass, the buck's antlers resembling the leafless branches behind him. Drew saw the terror in their eyes, a shock that rendered them immobile for an instant, frozen like a photograph.

The instant cracked. At once the deer burst into motion, turning their white tails up as they charged back into the forest, the sound of their hoofs like a rumbling rockfall. Lessening. Growing fainter.

The silence of the basin descended again.

Inhaling deeply, replacing the Mauser, Drew continued his cautious ascent across the shards.

7

At the base of the Horn, he peered up only once. The rule was, Don't look up, don't look down, just study the surface before you. But he couldn't resist appreciating the magnificence of this uncanny formation.

Securing the coiled rope and the nylon sling around his shoulder, he studied the deceptively easy task. Though the cliff went almost straight up, tapering inward near the top, its surface was so uneven that handholds and footholds would be no problem.

Until you started to climb, that is. And then you realized that the rock could snap as easily as a potato chip. No grip could be taken for granted. Each time you eased your weight down on a ledge or tensed your fingers around an outcrop, you had to test it—and test it again, slowly adding more pressure, never sure if it would hold. Only the most experienced, confident, and daring of climbers were qualified to attempt the Horn. Would *want* to climb the Horn. Two hundred feet to the top, that was all. But the ascent might last as long as two hours. One hundred and twenty nerves-stretched-to-the-snapping-point minutes. Thousands of stomach-contracting, sweat-dripping-off-your-forehead decisions. He understood why Arlene liked to climb the Horn when she needed to clear her head. You couldn't think of anything *except* the Horn when you climbed it.

But why was she so troubled that she needed the therapy of this cliff?

He shut the thought out. The Horn was a task for an existentialist. No preoccupations. Only instant-by-instant choices. Nothing before and nothing after.

Contrary to the expectations of an amateur, you didn't squeeze close to the cliff. You didn't hug it for support, for reassurance. The proper way to climb, to survive, was to lean out from the rockface. That position gave you a better view of the next hand- and footholds. It also allowed you to extend your arms and legs and thus relax them. Starting up, choosing his supports with suspicious care, Drew recalled the secret to climbing that Arlene had taught him. The secret to a lot of things now that he thought about it. Hang loose.

Nervousness wormed into his stomach. He felt both elated and frightened. Soon he would see her again.

8

The Horn was crowned with scraggly shrubs, barren now, but tangled and dense enough to give Drew cover. After squirming over the lip of the cliff, he forced himself to wait until he had crawled across a five-foot stretch of open rock before he allowed himself to rest in the deepest part of a thicket. The sun was above him, but though it gleamed from a pure blue sky, it gave little warmth. His sweat, formerly heated by exertion, began to turn cold. He shivered, reaching into his coat for sunflower seeds, dried fruit, and a Granola bar.

Chewing slowly, he unhooked a canteen from the belt beneath his coat and swallowed tepid water. Soon his strength returned. The top of the brush-covered Horn was roughly forty feet across, ample room for him to maneuver if he had to. He flexed his rock-abraded hands, relieving their soreness, and concentrated on the only entrance to the basin, the section of trees through which he'd come. Far above tree level, his vantage point made him feel small. He said a prayer of thanks for God's magnificence.

Sprawling flat on his stomach, trying to relax, he waited. In retrospect, the decisions he'd made seemed logical. If he'd stayed in New York, he might have had to wait several days before he saw a chance to get a message to Arlene without alerting the surveillance team. And the more he followed the spotters as they in turn followed Arlene, the more he risked being noticed by them.

But this way, knowing her destination, arriving here before her, he felt safe. After all, though the team would no doubt follow her to the Horn, they wouldn't dare show themselves by climbing up to find out what she was doing at the top. They might of course be tempted to climb to a neighboring bluff and watch from there, but the odds were that they didn't know the terrain and weren't experienced climbers. The main reason he didn't think the team would try to watch from a neighboring bluff was that it would take them too long to get up and down from there. Arlene, in the meantime, would have a chance to elude them.

Drew confirmed his decisions, confident that for a while, at least, he'd have the chance to talk to her alone, unseen, up here. As he pressed his stomach against the rocky earth, he saw Arlene step from the forest. A pulse throbbed in his forehead, and he fought to still the pounding in his heart. Tiny from Drew's perspective, she paused to survey the Horn, then straightened in satisfaction, shifting through the undergrowth, approaching.

She carried a coiled rope as he himself had. In addition, he saw a bulging heavy pack. Her clothes fit her loosely, rugged wool pants and shirt, both blue, and an open khaki jacket well supplied with pockets. Despite the austere shapelessness of those garments, however, she was unmistakably a woman. With her auburn hair tucked beneath a gray knit cap, she showed the sensuous angle of her neck. And even in solid climbing boots, her stride remained athletically graceful. Images of her body filled his brain. Drew shut his eyes to chase them away.

9

A hand appeared first. Abraded like his own, it gripped the lip of the cliff. Then another hand. He saw the gray knitted cap. And her effort-strained face, beaded with sweat, as she inhaled deeply, mustering a final surge of strength.

He watched unseen from the bushes, her features vivid before him. She pulled herself up, raised a knee to the edge of the cliff, and squirmed to the flat stretch of rock, rolling onto her back, her chest heaving.

She stared at the cloudless sky for several moments, swallowed, then reached for the canteen on her belt. As Drew expected, she drank in short measured gulps, taking care not to make herself sick. When the rhythm of her breathing had returned to normal, she wiped the sleeve of her coat across her brow and slowly sat, her back to Drew, peering toward the autumn landscape below.

She took off her cap, shook her head to release her hair, and combed her hands through the sides. Her back was as straight as a fashion model's.

Drew glanced past her down toward the dense forest but still couldn't see the surveillance team. He hoped that she'd stand and relax her legs by pacing through the bushes and thus approach him, but she continued sitting, peering down.

Finally he couldn't waste more time. He took a chance, depending upon her discipline.

"Arlene, it's Drew."

He whispered, but to her, it was likely a shout.

"No. Don't turn around."

A ripple of tension and surprise swept across her shoulders. But as he'd anticipated, her training took command. Accustomed to adjusting to instantaneous changes in circumstance, she showed no other reaction, maintaining her gaze toward the woods. A sinew tightened in her neck.

"Don't talk," he continued. "I'll explain why I'm here. But not in the open. You've been followed. They're watching from down there."

She took another sip from her canteen.

Yeah, you're the best, Drew marveled. "When it seems natural, stand, stretch your arms, get the kinks out. Pace a little. Since you're up here, what the hell, you figure you'll explore. Step into the thicket. But once you're out of sight from down there, sit and we can talk."

She swallowed more water and put the cap back on the canteen.

"I need your help," he added. "I'm in a mess."

A minute later, she stood, put her hands in her jacket pocket, turned to survey the bluffs at her end of the basin, and casually entered the thicket.

With all his heart, he wanted to hold her again, to feel her breasts, to kiss her opening lips. For Christ's sake, Drew agonized, what's the matter with you? You took a sacred vow!

Arlene sank beneath the bushes toward him, her hand in her jacket pocket. Her eyes disturbed him. They showed neither curiosity nor pleasure at seeing him again. Instead, they looked terribly calm. And her smile was fixed.

His pulse sped. As she knelt, she pulled her hand from the pocket.

And at once swung a piton hammer toward his left temple.

One end of it was curved, its underside serrated. Hearing

the point cut the air with a whistle, he toppled back, avoiding it, seeing its blur pass before his eyes.

"No." His voice was tense, hoarse. As she swung the hammer again, he rolled back in the opposite direction. Fear scalded his stomach. She was strong enough, the hammer deadly enough, that it would at least have shattered his jaw.

He rolled again, trying to gain the advantage, to overcome his shock.

"Arlene, *why?*"

Air rushed, the hammer going past.

"For God's sake!"

This time the hammer, misaimed, snicked the shoulder of his coat.

He kicked up as she struck at the spot between his eyes. His boot caught her wrist, deflecting the point. She groaned. He thrust up, grabbing her arm at the wrist and biceps, throwing her flat. His body pressed on hers, his hands restraining both of hers, conscious of his chest on her own. He was five inches away from the anger in her eyes.

Their harsh forceful breathing was indistinguishable. He smelled her.

"*You rotten bastard,*" she said.

He flinched.

She writhed, glaring hate. "Where the hell is Jake?"

His energy left him. Implications soared through his mind. "Jake?"

"You heard me, you sonofabitch. Where *is* he? God damn you, if you killed him."

Arlene thrashed, trying to knee Drew's groin.

He pressed her leg down, squinted deeply into her seething eyes, and, shaking his head in frustration, rolled away from her, staring bleakly past the bushes toward the sky.

The only gesture he could think of to mollify her. To show his innocence. Total exposure—surrender.

She scrambled up, eyes fierce, swinging the hammer. But he made no effort to repel it.

With a gasp, she buried the hammer's tip in the shallow ground beyond Drew's neck, the curved edge conforming to the contour of his throat, the serrated underside stinging his skin.

Neither moved. They glared at each other. On a bluff beyond them, a bird took off, fluttering.

Her chest began to heave, demanding oxygen. "You . . ."

"Bastard," he said. "I know. I got that idea. And God's going to damn me for being a sonofabitch. I got that idea, too. The thing is, tell me why."

She hesitated. Gulping more air, she slowly sank to the ground beside him. "I almost . . ."

"Decided not to miss my neck? Yeah, I figured that. But I also figured I had to take the chance."

"So I'd think you weren't a threat? I'm still not convinced."

"But at least you know I could have killed you when I was lying on you."

"And that's the only reason I didn't . . ." She scowled at the hammer pinned against his throat. "Same old Drew. You didn't even flinch."

He shrugged, removing the hammer, then sat up, hefted it, and gave it back to her. "Regrets? You want to try it again?"

Frustrated, she shook her head.

"Then what's this all about?"

Her eyes flared. "The same goes for you. What are you doing here? How did you know I'd be here?"

"You've been followed."

"I know."

He raised his eyebrows. "You do?"

"Three of them. One in a dark blue car down the street. Another lying on basement steps across the street, pretending to be a wino. The third sells umbrellas at a portable stand on the corner. When it's sunny, he switches to bratwurst and sauerkraut." She made a face. "They showed up five days ago."

Drew tensed. "On Saturday?"

She studied him. "Yes, Saturday. In the morning. Why? Is that important?"

Drew rubbed a hand across his mouth. Friday night, he'd arrived in Boston. He'd left his prisoner in the van at the parking ramp in Logan Airport. A few hours later, the death team—and whoever had ordered the attack on the monastery—would have learned that he was out of Vermont.

Jake? Arlene had wanted to know where her brother was. She'd assumed that Drew had something to do with Jake's disappearance. That was why she'd almost killed him.

"It tells me a lot," Drew said, still wanting to hold her, with difficulty keeping his voice steady. "What about Jake? You told me he disappeared. Before last Tuesday?"

Arlene's knuckles whitened on the hammer. "You *do* know something about him!"

"Not at all. Come on, we used to be close, remember? Take it easy. I made a guess at Tuesday because that's when my own troubles started. I'm beginning to think that what happened to Jake has something to do with me." His mind raced. "When exactly did he disappear?"

"Friday. Before that Tuesday."

"And why did you blame me?"

"Because of Janus."

"*What?*"

"You and Janus."

"A woman named Janice?"

"No. The name from myth." She spelled it. "J-a-n-u-s. You look as if you'd never heard of him. That's your new crypto-nym, isn't it?"

Janus? He abruptly remembered the voice of the Slavic

priest: "Yanus! I've got to talk to you about Yanus!" Had the accent distorted the word?

Drew's head began to throb. The ache swelled, squeezing the inside of his skull. Janus? The Roman god who looked backward and forward. The two-faced.

Insanity.

"I don't know what you're talking about," he said.

"But the cryptonym, it's *yours*. The newspaper articles. The photographs."

As much as he wanted to hold her, madness was added to madness. Nothing made sense. "Of me?" He feared that his mind would crack. "But there *can't* be any photographs. It isn't possible."

She glowered.

"What is it?" he asked.

"There can't be any photographs . . . Not possible . . . That's what Jake kept saying."

"You bet he said it. He ought to know."

She slammed the hammer into the dirt. "Damn you, stop playing games with me!"

"Janus. Who is he? Why is he so important?"

"If you're Janus, you should know."

"Tell me."

"A freelance assassin. An international killer. A rogue. He executed twenty people in the last two years."

Drew felt the blood drain from his face. "And I'm supposed to be him?"

Her hard gaze became uncertain. "The more Jake heard about you, the more he became upset. He wouldn't tell me why. Two and a half weeks ago, he finally said he couldn't wait any longer. He had to find out what was going on."

"And that's when he . . . ?"

"Disappeared. Last Saturday the surveillance team showed

up. I couldn't go anywhere without them. It didn't matter what tactic I tried. They outguessed me. That's why I'm here. To try to shake them. I planned to stay on top till dark, rappel down, climb a bluff behind the Horn, and lose them."

"Not bad." His chest aching with affection, Drew smiled at her cleverness. "Then you planned to find out what happened to Jake?"

"Believe it."

"You've got a partner." His voice was taut. "I want answers as much as you do. *To a lot of things.* Look, I'm sorry that I didn't tell you what happened to me." He studied her, almost touching her. "But you're wrong about the surveillance team. They're not watching you. They don't want to stop you from finding Jake."

"Then?"

"Me."

She narrowed her eyebrows.

"They're watching you in case. . . . They're after me," Drew said. "A while ago, you wondered why Jake was sure that I couldn't be Janus. Why the newspapers had to be wrong. Why there couldn't be photographs."

She waited, breathing deeply.

"Because for the past six years I've been in a monastery. *Because six years ago, Jake killed me.*"

10

"Killed?" Her face lost its color. She jerked her head back as if she'd been struck. "A monastery? What are you talking about? Jake *killed* you?"

"I don't have time to explain. Not now. You'd have more questions. And other questions after that."

"But . . ."

"No," he insisted. "Those men down there will be getting suspicious. They'll want to know what you're doing. You've been out of sight too long as it is."

She seemed to debate with herself.

"I promise. Later," he said.

With a sudden nod, she glanced toward the brush that concealed her from the surveillance team. At once she unbuckled her belt, undoing the button on her pants, pulling down the zipper.

He reacted with shock. "What are you doing?"

"You said it yourself—they'll want to know what I was up to."

His shock turned to understanding, then admiration. "Smart."

"But you're in this with me? You'll help me find Jake?"

"I *have* to find Jake. From what you've just told me, I'm sure he knows who's after me. We'll wait till dark, then leave together. As soon as we're someplace safe, I'll answer your questions. Between what you know and I do, maybe we can figure out where he is."

She studied him, smiling, her eyes loving. "It's been a long time. I always wondered what happened to you." She took his hand. "I'm sorry about the hammer."

"Forget it." Emotion made him tremble. "I figured that if you'd really wanted to kill me, you would have."

"I figured the same. You could have killed *me*." She squeezed his hand. "I can't tell you how glad I am to see you again. How I've missed you."

His voice was thick. "I've missed you, too." He felt torn apart, his love for her tugging him one way, his vow of celibacy the other. His turmoil increased as she leaned close, kissing him on the lips. He felt her breath on his skin. Badly he wanted to kiss her in return, to hold her, to feel the comfort of her flesh. But his crisis of will passed. What he felt now wasn't lust. He didn't want to make love to her. He wanted to show he cared. How could that be sinful? He held her tight.

"Those men down there," he said.

"I know." She grinned. "We'd better not get distracted." Sobering, she stood and left the bushes, pulling up the zipper on her pants.

Still feeling the touch of her lips against his own, straining to subdue his confusion, he peered unseen from a gap in the thicket, nervous for her. She closed the button at her waist, then buckled her belt, and sat on the flat stretch of rock at the lip of the cliff. Her gestures were convincing, he decided. The impression she'd give the surveillance team was that she'd gone out of sight to relieve herself. In their place, I'd accept the explanation.

He watched her eat some trail food. She drank more water and lay back on the rock as if to rest before her descent. Through the bushes, he saw that she closed her eyes. In a while, except for the rise and fall of her chest, she didn't move. Whether or not she'd actually gone to sleep, the surveillance team would think that she had.

He scanned the forest but couldn't find any sign of the team. Either they're awfully good, or they're not down there. Wouldn't that be a joke? he thought. To go through all this trouble when we didn't have to.

11

After dusk, he chose the best support on the rear side of the Horn—a boulder that his full strength couldn't budge.

Arlene came through the bushes, holding her rope and pack, kneeling beside him. "You found an anchor?"

"Here." He put her hand on the barely visible rock.

"You tested it?"

"It'll hold. With luck."

"Luck? Oh, brother." But she seemed to know he was joking. "We'd better get started." She reached in her pack and pulled out a nylon sling.

"I'll need your extra hardware. All I have is a rope and sling."

"That isn't like you, not to come fully prepared." Now *she* was joking.

"Well, I had a slight problem. A temporary shortage of funds."

As they spoke, keeping their voices low, Drew felt good to be working with her. He tied his nylon sling around the boulder. Arlene hooked a metal carabiner onto the sling, making sure that the carabiner's hinged flap was safely closed. She knotted the ends of her rope and looped its midpoint onto the carabiner. Drew knew that a simpler method would have been to attach the rope directly to the sling, but the rope, like the sling, was made from nylon, and nylon had a dangerously low friction point. If the rope and the sling were allowed to rub against each other, the weight of a climber could easily make them overheat and snap. This way, the metal carabiner acted as a buffer, reducing the heat.

Almost ready. Arlene tied a sling around her legs and waist in a pattern that resembled a diaper. She hooked a carabiner through it, at her crotch. Drew did the same, borrowing equipment from her pack. As night enveloped them, he was nonetheless able to see her shadowy outline, athletic and lithe. His love for her intensified.

She hooked the doubled rope into the carabiner, looped the two strands of rope around her left shoulder, down her back, and around to the right side of her waist. The carabiner at her crotch would thus take the main stress of the rope. Her shoulder and back would absorb the remainder of the stress, and if she needed to, she could use her right hand to press the rope against her waist, applying a brake.

"I'll take the pack and go first," she whispered. "There's a ledge sixty feet down. I'll rig another anchor. And another one farther down after that. It takes three separate rappels to reach the bottom."

"I know."

"Then you still remember how to do this?" She seemed to grin.

"I had a good teacher."

"Flattery. My, my."

She was gone, walking backward off the cliff, gripping the section of the rope above the carabiner, pressing the other section against her waist. He imagined the graceful ease with which she would drop. She'd always enjoyed a free-fall. A piece of cloth tied near the end of her rope would warn her when she would soon run out of rope. Then she would stop and rig yet another anchor.

That would be the dangerous part, searching for a solid spot on this brittle cliff. But after that, all she needed to do was balance herself on the ledge while she unhooked the rope from the sling around her crotch. She'd free the knotted ends of the rope and pull down on one side, tugging the other side up through the anchor at the top of the cliff, then down to her. She'd reposition the rope, this time on the new anchor, and continue her descent.

Anxious, his affection adding to his worry about her safety, he crouched, gently touching the rope, feeling it start to move. Okay. He relaxed temporarily. She would set up the other anchor. Soon, lower, she'd set up the third. When he judged that she'd had sufficient time to reach the bottom, to step back from the cliff and avoid any rocks that he might dislodge when he came down, only then would he begin.

Five minutes—that was all the time he'd need. He wondered what the surveillance team was doing. They must have become suspicious. Professionals, they presumably had an infrared scope that allowed them to see that Arlene had disappeared. They'd approach to investigate. If I don't get down there soon . . .

He quit counting, secured his rope, turned his back to the cliff, and as his stomach soared toward his throat, he dropped.

12

He stepped on a loose chunk of rock. It tilted. Lurching sideways, fighting for balance, he heard it clatter in the dark. He froze.

He'd reached the bottom. Behind the Horn, the wall of the neighboring bluff loomed close behind him, creating a thicker dark. The narrow enclosure smothered him. He felt disoriented, defenseless. Where was Arlene?

The snap of a finger told him where she stood. To his left. Across from him, near the other cliff. With as little noise as possible, he started in that direction.

He realized that anyone could have made that noise. In the dark, the surveillance team might have approached the base of the Horn, assumed that Arlene would descend from the back, and waited there for her.

For me as well, he thought. He strained to see a figure in the night. Again he heard fingers snap. He pulled out his Mauser, his muscles hard with tension, stalking forward.

A scream broke the silence. Unnerving, it came from above. Drew felt a rush of air—again from above—and stumbled frantically back as a massive object plummeted past him, walloping on the rocks. Though it seemed to be heavy and solid, it made a sickening plop, like a watermelon dropped from an overpass onto a freeway. Warm liquid spattered his face. He jerked a hand to his cheek.

His surprise became shock. His shock changed to urgency, commanding him. Though he knew what had fallen, he had to find out if this was Arlene. The fear made bile rush into his mouth.

But he felt Arlene suddenly next to him. This close, he recognized her shape, her smell. Then who had . . . ? He lunged forward, crouching with his Mauser in one hand, reaching with the other. His fingers touched bloody hair, a shattered skull, warm and sticky. He traced his hand along the torso. A man. The clothes were grimy, torn, buttons missing, a rope for a belt. The dingy clothes a wino might wear. Or someone disguised as a wino, one of the men who'd followed Arlene from her brownstone.

But how could this have happened?

As Arlene knelt beside him, he tried to think the problem through. The surveillance team must have become impatient. Suspecting that she would try to sneak down from the Horn at night, they'd split up. The wino must have tried to find a way up to the bluff behind the Horn. In turn, his partner, the well-dressed man with the earphones, had waited in case Arlene decided on the easy route and came back through the trees at the entrance to the basin.

So far, it made sense, Drew thought. The wino, hiding on top of the bluff in the dark, must have heard the scrape of our boots on the rocks when we touched down. If he leaned too close to the rim, he could have lost his balance and fallen. Easy enough to do at night.

But the explanation troubled him. It wasn't the kind of mistake you'd expect from a pro. Beside him, Arlene removed her hands from the corpse and slowly stood. He knew that she too would be trying to figure out the sequence. They didn't need—didn't *dare*—to discuss what had happened. The other member of the team was still in the area. Maybe up on the bluff, in fact. Maybe both men had gone up there, reasoning that the cliff behind the Horn was the logical spot for Arlene to try eluding them.

Too many variables. Too much uncertainty.

But this he did know. The falling wino's scream would have warned his partner. If the well-dressed man was in the woods at the basin's entrance, he might decide to come this way and investigate.

On the other hand, a professional wasn't supposed to allow a scream—even one from his partner—to lure him into what might be a trap.

Arlene touched his shoulder, communicating the same urgent need he felt to get away. They crossed the dark narrow chasm and stopped at the bluff behind the Horn. Behind them, the corpse made a gurgling sound, pressure forcing gas and blood from the torso.

Drew shut out the noise, concentrating on the problem he faced. Though a night climb was always difficult, the cliff behind the Horn offered one compensation. It wasn't as severely vertical as the Horn, and it offered more ledges, more outcrops. Arlene's shadowy form reached up, choosing a handhold, testing it, then raising her boot to fit it into a crack. Drew brooded. If the well-dressed man had gone with the wino up to the top of the bluff, we'll never get over the rim. We'll be pushed down here with his friend.

No, all of this felt wrong. He tugged the back of Arlene's jacket as she raised herself. She stiffened, resisting. He tugged again. She stepped back down, her indistinct face swinging toward him. He gripped her hand and used it to point away from the cliff, past the Horn, toward the entrance to the basin. He touched her hand to his chest, to hers, and again pointed past the Horn. The message, he hoped, was clear. It might be better if we went *that* way. She seemed to think about it. Two taps on his shoulder. Okay.

They crept from the chasm between the Horn and the bluff. If the well-dressed man was out there hidden in the dark of the woods, watching them through a nightscope, they'd be obvious targets caught in the open. But Drew had an intuition, an instinct, that the situation was even more confused than he imagined, that no bullet would pierce his chest, that he and Arlene had a better-than-even chance to get away.

They angled to the right, leaving the bluff on their flank, descending the slope of fragmented rock, entering the narrow exit from the basin. The woods they reached were still and cold but, because of their tangle, reassuring.

In keeping with their training, they stayed twenty feet apart, Drew taking the lead, shifting past deadfalls and boulders. Separated, they made less easy targets, and if a sniper shot at one of them, the other would have a chance to see the muzzle flash and return the fire. Drew felt reassured by the pistol that she'd taken from her pack.

This time, when he reached the stream, he didn't waste effort trying to find a log with which to cross, but simply waded, nervous about the inadvertent splashing sounds he made.

Then the stream was behind him, and hearing Arlene follow, he crept farther through the bushes and trees, easing his boots down on leaves that blessedly were still so soaked from yesterday's rain that they didn't crackle. With the stars to guide him, he headed east toward the two-lane road and the motorcycle he'd hidden near it.

His tension eased when he saw the blacktop. The moon had risen, casting a glow across it. The skeletal silhouette of a hydro pylon loomed against the pattern of stars to his right. When he'd arrived that morning, he'd chosen the pylon as a landmark to guide him back to where he'd hidden the chopper, and now heading right, through the bushes that flanked the road, he came to the Harley. He checked the bike; no one had tampered with it.

Still, he didn't want to start the motor and attract attention, so he walked the bike down the road, heading left of the pylon this time, soon reaching the spot where Arlene waited for him.

In the moonlight, he saw her gesture toward an overgrown lane that jutted into the woods. The bushes and saplings had been bent as if a car had gone along it. She motioned for him to follow, and thirty yards down the lane, he found the dark blue car almost indistinguishable from the forest.

It was occupied.

The well-dressed man sat motionless behind the steering wheel. A thin gash encircled the front half of his throat. The gash was deep, the obvious aftermath of powerful hands on a razor-sharp garotte. Moonlight filtered through the trees, revealing the blood that drenched the front of the dead man's overcoat.

Drew spun toward the black of the forest. The wino hadn't fallen from the cliff near the Horn! He'd been pushed! There was someone else in the forest!

Silence no longer mattered, Drew thought. Whoever's out there knows every move we've made.

He straddled the motorcycle, stomping down on the starter. The engine's roar broke the stillness. "Let's get the hell out of here."

13

Feeling Arlene's breasts against his back, her arms around his chest, he sped toward the gravel parking area where she'd left her car—a Firebird, the nameplate said, though he didn't recognize its design.

They quickly inspected it, but as with the Harley, no one

had meddled. Indeed, it started the instant Arlene turned the ignition key. Its tires throwing up gravel, Arlene raced from the parking area. Drew hurried after her.

But five miles down the road, just after a hairpin turn, he let her taillights disappear while he hid in bushes beside the road, watching for anyone who followed. He waited ten minutes.

No one came. It doesn't make sense, he thought. Whoever killed those men must have seen us leave. Why aren't we being tailed? Frowning, he left his hiding place and met Arlene ten miles farther along.

"There *has* to be someone," she said.

"I know." He glanced along the dark road. "I never thought I'd be bothered because I wasn't being followed."

"Let's try it one more time. After the next sharp turn, pull off the road again and wait."

No car followed. Distressed, he hurried to join her.

"That's it then," she said. "Let's put some miles behind us. Stay close. I'll use back roads."

"To where?"

"You said it yourself. We need to find a place that's safe, where you can answer my questions." She sounded exhausted. "And tell me what all of this has to do with Jake."

Troubled, they both glanced behind them. *What had happened in those woods?*

"We've *got* to find Jake," Arlene said urgently.

14

Heading south through Pennsylvania, they stopped at Bethlehem on the Lehigh River. The motel they chose was off a side street, a line of adjoining units with a parking slot outside each door. Facing a sleepy clerk, they registered as Mr. and Mrs. Robert Davis, requested the unit that was farthest in back ("So the morning traffic doesn't wake us"), and discovered that at 3 A.M. all the nearby diners were closed. They had to settle for the rest of their trail food along with stale cheese and crackers from a coin dispenser in the motel's lobby.

They parked the Firebird in front of the unit but left the motorcycle around the side out of sight from the street, locked the unit's door behind them, closed the drapes, and only then turned on the lights.

At once, Arlene sank across the bed, her arms outstretched. Against the white spread, she looked as if she were making angels in snow. She closed her eyes and laughed. "Just like the old days, huh? Reminds me of the time we holed up in Mexico City. You and me and—"

She opened her eyes, no longer relaxed.

"And Jake," Drew said.

She frowned. "It's time."

He didn't answer.

"You promised."

"Sure. It's just that . . ."

"Jake. You said you were in a monastery. You said six years ago Jake killed you. What does that mean?" Her voice hardened. "Tell me."

He'd known this was coming. During the troubled drive here (again the terrible question: *What had happened in those woods? Why hadn't they been followed?*), he'd tried to prepare himself.

But he still wasn't ready.

"I'm afraid it'll take a while."

"Then don't waste time. Get started." She stood, taking off her khaki jacket, beginning to unbutton her heavy wool shirt.

The intimate gesture surprised him, though clearly she didn't think twice about it, still relating to him as if they were lovers. Again he felt a rush of love for her, a bittersweet nostalgia for their former life.

"And while you're at it"—she opened the door to the bathroom—"I've got dibs on the shower." She turned impatiently, oblivious to the corner of one breast that showed through her partly opened shirt. "Come on, Drew. Talk to me."

His thoughts were in chaos, his subconscious struggling not to give up the nightmares it had buried. He glanced at the floor.

When he peered up, Arlene was gone. From the bathroom, he heard the scrape of hooks on a shower curtain, the spray of water into a tub.

The curtain scraped again, and he walked in. Her shadow moved behind the yellow-flowered barrier. Her dusty climbing clothes were piled beneath the sink. Steam rose, filling the room. "Drew?"

"Here. I'm trying to decide where to start." He bit his lip, closed the lid on the toilet seat, and eased himself down.

"But you said six years ago."

"No. It starts before then. Unless you know what happened before, the rest of it doesn't make sense." He stared at the steam that filled the bathroom. Despite their intimacy, he had never told her any of this before. The memories had been too depressing. "Japan," he murmured.

"What? I can't hear you. This shower."

"Japan," he said louder.

The mist swirled thicker. For a dizzying moment, he had the sensation of falling in.

PART FIVE

VISITATION

THE SINS OF THE PAST

⁜

1

Japan, 1960.

On June 10, prior to a planned visit by American President Dwight D. Eisenhower, a raging mob of ten thousand Japanese anti-American demonstrators stormed Tokyo's airport to protest a new Japanese-American defense treaty that permitted the continued presence of American military bases, and worse—considering the A-bombs the United States had dropped on Hiroshima and Nagasaki—the inclusion of nuclear weapons on Japanese soil. The immediate targets of their fury were the American Ambassador to Japan, along with several members of Eisenhower's White House staff. As a warning of worse riots to come if the American President arrived in Japan, the mob surrounded the limousine in which the American contingent had planned to drive to the embassy, so threatening the occupants that a U.S. Marine helicopter made an emergency landing among the protestors and flew the officials to safety.

Six days later, the Japanese government requested a postponement of Eisenhower's visit. However, the massive demonstrations continued.

2

Tokyo, one week later. The recent "troubles"—Drew had heard his father use the expression often lately—the "troubles" were to blame for the cancellation of his birthday party. He didn't know what the troubles were (something to do with the mysterious place called the embassy where his father worked), but he did know that last year when he turned nine there'd been twenty children at his party, and this year, tomorrow, there wouldn't be any.

"With the troubles, it isn't safe for Americans to associate with each other," his father had said. "So many cars and parents arriving. They'd attract too much attention. We can't afford further incidents. I'm sure you understand, Drew. Next year, I promise, we'll give you a bigger, better party than the one we planned for this year."

But Drew didn't understand—not any more than he understood why his father had told his mother at supper last night that they might have to move from their house to the embassy.

"Temporarily." Sometimes Drew's father used words too big for Drew to grasp. "Only until the situation has stabilized."

Whatever "stabilized" meant. The only sign Drew had of anything wrong was that during the past few weeks, most of their Japanese servants had resigned. And now that Drew thought about it, there'd been one other thing. His best friend in the neighborhood, a Japanese boy, no longer came to play. Drew often phoned him, but his friend's parents always said that the boy wasn't home.

"Hey, never mind the party, sport," Drew's father said, and playfully mussed his hair. "Don't look so glum. You'll still have presents. Lots of them. And a big chocolate cake, your favorite. I'll even stay home from work to help you celebrate."

"You mean you can actually get away?" Drew's mother asked, delighted. "Won't they be needing you at the embassy?"

"With the hours I've been putting in, I told the ambassador my son's more important than any damned crisis."

"And he didn't get angry?"

"All he did was laugh and say, 'Tell your son Happy Birthday for me.'"

3

A long black limousine stopped in front of the house at two the next afternoon. Drew watched, excited, from his bedroom window. The car had a small American flag on a metal post near the driver's side-view mirror. Its license plates were the same kind as on his father's car—from the embassy. A uniformed American got out, took a large red-white-and-blue package from the seat beside him, straightened the bow, and proceeded up the curved front walk, past an ornate Japanese garden, toward the entrance.

He knocked on the door and, while he waited, adjusted his chauffeur's cap, then turned, attracted to the song of an unseen bird in a nearby blossoming cherry tree. An elderly Japanese woman, one of the few local servants who hadn't quit working here, came out and bowed gracefully in her brilliant orange kimono.

The driver bowed slightly in return and then, from American habit, tipped his cap. "Please tell Mr. MacLane that the ambassador sends his compliments." The driver grinned. "Or I guess you should tell his son. And give him this birthday present. The ambassador hopes it makes up for the canceled party."

The driver handed the package to the servant, bowed again, and returned to the limousine.

4

Despite his growing impatience, Drew obeyed instructions and waited in his room while his mother and father made sure that everything was properly arranged.

"It's just the three of us," his mother had said. "But we'll have enough fun for twenty."

Eagerly he paged through the American comic books—Superman and Davy Crockett were his favorites—that his father had arranged to be specially delivered. "In the diplomatic pouch," his father had said, though Drew knew he was joking. "Nothing's too good for my son."

He lay on his bed, staring anxiously at the ceiling.

"Okay, Drew," he heard his mother call from the garden at the rear of the house. "You can come out now."

He leaped from his bed and scurried out of his room. The quickest way to the garden in back was through his father's study. As he passed his father's desk, he saw through the open sliding door to where his mother and father sat at a circular table piled high with presents, all sizes and colors. Sunlight glinted off the tall, frosted glass that his mother held.

"Why, even the ambassador sent you a present," she said, excited when she saw him coming, and raised the glass to her mouth.

"He didn't need to. Thinks of everything. Wonder what's in it," Drew's father said and shook the box.

Drew entered the garden.

The stunning blast deafened him, throwing him back through the open study door, slamming him hard against his father's desk. He must have blacked out for a moment. He didn't remember falling from the desk to the floor. The next thing he knew, he was staggering to his feet. The roar behind his ears made him sick. His vision was blurred. As he stumbled toward the indistinct wreckage of the study door, he realized—confused—that his clothes were wet, and peering down, frantic to clear his eyes, he saw that he was drenched with blood. The blood alone should have made him scream. But it didn't. Nor did he scream as he panicked, afraid of how badly he might be hurt, nor as he realized   no!   that the blood wasn't his.

He lurched through the shattered doorway, seeing his mother and father in fragments across the lawn, the grass wet from their blood. The birthday cake, the plates and cups and gaily wrapped presents that had covered the table no longer existed. The table itself had disintegrated. Acrid smoke from the blast swirled thickly around him, making him choke. A nearby bush was in flames.

But still he didn't scream.

Not until he focused on his mother's almost-severed head. The force of the blast had rammed the glass from which she'd been drinking into her mouth. Its circular base propped her lips apart. Inside her mouth, the rest of the glass had shattered. Blossoming shards protruded, dripping blood, from both her mangled cheeks.

Then he did scream.

5

The steam began to clear. Arlene's shadow was motionless behind the curtain. The bathroom was silent. Drew hadn't been aware that she'd turned off the water.

The silence was broken by the rasp of metal hooks on the curtain as she opened it part way, her features taut with sympathy. "I didn't know."

"You couldn't have. It's something I don't like to talk about. Even now, it's too painful." Except, Drew thought, once, in a moment of weakness, he had told Jake. He wiped what might have been steam from around his eyes.

"I'm deeply, terribly sorry."

"Yeah." His voice was flat.

"The present from the embassy—"

"With red-white-and-blue wrapping paper."

"—was booby-trapped?"

Drew nodded.

"But it didn't come from the embassy, and the limousine wasn't an official car, and the government license plates were fake," she said.

"Of course. And the driver—nobody knew anything about him. The embassy's security staff made me look at photographs. Nothing."

"Classic."

"Yeah." Drew closed his eyes. "Wasn't it, though?"

6

His mind blank, his body numbed from grief, he faced the ambassador in the large, oppressive office. From his ten-year-old perspective, the ceiling disturbed him; it was so high that it made him insecure, as if he'd suddenly become shorter. The hulking furniture was covered with leather and looked uncomfortable. The walls had somber wood paneling, brooding books on massive shelves, disturbing photographs of important-looking men. The carpet was so thick that he didn't know if he was allowed to stand on it with his shoes.

"Will that be all, sir?" an embassy guard—Drew's eyes had widened at the gun in the holster on his belt—asked the elderly white-haired man behind the desk at the far end of the enormous room.

Drew recognized the man, having met him several times before when his parents had brought Drew to the embassy for Christmas and Fourth of July parties. The man wore a gray pin-striped suit and vest. His closely trimmed mustache was as white as his hair. His lean face looked wrinkled, tired.

"Yes, thank you," the man told the guard. "Instruct my secretary to hold all my calls and appointments for the next fifteen minutes."

"Very good, sir." The guard stepped backward, leaving the office and shutting the door behind him.

"Hello. It's Andrew, isn't it?" The ambassador studied him, seeming to choose his words. "Why don't you come over here and sit down?"

Confused, Drew obeyed. The leather chair made a creaking sound as he settled onto it, his feet dangling off the floor.

"I'm glad you're out of the hospital. Did they treat you well?"

Bewildered, Drew only sighed. In the hospital, there'd been soldiers with guns that had scared him. There'd been no other children in the ward, and groggy from the injection he'd been given to make him sleepy, he hadn't understood why the nurses were called lieutenants.

"Your doctor tells me that apart from several cuts and bruises—and those flashburns on your eyebrows—there's nothing wrong with you. A miracle, really. He says not to worry, by the way. The hair on your eyebrows will grow back."

Drew frowned at him, mystified. His eyebrows? What difference did his eyebrows make? His parents—the shards of glass sticking out of his mother's bloody mangled cheeks—they were what mattered.

Grief cramped his stomach, rising cold to his aching heart.

The ambassador leaned forward with concern. "Are you all right, son?"

Drew wanted to sob but controlled the impulse, swallowing thickly, nodding.

The ambassador waited, trying to smile. "And your room here at the embassy? I'm sure that you miss your home, but under the circumstances, we couldn't very well let you stay there, even with guards. You understand. I trust that you're comfortable now, at least."

The bedroom Drew had been given reminded him of a hotel room—if he'd had the vocabulary, he'd have called it impersonal—where he and his parents once had stayed during a vacation trip to Hawaii. Again, he forced himself to nod.

"I know my staff's been treating you well," the ambassador said. "In fact, I've given orders to the kitchen crew that you can have all the ice cream you want. For the next few days, at any rate. Strawberry is your favorite, I believe."

The thought of strawberry ice cream, its color and consistency, reminded Drew of his mother's bloody cheeks.

"Is there anything else we can get you? Something you miss from home perhaps?"

My mother and father, Drew wanted to scream. He suffered in silence.

"Nothing at all?"

Aware of the tension, Drew struggled for something, anything, to say and murmured the first words that entered his mind.

The ambassador straightened. "I'm sorry, son. I didn't hear you."

Don't call me "son," Drew inwardly raged. *I'm not your son. I'm not anybody's son. Not anymore.*

But all he said, not caring, was "My comic books."

The ambassador looked relieved. "Of course. Whatever you like. I'll send a man out this afternoon to get them. Have you any preference, any you're especially fond of?"

"Superman." It made no difference. Drew wanted desperately to get out of the office. "Davy Crockett."

"I'll get a boxload for you." The ambassador pursed his lips. "Now then." He stood, came around to the front of his desk, and leaned his hips against it, bending forward to put his gaze at Drew's eye level. "I have a few things we need to discuss. This isn't easy, but it has to be done. Your parents' funeral . . ."

Drew winced. Though only ten, he'd been taught by yesterday's horror to have a sudden understanding of death. Certainly, after having seen his parents' fragmented bodies, he knew that they couldn't possibly be put back together.

". . . will be tomorrow morning. My assistants and myself have had several discussions on the matter. We know how painful this is for you, but we've agreed that you ought to attend it. To lay your nightmares to rest, so to speak. And to make you a symbol . . ."

Drew didn't understand the word.

". . . of what hate can do. Of what shouldn't be allowed to happen again. I know that this is all terribly confusing for you, but sometimes we have to make good things come out of bad. We want you to sit in the front pew at the funeral. A lot of photographers will take your picture. A lot of people—the world, in fact—will be watching. I'm sorry that you have to grow up so fast. For what it's worth, I feel confident that your mother and father would have wanted you to go."

At last Drew did cry. No matter how hard he tried, he couldn't stop himself.

The ambassador held him tightly, patting his back. "That's the stuff. Get it out of you. Let it go. Believe me, it's all right to cry."

Drew didn't need encouragement. He continued to sob, convulsing so hard that he thought his heart must surely break. Finally his spasms subsided. Wiping his eyes, feeling the sting of the tears on his cheeks, he frowned in pain at the ambassador. "Why?" His throat was so swollen that the word was a croak.

"I'm sorry, Andrew. I'm not sure I understand. Why what?"

"Who killed them? *Why?*"

The ambassador sighed. "I wish I knew. These days, America isn't very popular, I'm afraid." He named several countries, most of which Drew had never heard of—Cuba, Cameroon, Algeria, the Congo. "It's not just here in Japan that we've had riots against us. Everything's changing. The world's a different place."

"But isn't there *someone* you can punish?"

"I'm sorry. We just don't know enough. But I promise we're doing everything we can to find out."

Drew blinked through his tears.

"I hate to do this all at once. There's something else we need to discuss. A while ago I said that I've told the kitchen staff to give you all the ice cream you want for the next few days. The reason for the time limit is that after the funeral, after you've had a chance to rest, you'll be flown back to the States. Someone has to take care of you. I've spoken to your uncle and made arrangements for you to stay with him. You'll have a chance to speak with him on the overseas telephone"—the ambassador glanced at his watch—"in twenty minutes."

Confused, Drew tried to remember what his uncle looked like, but all he saw in his mind was his father's face, or rather, an indistinct image of his father's face. It alarmed him that he couldn't recall what his father looked like. Except for the fragments of the body strewn across the blood-soaked lawn.

7

"But who killed your parents?" Arlene sat beside him on the bed, clutching a blanket around her.

"I never knew. At the embassy, I heard a lot of talk. The American who'd dressed as a chauffeur and delivered the bomb was described as a free-lance, a mercenary. That was the first time I'd ever heard the word. The assumption was that he'd been hired by Japanese fanatics, but one man on the embassy's security staff—he'd lived in Japan since the end of the war—insisted that a bomb wasn't the Japanese style. He kept talking about samurai and *bushido* and a lot of other things I didn't understand. The code of the warrior. He said a Japanese worthy of that name was honorbound to kill his enemy in the open, face to face. Not with a bomb, not even with a gun, but with a sword. Three months later, in fact, a Japanese protestor did just that, shoving his way through a crowd to impale a Japanese politician who favored the new treaty with America. And the security guard also said that a true Japanese wouldn't have tried to kill his enemy's wife and child—only the husband, the father."

"But if the guard didn't blame the Japanese, who *did* he blame?"

"The Russians. Much of this didn't make sense to me at the time, of course, but I later got the idea of what he meant. The point of the new defense treaty was for America to help protect Japan from an attack by the Soviets. With our bases in Japan, we had our thumb on Southeast Asia and could try to stop communism from spreading. The guard's theory was that, if the Soviets could make it seem that the Japanese had blown up an American diplomat and his family . . ."

"The deaths would be so shocking they'd widen the gap between America and Japan. The treaty would be threatened," said Arlene.

"That was the guard's idea. But if so, the tactic didn't work. My parents' murders made everybody realize how out of control the situation had become. The Japanese, embarrassed that they were being blamed for the assassinations, began to stop demonstrating. The crisis passed."

Arlene took his hand. "But not your nightmares."

He looked at her with anguish. *"I wanted someone to blame."*

8

He'd often gone to mass with his parents, but he'd never realized until their funeral how many images of death surrounded him in church. Christ on the Cross, the nails through His hands and feet, His back slashed by whips, His head crowned with thorns, His side split open by a spear. In a prayer book, he found a colorful depiction of the tomb from which Christ had risen. Christ's disciples stood before the rolled-away stone, raising their faces in celebration.

But nothing could bring his parents back, he knew. He'd seen the bloody fragments of their bodies.

The thunderous organ music was scary, the Latin of the mass as meaningless as the English that the priest used to describe "this terrible tragedy." In the front pew, Drew felt everybody staring at him. Photographers kept taking his picture. He wanted to scream.

The ambassador had explained that the bodies would be flown to a place called Andrews Air Force Base, where his uncle and "even the Secretary of State" would be waiting. Whoever the Secretary of State was. It didn't matter. There'd be another service at his father's family plot in Boston, but to Drew, that didn't matter either, though apparently this first service was more important, a symbol—the ambassador had used that word again—of the need for friendship between America and Japan.

Drew noticed many hard-faced men, their suitcoats open, clutching what might have been guns attached to their belts.

And when the service ended, the ambassador took the American flags—one had covered each coffin—folded them, and brought them over for Drew to touch.

He pressed his face against them, soaking them with his tears.

9

"And that's why I couldn't be this freelance assassin you told me about. This mercenary terrorist." Drew said the words with disgust. "Janus. Because a man like Janus killed my parents. And he wasn't alone. The ambassador told me there were many other mercenaries like the one who'd disguised himself as a chauffeur." Drew bristled. "Without the honor of a Japanese. Cowards. Sneak thieves, who didn't have the dignity to face their enemies directly. Mothers, fathers, children—it made no difference to them who they hurt, what grief and pain they caused. Each night as I cried myself to sleep, I repeated a vow I made to myself." He clenched his teeth. "If I might never have the satisfaction of seeing the man who'd murdered my parents receive the punishment he deserved, I'd punish those who were like him. I'd make it my business to get even with all of them."

"You were—how old?—ten, you said?" Arlene looked astonished. "And you made that choice? You stuck to it?"

"There's nothing surprising about it." Drew swallowed bitterly. "You see, I *loved* my parents. To this day, I still miss them. I used to visit their graves. A lot." His voice cracked.

"Ten years old, I thought I could get revenge on my own. I didn't know how. But later, in my teens, I learned that others felt as I did. I went to work for . . ."

"Scalpel." She breathed the word.

The phone rang harshly, interrupting them.

10

Drew swung in surprise toward the bedside table. He glanced sharply at Arlene. Her eyes wide, she seemed as startled as he was. He stared again toward the table, where the phone rang a second time.

"Wrong number?" Arlene clearly didn't believe it.

Drew didn't even bother shaking his head. The phone rang a third time.

"The clerk in the office?" Arlene asked. "Something he forgot to tell us?"

"Like what?"

She couldn't think of anything. The phone rang again.

"Maybe we're talking too loud. Maybe we woke up somebody next to us," Drew said. "There's one way to know for sure." He leaned from the bed to pick up the phone. Despite his tension, he kept his voice calm. "Hello."

"Yes. Not to alarm you"—the voice on the other end was male, husky, heavily accented—"but I have no choice except to call you."

Regardless of that reassurance, Drew did feel alarmed, nagged by the terrible suspicion that he'd heard the voice before, though he couldn't identify it. Arlene left the chair, putting her head next to Drew's, listening as he held the phone slightly away from his ear.

The voice kept talking. "It's unfortunate, but even with the best equipment, I'm not able to hear everything you say in your room. The shower, in particular, presented a problem. And you're coming to the part that interests me."

Drew shivered from a cold spot between his shoulder blades as he remembered, with frightening vividness, where he'd heard the voice before. It belonged to the priest who'd suddenly appeared from the confessional when Drew had been attacked in the chapel at the retreat house in the Berkshire Hills. The priest with the gleaming red ring, the .45, and the Slavic accent. The priest who'd shot the two priest-assailants and chased Drew down the tunnel.

"I realize you need time to adjust to my intrusion," the voice said. "I've no doubt surprised you. But please, don't hesitate much longer. Time, as the saying goes, is short."

Drew gripped his Mauser. "Where are you?"

"In the unit next to yours. Note how freely I tell you. I put myself in your hands."

Drew scowled toward the opposite wall. "How did you find us?"

"Everything in due course. I want permission to enter your room. I'd prefer not to leave the building, however. A locked door separates our units. If you'll unbolt your side, I'll do the same on mine, and then at last we can meet."

Drew raised his eyebrows in question toward Arlene. She nodded, pointing at herself and then at the bed. Her next gesture told Drew to go to the wall beside the adjoining door.

Drew spoke to the phone. "If you show a weapon . . ."

"Please," the voice said, "I understand the rules. I took a risk by phoning you. Respect my candor. Unbolt the door."

Arlene nodded firmly again.

"All right," Drew said.

He set the phone on its cradle. Arlene got onto the bed, propping her back against its pillows. He aimed his Mauser and stepped toward the connecting door.

Hard enough to make an obvious sound, he twisted the bolt on the lock, then stepped toward the wall where he'd be out of sight when the door came open. But as an extra precaution, he shifted toward the corner, in case a bullet burst through the wall.

The lock on the other side was twisted. The door creaked, opening into the room.

On the bed, Arlene—in full view of the open door—separated the folds of the blanket she'd been clutching around her, revealing sleek, inviting breasts, their nipples hardening from the sudden comparative cold, her pubic hair . . .

Drew took advantage of the distraction. An instant was all he needed. He yanked the door completely open so it banged against the wall. Thrusting his Mauser hard against the man's kidney, he quickly, expertly, frisked him.

The priest groaned from the pistol's sharp jab. "No need. I left my weapon in my room." Having stooped in pain, he now straightened. "I told you, I understand the rules. I'm not a threat to you."

Drew finished his search, even thrusting a hand at the crotch of the priest's black trousers, probing the area around the man's testicles.

"And please," the man told Arlene, "kindly wrap the blanket around you again. I'm a priest. But I'm not immune to temptations of the flesh."

Arlene closed the blanket.

"Thank you." The man wore a black suitcoat, a black bib, a white collar. He was husky, of medium height, compact, muscular, with gray hairs in his thick dark mustache and hints of silver in his dense black hair. His face was square, craggy, strong-boned, ruggedly European. He seemed in his early fifties, but a deep brooding portion of his eyes, much blacker than his clothes, mustache, and hair, outlined by fierce strong wrinkles, suggested that his experiences had made him infinitely older.

Drew stepped cautiously back. "How did you find us?"

"At the retreat house, you were given clean clothes. A change of shoes." The priest waited for Drew to make his own conclusions.

Drew winced in disgust for not having suspected. "A homing device?"

"In the heel of one shoe. After you fled the seminary, I followed its signal. I found where you left the bishop's car—shockingly devastated, I might add." The priest allowed himself to chuckle. Drew started to talk, but the priest raised a hand. "Let me finish. I discovered that you'd switched the ruined Cadillac for a motorcycle. Resourceful of you. I followed you to Concord and Lexington. You made phone calls. From there, I followed you to Greenwich Village in New York and watched your efforts to contact this young lady. You gave me concern when you changed from the shoes with the homing device to those climbing boots at Satan's Horn. But I attached a homing device to your motorcycle. And"—glancing toward Arlene—"to your car."

For the first time since the priest had entered the room, she spoke. "And in the meantime?" She frowned. "You killed the men who'd been . . ."

"Following you? It was unavoidable, I'm afraid. I couldn't let them do the same to both of you. There were prior obligations. You see how open I'm being with you?"

"You pushed the man disguised as a wino off the cliff?" she asked.

The priest nodded slightly.

"And slit the other man's throat with a garotte?"

"It was necessary. Otherwise, you wouldn't be alive for us to have this talk."

"A priest who kills?" Drew looked at him in horror.

"I might ask the same of you, though you're not in fact a priest but only a brother. Even so, you're not unacquainted with killing. Or am I wrong?"

They stared at each other.

Arlene broke the silence. "What he says makes sense. With a homing device, he could have stayed far enough back that you didn't see his car when you waited at the side of the road."

"Quite true," the priest said. "I kept a distance. But finally we're together."

Drew shook his head again. "Why?"

"Isn't it obvious? The attack on the monastery."

"The bishop claims it didn't happen."

"He was told to pretend so. After we'd removed the evidence."

"*We?*"

"In good time."

"The bishop also claimed that Hal had *not* been killed at the retreat house. That I wasn't attacked."

"More instructions he followed. I stayed briefly at the retreat house to arrange the cleanup. The seminarians know only that a guest had a nervous breakdown. Nothing's been compromised."

Drew slammed his fist against the wall. "And I can't wait any longer! I want answers!"

"Of course. But, please, there's no need for dramatic gestures. I'm your guardian."

Drew froze. "My *what?*"

"The moment you came with Father Hafer to report to the bishop, I was sent for. I've never been far. Twice—at the chapel and at the Horn—I saved your life."

Drew's scalp prickled. "Saved my life? *Why?* And why didn't you let me know at the start what you were doing?"

"I didn't tell you at the retreat house because I didn't want to show myself. I wanted to see what would happen if you seemed alone, except for Hal. As I suspected, your apparent vulnerability invited an attack."

"You used me as bait?" Drew shook with indignation.

"It seemed an expedient way to draw out your enemies."

"You should have warned me!"

"I disagree. Even a professional such as yourself——"

"A *former* professional."

"That's the point. I wasn't sure how well you'd adapt to being back in the world. Extremely well, it turned out. But at the time, I wondered if six years of being a hermit would have blunted your skills. Suppose I'd told you I wanted to use you as bait to invite an attack? What if you were no longer capable of behaving naturally under stress? If you'd so much as glanced in my direction, you'd have warned your assailants of a possible trap. The two men who burst into the chapel weren't priests, by the way. They dressed to appear so and avoid attracting attention at the seminary. I want to emphasize, they didn't belong to the Church."

"Who were they?"

"We haven't been able to learn. They carried no identification, of course. We took photographs and made impressions of their fingerprints. Our contacts are trying to put names to them now, but I suspect we'll merely discover that they were mercenaries, that there's no way to link them to whoever hired them. After the attack at the retreat house, I tried to explain who I was and why I was there, but you ran. This is the first safe opportunity I've had. I should introduce myself." He held out his hand. "I'm Father Stanislaw."

Drew studied the hand, uneasy. "Stanislaw?"

"The name is Polish. I was born there, and it amused me to take the name of the patron saint of the country of my ancestors."

Reluctantly, Drew gripped the hand.

The priest's clasp was firm. Drew reached for the priest's other hand. His left. The one with the ring on the middle finger.

Father Stanislaw did not resist.

The ring had a thick gold band and setting. Its stone was large, distinctive, gleaming, red—a ruby with a symbol emblazoned upon it. A sword intersecting with a Maltese cross.

"I don't think I've ever seen this symbol. What order does it represent?"

"Order?" Father Stanislaw shook his head. "Not quite an order, though we've been in existence much longer than most orders. From the time of the Crusades, to be sure. But we call ourselves a fraternity."

Drew waited.

"The fraternity of the stone. We'll get to that in time," Father Stanislaw said. "But first, we have some catching up to do. If you'll allow me . . ."

The priest went into his room, came back with a briefcase, removed a folder, and handed it to Drew.

Puzzled, opening it, Drew discovered a dossier about himself—details about his youth. "Wait a minute." He looked up. "Where'd you learn all this?"

"It isn't important. What is," Father Stanislaw said, "is that you learn to trust me. I'm showing you the dossier to prove that I already know a great deal about you. As a consequence, I'm hoping that you'll tell me things I *don't* know. Think of this as confession. A confidence. A basis for understanding. Perhaps it will save your life. And more important, your soul."

Arlene leaned forward. Holding the blanket around her with one hand, she impatiently took the folder from Drew, set it down on her lap, and flipped through its contents. "What *is* this?"

"What happened to me after my parents were killed." Drew's voice was thick.

"But what does this have to do with Jake? My brother's in trouble. For all I know, he might even be dead!"

"To do with Jake?" Drew repeated. "Everything. Unless you know all of it, you can't understand."

11

"Here we are, Drew." His uncle stopped the red Mercury in front of a lawn that sloped up to a ranch house, as he called it. "We had it built last fall. There aren't many like it yet in Boston. The latest design. I hope you'll be happy here. You're home."

Drew stared at the building, feeling foreign and strange. Long and low, the house was made of bricks. It had a chimney; a crowded flower garden; a few short trees. It certainly didn't look anything like a ranch, and he couldn't help comparing it to the traditional Japanese house made of wood, with a high sloping roof, where he'd lived in Tokyo for half his life. Bricks? he asked himself. What would happen here in an earthquake?

And why was the garden so crowded?

"Home," his uncle had said, but it made Drew angry. No. This wasn't his home. His home was back in Japan. Where he'd lived with his parents.

A woman and boy came out of the house. Drew's aunt and cousin. Drew hadn't seen them since his parents had taken him from America when he was five, and he didn't remember them. But this much was clear. The two of them— and his uncle when he made the introductions—were awkward, uneasy. His aunt kept wringing her hands. His cousin kept scowling. And his uncle kept saying that every-thing was going to work out, you bet, yes, all of them would get along just fine.

"You'll be happy here."

Drew wondered, though. He had the terrible sense that he'd never be happy again.

The next day, he went to his parents' second funeral.

12

He spent the summer alone watching television or, if someone came into the den, reading comic books be-hind the closed door of what everybody still called the "guest room." Whenever his aunt told his uncle that it wasn't natural for a boy to stay indoors in summer, his uncle said, "Give him time to get adjusted. Remember, he's been through a lot. What's the matter with Billy? Tell Billy to play with him."

"Billy says he tried."

In truth, Billy hadn't, and Drew knew the reason—jealousy about the new kid in the house.

His aunt said, "Billy thinks he's strange. The way he never talks, and . . ."

"Wouldn't you seem strange?"

"You're at work all day. You don't know what he's like. He sneaks around. I'll be doing the ironing, and I won't even hear him. Suddenly he's right there beside me, staring. He's just like—"

"What? Go on and say it."

"I'm sure I don't know. A ghost. He makes me nervous."

"This is hard on all of us. But we'll have to get used to it. After all, he's my brother's son."

"And Billy's your *own* son, and I don't see why we have to pay more attention to—"

"So where's the kid supposed to go, huh? Tell me that. He didn't ask for somebody to blow up his parents. What the hell do you want me to do?"

"Stop shouting. The neighbors'll hear you."

"And so can the kid when you talk about him, but that doesn't seem to bother you!"

"I won't let you speak to me like that. I—"

"Never mind. I don't feel like eating supper, okay? Put something in the fridge for me. I'm taking a walk."

Drew, having listened out of sight in the hall, went back to the guest room, where he closed the door and read another comic book.

Batman now.

13

September was worse. The first day Drew came back from the local grade school, he had bubble gum stuck in his hair.

"How on earth did you manage that?" his aunt asked.

Drew didn't answer.

She tried to pull the gum out, tugging his hair till tears leaked from his eyes. Finally she cut the gum out with scissors, leaving a bald spot on the crown of his head that resembled a buck private's new haircut or a tonsure on a monk.

The next day, Drew returned from school with black indentations all down his left arm.

"My word, what have you been doing to yourself?" Pursing her lips, his aunt examined the indentations, went for the tweezers, and pulled the point of a pencil out of his skin. "How in heaven's name did that happen?"

The following day, the knee on Drew's new pants was torn, soaked with blood, his skin scraped raw.

"Those pants cost good money, you know."

The day after that, Drew's aunt made an urgent phone call to her husband at his real estate office.

She could hardly speak. But through her sobs, her husband understood enough. Shocked, he agreed to meet her at Drew's grade school after classes let out.

14

"Now I don't deny that your nephew had provocation." The principal had a wobbly double chin. "The Whetman boy is known to be a bully. I assume you're familiar with his parents? His father runs the Cadillac dealership over on Palmer Road."

Drew's aunt and uncle didn't recognize "Whetman," but they certainly recognized "Cadillac."

"So the situation's this." The principal mopped his forehead with a handkerchief. "The Whetman kid is twelve. He's big for his age, and he likes to throw his weight around. The fact is . . . I'll tell you this in confidence. I assume you won't repeat it. The kid takes after his father— pushy. But the father donates a lot of cash to our athletic fund. Anyway, the kid lets everybody know who's boss. So your nephew . . . Well, he didn't buckle under, is what it amounts to. I've got to give him credit. Tough little monkey. Everybody else buckles under. I don't know why your nephew didn't. When school got started, I guess the Whetman kid checked around to see who's new on the block and decided to pick on Andrew as an example. The way I hear it, the Whetman kid put bubble gum in Andrew's hair. And then he stuck pencils into him. And shoved him in the gravel at recess, ripping his pants."

Drew's uncle asked, "Why wasn't anything done to stop this?"

"It's only rumors, things I hear from the children. If I believed everything that the students told me . . ."

"Go on."

"Well, basically . . ." The principal sighed. "Today, the Whetman kid took a whack at Andrew. A pretty good one. He split Andrew's lip."

Drew's uncle squinted angrily. "And?"

"Andrew didn't cry. I'll give him credit for that as well. He sure is a tough little monkey. But the thing is, he should have complained to a teacher in the playground."

"Would it have mattered?"

The principal scowled. "I'm sorry. I don't understand."

"Never mind. Go on."

"Instead, Andrew lost his temper."

"I can't imagine why."

"He hit the Whetman kid in the mouth with a baseball bat."

Drew's uncle turned pale. "Oh, shit."

"Loosened the Whetman kid's front teeth is what he did. Now the kid had some discipline coming, sure. I won't argue that point. But a *baseball bat*? Overreaction, wouldn't you think? And Mr. Whetman was in here earlier. He's upset, I don't need to tell you. He wants to know what kind of school I'm running. He's threatened to go to the education board and the police. Thank God, I managed to talk him out of it, but the point is, until this problem is settled . . . Well, what I asked you here to talk about is that your nephew's suspended. I want him to stay home from school."

15

"It's a damned good thing for you," Mr. Whetman told Drew's uncle and aunt in their living room that night. "If my son had lost his teeth, I'd be suing you so fast . . ."

"Mr. Whetman, please. I know you've got every reason to be angry." Drew's uncle held up his hands. "Believe me, we're disturbed about this ourselves. I'll be glad to pay for any doctor or dentist bills. Your boy isn't disfigured, I hope."

Whetman fumed. "No thanks to your nephew. The doctor says that the stitches won't leave scars, but right now my son's got lips the size of sausages. I'll be direct. The principal told me about your nephew's background, about what happened to his parents. Terrible. It's the only excuse I can think of for his behavior. Obviously your nephew's disturbed. I've decided not to go to the police. On one condition. That the boy get professional help."

"I'm not sure what you mean."

"A psychiatrist, Mr. MacLane. The sooner, the better. Oh, yes, and something else."

Drew's uncle waited.

"I don't want that boy near my son. Have him transferred to another school."

Drew listened behind the partly open door of his room. His eyes stung bitterly. But he'd made a promise to himself, and he kept it. He didn't cry.

16

On the third day after his transfer, Drew's aunt heard the phone ring as she carried groceries into the kitchen. She hurried to set down the bags and answer it.

"Mrs. MacLane?"

The officious voice distressed her. "Speaking."

"I'm sorry to bother you. This is the principal over at Emerson grade school."

She tensed.

"I'm sure this is nothing. You probably, well, just forgot."

She gripped the cupboard.

"But since we didn't receive any word this morning, I thought I'd better call to find out if your nephew's sick."

She herself felt sick. "No." She swallowed something sour. "Not that I know of. He seemed perfectly well when he got on the bus this morning. Why? Has he been complaining about a stomach ache?"

"That's just it, Mrs. MacLane. No one here has seen him to ask him."

Inwardly, she groaned.

"I assumed you'd kept him home from school and simply forgot to let the attendance office know. It happens all the time. But because I'm aware of your nephew's situation, I thought there wouldn't be any harm in my asking. Just in case, you understand."

"In case?"

"Well, I don't think anything's happened to him, though you never can tell. But he wasn't here yesterday, either."

17

Standing next to the policeman, Drew stared down at the sidewalk in front of his aunt and uncle's house.

The screen door banged open. He peered up as his uncle stormed out. "It's after supper. Andrew, you had us worried. Where on earth have you been?"

"The cemetery," the policeman said.

"*What?*"

"Pleasant View. That's ten miles north of here."

"Yes, officer, I'm familiar with it."

"They've had some vandalism recently. Teenagers sneaking in, toppling tombstones, that sort of thing. I can't imagine why anybody would think that's funny. Anyway, the cemetery director asked us to keep a watch, so I've been driving through there on my rounds. Yesterday morning, I saw this youngster staring down at some graves. I didn't think much about it, mostly because I had a radio call about a burglary in progress, and I had to hot-tail it over to a liquor store. But this morning, I was driving through that cemetery again, and there was this youngster again, and I thought, 'Now wait a minute,' and stopped. He sure doesn't talk much, does he?"

"That's a fact," Drew's aunt said.

"Even when I walked up to him, he didn't pay me any attention. He just kept staring down at the graves. So I went around behind him and saw that the last names on the tombstones were both the same."

"MacLane," Drew's uncle said.

"That's right. A man and a woman."

"Robert and Susan."

"Right. So I asked him what he was doing, and the first and last thing he said to me was, 'I'm talking to my mom and dad.' "

"Dear God."

"Then he wiped at his eyes, but the funny thing was, I couldn't see any tears. I figured he must have someone with him, but when I looked, there wasn't anyone in sight. And most children, you know, this uniform makes them pay attention. Not him, though. He just kept staring down at those graves. He wouldn't tell me his name or where he lived. All by himself. Why wasn't he in school? So what could I do? I took him down to the station."

"You did right," Drew's uncle said.

"I even bought him a chocolate bar, but he still wouldn't talk to me, and his wallet had no I.D., so that's when I started calling all the MacLanes in the book. You say you're his guardians?"

"He was telling the truth," Drew's uncle said. "His parents are buried there."

"I sure feel sorry for him."

"Yeah," Drew's uncle said, "it's a long, sad story. Here, let me pay you for the chocolate bar you bought him."

"That's okay. My treat. Besides, he's a tough little kid. He never ate it."

"Right," Drew's uncle said. "A tough little kid."

18

Mrs. Cavendish set down the pointer she'd been aiming at multiplication lists on the blackboard.

"Andrew, I asked you a question."

The children giggled.

"Andrew?" Mrs. Cavendish stalked between rows of desks until she reached a seat near the back. Drew was slumped across the desktop, his head on his arms, asleep. She towered over him, glaring, her voice loud. "Andrew?"

He murmured in his sleep.

She nudged his shoulder. Nudged it again. "Andrew!" she barked.

He sat up bolt-straight, blinking.

"I asked you a question."

"I'm sorry, Mrs. Cavendish." Drew shook his head to clear it. "I guess I wasn't listening."

"Of course not. How could you? *When you were asleep.*"

The children had turned around in their desks to watch the

excitement. Now as Mrs. Cavendish shot an angry glance their way, they swiveled to peer ahead, their flushed necks the only sign of the laughter they struggled to contain.

"This isn't the first time. Do I bore you so much that I put you to sleep?"

"No, Mrs. Cavendish."

"Then it must be mathematics that makes you sleepy."

"No, Mrs. Cavendish."

"What is it then?"

Drew didn't answer.

"Well, young man, you can sleep on somebody else's time. From now on, you sit in the desk right in front of me. Stand up."

She marched him to the front and made him switch places with another student.

"And now, young man, the next time you're tempted to show me how boring I am by falling asleep, I won't have to reach far"—she picked up her pointer and whacked it hard against the front of the desk—"to wake you up."

Of all the children, only Drew didn't flinch.

19

Four A.M. A chilly October wind nipped Drew's cheeks as he stood with the policeman in front of the house.

"I hate to wake you up this late," the policeman said, "but I figured you must be frantic with worry."

Light spilled from the open front door. Drew's aunt clutched the front of her housecoat. Beside her, silhouetted in the doorway, Drew's uncle glanced nervously at the darkened houses along the street as if he hoped that the neighbors wouldn't notice the police car parked in front. "You'd better come in."

"I understand." The policeman guided Drew in and shut the door. "I'm sure you weren't expecting company. I'll just stand here in the hall."

"But where did you find him?"

The policeman hesitated. "The cemetery."

Drew's uncle blinked. "We didn't even know he was gone."

Drew's aunt raised a trembling hand to her hairnet. "I put him to bed right after supper. I checked him before we went to sleep."

"It seems he snuck out after. I've got his bicycle in the trunk of the car," the policeman said.

"He biked ten miles?" Drew's uncle slumped against the wall. "In the night, in this cold? He must be—"

"Exhausted," Drew's aunt said. She looked at her husband. "Dear Lord, do you suppose?" She shivered and stared at Drew. "Is that what you've been doing? Is that why you're so tired at school?"

"This time around, I managed to get him to talk to me," the policeman said. "Not a lot, but enough to get the idea. I gather that he's been biking over there at night and . . . maybe it's better if he tells you himself. Go on, Drew. Why have you been biking over there? I don't mean just to visit your parents. You can do that in daylight. Why at night?"

Drew glanced from the policeman to his aunt and uncle. He peered at the floor.

"Go on, Drew." The policeman crouched. "Tell them what you told me."

Drew's aunt and uncle waited sternly.

"Vandals," Drew said.

His aunt and uncle looked shocked. "Vandals?"

Drew nodded.

"The cat has his tongue again," the policeman said, "so let

me fill in the blanks. When I brought him home before, he heard me talk about the teenagers who've been vandalizing the cemetery."

"I remember," Drew's uncle said.

"Well, apparently that got him thinking. For starters, he didn't know what 'vandals' meant, so he says he looked it up in the dictionary. I don't know what he read, but it sure upset him."

"That still doesn't explain why he's been sneaking out at night to go to the cemetery," Drew's aunt said.

"It does if you think about it. What he's been doing is—" Drew fidgeted, self-conscious; they stared at him. "—protecting his parents' graves."

20

Saturday morning, bright and cold. As a group of neighborhood children played football in the distance, Drew sat alone on a swing at the far end of the lot.

A shadow loomed across him. From in back.

Drew turned. At first, with the sun angled toward his eyes, he couldn't make out the face of the tall man in the overcoat.

But as his vision got used to the glare of the sun, he suddenly grinned excitedly and rushed to the man.

"Uncle Ray!"

In truth, the man was not related to Drew, but from years of habit, that was what Drew had always called him.

"Uncle Ray!"

Drew threw his arms around the man's waist, feeling the soft brown cloth of the overcoat.

The man laughed, picked Drew up, and swung him around. "It's good to see you, sport. How's the world been treating you?"

Drew was too delighted to pay attention to the question. As the man continued laughing, Drew laughed as well, enjoying the wonderful dizziness of being swung around.

The man set him down and, smiling, crouched to face him. "Surprised?"

"Boy, I'll say!"

"I happened to be in Boston on business, and I thought, 'What the heck, as long as I'm here, I might as well visit my old friend Drew.'" Uncle Ray mussed Drew's hair. "A good thing I did, huh? When I saw you on that swing, you looked pretty glum."

Drew shrugged, remembering how he'd felt, returning to his somber mood.

"Got troubles, sport?"

"Yeah, I guess so."

"Any you'd like to tell me about?"

Drew scuffed his running shoes in the dead brown grass. "Just stuff."

"Well, it might be I know a few of them already. I stopped at the house. Your aunt told me where you'd gone." Ray paused. "She also told me what's been happening. Your problems at school." He bit his lip. "The other things. And I hear you've been getting in fights with your cousin."

"He doesn't like me."

"Oh? You're sure of that?"

"He's mad because I live there. He's always playing practical jokes on me or hiding my homework or blaming me for things I didn't do."

"I can see how that might happen. So you decked him, huh?"

Drew grinned, holding up his right hand. "Bruised my knuckles."

"It could be an even trade. At the house, I saw his black eye."

The man was as old as Drew's father had been. For some reason, "thirty-five" stuck in Drew's mind. He had neatly trimmed sandy hair, expressive blue eyes, and a narrow, handsome face, his jaw strongly outlined. Drew loved the sweet smell of his aftershave.

"Yeah, a lot of commotion," Ray said. "The question is, what are we going to do about it? You feel like taking a walk, sport?"

21

Puzzled, his heart thumping, Drew listened out of sight in the hall as the grown-ups talked about him in the living room.

"As you're aware, Drew's father and I were very close," Ray said. His smooth voice carried down the hall. "I knew him for years. We went to Yale together. We received our State Department training together. We were both stationed in Japan."

Drew's uncle said, "Then you were at the embassy when his parents were killed?"

"No, by the time the demonstrations started, I'd already been transferred to Hong Kong. When I heard what had happened, well, I couldn't believe that anybody would do such a horrible thing. I was involved in a diplomatic emergency at the time, and I couldn't leave Hong Kong even to go to the funeral. In fact, my assignment was serious enough that I wasn't free to get away till just last week. I'm sure you'll understand that I can't be specific about what I was doing. But as soon as I could, I wanted to come here to Boston—to pay my respects, to at least see their graves. It's hard to put this into words. Of course, he was your brother, Mr. MacLane, so I hope you don't take this wrong if I say that I felt . . . well, like a brother to him also. As I said, we were very close."

"I understand," Drew's uncle said. "The fact is, you probably knew him better than I did. I hadn't seen him in the past five years, and even before then, we didn't get together much."

"What about the boy?"

"I don't believe I saw him more than three or four times. Ever. My brother and I were the only children in our family. Our parents died several years ago. So naturally, when my brother called me to say that he was having a new will made out and would I take custody of Drew if anything happened to Susan and himself . . ."

"Yes, naturally you agreed."

"There wasn't anybody else he could ask, you see. But I never dreamed that I'd have to make good on my promise."

"What I want to talk to you about is this. I've always been fond of Andrew. I guess I feel like an uncle to him. Again, I don't mean any offense. I'm not trying to be presumptuous. But my wife and I don't have any children. It seems we're not able to. At any rate, given the difficulties you've been having with him . . ."

"Difficulties. That's putting it mildly."

"I wondered if you'd let my wife and me have custody of him."

"Have custody! Are you serious?"

"It could be the answer to several problems. The grief I feel for my friend. My fondness for the boy. My wife and I had already considered going to an adoption agency. Add to that the problems you've been having with Drew."

Drew's uncle sounded suspicious. "What makes *you* think you can do any better with him?"

"I'm not sure I can. But I'd like to try."

"And if it didn't work out?"

"I wouldn't bring him back to your doorstep, if that's what you mean. I'd abide by our agreement. If you're hesitant, though, if you think you'd want him back, we could arrange a compromise. Perhaps the boy could spend a month or so with my wife and myself, and after that, we all could talk about it again. This way, you'd have a chance to get your household back the way it used to be."

"I don't know. Where would you take him?"

"Hong Kong. For half of his life, he lived in the Orient. Hong Kong isn't Japan, of course. But perhaps he'd feel more at home if he went back to the Far East."

Drew's uncle sighed. "This is hard to . . . Your offer's certainly tempting. I confess I've been at wits' end. But there might be a problem. Suppose the boy doesn't want to go?"

"We can always ask him."

Hiding in the hall, his heart swelling, Drew silently shouted, *Yes*!

22

The bitter wind brought tears to his eyes, though he might have been crying for a different reason as he stared down at his parents' graves.

Uncle Ray pulled up the collar on his overcoat and shoved his gloved hands into its pockets. "I miss them too, sport." His sandy hair was blown by the wind.

"Maybe I . . ."

"Yes? Go on." Ray put an arm around him.

". . . should have brought the flowers anyhow."

"On a raw day like this? They wouldn't have lasted long. No, it's better that we let them live a while longer back at the flower shop."

Drew understood. There wasn't any reason why the flowers should die as well. Only the people who'd killed his parents ought to die.

"So what do you think?" Ray asked. "I know you want to

stay, but we've been here almost an hour. We have to catch that plane at five o'clock. It's not forever, you know. Someday, you'll be back."

"Sure. It's just . . ."

"Hard to leave them? You bet. But we've got photographs. You can still remember them while you're away. I mean, a guy can't very well camp here in the cemetery, can he?"

"No." Drew's eyes stung, misty, this time definitely not from the wind. He had trouble breathing. "I guess not."

23

Reading the dossier's objective summary, Drew recalled—and reexperienced—the emotions of his youth. As if a child again, he walked with Ray toward the car that would take them to the airport. In his painful memory, he glanced back, his throat tight, toward his parents' graves.

He knew that the priest's intention was to get him to talk about those days, and he did so freely, not caring if he gave the priest his wish. He needed to vent his sadness. "In later years, whenever I was in Boston, I used to go back to that cemetery. I went there before I became a Carthusian. Last week, though, I never had the chance to visit them.' "

"It was prudent of you not to," Father Stanislaw said. "Whoever wanted you dead would have put a surveillance team near those graves, just as Arlene was being watched in case you showed up." The priest retrieved the dossier. "Just a few more items. In Hong Kong, you began to run with a Chinese street gang. The man you called Uncle Ray understood your motive—to acquire the skills you thought you'd need to go after your parents' killer. To ensure your safety, he arranged for the grandson of a Gurkha to teach you street sense. Tommy Limbuk was the child's name."

"Limbu," Drew said. "Known as Tommy Two."

Father Stanislaw wrote a correction in the dossier. "And after that, wherever Uncle Ray was stationed—France, Greece, Korea—he arranged for you to learn the martial skills of the local population. Foot boxing, wrestling, judo, karate. When you were seventeen, your need for revenge had still not abated. During your stay in various countries, you'd learned an impressive number of languages—and acquired a remarkable liberal arts education, I might add. Uncle Ray, aware of your life's ambition, knowing you couldn't be dissuaded, approached you with a suggestion. The United States, nervous about growing anti-American sentiment in the world, had decided to form a counter-terrorist unit, designed to confront the very enemies you yourself had chosen. So you agreed to his suggestion and enlisted in the Rocky Mountain Industrial School in Colorado, a cover for military-intelligence instruction, a training facility much more secret than the farm in Virginia that the CIA used for its operatives."

"Scalpel," Arlene said.

Father Stanislaw glanced surprised at her. "You know about it?"

"I belonged to it. So did Jake. That's where we met Drew."

The priest leaned back in his chair. "Thank God. I was starting to think you still didn't trust me. I wondered if you'd ever volunteer information."

"You didn't ask the right questions. I'll tell you anything I can," she said, "if it helps me find Jake."

"Then tell me," Father Stanislaw said, "about Scalpel."

24

"1966: the year international terrorism became organized. In an effort to unite the struggles of Communist groups in Africa, Asia, and Latin America, Fidel Castro invited revolutionists from eighty-two countries to come to Cuba for an intensive training session, known as the Tricontinental Conference. A school for urban guerrilla warfare resulted, where members from almost every later infamous terrorist group received instruction. The IRA, the Red Brigades, the Baader-Meinhof Gang. The principles of terrorism worked out at that school became a Devil's bible. Qaddafi followed Castro's lead and organized training schools of his own in Libya. With Libya's enormous oil wealth, Qaddafi was able to accomplish more than Castro, not merely providing instruction to terrorists but also financing their operations. Random assassination; embassy takeovers; the slaughter of the Israeli athletes at the 1972 Munich Olympics. The kidnapping of the OPEC oil ministers in Vienna in '75. Commercial airliners destroyed by bombs. School buses blown apart. On and on. The list of horrors grew longer each year, but they all dated back to 1966, Castro, and Cuba. Even the fanatical Muslim sects from the time of the Crusades were not as barbarous."

At the mention of the Crusades, Father Stanislaw touched the ruby ring on his left hand, tracing the symbol of the intersecting sword and Maltese cross. Arlene continued.

"In 1968, the U.S. State Department, warned by intelligence sources about Castro's school for terrorists, financed its own school for counterterrorists. The State Department could, of course, have gone to the CIA for that kind of service. But given the notoriety that the CIA had acquired since the Bay of Pigs, the State Department chose instead to sponsor its own clandestine unit. A *truly* clandestine unit, spared exposure in *The New York Times* and *The Washington Post*. Only a few insiders knew about it."

As Arlene paused, Father Stanislaw nodded. "Scalpel." He glanced at Drew. "The unit into which your Uncle Ray recruited you."

"Now wait a minute," Drew said. "He didn't recruit me into anything."

"Then let's say he made a discreet suggestion," Father Stanislaw said. "We can play with words all you want. The end result is what matters. He approached you about it, and you joined. Why was Scalpel chosen as the code name for the unit?"

Drew tried to mute his anger. "Precise surgical removal."

"Ah, yes, of course. The terrorists were like cancer. As a consequence, their excision was morally permissible. An ingenious choice of name. It symbolized its justification."

"You find something wrong with the concept?" Arlene asked.

Father Stanislaw kept his eyes on Drew. "Obviously *you* did, or you wouldn't have resigned."

"Not wrong with the concept. Wrong with me."

"Ah," Father Stanislaw said. "In that case, we should perhaps have met earlier."

"Why?"

"To refresh your memory of St. Augustine. The concept that killing is necessary if a war is just."

"War?"

"Not nation fighting nation, not a conventional war. All the same, a war. The oldest, most basic one of all: good against evil. Terrorists, by definition, turn their backs on civilized standards. Their weapon is outrageous attack—to so disrupt the lives of average citizens that those citizens rebel against their government. But no end can justify such hellish means."

"You believe that?" Drew glared.

"Apparently you don't."

"There was a time when I would have."

"But?" Father Stanislaw asked.

Drew didn't answer.

"At last," Father Stanislaw said, "We're there. *The part I don't know about*." He sighed. "After graduating from the

Rocky Mountain Industrial School—a remarkable facility, I'm informed—you worked for Scalpel. From sixty-nine to early seventy-nine, you engaged in retaliatory strikes against whatever terrorists attracted your director's wrath. Sometimes, too, the strikes weren't after but *before* the fact. Preemptive. Made necessary by reliable intelligence reports. Terrorist activities were nipped in the bud, so to speak. Your urge to avenge your parents should have made you even more zealous. *What happened?* Why did you suddenly enter the monastery?"

Drew glanced toward the floor.

"No. Answer him," Arlene said. "I want to know as much as *he* does." She turned Drew's face, making him look at her. "What about Jake? *Is he involved?*"

Drew saw the anguish in her eyes. He hated what he had to tell her. "Eventually."

PART SIX

CHARTREUSE

MIRROR IMAGE, DOUBLE EXPOSURE

✤

1

"The assignment was complicated."

"When?" Father Stanislaw asked. "Be specific."

"In January of seventy-nine. In fact, I remember feeling puzzled—because I'd never been sent on a mission quite like it before."

Father Stanislaw prompted him. "What made it unusual? Its hazards?"

"No. The timing. You see, I hadn't been given one job, but two, and they had to be completed within forty-eight hours. They were both in France, so that didn't pose a problem, getting from one location to the next within the time limit. The difficulty was the method I was told to use. The same in each case. And in the first job, the geography was troublesome."

Drew paused, distressed, sorting through information, trying to organize it. Arlene and Father Stanislaw watched him intently. At last he continued.

"The other thing that made the assignment unusual was that I didn't get a briefing on my targets. Usually, I was told what the criminal was being punished for. How many innocent people he'd killed. What maniac he was working for. I learned all about his habits, his vices. And that made it easier. It's not hard to kill vermin."

Drew paused again, then resumed, "Sometimes the method

of execution was left up to me. Long-range sniping. A car-bomb in imitation of the bombs the terrorists so enjoyed setting off. Poison. Lethal viruses. The method was usually appropriate to the crime. But in this case, the mission had to be accomplished in a certain way. And as I said, there were in fact *two* missions. With a deadline. Quite unusual."

"That didn't bother you?"

"In Colorado, I was trained not to question orders. And after you've killed as many times as I have, when you think you're justified, you're bothered by nothing. Except . . ."

Arlene leaned forward. "Tell him everything. How you received your orders."

"I needed a cover that allowed me to disappear at any time for as long as a week without attracting attention. A job was out of the question, too restricting, too many people to account to. But I had to do *something*. So I lived in a college town and became a student. The cover was easy. I was always good at school. I've always enjoyed taking classes. Liberal arts. Literature mostly. I got a B.A. from one institution, then moved to another and got a second B.A. By then, I was too old to be an undergraduate, so I moved to a third school and got a master's degree. In fact, I have two of them, and I was working on the third when . . ."

"I still don't see the advantage of that cover," Father Stanislaw said.

"A student can be anonymous. But you have to pick a school that's large. The Big Ten was my preference. A college town, the type where the students outnumber the local population. The students are transient, so if I came to town and stayed for a year or two, then transferred to another school, and then another, well, a lot of students did that—I wasn't unusual. I took only large lecture courses, and I never chose the same seat, so if the lecturer didn't keep attendance records—and I made sure he wasn't the type who did—I wouldn't draw attention when I disappeared for a couple of days. I've always been a loner, so it wasn't hard for me to resist making friends with other students. The friends I did have, professionals like Arlene and Jake"—he smiled at her—"were all I needed. Between semesters or at term breaks, I went to visit them. At school, I was invisible. The only risk to my anonymity was, I went to a local gym every morning, to make sure I stayed in shape to be able to handle my assignments, and I went to a crowded diner every day at one, a bookstore at four, and a neighborhood grocery at seven."

"Why take the risk? Why those particular places and times?"

"I had to. The times were chosen arbitrarily. The places themselves didn't matter. I could have substituted a movie theater for the bookstore, and a desk at the library for the grocery. What did matter was the routine. So a courier would have several chances to contact me easily and, more important, inconspicuously. At the diner, someone might sit next to me and leave a Canadian quarter as a tip for the waitress. Or at the grocery, a woman might ask for Mexican beer. That would be my signal to go to my apartment as soon as I could. If a dish towel was over the sink, I'd know to look beneath my bed, and in my suitcase, I'd find everything I needed to get to where I was going. Plane tickets, a passport, identification under another name. Cash in various currencies. An address in a foreign city."

"Weapons?" Father Stanislaw asked.

"No," Drew said emphatically. "Never weapons. They were always made available to me from my contact at the foreign address. While I was gone, a lookalike would take my place and keep to my routine. It wasn't hard to make the switch. No one really knew me. Sure, they saw me. Mostly from a distance, though. I was merely part of the scene. The students and the locals didn't know me. That way, with someone doubling for me, a blur at the edge of the crowd, I had an alibi if something went wrong."

Father Stanislaw gasped.

"What's wrong?" Drew asked.

"Don't stop. You're telling me more than you think."

Drew glanced at Arlene. "What does he mean?"

"The pieces are coming together." Her voice was low. "I agree. Keep going. What about the assignment?"

He breathed deeply. "I received instructions to go to France but to do so indirectly, through London, where my double took my place. He went on a tour of literary landmarks— Stratford, Canterbury, that sort of thing, what a graduate student in English would find amusing. I'd been to those sites already, so if I had to account for my stay in England, I could do so easily. But while my alibi was being established, I flew to Paris, using another name, and received my instructions. Above Grenoble in the Alps of France, I learned that there was a monastery."

"Of course!" the priest said. "The Carthusian charter-house. La Grande Chartreuse."

"A man was scheduled to visit it, I'd been told. His car was described to me. Even the number on his license plate. I was to kill him." Drew bit his lip. "Have you ever been to La Grande Chartreuse?"

Father Stanislaw shook his head.

"It's extremely remote. In the Middle Ages, the founding monks selected its location carefully. They thought that the world was going to hell, which it always seems to be doing. They wanted to get away from the corruption of society, so they marched from the lowlands of France up into the Alps, where they built a primitive monastery. The Pope objected. After all, in the Middle Ages, what was the point of being a priest if you lived in deprivation?

"God seemed to side with the Pope by sending an avalanche

onto the monastery, destroying it. But you've got to give the monks credit. They simply moved the monastery a safe distance lower, protected from snowslides but still secluded from the world. And over the centuries, they built a magnificent cloister. It reminded me of a medieval castle. A mighty fortress for God.

"When the order spread to England, the monks were martyred by Henry the Eighth. Because he wanted a divorce and the Pope refused, Henry formed his own church, made himself its leader, and decreed that the divorce he craved was divinely sanctioned. When the Carthusian monks in England objected, Henry put them to death in the cruelest manner he could devise. They were hanged, cut down near death, disembowled but left sufficiently alive for them to see their guts being eaten by dogs. Molten metal was poured inside their body cavities. Their corpses were drawn and quartered, boiled, then thrown into ditches."

"You describe it vividly," Father Stanislaw said, his voice calm. "What happened at La Grande Chartreuse?"

Drew began to sweat. He could not fight down his emotion. "My assignment was to plant explosives at the side of a winding road that sloped up toward the monastery. The location was carefully chosen. A rock wall on the far side. A steep drop on the near side—toward me, where I was waiting on the opposite slope. After I planted the explosives at night, it took me half the next day to climb out of sight through gorges until I reached the opposite bluff. The mountains were thick with snow. A few miles either way, I could have been skiing. If only I had been." Drew shook his head. "But I crouched behind bushes, my boots in the snow, my parka not really warm enough for the weather, and as I watched my breath drift up before my eyes, I studied that winding road. Because soon, my target car wound up toward the monastery. The occupant was sight-seeing, you understand. Taking in the local attractions.

Of course, he could never have gone inside the cloister itself, never have seen the hermit monks. But he could tour the perimeter and walk through the central court and perhaps provide a generous donation in exchange for a sample of the famous Chartreuse liqueur." Drew felt the cold even now; he heard the squeak of the snow beneath his boots and recalled the stillness in those terrible claustrophobic mountains.

Blinking, he abruptly returned to the motel room, Arlene, and the priest. "I'd planted the explosives on the far side of the road. Against the rock wall. The thrust of the blast would send the car toward me, toward the cliff on the side that faced me. And the car, in flames, would fall. But this is the clever part. Someone at Scalpel must have thought long and hard about it. I'd been given a camera. Through its telephoto lens, I was to study the bend in the road that led up through the mountains. And when the car I was looking for came around the bend, when I made doubly sure it was the right car by verifying the number from the front license plate, I was to start taking pictures."

"That's all? Just take pictures?" Father Stanislaw stood and began to pace the room.

"Not quite all. You see, the trigger mechanism on the camera was also the trigger for the explosive. The camera had a motor-driven shutter, designed for rapidly repeating exposures as long as I kept the button pressed down. Click, click, click. The bomb went off. The car veered sideways, toward me. Its gas tank burst into flames. And remember, the shutter kept clicking. I saw a telephoto image of everything. Just as the car began to topple over the cliff, a door in back flew open . . ."

"And?" Arlene watched him anxiously.

Drew's voice rose. "God showed me a sign. He sent me a message."

"*What?*" Father Stanislaw roared the word. "You can't be serious."

"But He did." Drew's voice was suddenly calm. "You believe in the bolt of light that toppled Saul from his horse on the road to Damascus, don't you? Saul, the sinner, who understood at once that God was telling him something, who changed his life that instant to follow the way of the Lord. Well, this was my bolt of light. My sign from God. I'd call it a miracle, except a miracle's supposed to make you feel good and this . . . A kid fell out. A boy. I've studied the photographs often. The boy was . . ."

"What?" Again the voice was Arlene's.

". . . identical to me."

She stared at him. "You mean you noticed a resemblance. The same coloring perhaps. And size. Boys at the same age tend to look alike."

"No, it was *more* than that. I'm telling you the resemblance was uncanny. When he grew up, he could have been my double back at the college. While I went out and killed."

"Executed. Punished. Stopped them from doing it again." Father Stanislaw's tone was harsh. "Speak precisely. Don't exaggerate. You were under stress. You have to make allowance for . . ."

"The circumstances? For the moment? Listen, the moment is all I think about. That kid . . . *me*. . . tumbling from the car. Horror in his eyes."

Drew fumbled in his pants pocket, yanking out the four wrinkled photographs he'd taken with him from the monastery. He thrust them at Father Stanislaw. Arlene leaned quickly toward the priest to see them.

Drew's face was tormented. "They're all I kept from my former life. Before I joined the Carthusians, I went to every place I'd hidden money, passports, weapons. I got rid of them.

I canceled everything about my former existence, erased myself, even to the point of making it seem as if I was dead.

Shuddering, Drew glanced at the photographs. He knew the images by heart. "The one on top is me. In Japan in 1960. It was taken in the garden behind my parents' house. Three days before they were murdered."

Father Stanislaw set it aside.

"The next one," Drew said, "is my parents. Again, the same location, three days before they were killed. The others I took in seventy-nine below La Grande Chartreuse. After I detonated the explosives and the boy fell from the car. I had a section of the boy's photograph enlarged, to show his face. The picture's grainy, sure. And the smoke from the explosion was drifting in front of him, and snow had started to fall. But I think you get my point."

The priest peered up from the photograph, staring toward Drew. His hands quivered. "At first, I thought this third photograph was a poor reproduction of the first. I thought it was—"

"Me. But it isn't. If you look closely, really closely, you'll see it isn't. I tried to tell myself that the resemblance was coincidental. As Arlene said, kids often tend to look alike. But this is more than just a vague similarity. This is . . ."

"Unnerving."

"I'm just getting started. Look at the last photograph. I took it after the car had toppled from the cliff. But the car didn't drop all the way down the gorge. It snagged on an outcrop, its front end angling down, and by then, flames from the gas tank were streaking across the snow. That's when the two front doors burst open, and two adults leaped out. My instructions had been specific. Take as many photographs as you can. So despite my shock at seeing the boy, I stared through the viewfinder, aiming the telephoto lens, pressing the button, and then I realized God was still giving signs." His voice broke. "The man and woman looked like my parents. *Were* my parents."

"But they're in flames," Father Stanislaw said.

"Look closely!" Drew urged.

"I am!"

"They *are* my parents. I know they aren't, but they *are*. I couldn't get a focus on their faces when they leaped from the car. But before they burst into flames, their faces were quite distinct. On the cliff, on that freezing bluff, I was sure they were my mother and my father."

The room became silent.

"Of course—I don't mean any offense—we don't have any way to verify the comparison," Father Stanislaw said. "I grant that the boy from the car, even with the distortion of the smoke and the falling snow, could be your counterpart. At first, indeed, I thought it was you. But allowing for the coincidence, isn't it possible that your imagination carried you away? Could you have made the logical leap from the boy who looked like you, to the man and woman who, well, you *imagined* looked like your parents?"

"I know what I saw." Drew's voice was hoarse. "Finally I couldn't keep my finger pressed on the shutter button any longer. I lowered the camera. Across the gorge from me, the flames reached their faces. The gas tank exploded. My mother and father disintegrated. Just as in 1960. Only this time, I was the man who'd killed them."

"The circumstances were different."

"*Were they?* What we call a mercenary on their side is an operative on ours. I was the same as the man I'd been hunting. I was my enemy. Pieces of their bodies tumbled down the gorge, their clothes and flesh in flames. I *smelled* them. And on the top of the cliff, silhouetted against the snow, I saw the grieving face of the boy—I wasn't looking through the telephoto lens anymore, but I seemed to see his tears in close-up.

My tears. After nineteen years, my need for revenge had caught up with me. And nothing mattered anymore. Except to beg God's forgiveness; to save my soul."

Arlene touched his shoulder. He flinched, then gratefully accepted her comfort.

"To save your soul?" Father Stanislaw said, his voice raised in astonishment. "All the time you were an operative, you felt *religious?*"

"I had my own religion. The justice of the Old Testament's angry God. But God had a different idea. I'm more honored than Saul on the road to Damascus, thrown from his horse by a bolt of light. God sent me not one but *two* signs. He's certainly generous. Everything I've described happened in maybe ten seconds, though it seemed to take forever. The blast rumbled through the mountains, and as its echo dwindled, I heard something else—the shriek of the boy across the gorge from me, raising his hands to his face, trying to shut out what he'd just seen, his parents in flames. He screamed through his fingers. And after that? God's *third* sign to me. It wasn't enough that I'd recognized myself, that I'd come full circle and killed the parents I'd set out to avenge. As the rumble of the blast diminished, as the boy choked on his own screams, as the silence returned, I heard a chant.

"Later, I understood why. It was January sixth. The Feast of the Epiphany—when the Magi saw Christ and saved His life. Because the wise men, having seen the baby Jesus, having seen a light of their own, refused to go back to Herod and reveal where Christ could be found, though they'd promised Herod they'd do so. *That,* it seems to me, is why the Church decided that the Epiphany should be a major feast. Not because the Wise Men saw the baby Jesus, but because in a way they were double agents, who finally made a choice about which side to believe in. Just as I made a choice that day.

"The monks, in honor of the Magi and that crucial day in

Christ's continuing existence, must have scheduled a special convocation. Above me, from the chapel in the cloister in the mountains, I heard their chant. Their hymn in honor of that anniversary. It drifted down through the chasms, past the peaks, obscuring the echo of the explosions and the screams. The hymn praised God's will, His infinite foresight, His all-encompassing plan. But the words weren't nearly as powerful as the sound of the eerie voices of those hermits who'd divorced themselves from the falsehoods of the world.

"My knees bent. I found myself kneeling, staring toward that boy across the gorge from me. He tried to scramble down the cliff to find his parents. I wanted to stand up from the bushes that hid me and shout to tell him not to, that he'd fall and kill himself. Grow up! I wanted to shout. Hunt the man who murdered your parents! Who murdered my own! Come after me! And that's when I became religious. It was either that . . . or kill myself." He paused, exhausted.

Arlene studied his anguished face. Lovingly, she put an arm around him.

"And after that?" Father Stanislaw asked.

"I wandered for three days through those mountains. The length of time had appropriate religious overtones, don't you think? Of course, I didn't realize what I was doing. Later, it amazed me that I'd never dropped the camera. I don't know how I lived or where I slept or what I ate.

"It snowed while I wandered. I'm sure the authorities must have searched the area. But the storm hid my footprints. Was that a lucky coincidence, or another sign from God? I don't remember where or how I went. The next clear image I have is a village low in the mountains, smoke drifting up from chimneys, children skating on an icy pond, horse-drawn sleighs jingling down a road. Postcard stuff. And I later found out that I'd somehow walked a hundred kilometers, which is why the local police never linked me with the murders below La

Grande Chartreuse. I collapsed in front of a chalet. An old woman there took me in. She fed me soup and bread and the sweetest pastries I've ever tasted."

"Three days?" Arlene asked. "That's how long you wandered through the mountains? But . . ."

Father Stanislaw completed her thought. "Your assignment had been two missions in forty-eight hours. The deadline for the second mission had passed."

"At the start, I didn't think about the implications. I was alive, and that in itself amazed me. Not to mention the vision I'd had. The sight of my parents—*myself*—the circle closing, vengeance leading to . . . That boy, when he grew up, would hunt for me. When I was well enough to travel, I went to Paris to reach my contact. On the way, I checked back issues of newspapers to find out who my victims had been. The man, it turned out, was an American businessman, an oil executive, who'd brought his wife and son to France for a long-postponed vacation. The papers described the killings as senseless. I agreed. Of course, what you read in the papers isn't always true. But what if . . . I had the feeling that something was terribly wrong. What would an oil executive and his family have to do with terrorism? What motive could possibly justify those killings? I needed answers. I wanted to go to ground. To reach a safehouse. To rest. I guess God's messages hadn't quite come through. I still had some worldliness, and self-centeredness, left in me. That ended soon."

Father Stanislaw pursed his lips. "Because you'd screwed up. And now you were suspect."

2

In Paris, Drew left the train station, blending with the crowd. He walked to the next arrondissement, making sure that he wasn't followed, and only then used a public phone. Perhaps a needless added precaution, but under the circumstances advisable.

He called the number he'd been given when he'd first arrived in France—a week, a lifetime ago. He let it ring four times, then broke the connection and called that number again. The husky male voice that answered in French announced the name of a dress designer shop.

Drew responded in French as well. "My name is Johnson. I bought two dresses for my wife a week ago. One fit, the other didn't. I want a second appointment."

The proprietor gushed, "But yes, we later suspected that something was wrong with the second fit. We tried to contact you, but you weren't available. All we could do was hope that you'd call. We value your business. Can you possibly see us as soon as possible? We'd like to study the dress and find what went wrong."

"I'm free this afternoon."

"As you may remember, we're in the process of moving. Our new location . . ."

Drew memorized the directions. "Within an hour," he said.

The old house was made of stone and covered with vines. It was two stories high, with smoke swirling from the chimney. A fallow vegetable garden stretched to the left, two barren apple trees to the right. And beyond, the frigid, ice-covered Seine. Despite the ice on the water, Drew heard the subtle hiss of the river's current. He smelled dead fish and sulphurous smoke from factories upriver.

His breath coming out in vapor, he strolled around to the back as if he belonged here. The door creaking, he stepped inside a narrow hallway, smelling French bread, warm and fresh. His mouth watering, he opened a second door that took him into a shadowy kitchen.

He saw steam rise from a kettle on a large iron stove and felt a hand shove him forward while another hand twisted a pistol against his kidney. A third hand grabbed his hair from behind, touching a knife to his Adam's apple.

"You'd better have a fucking good explanation, boyo."

He flinched and tried to turn to see them, but they restrained him. Nor could he speak, his breath knocked out of his lungs as they threw him hard across the kitchen table, frisking him roughly.

He didn't have a weapon. The assignment hadn't called for one, and there'd been no need to go to his cache in Paris. Not that it would have mattered if he had.

"Why are—?"

He didn't have the chance to finish his sentence. They dragged him off the table, held him in the air, and let him go. He struck the floor with his face. At once, they jerked him to his feet, thrusting him through an open doorway into a living room. He toppled onto a dusty, threadbare sofa. It smelled of mildew.

The room was brighter than the kitchen. Logs blazed in a fireplace. The dingy drapes were closed. A well-worn carpet covered the middle of the floor. The only other furniture was a rocking chair, a stand-up lamp with no shade, a battered coffee table with circular water stains, and an empty bookshelf. Rectangular marks on the wall, rimmed by grime and dust, showed where pictures once had hung.

He straightened on the sofa, facing his assailants. "You don't understand." His heart pounded. "I was told to come here. I wasn't breaking in."

The tall one hissed. He wore a woodsman's sweater and hiking boots, gesturing with his knife. "No, boyo, *you* don't understand. We know you're supposed to be here. What we *don't* know is why the fuck you didn't finish your assignment."

The second man—he had a mustache, massive shoulders, and a brown-checkered sport coat straining against his muscles—

held a .22 Hi-Standard pistol with a silencer attached to it. An executioner's weapon. "How much did they pay you not to do it?"

"How did they contact you?" the third man said. In contrast with the others, he sounded genteel. He was thin and wore a business suit. His delicate hands opened a satchel, taking out a hypodermic and a vial of liquid, setting them carefully on the coffee table.

Their questions came so fast that, as soon as Drew opened his mouth to answer the first, he was interrupted by the second and third.

"Did you compromise the network?" the first man demanded.

"How many operatives are in danger? How much did you tell them?" the second man snapped.

"Tell *who*?"

"If you insist." The third man filled the hypodermic. He pressed the plunger, freeing air bubbles. "Take off your coat. Roll up your sleeve."

"This is crazy." Drew's stomach burned. He shook his head. "All you had to do was simply ask. You don't need all this . . ."

"His feelings are hurt," the second man said. "He wants us to be polite. He thinks we're here for coffee and croissants." The man flicked the switch on the stand-up lamp. The sudden stark light emphasized the anger on his face. "Just in case you still don't get the message, I want you to see this coming." His clenched fist was suddenly magnified.

Drew's head jolted back against the sofa. His blood tasted coppery. Stunned, he jerked his hands to his mouth. He touched the sticky warmth of his blood, feeling his lips ache and swell.

"Is that polite enough for you? Maybe not." The second man kicked Drew's left shin. Groaning, Drew dropped his

hands in pain to massage the leg, and the man punched his
mangled lips again. Drew's head snapped back.

"You were given questions to answer," the third man said,
his voice reedy, approaching with the full hypodermic. "I'd
prefer that we didn't waste time waiting for the amytal to take
effect. Please, save me the trouble. Why didn't you finish the
job?"

Drew's speech was distorted by his puffy lips. "After I blew
up the car, I was seen!"

"By the child who survived?"

"He fell from the car before it went over the cliff. No one
could have guessed that would happen. But that's not who saw
me!" Drew swallowed blood.

He took advantage of his injury, prolonging a coughing
spell, needing time to think. It was obvious now that if he told
these men what had really happened in those mountains,
they'd think he'd lost his mind. They'd decide that he was even
more undependable than they'd first suspected.

"It was someone else," Drew said, gagging. "When I ran up
the opposite slope, a car came around the bend in the road."
He coughed again. "It was headed down from the monastery.
A man got out. I turned. He saw me. The car had a two-way
radio antenna." Drew's breath whistled stridently through his
mangled lips. "I knew the police would be alerted. I didn't
dare go to the rented car I'd parked in a village down the road,
so I went the other way—up—through the mountains. A bliz-
zard set in. I got lost. I nearly died. It's taken me this long to
get back to Paris."

The first man shook his head. "You must think we're pretty
stupid. You're supposed to be an expert when it comes to survival in the mountains. That's why you were chosen to do the
job. The child you saw. Is that why you sold us out? Because
you lost your nerve?"

"I didn't lose my nerve! I told you the truth!"

"Oh, sure. But let's see if your story's the same when the amytal takes effect. For your information, the hit was necessary. The stakes were enormous."

Drew's mouth filled with blood; he spat it into a handkerchief. "Nobody explained a thing."

"Iran," the second man said.

("Hold on," Father Stanislaw said. "You don't mean they told you the purpose of the mission?"

"Everything."

"Dear God."

"Yeah, that's what I thought. I was hearing things I shouldn't know."

"They never meant for you to leave that house alive."

"It certainly looked that way. Till then, I'd thought I had a fifty-fifty chance of surviving. If I could bluff my way through. But when they started volunteering information . . .")

"Iran," the second man said. "The people are rioting. The Shah's about to be deposed. So the question is, who gets to take his place? The man you killed in the mountains"— and his wife, and almost his son, Drew thought—"pretended he was in France on vacation. Actually, he'd come to represent American oil interests, to negotiate for business-as-usual with the future ruler of Iran. You know who I'm talking about."

Drew shook his head, puzzled. "How the hell would I?"

"Quit it. Of course you know who he is. *Since you sold out to him.* An exiled Muslim fanatic. The Ayatollah Khomeini. He's living right here in Paris. And he's worse than the Shah. At least the Shah's pro-American. The Ayatollah isn't. So what are we to do? Let Iran—and all that oil—go someplace else?"

The first man interrupted. "Your job was to kill that executive, and then the Ayatollah. To take them out with explosives. And to make sure you came back with photographs. Because we wanted it to look as if the same nasty folks had done both hits. The photographs would be sent to the major newspapers, along with a bragging note from the Iran People's Movement."

"I've never heard of it," Drew said.

"Of course not. It doesn't exist. We made it up. What difference does that make? The note would have said that the Ayatollah—and the American oil executive—had been executed because they'd made a bargain to replace the Shah with the same old repressive government. And when Iran's indignation reached its peak, the next popular choice to rule the country, a man just behind the Ayatollah, would have taken over. But he'd have done what the Ayatollah should have. He'd have cooperated with the Western oil companies."

(Father Stanislaw nodded. "And because an American and his family had been killed, no one would have suspected that American interests were to blame. It might have worked."

"Except . . ."

"Indeed, except for you."

"And because of me, the Iranian hostage crisis occurred, the Soviets invaded Afghanistan, Reagan defeated Carter . . .")

"It could have worked!" the first man shouted at Drew, his face distorted with anger. "But, boyo, just one problem. It all depended on a timetable. Forty-eight hours from one hit to the next, *but you didn't stay on schedule*! On those two days, we knew for sure you could get at both the oil executive and the Ayatollah. We'd learned their itinerary. We'd found the spots where they'd be most exposed!"

Drew tried to shift the blame. "You should have allowed for contingencies. If the timing was so important, why wasn't another operative given the second assignment?"

"Because, you stupid bastard, the same man had to do both hits! *Because of the camera!* Both hits had to be recorded on the same roll of film. When we sent the photographs and the negatives to the press, we wanted the pictures to be in the same numbered sequence—to prove to Iran that whoever had killed the oil executive had also killed the Ayatollah. The Iranians had to be convinced that one of their own groups was responsible."

"Why blame me? You've got the camera. Reschedule the second assignment."

The first man sighed and looked at his companions. "You hear what he's saying? How simple he thinks it is to make things right again? Boyo, we *can't* reschedule! It's too fucking late! The Ayatollah's tightened security around him. We can't get near him anymore. Not close enough to use that camera. That first hit's worthless now! You did it for nothing!"

Drew heard the young boy's screams of grief.

"But the second hit—or rather, the one you didn't do," the aristocratic man said, "your failure earned you something, didn't it? How much did the Ayatollah pay for you to get conveniently lost in the mountains? You went to him, right?"

"That isn't true."

"I said quit it!" The first man stepped behind the sofa, yanking Drew's head back, pressing the knife against his throat again.

The third man continued. "Be reasonable. We want an excuse that makes sense. Later, after I give you the amytal, if your story's the same, we'll know you're not lying. And if we can sympathize with your reasons, we'll call it an honest mistake. We'll set you free. Of course, you wouldn't ever be hired again. But I don't think you'll object."

Drew's throat was stretched so taut that he couldn't speak. The man behind him seemed to understand; he removed the knife.

Drew coughed and swallowed. He had no more to invent. "All right." He massaged his throat. "I lied."

"Now there, that's better. At last, we're making progress," the third man said.

"But I didn't sell out. It's not what you think. Something—I don't know how else to say it—happened to me in the mountains."

"What?" The first man came from behind the sofa.

Drew told them. He'd anticipated their reaction correctly; they looked at him as if he'd gone mad.

"Boyo, not hire you again is right. Something happened to you for sure. You lost your nerve."

"There's one way to know," the third man said and gestured with the full hypodermic. "As I asked you earlier, please take off your coat. Roll up your sleeve."

Drew stared at the hypodermic, his spine feeling cold. They'd brought too much. His interrogators had enough amytal to kill him, as soon as they'd verified his story. He was being invited to participate in his own execution.

"Under amytal, I'll say the same thing," he insisted. "Because it's the truth." Standing, he took off his coat.

He threw it to his left, toward the man with the knife, obscuring his face. He had to reach the pistol. Lunging, he twisted the second man's wrist, tilting the silencer on the barrel toward the gunman's face. He pulled the trigger. The gun made a noise like the muffled impact of a fist against a pillow. The bullet went through the man's right eye, spewing blood and brain.

The man with the knife yanked the coat from his face. Drew shoved the sagging corpse at him. As they toppled, he pivoted toward the third man, jerked the hypodermic out of his delicate hand, and rammed the needle into the side of his neck. Blood flew, crimson spurting from a high-pressure hose, as he shoved the plunger all the way in. The genteel man collapsed.

Drew swung toward the upright lamp, clutched it like a

staff, and parried the knife that the first man, freed from the coat and the body, lunged at him. The cord on the lamp broke, extinguishing the bulb. Flickering light from the fireplace silhouetted their movements. Drew whipped the base of the lamp toward his enemy's shoulder, reversed his attack, and thrust the bulb-end of the lamp against the knife hand. He jumped back, using the skills he'd been taught in Colorado, struck his assailant in the crotch with the base of the lamp, and slammed the knife from his hand with the other end.

He grabbed the knife off the floor, ramming it up beneath his enemy's chin, through the tongue, through the roof of the mouth, into the brain.

Drew continued to hold the knife, feeling warm blood cascade down its blade and over his fingers on the handle. He kept the man standing up for a moment, feeling him tremble, scowling at his dying eyes.

Then he released his grip. The man fell backward, his head cracking sharply on the bricks in front of the fireplace.

Drew grabbed his boots and dragged him back from the flames, unable to bear the stench of burning hair. He shuddered, staring at the blood, the bodies around him. The odor of urine, of excrement, filled the room.

Though hardly innocent of the smell, he wanted to vomit. Not from fear but from revulsion. Death. Too much. For too many years.

3

"And then?" Arlene asked. She had taken his hand as he talked, giving him at least some comfort.

"I left the pistol in the house. All I wanted to do was run, though I made time to grab the camera. I'm sure a psychiatrist would find the choice interesting. But I did have a handgun in my emergency cache in Paris, along with money and a passport under another name. I rented a car and drove to Spain. I got rid of the gun, of course, in case I was searched when I crossed the border."

"Why Spain?" Father Stanislaw asked.

"Why not? I figured they'd be looking for me everywhere. At least"—Drew shrugged—"Spain was warmer. I left the car with the rental company and hired a private plane to fly me to Portugal. There, in Lisbon, I had another alias on a passport. And after that? Ireland. America. Three times, they almost got me. Once, at a service station, I had to set a car on fire. But at least I didn't need to kill anymore. And finally I was home. In America. I knew exactly where I was going. I didn't care about shahs and ayatollahs and oil and terrorists. None of it was important. I'd killed the equivalent of my parents. I'd caused a boy to suffer for the rest of his life as I had. The world was a madhouse. By comparison, those Carthusian monks lived in paradise. They had their priorities straight. They set their sights toward the long view. Toward eternity. Since I was ten, I've been a wanderer. But after I fled from that house on the Seine, faced with the prospect of wandering still more, I finally had a direction. I saw a goal. I wanted peace.

"A priest named Father Hafer was my sponsor. He arranged for me to go into the monastery. But before I entered the Carthusians, I had to get rid of all my possessions. Except these photographs, of course. But when I thought I'd finished, when I wondered if I'd canceled myself, I realized that there was one last thing I had to do. A sentimental weakness. A final breaking of the ties."

4

In darkness, Drew crouched behind bushes and jumped up with all his strength, his fingers clutching the concrete rim of the wall he'd been hiding against. It was March. His bare hands swelled from the aching cold as he scraped the soles of his shoes against the wall, struggling to climb.

He reached the top, sprawled flat upon it, breathed hard, then squirmed down the other side, supporting himself by his numbed fingertips.

He landed on frozen earth, his knees buckling, and surged up defensively, his only weapons his hands. He could have brought a pistol, of course, but he'd vowed that he wouldn't kill again. Subdue an enemy with his hands, that he could justify. But kill again? His soul recoiled from the possibility. If he in turn were killed tonight, it would be God's will. But no one challenged him.

He scanned the dark. After the glare of streetlights on the far side of the wall, his eyes would normally have needed a second or two to adjust to the deeper gloom. But he'd shut his eyes as he dropped from the wall. And now that he'd opened them, his irises were already wide.

He saw murky trees and bushes, a few waist-high upright pipes with taps, watering cans beside them. And tombstones. Rows and rows of them, their shadows stretching off until the night concealed them.

Pleasant View Cemetery, Boston.

He crept through shadows, passing trees and bushes, crouching by gravestones, sprinting stooped across gravel lanes, exhaling with relief as he reached silent grass again. Pressing his back for cover against the wall of a cold mausoleum, he studied the gloom. The darkness was eerily silent. The only disturbance was the lonely far-off drone of a car.

And at last, as he crept farther, he saw them, never confused for a moment as to where they would be.

The headstones, the graves, of his parents.

But he came at them indirectly, circling, checking every likely hiding place, remembering the vandals he'd protected his parents against so many years ago.

Finally he stood before them, staring down at the head-stones where the names would be if he could see them.

But even at night, he knew that this place was theirs. He traced his fingers lovingly across their names, the dates of their births, their deaths; then stepped back, brooding down at them for an instant that became a minute, two, then three, and said at last, "If only you hadn't died."

A voice made him stiffen.

"Drew."

He swung.

The voice was male. It was far away, hushed.

"Why did you do it?" The voice was ghostly.

Drew strained his eyes but couldn't penetrate the black-ness . . . over there, to his right.

He didn't feel threatened. Not yet, at least. Because he knew that the man could easily have shot him while he stood in front of his parents' graves.

Which meant that the man felt the need to talk.

He recognized the voice.

Jake's.

"Do you realize the shit you've caused?" Jake asked from the dark.

Drew almost smiled. A rush of friendship overcame him.

"Or how many men they've got hunting you?" Jake's voice was low.

"And what about you?" Drew asked. "Were you told to hunt me, too? You're a long way from New York. You're not here because you like cemeteries at three A.M. Are you going to kill me?"

"That's what I'm supposed to do." Jake's voice was reso-nant, mournful.

"Then go ahead." Exhausted, empty, Drew suddenly didn't care any longer. "I'm dead already. I might as well fall down and be still."

"But *why?*"

"Because you've got your orders," Drew said.

"No, that isn't what I mean. I want to know why you sold the network out."

"I didn't."

"They say you did."

"And I can say I'm the Pope. That doesn't make it true. Besides, you didn't believe them. Otherwise, you'd never have given me the chance to talk. You'd have shot me while I stood here. How did you find me?"

"Desperation."

"That's what I always liked about you. Your knack for long explanations."

"They sent a team to watch where you lived, just in case, but I knew you wouldn't go back there. In fact, the more I thought about it, the more I realized you wouldn't go back to *any* place that the network associates with you. My best guess was you'd holed up somewhere in the mountains. You know enough to survive there for months, years, even in winter. So that was that, I figured. The race was over. You'd won."

"That doesn't explain . . ."

"I'm coming to it. See, something kept nagging at me. A speck of a memory. There had to be *some* place that irresistibly tugged you. Even people like us are human. Where, though? What made you what you are? And then I remembered what you'd told me once—when a snowstorm forced us to camp for the night on a peak, the wind chill so bad we had to keep talking to each other to make sure we didn't fall asleep and die. Remember?"

Drew did. With fondness. "In the Andes."

"Right." Jake's voice came out of the dark. "And when you couldn't think of anything else, you told me what had happened to your parents and how you lived with your uncle and aunt in Boston."

"My uncle's dead now."

"Yes, but your aunt's still alive, though the way you'd described her I knew you'd never get in touch with her for help. But Boston reminded me of your story about how you protected your parents' graves. How you used to sneak into the cemetery every night. How, even as an adult, you still went to visit them whenever you could. It wasn't hard for me to learn which cemetery your parents were buried in or to find their graves. But I kept asking myself, before you went to ground, before you shut yourself off from the world, would you say your final goodbyes, would you still obey the old impulse? Or had you done so already and I'd missed you?"

"A long shot."

"Sure. But the only shot I had."

Drew squinted toward the dark. "I've been on the run since January. You've been watching these graves every night since then?"

"I told you. Desperation. But I gave myself till the end of this month." Jake laughed. "Imagine my surprise when you suddenly came out of the shadows. For a second, I thought I was seeing things."

"It's a good place for ghosts. And reunions. And executions. The undertaker might just as well skip the funeral and plant me where I fall. But you still haven't shot me. Why?"

In the darkness, Jake sighed. "Because I want to know what really happened."

Drew told him.

For a moment, Jake didn't react. "It makes a good story."

"It's more than a story!"

"But don't you see? It doesn't matter. *What they believe is what matters*. They came to me. 'You're his friend,' they said. 'You know his habits. You know what he'll do. He's dangerous. There's no telling who he might sell us out to next.' "

"I told you already. I didn't sell them out!"

"And they also said, 'We'll give you a hundred thousand dollars if you find him . . . and you kill him.' "

Drew lost his patience. He stepped ahead, stretching out his arms. "Then do it! What are you waiting for? Earn the bounty!"

"Don't rely on our friendship," Jake warned from the darkness. "Don't come any closer, and don't try to run."

"Run? I'm *sick* of running. Kill me, or let me go."

"If I let you go, you'd still be running."

"No. Tomorrow I'm supposed to enter a monastery."

"*What?*"

"That's right. I'm becoming a Carthusian."

"You mean you really did get religion? A Carthusian? Wait a minute. Aren't they the ones who live alone in a cell and pray all day? That's fucking weird. It's like crawling into a grave."

"The opposite. Like being resurrected. I'm in a grave already. And not because of the gun you're aiming at me. Think what you want. From your point of view, by joining the Carthusians I'd be dead already, wouldn't I? You wouldn't have to kill me."

"You were always good with words," Jake said from the darkness.

"I won't insult our friendship by thinking that you're tempted by the hundred thousand dollars they offered you to kill me. I won't insult you either by trying to tempt you with a larger amount if you let me go. The fact is, I don't have that kind of money anymore. I gave everything away."

"Weirder and weirder."

"What I *am* doing is counting on our friendship. I saved your life once. On that same climb in the Andes. Remember?"

"Oh, I remember all right."

"Nobody knows you found me. Return the favor. Save my life. Let me walk away."

"If only things could be that simple. See, there's something else I haven't told you. And more at stake here than just the hundred thousand. That's just the carrot on the end of the stick. But that stick has another end, a sharp end, and it's being jabbed right into my back. You really made them angry, Drew. A failed assignment. A *major* one. And those three operatives you killed. The network's sure you've become a freelance, a rogue."

"They're wrong!"

"But that's what they *think*. They're sure you sold out. The things you know, you could do a lot of damage to the network. So they're falling on you hard. They won't ever stop looking. And the angrier they get, the more they start falling hard on other people, too. Like me. It's like because I know you, because we're friends, they figure I should be able to find you. And if I don't, then I must be a rogue. Next month, I expect them to put the boots to me. So you see my point? I can't let you go."

Drew heard the sorrow in Jake's tone. "But do you *want* to kill me?"

"Christ, no! Why do you think I'm stalling?"

"Then maybe there's a better way."

"If there is, I don't know it."

"Go back and tell them you found me and killed me."

"What the hell good would that do? They wouldn't just take my word. I'd have to bring them proof!"

"So what's the problem? *Give* them that proof!"

"Make sense."

"Tell them you rigged a car-bomb and blew me up." Drew remembered the method of execution he'd been told to use in the Alps. "Take photographs. They like photographs."

"Of what? A bombed-out car won't . . ."

"No, of me getting in the car and driving away. Of the car blowing up, toppling into a river. Under the circumstances, if you tell them you couldn't get me except with a bomb, what more proof could they want? But I won't be in the car."

"You stop the car and get out before it blows?"

"That's right. Tomorrow, I'm supposed to report to the monastery. It's up in Vermont. But I can wait till morning to help you take the pictures."

Drew started forward, toward Jake's voice in the darkness.

"Stay where you are, Drew."

"I can't wait any longer. I have to know. It's time to put our friendship on the line. Shoot me, or help me. There's no other choice." He stretched his arms out again. A gesture of openness.

"I'm warning you, Drew." Jake sounded panicked. "Don't make me do it. Don't come any closer."

"Sorry, buddy. I've been running too long. I'm tired. And I want to see your face."

"For Christ's sake!"

"Yes, that's right!" Drew came within ten feet from the clump of bushes where Jake was hidden. Five. And stopped. He stared at the darkness. "So what's it going to be? Do you want to help me prove to them that you killed me? So you can get me off the hook, and I can spend the rest of my life in peace? Or do you want to kill me for real?"

He waited. Silence closed in.

The bushes rustled.

Drew tensed, fearing he'd miscalculated, imagining Jake raise his weapon.

A figure emerged from the darkness.

Jake approached, his arms outstretched as Drew's were. "God love you, pal."

They embraced.

5

"In seventy-nine?" Arlene scanned Drew's face, her voice as taut with emotion as Drew's had been.

"In March. In Boston. The day before I entered the monastery."

She slumped back into her chair. "You're right. I had to hear all of it before I could understand. It's like . . ."

Drew watched her struggle to find the words. "I came to think of it as a spiderweb," he said. "Everything interlocked, interwoven, coming full circle. For a terrible purpose. Because the ultimate spider's waiting."

She studied him. "And Jake did what you asked? He helped you?"

"We staged the photographs. I don't know what he told Scalpel. But he must have been convincing. From what you've said, there weren't any repercussions. In fact, until two weeks ago, you didn't notice anything unusual."

"That's right." She brooded. "But then he became nervous."

"And shortly after Jake disappeared, the monastery was attacked," Father Stanislaw said.

The room seemed to narrow with tension.

"Are the two events related?" The priest turned to Drew. "Did someone decide that Jake knew more than he was telling? Was he forced to admit that you were still alive, to reveal where you were?"

"But why the six-year delay?" Drew asked. "If Scalpel was suspicious about his story, why did they wait so long to question him?"

"Scalpel?" Arlene looked incredulous. "You're assuming *they're* responsible? That they caused Jake's disappearance and attacked the monastery?"

"I have to. Everything points to them."

"But—" She became more agitated.

"What's wrong? I thought you took that for granted the same as I did."

"No, you don't understand. It's impossible."

"But everything fits."

"It can't! Scalpel doesn't exist anymore!"

Drew's stomach dropped. *What?*

"The network was disbanded, in 1980. When you were in the monastery."

Drew flinched.

"She's right," Father Stanislaw said. "My sources are very firm about its cancellation. As you discovered, the program had gotten out of control. Far exceeding its mandate, it wasn't just counterattacking terrorists but had taken the potentially catastrophic step of interfering in foreign governments and plotting assassinations of heads of state. If the Ayatollah had learned that Americans were trying to kill him, he might have executed the hostages instead of merely holding them for ransom. For sure, he would have used the assassination attempt as proof that everything he said against America and its degeneracy was true. That's no doubt why Scalpel wanted you killed. Your failure to accomplish the hit and, worse, their suspicion that you'd become unstable enough to give away their secrets must have terrified them."

"But then they thought I was dead."

"And probably got their first good night's sleep since your failed assignment," Father Stanislaw said. "My sources feel that Scalpel decided it had come too close to disaster. A few even feel that someone in Scalpel was worried enough to let the State Department know how politically dangerous the program had become. Remember what happened to the CIA when the Senate's Church Committee uncovered the agency's assassination plots? Against Castro, Lumumba, Sukarno, the Diem brothers?"

"The CIA was almost disbanded," Drew said. "As a compromise, its powers were severely restricted. And seven hundred members of the covert operations branch were fired."

"Obviously Scalpel didn't want the same scandal. Protecting their careers, its administrators carefully and quietly dismantled the anti-terrorist network. The dismantling took a year from your failed attempt against the Ayatollah."

"Then who the hell tried to kill me? And why?" Drew asked.

"And what made Jake so nervous?" Arlene stared at them.

"Maybe the poison will give us a clue," Drew said. "If we knew the type used to attack the monastery."

Father Stanislaw considered him. "Yes. The bishop told me you'd kept the corpse of the mouse that saved your life. Your pet."

"Stuart Little." Drew had trouble breathing. "I figured the last thing he could do for me was to help me find the answers. With an autopsy, if the poison was distinctive, I might have the information that would lead me to whoever had ordered the attack."

"I wonder. Would you mind? May I see the body?"

"It isn't pretty."

"I expect that by now you know I'm not innocent."

Drew glanced at the eerie red ring, the intersecting sword and Maltese cross. "I got that impression. The fraternity of the stone?"

"That's right."

"You'll have to tell me about it."

"When the time is suitable. And in the meanwhile?"

Drew went to his coat. Remarkably, when he pulled out the plastic bag, the tiny cadaver seemed unusually preserved. It was dry and shrunken, like a mummy.

Father Stanislaw accepted it with reverence. "From tiny

creatures . . ." He glanced from the mouse to Drew. "I've explained that I had the corpses removed from the monastery. Your concern was well founded, the fear of scandal you expressed to the bishop. If the authorities had learned about the attack, their investigation would have led them to discover that *one* monk had survived. And when they'd dug more deeply, they'd have learned about your background. The Church protecting an international assassin? It wouldn't do. So after our own investigation, we erased the evidence. The corpses were buried in keeping with Carthusian custom. Respectfully, but humbly, without a headstone to identify them. We maintained the privacy that the monks had always wanted. But autopsies *were* performed. The poison *is* distinctive. And under the circumstances, appropriate."

Drew waited.

"Monk's hood."

The play on words was blasphemous. "If I ever get my hands on . . ."

"Patience," Father Stanislaw said. He set the plastic bag on the dresser and touched his priest's white collar. "I should have put on my vestments."

"For what?"

"Your confession, for that's what this has been. A difficult problem of canon law. I wonder if my oversight makes your confession invalid."

Drew's voice broke. "I don't think so."

"I don't, either. God understands. Is that the end of it? Have you told me everything you think is pertinent? Everything that leads up to the attack on the monastery?"

"Everything I can think of."

"Then bow your head, and complete the ritual."

"Father, I'm heartily sorry for these sins and the sins of all my life."

Father Stanislaw raised his right hand, making the sign of the Cross. The priest prayed in Latin. Drew recognized the petition to God for forgiveness.

Father Stanislaw paused. "To kill another human being is one of the ultimate crimes. Only suicide is greater. But the circumstances moderate your culpability. As does your lifelong ordeal. Make a good act of contrition."

Drew did so.

The priest said, "Go in peace." Then added, his voice suddenly harsh, "But stay right where you are."

Drew glanced up, startled.

"It's time to talk about Yanus."

Drew frowned. "You said that in the chapel at the retreat house. It took me a while to figure it out. Your accent. You mean *Janus*?"

"The assassin," Arlene interrupted.

Father Stanislaw nodded. "The two-headed god. Who's supposed to be Drew."

PART SEVEN

JANUS

THE SINS OF THE PRESENT

✣

1

In Ancient Rome, when an imperial army marched off to war, complex rituals had to be obeyed, lest ill fortune fall upon the venture. One of the most important of these rituals required that the army pass through a ceremonial archway while the favor of the gods—and one in particular, the god of good beginnings—was invoked. There were many such archways throughout the city, and most were not connected to walls or buildings but rather stood freely, as if their lack of practical purpose would emphasize their symbolic function. Likewise, small buildings were sometimes constructed for no other purpose than to provide a suitable setting for a priest or politician to walk into and out from.

The most respected of these buildings was a shrine to the north of the Forum. Simple, rectangular, it had double bronze doors on its east and west side, facing the rising and setting sun, as if to signify that, while the good beginning of a venture was hoped for, so too was a successful end. Like the archway through which Rome's mighty armies marched on their way to battle, this temple too was associated with war. Indeed, so frequently did the empire's generals pass into and out of the double doors facing east and west that by custom the doors were left open. Only when Rome was at peace were the doors closed, an event that happened rarely—during the first seven hundred years of the city's greatness, from the reign of Numa to that of Augustus, only three times.

The god to whom this shrine was dedicated was not, as might be expected, Mars. Instead, the statue that priests, politicians, and generals meditated upon as they passed from one set of doors to the next was that of a greater deity, Janus, whose likeness could easily be distinguished from those of all other gods because he had two faces, one in front, the other in back, peering toward each set of doors, the east and the west, the start and the finish.

When petitioned for success at the start of a day, he was known as Matutinus, from which comes matins, the Roman Catholic Church's word for the first canonical service of the day, just after midnight. But Janus was also petitioned at the start of each week and each month and, in particular, at the start of each year. Appropriately, the first month of the Roman calendar was named in his honor: January.

Janus, the two-faced, staring eternally forward and backward.

Toward the beginning. And the end.

2

"At the start," Father Stanislaw said, "what we had were mostly rumors. Almost a year ago."

"We?" Drew squinted. "Who's we?" He gestured toward Father Stanislaw's ring, the magnificent ruby, the intersecting sword and cross. "The fraternity?"

"Is it necessary to be explicit? A man with your experience. . ." Father Stanislaw considered him. "It shouldn't surprise you. The Church with its seven hundred million followers is virtually a nation unto itself. Indeed, in the Middle Ages it was a nation, composed of all of Europe, during the Holy

Roman Empire. It needs to watch over its interests. Just as all major nations do, it needs an intelligence network."

"Intelligence network?" Drew's voice hardened. "I'm beginning to understand."

"At least, you think you understand. But one stage of explanation at a time. The principal sources of our intelligence are various members of an ambiguous religious order that has come into prominence since you entered the monastery. The order is known as Opus Dei, the great work of God. I describe the order as ambiguous because its members—mostly successful middle-class professionals, doctors, lawyers, business people—continue to pursue their lay vocation despite their vows of poverty, chastity, and obedience. They dress according to the fashions of society, though many retreat at night to cloisters, and all bequeath their possessions to the Church. Their views are conservative. They're fiercely loyal to the Pope. Their membership in Opus Dei is kept a strict secret."

"In other words, an invisible order."

"Correct. The theory is that they can spread the Church's influence by using its doctrines in their daily business practice. A kind of Catholic fifth column, if you like. Imagine the effect if members of Opus Dei were elected to Congress, or if one became a member of the U.S. Supreme Court. But they aren't merely in America. Opus Dei exists in strength in over eighty countries. One hundred thousand professionals, using their ambition, striving to gain as much secular power as they can, for the sake of the Catholic Church. *They* are the basis for the Church's intelligence network. And it was from rumors they began to pick up that I first heard about . . ."

3

A freelance mercenary, who as if from nowhere appeared abruptly on the European scene and was reputed to be responsible for five assassinations in rapid sequence, all involving Catholic priests. In each case, the priests—politically active, influential, and fiercely opposed to Communist factions in their country's government—had died in ways that at first seemed merely unfortunate. A car accident, for example, a heart attack, a fire.

Widely separated, the deaths would not have attracted notice, but so many in quick succession, and most in Italy, prompted Opus Dei eyebrows to be raised. Powerful members of the order used their influence to make sure that investigations became more thorough. Soon, various factors in each death began to seem suspicious, though not conclusively incriminating. In the case of the car accident, the brakes had failed, and yet the brakes had recently been serviced. In the case of the heart attack, an autopsy on the victim revealed no weakness in his cardiovascular system. In the case of the fire, no one could recall the priest, who'd always been compulsively neat, ever allowing oily rags to accumulate in the rectory's basement.

At the same time, in Geneva, a young woman deeply in love made a frightening discovery. The man with whom she'd been having an affair, a pleasure-giving American, had recently installed a set of bookshelves in her apartment. One of the brackets that held the shelves to the wall had pulled from the plaster, causing the shelves to lean out alarmingly. Because the boyfriend, Thomas McIntyre, was out of the city on business (what kind of business she didn't know, something to do with imports and exports), she telephoned her brother to come to her apartment and advise her about the shelves.

When the two of them chanced to peer behind the shelves, they noticed a hole in the wall that had not been there before. And exploring further, they discovered a cavity filled with plastic explosives, detonators, automatic weapons, ammunition, and a metal container from which they extracted the equivalent of a hundred thousand dollars in various European currencies, along with three passports for Michael McQuane, Robert Malone, and Terence Mulligan. Despite the difference in names, the photograph on each of the passports was identical. It portrayed the face of the woman's boyfriend Thomas McIntyre.

After a long, intense, and violent argument, in which the woman defended her lover, threatening never to speak to her brother again if her lover wasn't given the chance to explain, the brother phoned the authorities. Three policemen arrived within the hour. They examined the objects concealed behind the bookshelves and proceeded at once to the apartment of the boyfriend, who—it turned out—had come back from his business trip early and, without informing his lover, was having a party. After the policemen knocked on the door and were with reluctance admitted by one of the guests, they faced a group of drunken revelers in the midst of which a man who resembled the photograph in the various passports agreed to answer questions in the bedroom. Once inside, however, the American pulled a pistol, shot the three policemen, and fled down a fire escape.

One policeman lived to tell the story. Further investigation revealed that the metal container concealed in the wall behind the girlfriend's bookshelves also held a notebook in which addresses in various cities and countries turned out to be those of the five priests who had died.

4

"Reactions so far?" Father Stanislaw asked.

Drew thought about it, troubled. "If this McIntyre's an assassin, he needs a few lessons in tradecraft. That rickety bookshelf. Panicking in front of the police." He shook his head. "An amateur."

"So it seemed to me. Unless . . ."

"I don't understand."

"Unless he was putting on an act."

"You think he *wanted* to expose himself?" Arlene asked, surprised.

"But why?" Drew added.

"To announce himself. To gain a reputation quickly," Father Stanislaw said. "And once he'd been exposed, no doubt deliberately on his part, he suddenly became professional. The authorities did everything possible but couldn't find him, and in rapid succession, three other politically active priests were killed. Then Opus Dei members themselves began to be killed. Corporation executives, publishers, but mostly politicians. And it now was clear, this Thomas McIntyre, and his various other similar names on other bogus passports, was engaged in systematic terrorism against—"

"—the Catholic Church." Sickened, Drew turned to Arlene. "You told me he'd been killing politicians, but you didn't tell me—"

"—they were in Opus Dei? How could I have known?"

"You couldn't have," Father Stanislaw said. "How could anyone outside the intelligence network of the Church have known? That's the whole point. The members of Opus Dei are a secret."

"Not anymore," Drew said.

"And now we come to you." Father Stanislaw sat down next to Drew. "As the authorities investigated, spurred on by powerful members of Opus Dei anxious to find the man who was stalking them, other rumors began to surface. A man with the code name Janus was buying weapons and explosives on the European black market and at the same time hiring freelance investigators to document scandals involving the Catholic Church. These scandals ranged from mistresses whom various Church officials maintained, to homosexual affections, to rich estates that no priest, given the vow of poverty, ought to have the resources to own. Alcoholism. Drug addiction. Deadly sins. If a priest or a member of Opus Dei had a vice, Janus wanted to know about it. And be given the proof. Sometimes he merely sent the documentation, including photographs, to the newspapers. Other times, he killed the priest or the Opus Dei member and *then* sent the documents, apparently to justify the assassinations."

"Janus," Drew said.

"The connection was obvious. Thomas McIntyre, the assassin with the same ambition? Could *he* be Janus? Indeed, when the authorities tracked down one of Janus's contacts and made him talk, the man identified the passport photograph of Thomas McIntyre as his employer."

"Identified?" Drew stiffened. "You're telling me that this Janus—this McIntyre—actually let his contacts see him? He didn't even have the sense to use a safe phone? Something's wrong. The tradecraft's so clumsy it almost seems . . ."

"Intentional?" Father Stanislaw asked. "Almost as if he *wants* to be caught? Indeed. The same pattern. And yet, despite the efforts of the most powerful members of Opus Dei, and their considerable influence on Interpol and MI-6, no one's been able to find him."

"But *you* thought I was Janus," Drew told Arlene. "Or at

least you did till I made you give me the benefit of the doubt. Why were you tempted to make the connection in the first place?"

"Because of the photograph in all those passports," Father Stanislaw answered for her. "It took some time, but finally the American authorities managed to find the same face in its files. Part of the difficulty was that your own legal passport had now expired. But as they searched their previous records . . . Younger. Thinner, though not as thin as you are now. Nonetheless an obvious likeness. Andrew MacLane. The similarity of your last name with Janus's many last names attracted immediate attention. McIntyre, McQuane, Malone, Mulligan. Granted, an odd blend of Irish and Scot. But nonetheless the parallel could not be ignored. Janus, the authorities decided, had to be you.

"Your choice of code name seemed puzzling for a time. But intelligence officials soon understood. You'd worked for a now defunct American anti-terrorist network, though what you did for that network was naturally never revealed. In seventy-nine, you'd sold out to Iran. You'd dropped out of sight for several years, but now you were back, ignoring your former loyalties, working for whoever paid you the most. Janus. The code name then seemed perfectly apt. The Roman god who stared forward and backward."

"Janus, the two-faced," Drew said bitterly.

"When the story went public," Arlene said, "Jake and I were stunned. How could you be an assassin attacking the Catholic Church? It didn't make sense. But the proof was overwhelming. Jake got more and more upset. He began to act strangely. And disappeared." She clenched her fists. "*Why didn't he tell me what was going on?*"

"He couldn't," Drew said. "Not until he was sure it was me. After all, Jake knew I was supposed to be dead. He was the man who claimed to have killed me, and Scalpel had accepted his proof. But as far as Jake could tell, I was in a Carthusian monastery up in Vermont. So how could I be killing priests and politicians in Europe?"

"Unless you'd left the monastery," Father Stanislaw said. "Unless you'd simply used him. So you think he went to the monastery to find out?"

"I never saw him there. But my guess is he didn't."

"What then?"

"Let me put it this way. Whoever Janus is, he's taken a lot of effort to make the authorities think—"

"—that he and you are the same," Arlene completed his thought.

Drew struggled to concentrate. "*Why* would he do that? Why would he be so determined to blame the killings on me? If the authorities found me, I could prove that I hadn't done them."

"True," Father Stanislaw said. "If you were in a monastery, your alibi would be perfect."

Drew's scalp tingled. "But Janus couldn't have known I was in that monastery. And yet he was sure I'd never be able to prove I wasn't Janus. Why?"

Arlene spoke, her voice somber. "He thought you were dead."

The three of them stared at each other.

"If the authorities were hunting a dead man, Janus wouldn't have to worry. I'd be a perfect distraction for them. While they went after a ghost, he could . . ."

"Be invisible and do what he wanted." Arlene stood, distressed. "Then did Jake investigate his former superiors in Scalpel?" Her voice shook. "Because he believed that one of them was using the fact that you were dead—or *supposed* to be dead—as a cover for Janus?"

Drew nodded.

"And whoever invented Janus found out what Jake was

doing?" She shuddered. "I hate to think it, let alone say it. Did someone kill Jake to prevent him from finding out who was masquerading as you?"

"Arlene, we don't know that."

"But is that what you suspect?"

Drew looked at her with pain. "I'm sorry."

Her face went pale. Her eyes became frightening. "Whoever did it will be even sorrier."

"But the sequence didn't stop there. Whoever invented Janus must have forced Jake to admit why he was investigating them," Drew said. "If they found out I was still alive, in the monastery, they'd have had to kill me as well. To protect their cover for Janus. And that presented a problem. Because the Carthusian monks are anonymous, the entire monastery had to be taken out to make sure I was really dead this time. And then, I assume, my body would have disappeared."

Father Stanislaw's mouth tightened. "And the Church, when it investigated, would have wondered why. Which brings us back to the concern you expressed to the bishop. No one could know that the Church inadvertently was sheltering an assassin, albeit one whose motives could be justified. The controversy would have been intolerable, undermining the authority of the Church."

Drew's voice was guttural with rage. "Like a spiderweb. Everything interconnected. Janus must have found it amusing. Thinking I was dead, he used me as an alias to attack the Church. Then, realizing I was alive, he decided he could kill me without the authorities ever finding out. Because the Church, to protect itself, would have to cover up the mass murder. The Church in effect would be helping him. Clever to the point of genius. And if I have my way, I'll see that he suffers in a clever part of Hell.

"*My double*," Drew suddenly added. The rush of understanding made him shiver.

Father Stanislaw squinted, rubbing the sword and cross on his gleaming ring. "So he occurred to you as well?"

Arlene nodded forcibly. "When you mentioned him earlier, I started to wonder."

Drew shivered again.

A turncoat assassin . . . assuming Drew's identity, resembling Drew's passport photograph, sufficiently similar to convince those who met him that he was Drew.

"Dear God," Drew said. "It sounds like the double I used when I was in Scalpel. My alibi when I went on a mission. They disbanded Scalpel. But they must have contacted some of its former members and created another network like it. Under another name, Scalpel still exists!"

"But what network?" Father Stanislaw studied Arlene. "Were you and your brother asked to join another intelligence unit?"

Arlene shook her head. "These days, I'm a civilian. I teach outdoor survival and climbing techniques."

"What about your brother?"

"He worked for another network. That much I know. But he never told me which one, and I followed protocol by never asking. He wouldn't have told me if I had. I wouldn't have expected him to."

"Janus," Drew said with disgust. "Like monk's hood, the poison used at the monastery, Janus is another Goddamned pun. The two-faced. The hypocrite. Sure. But *literally* Janus is a man with two lookalike faces. And the only person I can think of to tell us who's behind this is my double."

"Do you know where to find him?" Father Stanislaw asked.

5

The bond that Drew and his classmates had shared at Scalpel's training school in Colorado had been too strong to be dissolved by their dispersal after graduation. He, Arlene, and Jake had kept in touch with each other, for example, maintaining their friendship; eventually Drew and Arlene became lovers.

But Scalpel had forbidden Drew ever to associate with Mike, his double, lest their remarkable resemblance attract attention and jeopardize assignments. It hadn't been a burden for Drew to accept this separation, for among all his classmates at the training school, the only one he'd never gotten along with was Mike. Their similarity had produced a rivalry, particularly on the part of Mike, that prevented them from ever feeling close to each other. Drew had nonetheless remained curious about the man upon whom he depended for his life, and whenever he'd had the chance, he'd asked former classmates what his lookalike was doing. In '78, Drew had learned that Mike was taking courses at the University of Minnesota. American Lit. The same kind of master's program that Drew had been taking at Iowa. It figured. He and his double didn't just look alike; they thought alike. They preferred the same cover as literature students in college towns.

"One of the few differences between us was that I liked classical American authors, and he liked the moderns," Drew said. "I heard that after he finished his degree at Minnesota, he planned to go to the University of Virginia to work on Faulkner. After Faulkner, he wanted to become an expert in Fitzgerald, then in Hemingway. Figure two years for each master's degree. If the timing's right, he should be working on Hemingway now."

"Assuming he kept to that schedule. Even if he did, it won't help us find him," Father Stanislaw said. "Every university in the country teaches Hemingway."

"No, the two top specialists on Hemingway are Carlos Baker and Philip Young. Baker's at Princeton; Young's at Penn State. Their approaches are so different that someone determined to be an expert in Hemingway would have to work with either or even both of them. Believe me, I've got enough advanced degrees to know what I'm talking about."

Princeton or Penn State? But how to be certain? How, among tens of thousands of students, to find the quarry? The literature department would be the focus of the search. So would the local gyms. Because Drew's double had to keep himself in shape for his missions, he had to work out every day. But he'd want to be invisible, so he'd go to the gym as early as possible when hardly anyone was around. Drew knew—he was sure—because he himself had followed that schedule.

Father Stanislaw made phone calls to his Opus Dei contacts. Seven hours later, the priest received a call from the Penn State campus about a man who matched Drew's age and description, who was taking graduate courses in American Lit, who worked with Philip Young on Hemingway, and went to a local gym every morning at six.

The man was a loner.

A half-hour later, Drew, Arlene, and Father Stanislaw were on the road.

6

A cold wind nipped Drew's cheek as he crouched with reverence at the side of a meadow halfway up a slope where he was concealed by thick leafless trees. He, Arlene, and Father Stanislaw had traveled together in the priest's black Oldsmobile, leaving Arlene's Firebird at a parking garage that offered long-term rates, paying several weeks' rent in advance. Drew had driven the motorcycle to the sleaziest bar he could find, making sure that no one saw him take off the license plate when he left the chopper next to the garbage cans in back. The police would eventually find it, but without the plate, they'd be slow to link the Harley with one stolen in Massachusetts. And because he'd wiped off his fingerprints, no one could link it to him.

While Arlene slept, Drew sat next to Father Stanislaw, still smelling the acrid smoke from Bethlehem's steel plants. He peered toward the Appalachian slopes before him. "I guess this place will do." He pointed toward a wooded ridge that loomed ahead on his right. "As good as any."

"Do you think you'll be long?" Father Stanislaw asked.

"We've got a schedule to keep. Not long. Leave the motor running."

Father Stanislaw parked on the gravel shoulder, and though the sun was bright, Drew felt a stinging wind as he got out. His eyes narrowed, he climbed the dead grassy slope. For all a passing motorist might guess, he was headed toward the trees above to relieve himself.

But when he reached the trees, he continued through them, pausing only when he came to the edge of this upper meadow. He glanced around, seeing game trails through the grass, smelling autumn's sagelike fragrance. Yes, this place would do.

With a sturdy branch, he dug a tiny trough in the grass, two inches wide, ten inches down. The semifrozen earth resisted. The tip of the branch broke. Finally, though, he was finished. Crouching, he reached in his coat and pulled out the plastic bag that contained the body of Stuart Little. Strange that the mouse hadn't rotted. Was that a sign? he wondered. A message of approval from God? He dismissed the thought, unable to allow himself to pretend to know God's mood.

Untying the plastic bag, he gently dropped Stuart's body into the bottom of the trough, then used his hands to fill in the dirt, covering it with a clump of grass. To complete the ritual, he gingerly stepped on the grass, tamping down the earth, making everything smooth. The edge of the meadow now looked undisturbed.

He stared down, for a distressing instant reminded of his parents' graves.

"Well," he said, "you saved my life. The fact is, you brought me *back* to life. I'm grateful." He almost turned before he thought of something else. "And I'll get even for you, pal."

He left the trees, grimly descended the windy grassy slope, and got in the car.

"Drew?" Arlene was awake now, frowning with concern.

He shrugged.

"Are you okay?"

"Fine."

"You're sure?"

"You were up there twenty minutes," Father Stanislaw said. "We almost went looking for you."

"Well, now I'm back," Drew said. "I made a promise up there. So let's put some miles behind us. I want to see this damned thing finished. I want to make sure I keep my promise."

"The look in your eyes," Father Stanislaw said. "God help the people we're after."

"No, that's wrong."

"I'm not sure what you mean."

"God help us all."

7

One range blended with another, then another. By mid-afternoon, they reached the Alleghenies, following the twists and turns of roads that led past barren strip-mined slopes and dying towns. Massive oil pumps were sometimes visible among skeletal trees, their metallic beaks rising and falling, rising and falling, their relentless thump oppressive even through the car's closed windows.

In contrast with their long intense discussions back at the

motel room, neither Drew, Arlene, nor Father Stanislaw spoke much now, each brooding privately.

They reached their destination, zigzagging down a road that took them into a circular valley, located at almost the exact midpoint of Pennsylvania. And there, in the middle of the valley, they came to State College.

It was one of those towns that Drew had said was best for cover. The sprawling campus was large, with majestic vine-covered buildings and rows of towering trees. Because the town had no other major business, the local population had been forced to adjust to the vagaries of the more than twenty thousand students upon whom they depended for their livelihood. Typical of any large college town, half the population was constantly in flux, students coming and going, enrolling and graduating. An operative who liked to fill his time between assignments by reading and going to classes could have a satisfying life here and, more important, could have a cover that no one questioned. As long as he didn't need a social life, he'd be invisible. He could disappear.

8

Father Stanislaw used a pay phone in a supermarket on the outskirts of town, getting directions to the local Catholic church. The church had a modern design, low, long, made of concrete, with an iron statue of Christ on the Cross in front. They parked the car and entered the front door.

A tall, balding man in a business suit sat on a chair beside the holy water fountain in the vestibule, reading a prayer book. He glanced up as they came in.

"God be with you," he said.

"And with your spirit," Father Stanislaw added.

"*Deo gratias.*"

"Amen," the priest responded. "I must say it's good to hear Latin spoken in a church."

Drew stood with Arlene in the background, watching with interest.

"Is the suspect still being followed?" Father Stanislaw asked.

Nodding, the businessman set down the prayer book and stood. "He doesn't seem aware of it. As you suggested, we're keeping a cautious distance and tailing him—is that the right word?—in shifts." He permitted a smile. "It's almost like taking turns for forty-hours devotion."

"You know where he lives?"

The businessman nodded again. "It was difficult to learn. The university sends his mail, grades and such, to a postal box. He isn't listed in the phone book. But our source at the phone company discovered that he did indeed have a phone, unlisted. The computer's billing file had his address." The businessman reached into his suitcoat and pulled out a folded piece of paper, giving it to Father Stanislaw.

"It's a section of town where a lot of students live," the businessman continued. "I've marked it on this map. Years ago, the landlord owned a rundown mansion that he divided into as many single-room apartments as he could. He made so much money that he couldn't resist adding on to the mansion. Sections on the sides, in back, in front, each with tiny rooms. After a while, you couldn't see the mansion for all the additions. And still not satisfied, he started buying houses along the block and in back. He built additions onto those as well until all the additions came together and you couldn't tell one house from another. It's as if the block imploded. Only God knows how many apartments he's got there. The place is crammed with intersecting hallways and alleys so the students can get to the inner apartments. It's a maze. You can get lost in there."

Father Stanislaw glanced at the paper. "Number eighty-five?"

"The sequence isn't always in a continuous line. You'll have to do your best and then ask directions."

"But he's not at home right now?"

"Not that I know of. There's a pay phone here in the basement. I've been getting reports every hour. The last I heard, he finished a class in Depression novelists and went to the library."

"Is there anything else I should know about where he lives?"

"Only that the students don't take well to strangers. They realize how unusual the place looks, and they get tired of sightseers."

"Perhaps they won't object to a priest. You did good work. All of you. Your Church is grateful. Tell the others."

"We're the ones who are grateful. As long as it was necessary to preserve the faith."

"Believe me, it was."

"For the honor and glory of God."

"And the protection of His Church."

Father Stanislaw raised his right hand in blessing. "Please continue to receive your reports. Periodically I'll phone in case you have any change in the target's status."

The businessman bowed his head. "God's will be done, Father."

"Indeed it will. And thank you again."

Father Stanislaw turned, gesturing for Drew and Arlene to leave the church with him.

The heavy door thumped behind them.

Outside, the air was nippy, the dark sky bright with stars. A car drove by, its muffler streaming frosty exhaust.

"Opus Dei?" Drew asked.

Father Stanislaw didn't answer.

9

Drew stood in shadows across the street from the complex. Filling an entire block, it was situated at the level top of a gentle slope, bordered by shrubs. The shrubs and the night made it almost impossible to tell where one house ended and the next began.

But this much was sure, there were many houses. Twenty? Drew wondered. Thirty? The house had been expanded with no consideration for consistency of style or materials. A plain cinderblock structure abutted an ornate wooden chalet attached to a modernistic glass-brick tower, and these all protruded from a Victorian mansion with gables and dormer windows. The mansion in turn adjoined a two-story log cabin, and then something that resembled a castle.

Jammed together, the entire hodgepodge seemed the work of an architect gone insane from the wondrous possibility of choice, though the prosaic truth was probably that the owner had simply built each new addition in whatever style was necessitated by the cheapest materials he could get his hands on from year to year.

Drew scanned the lit windows in the jumbled levels across from him. He stepped deeper into the shadows, watching silhouettes disappear among the crazily contrasting buildings.

Nervous, he turned from the eerie glow of gaslamps up there to frown at Arlene. "Father Stanislaw should have been back by now."

She shrugged. "He might have had trouble finding his way."

"Or else . . . Another five minutes. Then we'd better find out what happened to him."

"We?"

"Okay"—he allowed himself to grin—"I mean you."

She grinned back.

They both understood. Because of Drew's resemblance to the man they were looking for, he couldn't risk attracting attention by wandering the complex.

Five minutes lengthened to ten.

"That's it. Now I'm worried, too," she said. "I'm going in there. He should have . . ."

A shadow emerged from the bushy slope across the street. Drew relaxed as he recognized Father Stanislaw.

The priest approached, exhaling frost. "I found it. *Finally.* That place is like a rabbit warren. It's astonishing how easy it is to get lost up there."

"The apartment?"

"In a narrow alley. It's got an outside entrance, with no doors on either side, and it faces a cinderblock wall."

"So the neighbors can't see him going in and out. And if he disappeared for a couple of days, no one would notice."

"Or probably care. These people aren't what you'd call friendly. Twice, I needed to ask directions; not to his apartment, of course, just near it. They treated me as if I'd demanded their youngest child. By the way, his apartment has an opaque glass window with its curtain closed, but I could tell that the lights were on."

"Timers, probably," Arlene said. "The last we heard, he was still downtown."

"An hour ago," Father Stanislaw warned. "Be careful."

"How do I get there?" Drew asked.

"At the top of the slope, you'll face three alleys. Take the middle one. You'll come to a tree carved into a totem pole."

"Totem pole?"

"Turn left till you reach a statue that looks like twisted airplane propellors. Then turn right." Father Stanislaw sighed. "I think I'd better draw you a map."

10

A gaslamp hissed, barely dispelling the gloom. When Drew passed the statue, he had to stoop beneath an arch and found himself in one of the buildings. To his right, along a musty hall with pale bare bulbs dangling from the ceiling, he saw doors. To his left, a rickety wooden stairwell led down to an earthen floor. And down there, beyond in the shadows, he saw other doors. Father Stanislaw had called this place a rabbit warren. Drew's own impression was that of an anthill, except that ants didn't play rock music or cook onions.

He left the building and entered a courtyard where another gaslamp revealed a One Way Only traffic sign that stood in front of three tunnels. The map that Father Stanislaw had drawn told Drew to angle left. The tunnel led him through a further building to a courtyard that housed a chicken coop. He heard fowl clucking in there. And later in another courtyard, he saw a goat in a pen. Glancing down, he found that the long stone slabs he was walking on were tombstones. Madness. The deeper he followed the zigzagging corridors into the chaos, the more he accepted the bizarre.

His double had chosen his lodging well. In this environment, a man who stayed to himself would hardly be noticed. Indeed, everyone here seemed to want to be alone, as if convinced that the rest of the tenants were crazy. Drew realized why Father Stanislaw had encountered suspicion when he knocked on doors to ask for directions. Here, a priest would be inappropriate.

Several times, tenants stared suspiciously at Drew. But he didn't give them a chance to see his face, and as he moved purposefully forward, appearing to belong here, they relaxed.

As soon as he was out of their sight, he checked his map again, and at last he came to his destination. The narrow alley.

The cinderblock wall to the right. The single door on the left, and the opaque window with the curtain behind it, the faint projection of light from inside.

He paused, his cheeks cold. From an apartment somewhere behind him, he heard muffled voices arguing about Plato and Aristotle.

Read St. Augustine, Drew thought, as he shifted toward the end of the narrow alley. He stood in the dark at the corner farthest along, shifting behind a head-tall stack of boards, leaning against the crook in the wall, his insulated coat protecting his back from the chill of the cinderblocks.

He waited.

11

Just before midnight a shadow came around the opposite end of the alley. The timing was right. Drew had often followed this schedule himself. Don't head home till the neighbors have settled down. In the meantime, go to a movie. Maybe one of those retrospectives of Truffaut at the Student Union or, for a laugh, the latest James Bond movie downtown. In a college community, there were many other distractions: a lecture by this year's notable literary critic, a touring company's version of *Measure for Measure,* the music department's Mozart concert. If you wanted soothing diversion, especially in Drew's former line of work, a university was perfect. The next best thing to becoming a priest.

All the same, this approaching shadow might just be a student using the alley to reach an apartment farther back. But as the figure moved closer to the door across from the cinderblock wall, Drew became certain. The man approaching him was himself!

Drew held his breath; the figure stopped. He had Drew's proportions—the same build, the same height. The facial resemblance was uncanny, making Drew shiver. I wonder if he's been told I'm not dead, Drew thought. Or if he knows about the monastery. Then wouldn't he have gone into hiding?

The shadow reached into his coat, pulling out a key. Drew hadn't known quite how to act, but now he followed his instincts, deciding to play it casual. Good buddy time.

"Hey, Mike." His voice echoed.

The shadow turned, on guard, toward this dark corner. "What?"

"Hey, don't get panicky," Drew said heartily. "It's your old classmate. Drew. I've been waiting to talk to you. Man, I'm in trouble. Please, you've got to listen. I need your help."

Mike stiffened, staring toward the darkness. "Drew?"

"Remember those Colorado jack rabbits Hank Dalton made us use for target practice at the school? How Hank's dog used to eat them?"

"No. It can't be you." There was fear in Mike's voice.

"How about that coffin Hank used to keep our guns in?"

"Christ, it *is*!"

"Good to see you, man."

"But how did you find me?"

"I'll tell you later. Right now, you've gotta help me. Find me a place that's safe. Man, I'm in shit."

"Oh, sure, I'll help. The thing is, who else is with you?"

"With me? Why would—? I just told you. Who'd be with me when I'm in trouble?"

"Yeah?" The shadow glanced around nervously.

"How many years has it been?" Drew asked. "Enough to make us wonder where our youth went, huh?" He took a chance and stepped from the darkness, holding out his hand in greeting. "For God's sake, will you help me out?"

"You're sure nobody's with you?"

As Drew came closer, Mike's likeness to him became more unsettling. "With me? What makes you keep asking that?"

"Because, good buddy"—Mike held out his hand and grinned—"it's been so long that—"

"Yeah?"

"—I heard you were dead."

Mike lunged in Drew's direction. Heart thumping, Drew crouched protectively. Boards suddenly clattered behind him, from the end of the alley where he'd been hiding. Startled, sensing a trap, Drew pivoted sideways, ready to defend himself not only from Mike but from men who'd been guarding Mike in case Drew showed up. I walked right into it! Drew thought in alarm.

But no one lunged from the end of the alley.

Instead, Mike seemed as startled as Drew. Freezing in mid-attack, staring toward the clattering boards, he seemed convinced that Drew had lied about being alone. Jerking back, on guard against unseen assailants, he cursed and swung around sharply, racing toward the opposite end of the alley, unaware of the Irish setter that emerged from the dark to nose at something beneath the boards it had toppled.

12

Drew scrambled in pursuit. He had to keep Mike in view. His lungs burned, but he knew that in this maze of alleys, courtyards, and tunnels, Mike needed only seconds to make Drew lose him. Mike knew all the twists and turns. He'd no doubt scouted the place for dozens of emergency places in which to hide.

Mike ducked around the alley's corner. Wary, Drew pulled out his Mauser. His query might continue running away—or he might stop abruptly, taking Drew by surprise as Drew charged around the corner after him. Drew had to reduce his speed, cautiously rounding the corner, using up precious seconds. He didn't think Mike would have a handgun on him. Why would Mike take the risk of destroying his cover if someone happened to bump against a gun beneath Mike's coat in a throng of students leaving class?

But a knife? Mike could easily carry one. A stiletto in his boot, or a pocket knife. No one would question that. For that matter, Mike didn't need any weapon except his hands. Like Drew, the man could kill with one sharp blow to the chest or the larynx.

But Mike didn't attack as Drew crept around the corner. Instead, Drew saw him racing down the continuation of the alley. His chest heaving, Drew rushed after him. Even in the shadows, he had a sufficient target to shoot at. But he didn't dare. Not only because of the noise, the commotion it would cause, a crowd, the police. But because he might kill Mike instead of wounding him. And Mike had to be kept alive to answer Drew's questions.

Mike charged around another corner; Drew followed. Beyond a courtyard, its gaslamp hissing, he saw Mike veer past a greenhouse made from storm windows, then sprint inside an imitation English manor. Now Drew could rush ahead again. As he entered the building, he bumped past a man coming through a door to the left. The man toppled back inside his apartment, sprawling hard on the cracked linoleum floor. "Watch where the hell you're—!"

Drew didn't hear the rest. He was already through the building's central hallway and banging out the exit door, not worried that Mike might be lurking behind it because before the door had swung shut he'd seen his double charging ahead across another lamplit courtyard. This one had a sandbox and swing set.

The building beyond it was a barn. But instead of darting into it, Mike swung to the right, rushed down another alley, leaped over a bicycle, raced left past a wishing well, and, with a furtive glance behind him, scurried down wooden steps to the basement entrance of a looming Victorian house.

The door creaked as Drew stalked into the basement. He wasn't surprised when he faced another corridor. The floor was earthen, like the one he'd seen earlier. Doors lined the hallway. Only half the dangling bulbs were illuminated.

At the far end, Mike lunged through another door. Rushing after him, Drew heard the crunch of broken glass beneath his shoes. He frowned. The earth floor should have absorbed his weight. The fragments of glass should have been squeezed down into the earth instead of cracking now.

The detail troubled him, but he couldn't become distracted. There was too much else to think about. He was gaining on Mike, and in the alley outside this house or in the next court-yard, he had a good chance of catching him. Drew neared the door through which Mike had disappeared.

He aimed the Mauser, pushed the door open, and faced a brick wall directly in front of him. A hurried glance showed another wall on his left, behind the door. He darted right. The door swung shut. His bowels contracted as absolute darkness smothered him. Oh, Jesus, he prayed. Spiders scuttled inside his stomach. Total darkness.

Frantic, he pressed his back against the wall, and though his lungs ached after his urgent chase, he struggled not to breathe. Because the rasp of his breath could now get him killed. Oh, Jesus and Mary. He was trapped inside a black room.

The broken glass on the earth floor of the hallway outside made sense now. Most of the dim bare bulbs in the ceiling out there hadn't been illuminated. Mike, in rushing along the hall-way, had hit at the bulbs, smashing them. That accounted for the broken glass Drew had heard beneath his shoes.

The extinguished bulbs had been at this end of the hallway—the approach to the door through which Drew had entered this black room. If the entire hallway had been lit, Drew might have been able to see inside this room and notice where the light switch was and turn it on to find where Mike was hiding. Or maybe Mike wasn't even here. He might have ducked out a now-unseeable door and left Drew to think he was trapped in here with an equally unseeable opponent. Mike might be racing out of the complex by now while Drew tried to guess if he was in danger.

But Drew had to assume that Mike was here. The implications made his heart contract. A completely black room. He knew the situation well—from the black room in the airplane hangar at the Rocky Mountain Industrial School. Fighting in the dark had been their chief instructor's specialty. And Hank Dalton had mercilessly drilled his students in the principles of that unnerving form of combat. But Mike had been trained just as thoroughly. Drew was fighting someone just as good. He was fighting himself.

13

In Colorado, Drew and the other students—including Mike and Jake—had gone to the gym as usual for their first class at 8 A.M. They'd studied the double doors through which Hank Dalton always pushed the gleaming copper coffin. Though proud of their eighteen-year-old maturity, they nonetheless felt the anticipation of children about to play with toys. Soon Hank would open the coffin and give them their weapons, urging them to see who could take apart and reassemble them in the shortest time. Jake was always fast. But Drew and Mike were faster, rivals in this as in everything else, their physical similarities seeming to make them want to test their resemblance in other ways.

That morning, they waited for the class to begin. Fifteen

minutes later than usual, Hank Dalton came through the double doors. But without the coffin.

"Outside on the double!"

The sharp edge in his voice made the students think that Hank was angry at them. Anxious not to make him angrier, conditioned to be obedient, they snapped to attention and ran through the double doors, down a corridor, and outside, where they squinted from the morning sun toward an unmarked bus parked in front of the obstacle course. The motor was rumbling.

"What are you gawking at?" Hank barked. "You never seen a bus before?" At once he grinned and scratched his leathery cheek. "It's time for a little field trip. Hustle aboard."

Relieved that Hank wasn't angry, everybody scrambled in, and with Hank himself driving, they left the chain-link fence of the compound, following a dirt road into the mountains.

Two hours later, after a seemingly aimless route, with nothing but pine trees and sagebrush to look at, Hank drove through the open gate of another chain-link fence and parked in front of a corrugated-metal airplane hangar. There were no other buildings. In the distance, a small dirt airstrip cut through the scrubgrass of this small valley.

Not that the students had a chance to study the place. Hank hustled them into the hangar, and that was the last they saw of the sun for what they later learned was twenty-five days.

He shut the door and marched the students forward. They bumped against each other in the dark.

"Having problems with your eyes?" Hank asked. "Well, we'll fix that. You'll soon think the dark is home." He laughed good-naturedly.

Indeed, as their eyes adjusted to the dark, the students glanced around with interest. Helped by hints of light that showed through the cracks in the metal walls, they noticed something large in the middle of the building—so large that it might have been a one-story house without windows.

"Wonder what *that* is," someone murmured.

"All in good time," Hank answered, directing them toward a shadowy area to the right of the structure. Here they found a row of bunkbeds, each with two dark sheets and one dark blanket, and on top of each blanket, the top and bottom of a plain black garment.

"Pajamas?"

"More or less." Hank's voice drifted out of the shadows. "Strip and put them on. They'll be your uniform."

More puzzled, the students obeyed. Their eyes adjusted further to the shadows, allowing them to see that Hank had changed from his usual cowboy boots, faded jeans, denim shirt, and battered stetson to the loose black pajamas.

"You'd better get some rest now. 'Cause from here on in we'll train at night."

Rest? In the middle of the day? Drew didn't feel tired, and yet he yawned as soon as he stretched out on his bunk.

Abruptly he wakened to Hank's voice echoing from a loud-speaker somewhere in the hangar.

"Rise and shine."

At night?

"He sounds like God," someone said.

Supper—or was it breakfast?—consisted of rice and fish in something that tasted like oyster sauce. It was followed by tea.

The training began immediately. Hank led them to the back of the hangar, where, by feel, they learned that sandbags had been stacked against the wall. Drew heard Hank move, leaning toward something beside the bags, and at once, a pale yellow light came on behind them from the opposite side of the hangar. It struggled through the otherwise absolute darkness toward the sandbags.

Hank shrugged, looking Oriental in his black pajamas.

"Even the night has stars. And a moon, though of varying brightness. Unless there are clouds. And then you believe in demons."

Drew's eyes strained, fighting to admit as much as possible of the pale yellow light on the other side of the hangar. He was amazed at how much better he began to see the sandbags against the wall; his imagination learned to add the dimensions concealed by the shadows.

Hank instructed them on the proper way to hold a throwing knife. For hours, he made them hurl the knives against the sandbags. He made them hurl straight razors, Japanese throwing stars, even sticks, ashtrays, and rocks.

The exercise didn't seem to be a rehearsal for killing, though often Drew felt confident that his opponent would have been felled by the deep blow of his knife. Rather, as Hank clapped his hands, the purpose seemed to be the speed with which they hurled the object on command and the accuracy with which the object struck.

"Because you can't know in the dark if your target's dead," Hank barked. "The instant you hear your weapon hit, you've got to assume your enemy's been distracted and—"

But the "and" was apparently for the next day—or night, given the reversal of their normal schedule—because Hank interrupted himself to correct the throwing stance of one student.

He made them turn their backs to the sandbags. Now, when he clapped his hands, the group had to pivot in order to throw.

He shouted commands about their balance, the need to keep their feet spread—not too much, just the width of the hips. And to keep their legs bent, so their knees—in that flexible position—could act as a better pivoting mechanism. They learned to hunch slightly forward, so their hips could help the body twist better.

Often the sharp objects they threw at the sandbags fell clattering to the concrete floor.

That too had its value, Hank insisted. "Because you can't allow yourself to pay attention to any noise you can anticipate. By the end of your stay here, I plan to make you familiar with the sound of any weapon you can imagine as it falls on any surface you can imagine. Not just this concrete floor. But sand and carpet and grass and shale."

Drew crawled exhausted into his bunk that morning, seeing the glow of the rising sun creep through the cracks in the hangar's metal walls.

But the difference in time didn't matter, he thought, as Hank turned off the pale yellow light and Drew snuggled naked between the dark sheets, beneath the dark blanket. What mattered was sleep. In his dreams, he threw Coca-Cola cans at sandbags.

The next night, Hank continued the throwing exercises. They became so repetitious that Drew no longer flinched from the sound of the various objects as they fell on the floor in the darkness.

In nights to come, Hank added refinements. The students now had to lunge at their target, holding a felt-tipped pen as if it were a knife, attacking the sandbag in the shadows and slashing upward.

After each assault, Hank would inspect the sandbag, using a shielded penlight, commenting on the accuracy of the thrust. His command was always the same. Use what little light you have, and learn to judge the rest of the target from the part you see.

Next, Hank had the students throwing fragile objects at each other in the almost total dark, then lunging with felt-tipped pens to slash at the opponent's pillow-buffered chest.

And each time, Hank used the shielded penlight to assess the theoretical damage.

Eventually the students weren't allowed the advantage of pillows. If a felt-tipped pen bruised your stomach, well, you should have been more careful. Imagine if the blow had come from a knife.

In these and many similar ways, Hank trained his students to develop reflexes in the dark.

They were taught to move with a knife as if it were an extension of the hand. In turn, to make the hand an extension of the arm. To sweep the arm, to make the hand follow it. And thus the knife to follow the hand. Fluidity.

How to crouch while shifting sideways, never extending the feet beyond the width of the hips. Always slowly, *gradually*, shifting weight. Never to the rear, and never forward. Silently.

They learned the parts of the body: spleen, epiglottis, testicles, sphenoid, maxilla, thyroid, transverse sinus, septum, carotid, humorus, orbital. And lunged through the dark at the sandbags or at each other with felt-tipped pens, and later with the palms of their hands or the tips of their elbows.

As their training became more intense, they had the sense that Hank was preparing them for an ultimate test. Night followed night—how many, it became impossible to know. They couldn't help glancing more often toward the single-story structure that waited for them in the middle of the hangar's darkness.

At last, after they'd successfully demonstrated their skill in stalking an opponent through the darkness across various surfaces that resembled a sand shore, a thick carpet, a slick waxed floor; after they'd learned how to step silently around and over shadowy obstacles with the same grace that they'd developed in their ballet classes back at the school, Hank said, "Okay, it's time. You're ready to find out what's in the compartment."

Eager, they followed him through the shadows to its door. Hank opened it, but neither Drew nor anyone else was able to see inside.

Hank pointed to Jake. "After I go in and shut the door, give me fifteen seconds. Then you come in and shut the door."

Jake hesitated. "And?"

"You never played hide-and-seek? Try to find me. Just one thing, though. I'm supposed to be your enemy. If you give me a chance, if you're not careful and you let me hear you or sense you, well, in real life, I'd be able to kill you. For now, we'll play the game this way—whoever surprises the other first, with a touch, is the winner. Simple enough?"

"Sure."

Hank went inside. Fifteen seconds later, Jake followed, closing the door behind him. In thirty seconds the door opened again, and Jake stepped out. Drew saw the frustration on his face.

"What happened in there?" someone asked.

"I'm not supposed to talk about it. He wants you all to line up, and one by one to go in."

Drew felt uneasy. Standing near the end of the line, he watched each of the others go in. None lasted any longer than Jake had.

Mike took his turn, and he too came out almost at once. Drew sensed his humiliation. Always competitive, Mike seemed to challenge Drew to do any better.

Then it was Drew's turn.

He opened the door, concentrated to heighten his reflexes, stepped inside, and nervously closed the door behind him. Almost at once he felt stifled, as if the air was thicker in there, squeezing him.

And the darkness. He'd thought that the hangar was dark. But now he understood what darkness really was.

In here, it was absolute, compressing him. The silence made his eardrums hiss; he debated what to do. Stepping forward in search of Hank, he bumped against a table. Its legs screeched on the concrete floor, and at once Hank grasped his right elbow.

"You just got killed." Hank whispered so close that his breath tickled Drew's ear.

Leaving the black room, trying not to look embarrassed, Drew noticed Mike's satisfied expression, his delight that Drew had been no more successful than himself.

Hank called the group together and asked them to assess what had happened. He made them repeat the exercise, debriefed them again, and gradually instilled in them the principles of this type of confrontation.

"All of you tried to find me too soon. You didn't let yourselves feel the stillness. Your anxiousness betrayed you. Take your time. It might be the last time you ever have, so why not prolong it? Sense it fully."

Hank taught them patterns with which to search the room instead of merely moving blindly forward. He encouraged them to use the skills which they'd already developed in attacking the sandbags and avoiding obstacles in the hangar.

"But this is different," someone said.

"How?"

"In the hangar, we had plenty of room. And the darkness wasn't total. Besides, you were in there first. You had the advantage of being able to hide."

"Imagine that. And if you're up against an enemy, I suppose you'll complain to him that he isn't playing fair if he too has an advantage. In this game, you have to make your own advantage," Hank said. "By being better than your opponent. The most important thing you have to remember—apart from the pattern I told you to follow once you're in the room—the most important thing is to move so slowly that you're barely moving at all."

They tried the exercise again and yet again, and each time they lasted a little longer before Hank touched them. Five seconds longer perhaps. Then ten. But that slight extension of their endurance was, by comparison, a major accomplishment. And the first time Drew survived for a *minute*, he had the exhausted but giddy sense afterward of having been in the room much longer.

"You're still not moving slowly enough," Hank insisted. "You're still not feeling the dark. Did you ever watch the way a blind man knows an obstacle's in front of him, even if he doesn't have his cane? It's because he's so used to living in the dark that he can feel the air bounce off his surroundings. He can sense things around him, almost as if they give off vibrations. And that's what *you've* got to learn to do. Compensate for your lack of sight by heightening all your other senses. Jake, you moved silently, I have to give you credit. But you're a smoker. I smelled stale cigarettes on you and knew your exact location, even though I couldn't see or hear you. From now on, nobody on this team is allowed to smoke. And I don't mean just while we're here. Ever. Mike, you use deodorant. I smelled you coming too. Get rid of it."

"But we can't help giving off some kind of odor," Mike said. "Sweat, for instance. That's natural under stress."

"No. The kind of stress we're dealing with makes your sweat glands dry up. They stop functioning. Oh, maybe one or two of you aren't typical, and your glands won't quit. We'll soon find out. And you'll be out of the school."

Soon the students were able to survive the exercise for an even longer time. Two minutes lengthened to five. And then to ten.

Drew gradually learned about the objects in the room. Proceeding slowly, methodically, he discovered that the layout resembled that of a living room: chairs, a sofa, a coffee table, a television set, a lamp, a bookshelf. But one night, the furniture had been rearranged, and instead of a concrete floor, there now was a rug. Another night the set-up had been transformed into a bedroom. Yet another night, the room was filled with crates at random, as if in a warehouse.

"You can't assume anything," Hank warned.

At last, each member of the class was able to stalk Hank for an hour without being touched. Then Hank changed the exercise. "From now on you stalk each other. One of you goes in, then someone else goes after you. After that, you'll do it in reverse, the second man going in first, so the hunter becomes the hunted. And you'll keep changing partners. Everybody gets a chance to go against everybody else."

Drew glanced at Mike, who returned his look, clearly anxious for the chance to test his skills against Drew. They weren't paired right away. Only after four other partners did they find themselves in the room together. Drew, the hunted, won the first time. But when Mike became the hunted, he won. And later when they were paired again, their score again was tied. The final time, after they stayed in the room for three hours, neither winning, Hank broke up the game.

14

Now, after sixteen years, they were paired again. But their weapons would not be felt-tipped markers, and Hank wasn't here to stop the exercise. Their rivalry had reached the ultimate. There'd be no question about who was better. And no rematch.

Drew didn't *want* to kill. He had to keep Mike alive, to make him talk about Janus. But his reluctance to kill was a liability. Because Mike for sure wouldn't hesitate.

The instant Drew realized the terrifying implications of this pitch-dark basement room into which Mike had lured him, he automatically bent his knees, assuming the crouch Hank had made second nature for him. He spread his feet apart, the width of his hips, and stretched his arms before him, also spread apart, the width of his shoulders, testing the dark with his hands. He spread his arms farther apart, feeling the emptiness to his right and left. At once, he changed his location, shifting to the left, not far, just a body's width, and stopped.

These initial tactics had one purpose only—to move from where he'd been as he came into the room, lest Mike take advantage of the inadvertent sounds Drew made and attack while he was still unprepared. But now Drew was one with the dark, just as Mike was. The stalk would begin.

Drew was even more sure that Mike had not been carrying a gun; there'd been too many chances for him to use one. Certainly as Drew came into this room, an instant before the door swung shut, cloaking him with total darkness, Mike would have had a reliable target.

Even so, Mike might have a knife. Drew considered that risk and decided that Mike would have thrown it when Drew first entered the room. The moment Mike heard the knife hit Drew, he would have attacked, taking advantage of the blow's distraction to kill Drew with his hands if the knife hadn't done the job. Hank Dalton had drilled that tactic into them. Second nature.

So there had to be a reason for Mike to hang back. The only explanation Drew could think of was that Mike didn't have a weapon, that he was depending on his skill in hand-to-hand combat. Which meant that Mike would wait for Drew to come close and then take him by surprise.

Drew did have a weapon, the Mauser he clutched, but in the dark it was useless—even a liability, because it limited the right hand with which he held it. Under the circumstances, Drew would have preferred to have his right hand nimble, so it could better sense the feel of the stillness, the subtle vibrations of the dark. But he didn't dare risk the sound of putting the gun in his pocket.

He waited, crouching, on guard, for five minutes, listening intensely. This room was apparently so deep within the ground, its walls so thick, that no outside sound intruded. He strained to hear subtle breathing. Or the brush of a footstep. But he heard nothing except the pounding of blood behind his ears.

Inhaling slowly, he assessed the smells in the room, separating and identifying them. A turpentine odor. Paint. Something like varnish. A vague whiff of gasoline.

A storeroom? he wondered. The more he judged the odors, the more his conclusion seemed correct. Maintenance supplies. Maybe even a lawnmower. Maybe tools.

He'd soon find out. Because he had to begin the hunt, just as, he assumed, Mike had started to hunt for him.

"Never head directly into the room," Hank Dalton had insisted. "Avoid the middle. Check the perimeter first. Which means you've got two choices. Right or left. Keep your back against the wall. The layout of the room—its obstacles—will determine which direction seems better."

In the present case, neither right nor left seemed to offer any advantage. True, he'd moved to the left when he entered and recognized the trap. Mike might assume that Drew would continue toward the left. The way to fool him, then, would be to shift in the direction Mike didn't expect, to the right.

But guessing, and second-guessing, and triple-guessing, were part of the hunt. Mike might anticipate Drew's logic. He might assume that Drew, having started toward the left, as a feint, would then switch direction. Eventually, no matter what logic either opponent used, there was no way for one or the other to anticipate in which direction the hunt would begin. To think about it too long would lead to paralysis.

Arbitrarily, Drew decided to keep going left. With agonizing slowness. Shifting his arms, his hands, testing the darkness. Gently moving his feet.

The floor, like the hallway outside, was earth. But at least the dirt was packed solid, absorbing his weight as he slowly eased his foot down. No crunch communicated his position.

He paused again, listened, smelled, sensed. Again he tested the darkness with his hands and slowly crept a few inches farther to his left.

Gingerly moving his feet, he stiffened as the edge of his left shoe touched an object. Almost imperceptible pressure against his left leg and hip warned him that the object was large, but when he moved his left hand in its direction, he felt nothing. Whatever it was, the object rose no higher than his waist. When he lowered his hand to that level, he felt wood, gouged and battered, heavily grained, somewhat oily.

A workbench. Silently exploring with his hand, he felt a metal vice clamped onto the side of the bench. A pockmarked pair of pliers. A gritty oil can with a spout.

From now on, the complications multiplied. For all he knew, Mike was waiting on the other side of the workbench, ready to attack as Drew inched around the bench to return to the wall. Or maybe Mike was directly across from him, against the *opposite* wall, and as soon as he sensed that Drew's attention was fully occupied with the problem of getting around the bench . . .

Second-guessing, triple-checking. As Drew began to ease around the table, he imagined Mike's thoughts.

Hey, Drew, it's just like back in Colorado, when we were rivals. Sure, we looked so much alike everybody wondered which of us was better, didn't they? But we never settled the issue. Not to my satisfaction. Of course, the higher-ups had their own stupid idea that you were better than me. Otherwise, they wouldn't have chosen me to act as a double for you instead of the other way around. You were the star; I was the stand-in. Shit. But I outlasted you. You're supposed to be dead. I got to take your place. I *became* you, and I like it that way just fine. I won't switch places again. I won't go back to being second-best. This time, I plan to make damned sure you *stay* dead.

His muscles aching from tension, Drew inched through the darkness around the bench. But to check out the corner between the bench and the wall, he'd have to leave himself partly vulnerable to an attack from across the pitch-black room. He sharpened his senses, on guard against the slightest sound or shift in the dense, still air.

Subtly, silently, he waved his left hand in front of him, toward the continuation of the wall. He wanted to cause a gentle waft of air that might make Mike think Drew was closer than he was, that might prompt Mike to attack prematurely from the corner of the wall and the bench.

But no attack came, and as Drew eased around the other side of the workbench, coming closer to the wall, he aimed his Mauser toward it. If Mike indeed were hiding there, if he attacked, Drew would shoot as soon as he felt Mike's body.

But nothing happened. And with a mental exhalation of relief, Drew reached the wall, pressing his back against it again. He waited in the darkness, mustering energy, concentrating.

"Discipline," Hank had told them. "Patience. Those are the secrets to winning this game. One thoughtless move. One careless gesture. That's all it takes, and you're dead. You have to ignore the future. You can't let yourself imagine how good it'll feel to win and leave the room and relax. Because *now* is what counts, and if your enemy's concentrating on now while you're in the future, well, pal, you'll never see the future. You'll be history."

Drew continued to shift along the wall to his left. As before, he used his feet, the side of his leg and hip, to test for obstacles. Aiming the Mauser with his right hand, he moved his left hand before him, almost caressing the dark. His silent foot touched an object to his left; indeed, he sensed that the object was there even before his shoe touched it. The object was wood. It projected sixteen inches into the room. He felt it with his left hand. The object rose all the way to the ceiling. And when he eased his fingers around its side, he touched cold circular metal. Paper, wrapped around it, was partly peeled away. Here, the odor of turpentine was stronger. A paint can? Yes, he decided. Ceiling-high shelves of paint cans. Keeping his back against the shelves as if they were the wall, he continued to his left.

He'd progressed no more than ten or twelve feet and had been in here for possibly forty minutes, maybe longer. It was hard to know. In a black room, time was distorted by the agonizing slowness of movement. Every second seemed eternal. Terribly full.

Breath held, he came to the end of the shelves, felt around them toward the wall, but touched another wall instead. It extended to his left. He tested that corner.

With alarming abruptness, something hit the shelves to his right. The object clattered down, thumping onto the floor.

Drew flinched. He couldn't help it. His heart expanding as if it would burst, he fought not to gasp. In fact, he made no sound at all. Instead, as his training spurred him, he crouched reflexively—so low that his hips touched the back of his legs. With his back wedged into the corner, he raised his hands, his Mauser aimed.

The reaction was so instantaneous that even before the object had finished thumping onto the floor he was ready.

Mike might be attacking. That had been one of Hank Dalton's tactics. Startle your opponent. Throw something. The moment it clatters, take the advantage. Go for him.

But as silence again filled the room, as the stillness once more gelled, Drew felt no impact, no body charging into him. He waited, his stomach contracting, his nerves stretched taut.

Nothing happened.

He tried to calculate the direction from which the object had been thrown. Couldn't. But at least he knew that Mike was in here, that his lookalike had not ducked out an unseen exit before Drew entered this room.

Most surely now, this was to the death.

But something else bothered him. Why hadn't Mike attacked? Drew debated, tense, deciding.

Because Mike hasn't figured out where I am. In the dark, if he rushes me but misjudges my location, he knows I can kill him. He threw something toward where he thought I might be and hoped that I'd lose control, that I'd make a sound. But because he missed, he'll throw something else. If he hits me, as soon as he hears the impact against my body, he'll assume I'm distracted, and he'll attack.

Another Hank Dalton strategy.

As Drew crouched with his back to the corner, facing the dark of the room, a second object struck the shelves on his right. The clatter was nearer, sending a vibration against Drew's shoulder.

But this time Drew had expected the noise. He took advantage of the object's fall to shift toward the left along this new wall.

Sure, Mike decided I moved in this direction. He's trying to box me in. The moment he hits me, he'll rush.

A third object whacked against the corner where Drew had been crouching. Again he took advantage of the sound to shift a little farther along this new wall.

And now he had more information. The deflecting angle of the various objects, the direction of their sound when they hit the earthen floor, told him that Mike was on the far side of the room, probably in the corner opposite to the one in which he himself had just been crouching.

Or at least Mike had probably been there a moment ago.

For all Drew could tell, his double had taken advantage of the clatter to shift position as Drew had.

In which direction would Mike have shifted, though? Toward the wall Drew was following—to meet Drew head on? Or toward the wall Drew first had crept along—to come at him from behind?

Drew wondered if he should reverse his direction. A flip of a coin. A fifty-fifty chance. They could go on like this, double- and triple-guessing, all night. He imagined them circling the room forever.

A fourth object clattered. But this time, it rebounded off the wall Drew first had crept along, thumping onto the floor.

Does Mike think I've doubled back? Or is he trying to trick me into thinking that's what *he* thinks?

As Hank Dalton had repeatedly stressed, that was the point of the exercise. To confuse your opponent until his mind was tired, off-balance.

And then to kill him.

"The rules. Trust them. Depend on them," Hank had demanded. "It took me almost twenty-five years to discover them. And they're one reason I'm still alive."

But as Hank had pointed out, few other warriors knew those rules. In actual combat, one of Hank's students shouldn't need to exhaust himself, stalking an opponent. Because Hank's system of fighting in the dark wasn't standard training anywhere else. "Remember," he'd said, "you've got the advantage. Don't be overconfident. But don't feel overwhelmed. Because, if you follow the rules, you've got a better-than-even chance of winning."

Sure, Drew thought. Just follow the rules. But listen, Hank, tell me this. What do you do when your opponent also knows the rules? Back in Colorado, I had an awful lot of stalemates with him. He not only looks like me. He's been *trained* like me. What's to prevent another stalemate? Except that this time the stalemate must be broken. And exhaustion will probably do it. Since the monastery, I've been running too long. If stamina's the deciding factor, I'll probably lose.

He didn't panic. Instead, as his spine tingled, he had a sudden inspiration. What do you do when you're up against someone who also knows the rules?

Do the completely unexpected. *Break* the rules. Go back to the way you behaved when you first entered that black room in the hangar in Colorado. Circle the room, follow its walls, the way Hank insisted? No. Go straight across. Crouch in the middle and wait for Mike to throw again.

And then, when you sense exactly where he is, go after him.

His shoes seemed not to touch the earthen floor as he crept silently toward the middle of the room. He maintained his slow careful pace, shifting his left hand before him while he aimed the Mauser with his right, testing the dark.

And when he judged that he'd reached the middle of the room, he hunkered down, resting as comfortably as possible on his haunches while he waited for Mike's next move.

He felt the shift of air from the object as it hurtled past him, only inches above his head, cracking against the wall he'd been following. There. In the opposite corner. Drew inched closer.

Another object whipped air past his head, whacking the wall behind him.

Drew inched even closer.

It happened with startling suddenness. Drew sensed an obstacle abruptly in front of him. He didn't touch it. No, as Hank Dalton had insisted, he didn't need to touch it. If he was alert enough, he'd actually be able to feel the vibrations coming off it.

The obstacle was a man.

Mike, who looked like Drew, who'd been trained the same

as Drew, also *thought* like Drew. Mike, as well, had debated how to stalk an opponent who had the same advantage of Hank Dalton's training, who could anticipate.

Because of the rules. So break the rules.

And with unexpected abruptness, Drew found himself grappling chest-to-chest, face-to-face, with his double.

The shock was sickening. As they stumbled one way, then the other, Drew no longer feared making noise. Instead, he breathed stridently, desperately needing oxygen, pushing, straining against the man he held and who held him.

He groaned from a knee that struck his thigh, barely missing his testicles.

He winced as he lurched back against the sharp edge of the workbench, hitting his kidneys.

"Mike . . ."

He rammed the heel of his left palm into his attacker's solar plexus.

Mike groaned.

"For God's sake, listen . . ."

Drew gasped from a crushing blow to the side of his neck.

"We have to talk!"

But when the blunt edge of a screwdriver tore—shockingly, oh, blessed Jesus—into Drew's left shoulder, his coat buffering the damage, he understood that Mike was determined to win.

What choice did Drew have?

He shoved Mike away and squeezed his finger on the Mauser's trigger.

Shot.

And shot.

He emptied the magazine, his ears stunned by the repeated blasts, his eyes offended by the muzzle flashes.

Yet despite the various injuries to his body, he spread his bullets skillfully. And when he heard a bullet hit home, he narrowed his aim, his nostrils flaring from the acrid stench of gunpowder and flashburns, scorched fabric and flesh.

He blew his lookalike to Hell.

As blood pelted onto the earthen floor, as it splattered warm and salty across his lips, he felt Mike lunge against him once more, still determined to keep up the battle. But Mike shuddered in death. The two men embraced each other, almost as lovers.

Mike sank toward the floor, his flaccid jaw sagging past Drew's chest, stomach, groin, and knees.

"Why didn't you listen?" Drew whispered, though he wanted to shriek. Damnable discipline kept him in control. "*You should have listened*. All you had to do was tell me who you were working for. You stupid . . . You'd still be alive. Maybe finally, we could have been friends instead of . . ."

Rivals? Doubles?

Janus. He'd killed Janus, but the man behind Janus was still alive!

Enraged at the pointlessness of the death, Drew wanted to kick Mike's corpse, to smash its teeth, to crush its nose.

You stupid . . .

Instead he sank to his knees in the dark.

With tears streaking down his cheeks, he prayed for Mike's soul.

And his own.

15

Time had been so distorted in the black room that, when Drew left the building, he blinked in surprise. The night had passed. A cold October sun was rising. Now, all the gaslamps were extinguished, the apartments silent, though chickens clucked eerily from somewhere. Obviously the people who lived here had not heard the shots or else had deliberately ignored them, not wanting to get involved. He followed the zigzagging hallways, passages, and tunnels back to the narrow alley with a cinderblock wall on the right, where an eternity ago he'd stepped from the stack of sheltering boards and confronted his double.

He'd used a handkerchief to wipe Mike's blood from his face and hands. He'd used the same handkerchief to staunch the flow of blood from his shoulder where Mike had struck it with a screwdriver. Then he'd taken off his coat and carried it folded across his shoulder to hide both the wound and the bloodstains on the coat. The precaution was needless. This early, he encountered no one.

Cold, his shoulder throbbing, sick at heart, he used a key that he'd taken from Mike as he searched the body, and unlocked the door to Mike's room. He had no fear of booby-traps or anti-intruder alarms. Earlier, Mike had taken no precautions as he pulled out this same key and aimed it toward the lock. So Drew's assumption was that the apartment was unprotected. And if it wasn't?

Drained, he didn't care. He had killed again, and nothing else mattered.

Nothing. Except the continuation of his quest. The need to avenge the monks in the monastery. To discover who Mike had been working for.

He turned the knob and opened the door, frowning when he saw no light in the room. His instincts quickened in alarm. Last night, there'd been a glow beyond the closed drapes and the opaque window. Who'd been in here to turn off the light? As his chest tightened, he scanned the room. Even with the light off, it wasn't pitch-dark. The rising sun illuminated the open doorway, dispersing the shadows.

Despite his uneasiness, he made two assumptions. The first was that the room was deserted. After all, anyone hiding here had already been given ample opportunity to attack him.

The second was the consequence of the first. The lights were off because, as Arlene had suspected last night, they were on a timer.

Stepping farther in, he saw brick-and-board bookshelves, a desk with a typewriter, a sofa-bed, a dinette table, a television and stereo.

Nothing fancy. The furnishings a graduate student would have. The same sort of furnishings Drew had once had, though he—like Mike—could have afforded much better.

The apartment was all in one room; a stove and fridge were set off by a counter.

Something moved near the sofa. Drew bent his knees, raising his hands, preparing to defend himself. Then his scowl changed into a grin, which broadened as he remembered Stuart Little. For now he was crouched defensively against a cat.

It meowed, approaching. Not a kitten, but not full-grown either. Orange with white spots. Another cat appeared from beneath the desk, and another from behind the counter, one totally black, the other a Siamese, its blue eyes distinctive even in the shadows.

He almost laughed but stopped himself, his injured shoulder throbbing, again reminded of the parallel between Mike and himself.

In the old days, before the monastery, Drew had enjoyed keeping cats. They'd been his luxury; his social life. And later, when not a cat but a mouse had entered his cell in the monastery, he'd once again felt alive. Because, despite the Carthusian insistence on effacing oneself from the world, the one thing he'd missed was the chance to share his existence with another creature.

"Cats, I bet you wonder why no one came home last night," he said, with a sudden vision of Mike dead in that black room. Shuddering, he tried to stifle his terrible emotion. His voice sounded hoarse. "I bet you're awful hungry."

He closed the door behind him, locked it, noticed a murky light switch on the wall, and flicked it up.

Two lamps came on, one beside the sofa, the other on the desk. He flinched, stumbling back. A door came open to his left. And across from him, a figure rose from behind the counter. He braced himself.

Father Stanislaw appeared from the door. Beyond it, Drew saw a closet. He swung toward the counter where Arlene stood all the way up.

She came to him. He wanted desperately to hold her.

"Thank God, you're alive." She hugged him longingly. "When you didn't come back to the car . . ."

He felt her arms around him, her breasts pressed against his chest. Reflexively, he leaned to kiss her.

Father Stanislaw cleared his throat. "If I can interrupt."

Drew glanced at him in confusion.

"We waited till just before dawn," Father Stanislaw said.

Arlene stepped back slightly, still keeping her arms around him. But Drew's chest retained the sensation of her breasts. He remembered the way he'd held her, lovingly, so often in the old days. To camp and go climbing. And hold her, as she held him, in the sleeping bag they shared.

"By then, we didn't know what else to do," she added. "We *had* to come in and find you."

"From the outside, the apartment was quiet." Father Stanislaw stepped closer. "Everything seemed peaceful. But we reasoned that, if there'd been trouble, your counterpart would have fled instead of staying here. The risk seemed acceptable. But we even knocked on the door before . . ."

"You picked the lock?"

Arlene still had her arms around him as he glanced toward the priest. Seeing a nod, Drew shook his head. "You keep surprising me."

"Well"—Father Stanislaw shrugged—"the Lord is with me."

"And with your lockpicks."

The priest grinned.

"When you stepped through that door," Arlene said, "I almost thought you were . . ."

"My double?"

"You were carrying your coat instead of wearing it. For a moment, I thought he'd taken it off you."

"No." Drew swallowed. "He's dead." He slid his coat off his shoulder, revealing his bloody shirt and the bulge beneath it where he'd stuffed the handkerchief.

"Drew!"

"He stabbed me with a screwdriver. My coat helped to ease the blow."

Before he could argue with her, Arlene had unbuttoned his shirt. The intimacy made him feel weak. Gently, she took out the bloody handkerchief, peering beneath the torn cloth.

"It could have been worse," Drew said. "At least, the bleeding stopped. I don't think it needs stitches."

"But it sure needs disinfecting. Take off your shirt. I'll get a washcloth and soapy water."

"It can wait."

"No, it can't." Again he didn't have the chance to argue. *"Hold still."*

It made him feel oddly good to accept her orders. While she cleaned the wound, using a first-aid kit from the bathroom to dress it, he told them what had happened.

Father Stanislaw raised his right hand and gave Drew absolution. "I'm sure you're forgiven. You had to defend yourself."

"But his death was so pointless." Drew's throat constricted, only partly because of the swelling from the fist Mike had struck against it. "What did it accomplish?"

"Your life," Arlene insisted.

"Insignificant. The answers. *They* were what mattered."

"We've been looking for them," she said.

He listened intently.

"We went through his papers. Receipts. Canceled checks. Bills."

"What did you find?"

"Exactly what you'd expect," Father Stanislaw said. "The man was a professional. Nothing."

"Nothing?" Drew thought about it. "Maybe. At least, that's how it seemed."

"I don't understand."

"From what you just said, you saw it, all right. But you didn't know what you were seeing. What to look for."

"I still don't know what you mean."

"Receipts, you said? Canceled checks, bills?"

"That's right."

Drew glanced tenderly toward Arlene. "You couldn't have understood. Because you"—he turned toward Father Stanislaw—"and *you* didn't have my cover. The way the system worked, I used a post office box for my mail. Anonymous. As long as I made sure I wasn't being watched when I picked up my magazines, tuition bills, whatever. But I had another post office box in the nearest town. And *that* was where I picked up the stuff that mattered . . . Like my pay."

He let it sink in.

"Of course." Arlene got it first. "Scalpel was part of the government."

"A buried branch of it. The government itself never knew what was going on."

"But records had to be kept," she said. "And payrolls justified. Because the network had a budget, no matter how buried. The ledger had to be balanced."

Father Stanislaw understood now. "The same way the CIA or any other intelligence network has to keep accounts. But not directly. Its budget might be channeled through the Department of Agriculture or the Interior."

"However it's channeled, the money has to come from somewhere," Drew said. "If the funds belong to the system, there's a paper trail. There has to be."

"But if Scalpel's defunct"—puzzled, Arlene glanced from Drew to the priest—"if the network was canceled but someone reactivated it, someone not in the government, then the money comes from the private sector."

"All the more reason to need ledgers, explanations for where the money went," Drew said. "The IRS is ruthless. It demands an accounting."

"So?"

"We follow the paper trail," Drew said. "Canceled checks. You told me you'd found them. What's the name of the local bank? And"—Drew turned toward Father Stanislaw—"who's the most powerful Opus Dei contact here? The one in banking and business?"

"Ah," the priest said, understanding.

"Yes," Drew told him.

Father Stanislaw glanced at his watch. "It's only seven in the morning. We'll have to wait till—"

"Fine," Drew said. "I've got something almost as important to keep me busy."

16

He found an opener in a drawer beside the sink and took the lids off every container of cat food in the apartment. Ten, all told. Some were chicken, others liver and fish, and one, Gourmet Delight, seemed to be a combination of everything.

He found two bags of dry food underneath the sink and opened them as well, then carried all of it to the alley outside and in the cold morning air spread the goodies along the cinderblock wall.

The cats ate voraciously.

"Enjoy," he said. "That's all there is. There won't be any more."

He felt an ache in his chest.

Because your master's dead. I killed him.

17

At five after nine, as Drew and Arlene watched, Father Stanislaw used the phone in the apartment to reach his contact. He explained what he needed, hung up, and ten minutes later received a call from someone else.

Again he listened. He nodded and thanked whoever was calling. At once, he phoned someone else, received more information, and called yet another number.

The process took fifty minutes. And when for the final time he set down the phone, he leaned back exhausted on the sofa.

"Well?" Drew asked.

"When you cash a check, the bank keeps microfilm records of the transaction. Mike's inheritance—sometimes it's called a scholarship; never mind, let's say his checks—came from the Fairgate Institute. So what's the Fairgate Institute? I charged long distance to this number. I didn't think the occupant would mind. According to my contacts in New York and Washington, the Fairgate Institute is part of the Golden Ring Foundation. A non-profit help-to-the-needy, et cetera, et cetera. And the Golden Ring Foundation . . . remember the IRS insists on these records . . . God bless bureaucracy . . . the Golden Ring Foundation is part of . . . well, the bottom line is, when layer after layer is peeled away, the Risk Analysis Corporation. In Boston."

Drew shook his head. "Am I supposed to make a connection?"

"No. At least, not on the face of it. You won't like this," Father Stanislaw said. "My contact in Boston found out the name of the man who runs this Risk Analysis Corporation."

"And I know him?"

"Oh, indeed," Father Stanislaw said. "The coincidence is too shocking to be dismissed. I think it proves that Risk Analysis is Scalpel, and that this man ran it as well."

"*Who?*"

When Father Stanislaw told him, Drew ignored everything—Arlene's hand on his shoulder, the meow of the cats outside, the memory of Mike's blood dribbling salty past his lips.

The name.

Oh, yes, the name.

It and nothing else mattered.

His world came together.

The name was the secret to his life.

PART EIGHT

JUDGMENT

THE FRATERNITY OF THE STONE

✣

1

The woman's voice was prim, professional, precise. "Good morning. Risk Analysis Corporation."

In a phone booth on Boylston Street, just down from Boston's public library, Drew managed to subdue his anger, to force himself to sound equally businesslike. "Mr. Rutherford, please."

"I'm sorry. He's in a meeting right now. But if you'd care to speak to his executive assistant."

"No. It has to be Mr. Rutherford. I can't do business with anyone else." Drew let her think about it. The phone booth muffled the roar of 10 A.M. traffic.

"Of course," the receptionist said. "I understand. In that case, why don't you give me your name and phone number? Mr. Rutherford will . . ."

"I'm afraid that isn't possible. My schedule's rather uncertain at the moment, and I'm not sure where I'll be. It's better if I call him."

As he expected, the receptionist for the Risk Analysis Corporation didn't think his evasion was unusual. Her voice became more alert. "By all means. If you have the chance, phone back at eleven-fifteen. He should be available then."

"I hope so."

"And your name?"

He gave her credit for trying again. "Just tell him the matter's urgent."

He hung up. Outside the phone booth, he stared at the clear cold October sky, then lowered his gaze toward the traffic on Boylston Street.

His eyes narrowed. Soon now, he thought. He shoved his hands in his new coat and started down the street. Yes, everything was coming together. He felt it. In his soul. Even his return to this city seemed appropriate. Boston, the graves of his parents, the start of everything. And now the end. Soon. Very soon.

Yesterday, he, Arlene, and Father Stanislaw had driven here from Pennsylvania, each taking a turn at the wheel while the others had a chance to sleep. Or in Drew's case, *tried* to sleep. His throbbing shoulder, his troubling thoughts, had kept him awake. When the others had been alert, he'd explained what he wanted to do. His plan had made them uneasy.

A minute ago, he'd told the receptionist, "My schedule's uncertain. I'm not sure where I'll be." He'd lied. His schedule was quite precise. And so were those of Arlene and Father Stanislaw. As he'd instructed, at this moment Arlene would be approaching an office building across the Charles River in Cambridge. Father Stanislaw would be leaving the northern limits of the city, about to reconnoiter a mansion on the Bay. Yes, soon. His anger accumulating, Drew stalked down Boylston Street. It would all come together soon.

2

Intelligence officials seldom leave their profession willingly. True, a few become disillusioned and walk away, but most are forced to retire or asked to resign. Outside their network, they feel lost. Addicted to secrets and the intrigue of high-risk gambles, they look for ways to satisfy their craving. Their choices, as a rule, come down to three.

First, to accept an offer from an international corporation anxious to have an intelligence expert on its board of directors. Such an expert, the corporation feels, can be of critical value in solving business crises that occur in troublesome, but lucrative, countries. This tactic was especially useful, for example, when in the early seventies Salvador Allende, the Marxist president of Chile, attempted to nationalize American business holdings there. Dissidents, rumored to be funded by American corporations with advice from former CIA officials, began a coup. Allende eventually "committed suicide."

The second option is to accept an offer from a war-games think-tank, where a top intelligence officer's knowledge of global intrigue adds data to the computer's calculations of which major power, under which circumstances, will use which tactic to blow the others to hell.

The third option is to refuse such offers and go into business for oneself. Specifically, to organize a company in which the former intelligence official creates a network of his own. But this time, the network isn't affiliated with his government. It belongs in the private sector, and its purpose—like the former intelligence official's on the board of directors for an international corporation—is to advise major companies, to encourage or else to warn them about the ever-shifting global situation. Should a company drill a testwell for oil in X? Or build a smelter for copper in Y? A factory for potash in Z? Will anti-American factions sabotage those operations? What about the banana pickers here, the dockworkers there? Do they plan to go on strike? Is there any basis to rumors about a coup? What about the bad health of this bought-off dictator? How long will he last? Who's likely to take his place?

The private intelligence network, extremely lucrative,

funded by global companies, even foreign nations, was typi-
fied by the Risk Analysis Corporation.

Here in Boston. Owned by Mr. Rutherford, though Drew
had called him by another name.

Again he thought of Janus.

3

"Mr. Rutherford, please."
At 11:15, as instructed, Drew clutched the phone
in another booth, this one on Falmouth Street, down from the
Prudential Center. He imagined what Arlene and Father
Stanislaw were doing—at the office building in Cambridge, at
the estate on Massachusetts Bay.

Yes, soon now, he thought, and waited.

The receptionist spoke. "Sir, are you the same party who
called at ten?"

"That's right. To discuss an urgent matter."

"One moment, please. Mr. Rutherford's been waiting for
you to phone back. I'll put him on the line."

Drew heard a click.

"Yes? Hello?"

The resonant voice was so familiar, so friendly, so formerly
reassuring, that Drew's stomach dropped, making him sick.

"This is Mr. Rutherford."

Drew had to muster all his discipline, to force himself to
sound equally friendly. "Long time no see. How are you?"

"What? Excuse me? I'm not sure who this is."

"Come on. You don't mean to tell me you don't recognize
my voice?"

"No. That is, not exactly."

"I'm really disappointed. A long-lost relative, and . . ."

"Long-lost . . . ?"

"How are you, Uncle? It's good to talk to you again."

"Uncle?" The voice sounded more and more puzzled. "I don't have any nephews."

"Well, that's true, I'm not exactly your nephew. I mean, we're not related by blood. But I think of you as a relative. And that's what I used to call you. Uncle Ray."

The man on the other end breathed sharply. "My God, it's . . . No, it can't be. Drew? Is this *Drew*?"

"Yep, me. None other. The one and only."

Ray burst out laughing. "I can't believe it! Drew! Why didn't you tell me right away?"

"A practical joke." Drew chuckled. "I just felt like putting you on. Remember how you rescued me from my *real* uncle and his family? How you took me to Hong Kong?"

"Remember? Christ, sport, how could I ever forget?" Ray laughed again. "But it's been *years* since we talked. What happened to you? Where have you been keeping yourself?"

"Well, that's the problem."

"What?"

"It's the reason I'm calling." Drew swallowed hard.

"Go on. Say it, Drew. What's the matter? Is something wrong?"

"I really hate to get you involved in this, but I don't know who else to ask. Uncle Ray, I'm in trouble. I need your help."

"Trouble?"

"The worst. Some people are trying to kill me."

"Wait a second. You'd better not say any more. I'm using one of our open phones. We get tapped a lot, and if this is as serious as you believe, we don't want to take any chances. I'll switch to a phone that's secure."

"Good idea. I'll call you right back. Hold on. I'll get out my pen and pad. What's the number?"

"It's . . ." Ray started to dictate the number and stopped.

"No, that won't work. It's better if I call you. I've got a client coming in at eleven-thirty. I can't put him off. But I'll deal with him fast. Half an hour, and I'll get back to you."

"Noon?"

"Even earlier if I can. Stay close to your phone. What's the number?"

Drew told him.

"Fine. Now just relax. I'll call as soon as I can. But, sport, you shouldn't have worried about asking me to get involved. Believe me, I'm glad to help."

Drew swallowed again. "I knew I could count on you."

"Well, I'm your uncle, aren't I?"

"Hey, you bet."

"Don't worry."

"Uncle Ray, I mean it. Thanks."

"Come on, we go back a long way. You don't need to thank me."

4

From his hidden vantage point near the Prudential Center, Drew studied a pizza store down the street, and the phone booth outside, the phone whose number Drew had given to Uncle Ray.

At ten to twelve, amid the chaos of traffic and the swarm of pedestrians, he spotted the surveillance teams. As he'd anticipated, he didn't have any difficulty. Just before noon, with everybody in a rush, those who weren't hurrying were bound to attract attention. It wasn't their fault. To watch the phone booth, they had no choice except to stay motionless. After all, they'd been given short notice. There wasn't time for anything skillfully complicated. A woman on one corner glanced too often down the street toward the booth. A man on the opposite corner kept peering down at his watch as if a friend was late to meet him, but the phone booth was apparently more important to him than his friend or his watch. A taxi, double-parked, waited for a never-arriving fare. A van with several antennas circled the block. A pizza delivery boy didn't seem to care that his boxes were getting cold.

No doubt there were more. Drew had to give them points for mobilizing this well in such a hurry. But not well enough.

The message was obvious. The surveillance team was waiting for Drew to appear from his hiding place at noon and answer his "uncle's" call. After that, Drew thought, the team would converge while I was distracted by Uncle Ray on the phone. I'd be killed on the street.

Or better, from a tradecraft point of view, I'd be dragged inside the van and killed out of sight by the kid with the pizzas. At night, a fishing boat would take me far out into the Bay.

Drew clenched his fists as he left his hidden vantage point beside the Prudential Center, heading west on Belvidere Street, away from the pizza store.

5

"Mr. Rutherford, please." Despite his disciplined, calm tone, Drew shook from the rage in his chest.

"I'm terribly sorry," the receptionist said. "Mr. Rutherford isn't . . ."

"No, listen carefully. I called at ten. And again at eleven-fifteen. Believe me, Mr. Rutherford wants to talk to me again. Just tell him I asked for Uncle Ray."

The receptionist paused. "I must have been mistaken. Mr. Rutherford *is* available."

Almost at once, the familiar reassuring voice was on the

line. "Drew, where the hell *are* you? I called the number you gave me, but no one answered. I got worried! Did something happen?"

"You could say that. Imagine my surprise when a hit team showed up."

"A *hit* team? How—?"

"Because you traced the location of the number I gave you. Look, Ray, I'll save us a lot of time. When everything started to point in your direction, I told myself, 'It can't be Ray. He's my friend. I lived with him from the time I was ten till I was seventeen. He took me in when no one else really wanted me.' You took me in, all right."

"I don't know what you're talking about. I've always felt close to you."

"Save it. I'm not impressed. So I figured I'd better not jump to conclusions. But I didn't want to be stupid, either. I decided to test you. A phone call; a plea for help to someone I'd once depended on. A chance for you to prove your loyalty. And Uncle Ray, guess what? You failed."

"Now wait a minute."

"No. *You* wait. You've had your chance. I want an explanation. For Christ's sake, *why?* I know you used what happened to my parents to recruit me for Scalpel."

"Drew, stop. Don't say any more!"

But furious, Drew kept on. "At the time, that was what I wanted, though. A chance to get even for what happened to my parents. I can almost forgive you. But why did you hit the monastery?"

"I told you to stop! We're still on an unsecured phone! I can't discuss it on . . ."

"Okay, I'll call you back, and then, by God, you'd better have a phone that's safe. Give me the number."

Ray did. Drew made him repeat it, writing it down.

"There's just one other thing," Drew said. "After you hang

up, I want you to leave your office, go past the receptionist, and look in the hall."

"What will *that* prove?"

"You'll understand. After you've looked in the hall, I think you ought to phone home. The mansion north of the city? The estate by the Bay?"

"How did you know about that?"

"I've got contacts, too. Just do what I told you. I know you're trying to trace this call, so I'll hang up now. I'll phone back in fifteen minutes. On another line."

"No, wait!"

Drew broke the connection. He made another call, this one to Arlene, who was at a phone booth across the Charles River in Cambridge. The phone booth was near an office building, the fifth floor of which was rented in part by the Risk Analysis Corporation.

Early that morning, Father Stanislaw had driven Drew and Arlene past the building. They'd chosen the phone booth and written down its number. Since 10 A.M., Arlene had been waiting there for Drew to report to her. He'd done so periodically, and now, as before, she answered quickly.

"Is everything ready?"

"No problem," she said.

"Then press the button."

He left the phone booth. Heading north toward Commonwealth Avenue, he smiled with angry satisfaction, imagining what was now taking place. The button he'd told Arlene to press was on a radio transmitter that sent a signal to a detonator in a shopping bag she'd left in the fifth-floor hall of the office building, outside the suite rented by the Risk Analysis Corporation.

Uncle Ray—curious why Drew had told him to look outside in the hall—should have seen the bag by now. With luck, he would even see it explode.

But the blast would be small. Drew didn't want people hurt, though they'd certainly be alarmed and inconvenienced. The minuscule blast would fill the hallway with smoke, and the smoke would have such a horrible odor that the entire floor, perhaps the entire building, would need to be evacuated.

To add to the confusion, Arlene would by now have phoned the fire department, the police, the 911 line, the bomb squad. The street outside the building would soon be in chaos as police cars and fire engines converged, lights flashing, sirens wailing; they'd snarl traffic during rush hour. Drew's satisfaction swelled. It would be a mess, all right. A wonderful mess.

But there was more. As soon as Arlene completed her calls to the authorities, she'd make yet another—this one to Father Stanislaw, who'd earlier checked in by phone with her, just as Drew had been doing, and who had told her the number where he could be reached. In the village near Uncle Ray's country estate.

6

Halfway through the first ring, Ray picked up the phone. "You son of a bitch! What the hell do you think you're doing?"

"Watch your temper."

"Temper? I'm just getting started! For Christ's sake, the stench of that smoke, I swear to God it's in the walls—in the carpet, the *furniture*! I'll never get rid of it. I might have to move the fucking office!"

"Such language. Did you call home?"

"That's something else, you bastard! Somebody set a bomb off in my front yard! I don't mean a stink bomb like the one in the hall. I mean a *bomb*!"

"It must have been local vandals," Drew said, his heart cold.

"Local, my ass! Just what do you think you're—?"

"Uncle Ray, don't disappoint me. I thought the message was perfectly clear. I'm angry. You betrayed me. Not just with that hit team you sent. I sort of expected that. But you used me from the start. You took advantage of what happened to my parents to recruit me for Scalpel. The thing is, I guess it slipped your mind at the time, huh? You forgot to tell me that you organized Scalpel, that you were in charge of it."

"I won't apologize. I *loved* your parents. Your father was the closest friend I had! You and I, both of us wanted revenge."

"But you reached too far. You weren't satisfied with fighting back at mercenaries and terrorists."

"The same type of scum who killed your parents. Remember that!"

"I never disagreed. I did my share of killing. For the sake of my parents. But you weren't satisfied with exterminating rabid dogs. You had to start predicting the future, judging which leaders fit your standards. In Iran, the Shah had his terror squads and his torture chambers. But you didn't hit him. Instead, you had to try to assassinate the man who replaced him."

"The Ayatollah's insane."

"In hindsight. But you didn't know that at the time. You were playing God. The trouble is, I screwed up the hit. *And so did you.* Because you made the mistake of sending me to kill that American family first, that oil executive who was trying to grease the wheels with the Ayatollah. I have to give you credit. The alibi for Scalpel would have been perfect. After the Ayatollah was killed in the same way that American family was—after a nonexistent radical sect of Iranians claimed both hits—no one would have suspected that an American network was actually responsible. Brilliant in its own twisted way. But you screwed it up. You should have sent someone else to do the

job. When I saw the parents I'd killed, and the boy who survived like me, who now has to suffer the nightmares I did . . ."

"You're not making sense!"

"*Perfect* sense. I'd turned into the maniacs I was hunting.
Worse, I'd got religion. I wasn't dependable any longer. I
might have even talked about Scalpel. So I had to be termi-
nated. To protect your glorious plan."

"Drew, listen, you've got it wrong. This is all a misunderstanding."

"You bet it is. And you're the one who doesn't understand!"
Drew fought to get control of himself.

"Believe me, Drew, you don't realize how important—"

"You're right. I *don't* realize. After you thought I was dead,
why did you use my double to pretend he was me? Why did
you create Janus to attack the Church?"

Uncle Ray didn't answer.

"I asked you a question!" Drew screamed.

"No." Ray swallowed. "Even on a safe phone, I won't answer that."

"Oh, you will." Drew raged. "Believe me. That stink bomb
at your office . . . The explosion at your home. You wondered
why? *To get your attention.* Because the shopping bag in the
hall outside your office could have been a *real* bomb. It could
have blown you and your staff to hell. And the explosion at
your home? It could have been bigger. It could have blasted
your whole damned mansion apart—when *you* were in it!
Next time, maybe that'll happen. Count your blessings. Count
the seconds. I'm about to give you a taste of your enemy, Uncle
Ray. You're about to get a crash course in terrorism. From the
victim's side."

"No, listen!"

"I'll be in touch."

7

Arlene was puzzled. "But . . ."

"What's wrong?" Drew asked. "What is it?"

Father Stanislaw waited, curious.

They'd rendezvoused across from Boston Common at the Park Street Church; from there, they'd driven to Beacon Hill, where they sat now at a gleaming glass-and-metal kitchen table in an oak-paneled townhouse. One of Father Stanislaw's Opus Dei contacts had arranged to have it lent to them for the next few days.

"I don't understand," Arlene said. "If you told Ray you planned to blow up his home and his office, he'll have them guarded. He'll stay away from them."

Drew nodded. "That would be my guess."

"But doesn't that make it harder for us?"

"Maybe easier." Drew shrugged. "I hope. What I'm trying to do is skip a few steps. We knew from the start that we couldn't just make a grab for him. Since the monastery, he's been hunting me. He'd be a fool if he hadn't increased protection around himself, in case I figured out who was after me and decided to start hunting *him*. Believe me, I know him well. He isn't stupid."

"All right." Arlene raised her hands. "I see that. I agree. As soon as we tried to grab him, we'd have been killed. But why did you warn him there'd be other bombs?"

"I want to weaken his defenses, to surround him with distractions. The guards he orders to watch his home and his office will mean he has less guards to protect himself. You're right. He'll be so nervous he'll stay away from those places. But that's to the good. We've restricted his movements. We've gained the same effect as if we did blow them up. What I want to do now is escalate our attacks. Make each one more serious than the last. Strike where we're least expected. Do it more often. Use the basic principles of terrorism."

"But *why*?" She seemed distressed by his evident joy in terrorizing Ray.

He avoided her searching eyes. "I'm not sure what you mean."

"But I do," Father Stanislaw said. "I think she wants to know where all of this is leading. Is your ultimate purpose to kill him?"

Drew tensed, evading the question. "We have to get our hands on him. We need more answers."

"To learn about Jake. To find out what happened to him," Arlene said quickly.

"But in the end?" Father Stanislaw asked.

They stared at Drew.

"In honesty?" the priest asked.

They waited.

Drew sighed. "I wish I knew." He frowned at his grim reflection off the shiny glass table. "For so many years, I fought back at substitutes for the bastards who killed my parents. I let them know how terror feels on the receiving end. But then I walked away in disgust. I made a sacred vow that I was through. And now, here I am, right back doing it again. The truth? I hate to admit this. Today, it felt as good as it used to." Drew stared toward Father Stanislaw. His eyes felt hot and moist.

"Even God gets angry sometimes," the priest said. "If the cause is just. And make no mistake, *this* cause—to protect the Church, to stop the attacks against it, to find out what happened to Jake—this cause is just. God will forgive your righteous anger."

"But will I forgive myself?"

The phone rang, startling them. As Drew and Arlene

glanced uneasily at one another, Father Stanislaw crossed the kitchen toward the phone on an oaken wall. "Hello?" He listened. "And with your spirit. *Deo gratias.*" He reached for a pad and pencil. "Good." He finished writing. "Your Church is pleased."

Hanging up, he turned toward Drew and Arlene. "My contacts apparently aren't as well placed as Uncle Ray's. He needed only twenty minutes to trace the number you gave him, the phone booth on Falmouth Street. But we needed several hours to trace the number of the safe phone he gave you."

"You've got the location?" Drew asked.

Father Stanislaw nodded. "As you suspected, the phone isn't in the Risk Analysis office. Instead, it's two blocks down the street. A florist shop. But not the business phone. A private number, unlisted."

"Is he there now?"

The priest shook his head no. "But he's been calling there, checking in with his surveillance team. It seems they're still checking the area in case you're around. We managed to trace one call he made to that number." Father Stanislaw set the slip of paper on the glass table. "As close as we can tell, this is where Uncle Ray is."

Drew studied the address.

8

In the night, Drew walked yet again around the block. An expensive residential section of Cambridge, it was near the target area, yet far enough away that he wouldn't be noticed by Uncle Ray's guards. For the same reason—to avoid attracting attention—he'd decided not to stand in one place and wait but rather to appear to be taking a late-night stroll.

The exercise helped to dispel the cold. Passing streetlights, he noticed puffs of frosty breath coming out of his mouth. With a shiver, he pulled the hood of his coat up over his head and kept his gloved hands inside his pockets.

It was after midnight. He noticed few cars or pedestrians, though he did see occasional activity beyond glowing windows in magnificent homes. The trees were leafless, their branches scraped by the wind.

He heard a car and, glancing behind him, saw headlights turn a corner, coming his way. In the glow of a streetlight, he saw that the car was black, an Oldsmobile. He recognized Father Stanislaw's profile behind the steering wheel and quickly got in when the car stopped beside him.

The heater was on. Drew took off his gloves and warmed his hands.

"The house we want is on a corner," Father Stanislaw said. "It's surrounded by walls. It belongs to a friend of his."

"Any lights on the grounds?"

"None at all. The house has all its lights on, though."

"Sure. A flame for the moth. In case I found out where he was. Any guards?"

"I didn't see any. Mind you, I didn't have much chance. I had to keep driving by. But the entrance to the driveway has a large metal gate. It's closed. Beyond the gate, I saw several cars."

"So the guards must be waiting out of sight in case the shadows look tempting and someone comes over the wall. That's when the grounds get lit up."

"So I suspect," Father Stanislaw said. He drove around the corner and stopped at the darkest part of the block.

A sports car—Drew didn't recognize the model—pulled up behind them. A figure emerged, approached the Oldsmobile, and opened the door.

Arlene got in back. "I checked the house the same as you did," she told the priest. "I didn't see any guards."

"So what do you think? Should we risk it?" Drew asked.

Their gazes were steady.

"It's time." Drew turned toward a wooden case of soft-drink bottles on the back seat. But the bottles contained something stronger than soda pop.

9

Gasoline mixed with liquid detergent, each bottle's mouth stuffed with a tampon. Homemade napalm. The burning gasoline would cling to whatever surface it struck.

They divided the bottles evenly, each putting eight in a knapsack. Leaving the Oldsmobile, they walked to the corner. Father Stanislaw went straight across the street and continued down the block, while Drew and Arlene turned right and proceeded down the adjacent street. When the two of them reached the next corner, they faced each other.

"Be careful," Drew said, a wave of sadness rushing through him. What was he forcing her to do?

"When this is over . . ."

He waited, uncertain if he wanted her to continue.

"You and I have a lot to talk about," she said. A streetlight reflected off her intensely probing eyes.

He knew what she meant, but as his sadness deepened, he didn't know what to tell her. He hadn't given himself time to decide.

"I never stopped missing you," she said.

He still didn't know what to say. But he didn't resist when she kissed him. Indeed, not allowing himself to think, he returned the kiss, holding her close.

"All right. When this is over"—he breathed painfully—"we'll talk."

10

Cautious, holding his knapsack, he walked along the murky street in back of the target area. He passed two darkened houses and left the sidewalk to creep between them, using hedges and bushes for cover. In a moment, his eyes adjusting quickly to the greater blackness, he saw the lane that ran parallel to the street he'd just left. And beyond the lane, he saw the ten-foot-high brick wall that separated him from the back of the house.

From this perspective, with the wall partly shielding it, he saw only the upper levels, but as Father Stanislaw had said, lights were on inside. To protect his night vision, Drew didn't look at them. He scanned the lane—it was gravel, he saw now—and studied the sheltered spots where someone might hide. There was always the risk that Ray had posted sentries outside the walls, though Drew doubted that he had done so. For one thing, a neighbor might notice the sentries and call the police to complain about prowlers. For another, with Ray's forces now dispersed—some at the office, some at his estate on the Bay—he'd probably want to concentrate his remaining men on the inside of the property, spacing them effectively so they could make sure that no one came over the wall.

All the same, no harm in being careful, Drew thought. Besides, as he cupped a hand over the luminous dial of his watch, he saw that he still had a minute to wait while Arlene and Father Stanislaw got in position. So he might as well use that minute to double-check the darkness of the lane.

A light came on in the house behind him.

He squirmed beneath the spreading boughs of a fir tree. Smelling its resin, he squinted through needles toward the light. It was on the second floor of the house. The curtain was drawn. He saw a silhouette stand sideways, motionless for several seconds. Then the silhouette reached down, pressed something, and walked out of sight. The light went off.

A bathroom? Drew wondered. A man relieving himself? Whatever, the silhouette hadn't peered outside. There seemed no cause for alarm.

But as he returned his attention toward the wall, a whoosh of flame erupted on the other side of the wall, toward the front of the house. Another fiery roar. Then another.

While he'd been studying the light in the window, concerned that he'd been spotted, the others had reached their positions on either side at the front of the house. The minute had passed. They'd started lighting and throwing their napalm-filled bottles. The grounds at the front—and to the right and left—exploded with flames.

They'd calculated that for each of them to light and throw eight bottles would take thirty seconds. Possibly less; an adrenaline rush could make a person move awfully fast. Then they had to scramble out of the area. Because after thirty seconds the element of surprise would have dissipated. Ray's guards would come charging out of the compound, guns ready, searching.

Drew had to get started. But as he braced himself to surge from beneath the branches, he froze.

Someone else was out here. A shadow detached itself from the blackest section of the wall. A man with a gun, a silencer projecting from it. He turned to stare toward the top of the wall, toward the reflection of flames off the house.

Their roar grew louder, fiercer. Sixteen bottles thrown evenly around the front and sides of the house. And the bottles didn't have to shatter when they landed. The heat of the burning tampon would ignite the napalm inside, causing the glass to explode, scattering the fiery gasoline-and-detergent mixture. The house would be surrounded by flames.

At least, the house was *supposed* to be surrounded by

flames if Drew accomplished his part of the mission. He stared at the man with the gun who'd appeared from the blackness of the wall.

Drew's approach had been such that bushes concealed him. But if it hadn't been for the sudden light in the house behind him, he would have crept a little closer and been seen, been shot.

Distraught, the man abruptly raced down the lane, around the corner, toward the front of the house.

Drew's instincts told him to use this chance and get away. But he couldn't let himself. The plan depended upon the full effect of all the explosions. If Uncle Ray were inside, he had to be made to feel totally trapped, completely vulnerable. Taking several deep breaths, an athlete preparing himself, Drew lunged from beneath the fir tree, pulled the bottles from the knapsack, and hurriedly lit them, then frantically threw one, two, desperate to make the bottles land as far inside the compound as possible.

Three, four.

Heaving them as hard as he could, he kept darting his eyes toward the corner of the lane.

The bottles exploded.

Five, six.

Flames roared, cresting the wall. On the other side, men shouted.

Seven.

His heart pounding, he lit the eighth. Lights came on in several houses behind him. Their manifold gleam, added to the glare of the flames, made him feel exposed as if in daylight.

Attracted by the explosions at the rear of the house, the man with the gun came running back around the corner of the wall. Sprinting along the lane, he skittered to a stop when he saw Drew, and raised his gun.

Drew had no chance to reach for his own. He realized that

the only weapon he had available was the bottle, its tampon burning closer to the napalm.

The man aimed. Drew flung the bottle toward him, diving for the cover of the fir tree. The man, distracted by the flame on the bottle streaking toward him, shot at Drew but missed.

The bottle struck the gravel in front of the man. Drew had thrown with such force that the glass broke on impact against the stones, and a wall of flames erupted, blocking the lane.

The man stumbled back, his hands up, protecting his face. But he lost his balance and fell as the blaze streaked toward him. He rolled to avoid the splatter of the fire. Swatting at specks of flaming detergent that clung to his coat, he screamed.

Drew lunged to his feet. As he raced between the houses, a man in pajamas burst out the side door.

"What the hell's going on?"

Drew jolted against the man, toppling him against the house, and continued racing toward the street. Behind him, he heard the increasing roar of the fires in the compound. Screams. Shots, though he didn't know if they were aimed at him. He saw the reflection of the blaze off clouds in the sky.

His lungs in agony from exertion, he ran across the street, between more houses, across another street. His shirt was drenched with sweat beneath his insulated coat. He vaulted a fence, turned right at the next street, and sprinted along the sidewalk. He ducked left down a lane, glanced behind him, banged his hip against an unseen barrel, but ignored the ache in his muscle, and ran.

In the distance, sirens shrieked.

11

Limping from fatigue, at last he reached the rendezvous point. He'd been forced to approach it in a roundabout fashion, using precious time to hide every time he saw headlights or thought he saw someone searching the street. But finally he was here, a parking lot near MIT. Their fall-back position. After the attack on the house, Arlene and Father Stanislaw were supposed to have hurried to their cars, making sure they weren't followed. Drew, on foot, was supposed to have joined them at this parking lot an hour ago.

But the only two cars in the shadowy lot were neither an Oldsmobile nor a sports car.

He paused, exhausted. Had Arlene and Father Stanislaw been caught? Or, like him, had they been forced to flee at random till they couldn't get back to their cars or couldn't reach the rendezvous point in time?

Or perhaps they had reached this parking lot on schedule, waited, and finally decided that prudence required them to leave before the authorities widened their search.

In that case, he had to cross one of the two near bridges to get to the townhouse in Beacon Hill on the other side of the river. If the townhouse was safe anymore. What if Arlene and Father Stanislaw had been caught? What if . . . ?

No, he thought, angry at himself. Neither Arlene nor Father Stanislaw, if they were caught, would talk. Unless chemicals were used.

Soaked with sweat, he shivered. Headlights caught him in their glare. From the side of a building to his left. He stiffened, debating whether to trust that this was Arlene, or whether to run.

The headlights came toward him.

In case this was a cop, he decided that he'd better keep walking—straight ahead, away from the approaching headlights. He tried to look natural, as if one of the two cars in the lot belonged to him.

The headlights veered to follow. His reflexes quickened. He turned to look.

And sighed, recognizing Arlene in the sports car.

She stopped and he got in, his body welcoming the heat, the chance to relax.

"Some date *you* are." She put the car in neutral. "I was beginning to think you'd stood me up." But despite the joke, her voice didn't hide her concern, and she leaned over, touching him.

"Sorry. I had this marathon to run first," he said.

"Excuses, excuses."

He couldn't help it; he returned her embrace. "But I'm here now. Are you okay?"

"It's a good thing I've got long legs. They came in handy running tonight," she said. "But I missed the rendezvous time. In fact, I didn't get here till twenty minutes ago. I thought maybe something had happened to you. Or you'd been here already, got afraid of waiting, and left. I kept expecting a police car to check out the lot."

"That's what I thought you were." He studied her face. "Thanks. For taking the risk. For waiting for me."

"Shut up. You want to thank me? Monk or not, hold still for this."

She kissed him on the lips, a gentle kiss, soft and full of love.

In this night of surprises, his body responded. At once, self-conscious, he leaned back. "It's been a long time." He shook his head in torment. "Too much has happened. I vowed to be celibate."

"That means not marry. I'm not proposing. I'll give you all the time you want."

He stared at her. "I can't promise anything."

"I know it."

"Fair enough," he said.

She put the car in gear, and drove from the lot.

"Where's Father Stanislaw? Did he go ahead to the town-house?"

"He was shot." Her voice became professional.

"Dear God."

"He's alive. Bleeding heavily. But it looked to me like the bullet passed through his shoulder. I don't think anything vital was hit. He's one of the reasons I was late. I had to take him for help."

"A hospital? The police will . . ."

"No, he made a phone call to one of his contacts. They gave him the address of a doctor we can trust. And they sent someone to get the Oldsmobile."

"Father Stanislaw and his contacts." Drew's voice was filled with admiration.

"Their motivation's powerful."

"To save their souls."

She turned a corner. Ahead, Drew saw the bridge that would take them to Beacon Hill.

"What if the police have a roadblock?"

"Then we'll just tell them the truth," she said.

He didn't understand.

"We were back in that parking lot necking," she said. Her eyes crinkled. "Well, sort of necking, anyhow."

12

The woman's voice was the same—prim, precise, professional. "Good morning. Risk Analysis Corporation."

"Mr. Rutherford, please," Drew said in a Charlestown phone booth down the street from the Bunker Hill Monument.

"I'm sorry. Mr. Rutherford won't be coming into the office today."

"I had a hunch he wouldn't be. But I wonder if you can get a message to him."

"I'm not sure if . . ."

"To Uncle Ray? Could you tell him his nephew would like to speak with him?"

The woman's voice became alert. "He did mention he hoped you'd be calling. He left a phone number where you could reach him."

"Good. I look forward to talking to him."

She read the number to him; he wrote it down.

"If you speak to him in the next few minutes, tell him I'll phone that number as soon as—"

The receptionist interrupted. "Mr. Rutherford asked me to tell you that his schedule is extremely crowded today. The only time he'll be at that number is four o'clock this afternoon. He said if you called any earlier or later, you wouldn't be able to reach him."

Drew's head ached as he hung up.

Arlene stood next to him. In the background, tourists surveyed the Bunker Hill Monument.

"So?" she asked.

Drew explained what he'd been told, then showed her the number he'd written down.

"Four o'clock. Okay, what's the matter? How come you're frowning?"

"I'm not quite sure yet. Something. I don't know—call it a premonition. I feel like I'm being manipulated."

"We have to expect he'll want to get back at you."

"That's the point," Drew said. "Why would he let me have all day to learn the address of this new number?" He studied the tourists on Bunker Hill. "Maybe I'm overly cautious, but we'd better not hang around this phone booth."

They started down Monument Avenue.

"If it makes you nervous, don't call him," she said.

"I have to."

"Why?"

"To say I want to meet with him."

She turned, surprised. "*Meet* with him? He'll set up a trap."

"Of course. But I won't show up. I'll make an excuse and arrange another meeting. But I won't arrive for that one, either. In the meantime, we can think of other ways to put pressure on him. I want to keep aggravating him, make him nervous. Or better yet, maybe we could plan a meeting in such a way that we could turn his trap around." Drew couldn't quell his uneasiness. "That new number he gave me. To call at four o'clock. What's he up to?"

"You're right—he has to assume you'll learn its location."

Drew stopped abruptly and studied her face. "Is *that* it? He's trying to trick me into going to that location? He wants me to try to grab him while he's making the call?"

"And his men would kill you instead."

He shook his head. "No. He gave us too much time to anticipate the trap. Whatever he's got in mind, it isn't that. His tactic's working, though. He's got us confused. He's put us on the defensive. I told you. He isn't stupid."

13

At noon, a van arrived outside the Beacon Hill house. Two men helped Father Stanislaw get out. The priest was pale, his arm in a sling. Supported by his escorts, wincing from the strain, he mounted the steps of the townhouse; but once inside, with the door closed, he crumpled into their arms. Gently, they lowered him onto a sofa.

A middle-aged woman came in behind him. Handsome rather than pretty, with a conservative haircut and no makeup, she wore a blue London Fog overcoat and a gray wool suit. As the two men left, never saying a word, shutting the door again, she explained that she was there to take care of the priest. His wound wasn't critical, but he'd soon be needing another sedative, she said, and there was always the danger of infection. She carried a medical bag. Drew noticed that she didn't volunteer her name, and neither he nor Arlene asked for it.

They helped Father Stanislaw up the stairs to a bedroom, made him as comfortable as they could, and left to allow him to sleep.

"His constitution's remarkable," the woman said when they returned to the living room. "Polish, I believe. Hardy Slavic stock. He barely has a fever."

"We need to wake him up soon."

The woman spoke sharply. "I'm afraid I can't allow that."

"We wouldn't do it if we had a choice."

"I'll be the judge of that." She stood with her back to the stairs, as though to bar Drew from going up again. "What did you wish to speak with him about?"

He had a sudden intuition. Remembering how Father Stanislaw had addressed the businessman in the church in Pennsylvania, he said, "The Lord be with you."

"And with your spirit."

"*Deo gratias.*"

The woman relaxed. "Then you're one of us."

"Not exactly. Close enough. For six years, I was a Carthusian."

"In New Hampshire."

Drew sensed he was being tested. "No. In Vermont."

She smiled. "The Carthusians are saints on earth."

"Not this one, I'm afraid. I'm a sinner."

"Aren't we all? But God understands human weakness."

"I hope so. We have to talk to Father Stanislaw so we can get in touch with his contact at the telephone company. We need to find the location of a number we've been given."

The woman reached out her hand. "Give the number to me."

"But . . ."

"If that's the only information you want, there's no need to wake Father Stanislaw. I'll take care of it myself."

Drew blinked.

"Surely you don't think I'd have been allowed to attend him if I weren't responsible," the woman said. "Please, give me that number."

Drew did.

She walked to a phone, dialed, and, in a soft voice, gave instructions. She hung up, and they waited.

At two o'clock, the phone rang. The woman answered, listened, said, *"Deo gratias."* And hanging up, she turned to Drew. "A pay phone near the Paul Revere statue and Old North Church."

"A pay phone?"

"In North End," the woman said.

"But . . ."

Arlene leaned forward from a canvas director's chair. "What's wrong?"

"A pay phone? Near the Paul Revere statue—a tourist area?" Drew's stomach felt packed with ice. "And Uncle Ray gave us the day to find where it was? That doesn't make sense. He wouldn't *dare* to use that phone. It's too exposed. If we staked out that location, we could tell right away if Ray was setting up a trap. He'll *never* go there. But he'll spread men through the neighborhood in case *we* do."

"Which means we won't," Arlene said.

"Right. But Ray expects that, too. He wants to use that phone for another reason. Someone, not Ray, will answer my call. And give me another number. That pay phone's just a relay. We'd better get moving."

"No," Arlene insisted. "I'm staying right here till you tell me what's going on."

"It's a setup, all right. For sure, a trap. But not the one we expected. This is algebra turned into trigonometry. He's skipped a dozen steps. But I know what he's doing. I learned from the same set of rules. I used the same trick in . . ." He shuddered at the memory.

"If you don't explain what's going on."

"When we get in the car. Hurry." He swung toward the woman with the medical bag. "We need a room with a door that has a window. I have to be able to stand outside and look through the window into the room. An isolated location. And the room needs to have a phone."

The woman considered. "I don't . . . No, wait a minute. There's a local parish hall with a kitchen in the basement. The kitchen has a swinging door with a window so people coming in and out can see and not bump the door against each other. The kitchen has a phone."

"What's the address?"

The woman told him.

Drew wrote it down. "Call and make sure no one's there." He glanced at his watch. "We don't have much time till four o'clock."

"For what?" Arlene asked.

"To buy a tape recorder. And, God help me, a mouse."

14

It was white—unlike Stuart Little, who'd been gray. Drew bought it with a cage. He paid the pet shop owner. "Have you got any mouse treats?"

"Mouse treats?" The overweight man with thinning hair and a bird-dung-stained apron raised his eyebrows.

A parrot squawked in the background.

"Sure. Whatever a mouse likes to eat the best. Something he'd really love. Gourmet."

"Gourmet?" The man looked at Drew as if he were crazy.

"Hey, listen, I could cheat you, but I want my customers happy. There's no reason to spend a lot of money on mouse food. This stuff over here, it's cheap, it's filling, they don't know the difference. I mean, a mouse, what the hell does a mouse know?"

"He's only the one who's eating it, right?"

"Yeah, except this particular mouse is female."

"Then *she*. I want the best for her. I want her to stuff herself with the best meal she ever had. And I don't care about the cost."

The man sighed. "Whatever you say. It's your wallet. Step right this way. What I've got here on this shelf, it's what you might call the Rolls-Royce of mouse food."

Drew paid another ten dollars and left the pet shop, a five-pound bag of food in one hand, the mouse in the cage in the other.

At the curb, Arlene sat waiting in the sports car, its motor rumbling. "Cute," she said. "Personally, mice never bothered me. Have you given it a name?"

His voice was grim. "Stuart Little the second."

She suddenly understood. "Oh, shit." Her look was consoling. "I'm sorry I tried to be funny."

Drew shut the door, clutching the cage. "No problem. It's Ray who has to be sorry."

15

Even at half-past three, the basement of the parish hall was shadowy. As the autumn sun drooped low, the church on that side of the hall blocked out its descending brilliance. The windows at the top of the basement's western wall were shrouded with gloom.

The place was damp. Drew felt the chill as he came down concrete stairs, pausing while the echo of his footsteps diminished.

Silence.

He squinted at rows of long plastic-topped tables that smelled from years of church socials, beans and hot dogs, potato salad, coleslaw.

Arlene descended quickly behind him, holding a box that contained a tape recorder.

"Is anyone here?" Drew called. His voice echoed. Silence. "Good."

The mouse skittered in her cage.

Scanning the shadows, Drew pointed toward a door with a window halfway along the wall to his right. "That must be the kitchen. Now if only our friend remembered correctly and there's a phone."

There was. As Drew pushed open the swinging door and flicked on a light switch, he saw a phone on a counter between a stove and a humming refrigerator. "Let's make sure." He picked up the phone, exhaling when he heard a dial tone.

He set down the scrambling mouse in her cage and again glanced at his watch. "Less than twenty-five minutes. The tape recorder worked in the store. It had better work now."

Indeed, when he took the box from Arlene, unpacked and plugged in the recorder, it functioned perfectly. He dictated into the microphone and played the tape back.

"Does that sound like me?" he asked with concern. The recorded tone of his voice didn't seem like the tone inside his head.

Arlene said, "Lower the bass."

He did and played the tape again.

"That's you," she said. "It certainly ought to be. That machine's worth a fortune."

Drew rewound the tape. "Fifteen minutes. Time to feed our friend."

He opened the bag of mouse treats and sprinkled the tiny chunks through the top bars of the cage. The mouse became frantic with ecstasy.

"Good," Drew said. "Enjoy." He rubbed his forehead. "What else? I'd better rig the remote control." He pulled an electrical cord from the cardboard box, plugged it into the tape recorder, and led it across the kitchen floor, through the swinging door, and into the murky hall. The space beneath the kitchen door was sufficient for Drew to be able to close the door over the cord. The last thing he did was attach a remote control hand switch to his end of the wire.

In the light that came from the kitchen through the door's window, he studied the buttons on the hand switch. "On. Off. Pause. Play. Record." He nodded. "Ten minutes. Have we forgotten anything?"

Arlene thought about it. "Just in case, you'd better test that hand switch."

He did. It worked. "Then I guess there's just one thing left to do."

She didn't need to ask what he meant.

"Pray."

16

At four o'clock, Drew picked up the phone in the kitchen. A fist seemed to squeeze his heart. He'd know soon if he'd misjudged. Everything depended upon the logical assumptions he'd been making.

But what if Ray had anticipated those assumptions?

Drew stared at the phone. It was black, with an old-fashioned rotary dial. As his apprehension strengthened, he dialed the number that the Risk Analysis secretary had given him. The digits clicked ominously. He glanced at Arlene, reached out, and held her hand.

Relays connected. Drew heard a buzz as the phone at the other end—near the Paul Revere statue in North End—began to ring.

Someone answered it almost at once. In the background, Drew heard sounds of traffic. A gruff voice said, "Hello?"

"Mr. Rutherford, please."

"Who?"

"Uncle Ray. It's his nephew calling."

"Why didn't you say so? He isn't here."

"But"—Drew made himself sound puzzled—"I was told to call at four o'clock."

"He had an unexpected appointment. You can get in touch with him at . . ." The husky voice dictated a number. "You got it?"

Drew read the number back.

"Perfect," the voice said. "That housewarming you gave us last night? Cute, pal."

The man hung up.

Drew slumped against the counter.

"We were right?" Arlene asked.

He nodded. "Ray never intended to go near that phone. It was only a relay. I'm supposed to call another number."

"As you expected. But you could be wrong about the next call. It might not mean what you think. Suppose Ray was only being careful. Suppose he took for granted that we'd learn the location of the number you were given this morning. This way, by using that phone booth as a relay, he was simply protecting himself. He knows you can't possibly find the location of this new number before he finishes the call and leaves."

Drew's shoulders ached from nervousness. "Possibly. But I don't think that's what's going on here. In sixty-eight, a man named Hank Dalton taught me a procedure. I used it once on a mission. Against a hit man for the Red Brigades. And Uncle Ray was Hank Dalton's boss. I have to suspect Ray'll try it on me." He paused. "Let's put it this way. If I'm wrong, we've lost nothing."

"But if you're right . . ." She nodded soberly.

"There's no more time," Drew said. "Ray's expecting my call. I don't dare let him wait."

Drew set the tape recorder next to the phone. His hand trembled as he set the cage beside the tape recorder. Inside the cage, the white mouse kept eating greedily, its sides bulging, mouth full, chewing ecstatically.

"I hope you're as happy as you look," Drew said. He turned to Arlene. "You'd better go out to the hall."

She went through the swinging door.

He stared at the slip of paper, put his index finger into the first digit's slot, and dialed.

He waited, hearing the phone ring at the other end. Ray was playing this cool, not answering right away. But after the fourth ring, Drew wondered if anyone was going to answer at all.

Halfway through the fifth ring, the phone was picked up. "Hello?" a voice said.

Drew didn't reply.

"Hello? Drew? Come on, sport, talk to me. I've been waiting for you to call."

No question now. The voice belonged to Uncle Ray.

As gently as possible, he set the phone down onto the counter, making no sound. The speaking end was next to the tape recorder, the opposite end next to the mouse.

Faintly from the receiver, he heard Ray's voice. "I'm anxious to talk, Drew. To get this settled."

But Drew left the kitchen. Outside in the murky hall where Arlene waited, he picked up the tape recorder's remote control and pressed the play button.

The door was solid enough that he barely heard his recorded voice. No matter. It would be sufficiently loud against the phone.

"Uncle Ray, I want to arrange a meeting," the recorder said.

"I could blow up everything you own, but that won't get me the answers I want. I need . . ."

Staring through the window in the kitchen door, Drew didn't concentrate on the tape recorder. Or on the phone.

He focused all of his attention on the mouse.

". . . to see your face, you bastard," Drew's recorded voice said, *"to watch those damned lying eyes of yours when you try to justify—"*

With frantic speed Drew pressed the stop button, cutting off his recorded voice. Because a jet of blood had burst from the mouse's ears. The mouse toppled, trembling, the white fur around its neck turning crimson.

Drew stooped, tugging at the cord that led from the remote control to the tape recorder. He pulled the cord, feeling pressure against it now. "Come on," he whispered urgently. "Come on."

He slumped in satisfaction as he heard a clatter from inside the kitchen.

"Did it fall?" he asked Arlene.

Peering through the window in the kitchen door, she nodded.

His knees felt weak as he stood. Through the window, he saw where the tape recorder had been pulled off the counter to crash on the floor.

"That's it, then," he murmured. "We did it. When that recorder fell, Ray must have heard it."

"And now he hears nothing," she said, her voice low.

"He thinks I'm dead." His tone matched hers. "The clatter of the tape recorder falling—he'll figure it was me when I fell, still clutching the phone."

The tactic that Hank Dalton had taught Drew in Colorado in 1968 was a way to kill a man remotely, using the phone. If the target was sufficiently distracted, if the arrangements were properly made, the man would never suspect the means of assassination.

Dalton had called it a supersonic bullet. With sophisticated electronics equipment, a super-high-pitched tone could be transmitted through the phone line, rupturing the victim's eardrum, piercing his brain, and killing him instantly.

As the mouse had been killed, its cage against the receiving end of the phone.

Customarily, the assassin would then hang up. But Drew suspected that Uncle Ray planned to add a variation to this tactic. He imagined Ray hearing the sudden interruption of Drew's voice, the clatter as Drew in theory collapsed, still holding the phone.

But what would Ray do after that?

Keep listening, Drew guessed. If I had someone with me, Ray knows he ought to hear shouts, cries for help.

But if there *weren't* any shouts? If Ray heard only silence on this end of the line?

Drew concentrated. He'll have to assume that I was alone when I made the call.

And in his place, I'd want to make doubly sure that my hunter, my enemy, was really dead.

Drew brooded about the final step. For the past two hours, he'd been analyzing the conclusion he'd reached, testing it for flaws. But it still made sense. Excitement jolted him.

If my end of the line stays open, Ray can trace my call. He can find out where I was phoning from. Provided he doesn't hear any sounds from this end of the phone, he'll think it's safe to send a team here to verify that I'm dead.

And just as important, to get my body.

The authorities think I'm Janus. If he wants to continue using Janus as a cover for his other assassinations, he can't let my corpse be found.

With painstaking care, Drew opened the swinging door, making sure it didn't creak. Gently, he stepped toward the phone.

"It's been five minutes. Any sounds yet?" Drew recognized Ray's voice.

"Nothing."

"Okay, keep listening, just in case. But I think it's worth a try. Start the trace."

Drew silently left the kitchen. In the murky hall, he gestured for Arlene to follow him. They walked a safe distance, stopping at the stairs.

"Here's the slip of paper with the second number I called. Find a pay phone outside and call the townhouse. Tell Father Stanislaw's contacts to learn where this number's located."

She took the paper. "And you?"

"I think I'd better stay here. In case Ray's people arrive sooner than we expect."

"If they do?"

"I'm not quite sure how to play it. For starters, I want to take a look around this hall and find a good hiding place. As soon as you get the address, come back. But be careful. And make sure Father Stanislaw's contacts go to that address."

Her eyes were frightened. "Drew."

"I know," he said. "From here on in, it gets dicey."

He didn't reconsider his impulse but simply obeyed it. He kissed her.

In the gloom, they held each other for a moment.

Her voice sounded thick. "I'd better get going."

He felt hollow. "See you."

"God, I hope so."

She paused once halfway up the concrete stairs, looking back at him. Then she went up the rest of the way and out the door. In a moment, the hall again was silent.

To his amazement, what he experienced now was disturbingly unfamiliar. Loneliness. Inexplicably, his eyes felt warm. *What if he never saw her again?*

17

Just before six, the autumn sun now almost completely gone, the basement hall in deeper gloom, Drew heard the door at the top of the stairs creak open. From where he hid, between rows of stacked chairs against the middle of the left wall at the bottom of the stairs, his first thought was that Arlene had returned, and he felt a wave of joy. But as the door snicked shut, whoever had entered didn't come down.

Drew waited. Still, no one descended.

Arlene would be careful when she came back, he knew. She might be taking the time to sense if something was wrong. Or she might be waiting for Drew to call to her. But he couldn't allow himself to do so.

When sufficient time had passed that the memory of the sound of the door seemed a fantasy, Drew heard another sound. Softly—so softly that it too might have been imagined—a shoe touched a concrete step.

And stopped.

Drew's position between the stacks of metal chairs was comfortable. Hank Dalton had always insisted that his students should take that precaution. "You don't know how long you might have to wait. So make sure you like where you're hiding. Otherwise someone might hear you stretch your leg to relieve a cramp."

Yet despite Drew's comfortable position, tension had made his body stiff. He strained to keep silent as he listened for yet another soft footstep on the stairs to his right. He breathed imperceptibly.

Yes! A sound. But not from the stairs, as he'd anticipated.

Instead, the sound came from the opposite end of the hall, from the darkness across from him on the left. It could have been anything, the brush of wind against a window at the top of the wall over there, or the settling of a joist in the ceiling.

But he heard it again and now identified it—the subtle easing down of a sole on the concrete floor.

Not one, but two intruders were down here. Earlier, after Arlene had gone and he'd scouted this basement, he'd found a set of stairs in that other corner. Unlike the stairs that he and Arlene had used, to his right, those other stairs didn't have a door at the top, so he'd felt secure. Now he realized, his pulse hammering, that he should have followed the stairs where they turned to go up to ground level. He should have checked the main floor. Because it was clear that the second intruder had entered through an upstairs door Drew had not discovered. While Drew had been distracted by the door at the top of the stairs to his right, the other intruder had crept down the stairs on the far side of the room.

Two of them, Drew thought. Okay, as long as I know where they are, I can deal with them. He directed his attention back to the stairs on his right, seeing a shadow reach the bottom.

He understood. This first intruder's a decoy. He's supposed to attract attention. If somebody moves against him, his partner's across the room, ready to protect him.

The light through the kitchen door's window beckoned the shadow. Across the hall, the subtle sounds of the second intruder stopped. Drew watched from the dark between the stacks of metal chairs as the shadow on his right crept toward the window. A man, he saw now. Holding a pistol with a silencer on the barrel, the shadow paused at the side of the swinging door.

Before Drew had chosen his hiding place, he'd returned to the kitchen, and silently, terribly conscious of the telephone receiver lying on the counter, he'd picked up the dead mouse in its cage and hidden it outside in the hall. He'd done the same with the tape recorder. As a final precaution, he'd set the open tape recorder box over the telephone.

Now, when the intruder went into the kitchen, he wouldn't see anything to alarm him. He'd decide that the phone—and the body—had to be somewhere else down here. He and his partner would continue searching.

But I don't dare try anything, Drew thought, clutching his Mauser, unless I've got them both together.

The shadow next to the kitchen door risked a furtive glance through its lighted window. He ducked back. Ten seconds later, he risked another glance.

On the opposite side of the hall, the other shadow moved, creeping forward to join his partner beside the kitchen door. This second shadow, too, had a pistol with a silencer. They flanked each side of the door. One man charged in, the second lunging directly after him. Before the door swung shut, Drew saw them standing back to back, their pistols aimed at opposite sections of the kitchen.

Now!

He shifted from his shelter between the stacks of metal chairs. Mauser ready, he braced himself, crouching in the darkness. As he'd expected, he didn't hear any conversation. Until the men were confident of their safety, they'd remain as silent as they could.

I'll have to shoot them both, Drew thought. While I've got them together.

But not to kill. I need them alive. I need them to tell me where Ray is. When I'm through with them, they'll talk. They'll *beg* me to ask them more questions.

The kitchen door swung open; the two men slipped out, silhouetted by the glow through the kitchen window. Facing the hall, one gestured to the other to check the left side while he took the right.

"Don't move!" Drew shouted. Prepared to fire, he meant to order them to drop their guns. He didn't get the chance.

A shot filled the darkness. But not from the men. Deafening, it came from the opposite end of the hall. Drew dove to the floor, the concrete jolting his chest. A second roar walloped his ears. He fired, but not toward the sniper across the room, rather toward the targets he could see—the two men in front of the kitchen door. As they darted for cover, still exposed by the light through the window, he shot again and again. Screaming, both went down.

He rolled, afraid that the muzzle flashes from his Mauser would attract the sniper's aim. Sprawling on his stomach, he glanced back and forth from the shadows of the two men he'd shot toward the unseen gunman on the other side of the hall.

He blinked, his eyes in pain, as the overhead lights blazed. Blinded, he firmly closed his lids as he'd been trained to do, then barely opened them, allowing his corneas to adjust to the sudden illumination, opening his lids a little more now, desperate, aiming.

He found himself peering beneath rows of tables toward the body of a man on the floor near the opposite stairs. The man wasn't moving. Blood poured from his chest. A pistol lay near his hand.

But how the hell—?

His spine cold, Drew glanced toward the two men on the floor outside the kitchen. One lay still. The other clutched his stomach, moaning.

Drew stared back toward the man on the floor across the room. Two shots had come from that direction. But who had killed the sniper?

He heard footsteps scrape on the concrete stairs over there. The sounds were unsteady, slow. He grimaced, aiming, unable to see who was coming down.

A shoe appeared. Then another. He steadied the Mauser.

Dark trouser legs came into view. Drew squinted down the Mauser's sights. The footsteps paused.

A man spoke. His voice, though husky, was weak. "Drew? Are you all right?"

The Slavic accent was unmistakable. Father Stanislaw.

"All right?" Drew exhaled with nervous relief. "I suppose so."

The priest coughed. With painful slowness, he came down the rest of the stairs. His left arm was in a sling. His right hand clutched a pistol. Wavering, the priest leaned back against a wall and took several deep breaths.

"But *you* don't look all right." Drew stood.

"How do they say it on television? It's only a superficial wound? Don't believe the 'only' part." Father Stanislaw winced. "Even with sedatives, it hurts."

Drew had to grin. "I thought you Poles were supposed to be tough."

Father Stanislaw forced himself to stand straight. "Believe me, we are. If you've ever eaten *pierogies*, you know how tough I mean."

Drew's grin broadened.

But he didn't let his growing affection for this man distract him from being practical. He glanced toward the men he'd shot. One lay as still as before. The other continued to clutch his stomach, groaning. He searched them and took their guns. Then it seemed all right to cross the room and help the priest.

But Father Stanislaw mustered his strength and approached Drew's side of the hall, motioning to Drew to stay where he was. "I made it this far on my own. I don't need any help."

"How did you get here?"

"Arlene called the townhouse. With another phone number and instructions to find its location."

"I know. I asked her to."

"I was awake when she called. I insisted on talking to her. She told me what had happened while I was asleep. Then I insisted on coming back here with her. My friend, you tried to accomplish too much by yourself."

"I had no choice."

"Perhaps. But recent events"—Father Stanislaw gestured toward the men on the floor—"prove that I was right."

"Arlene." Drew whispered her name. "Where is she?"

"Outside, watching in case these three weren't alone. When we got here, we realized that we couldn't enter the building without alarming you. So we decided to act as your surveillance team. We saw three men enter, one on the side, two upstairs through two different doors. It seemed obvious that they were planning to use the first man as a decoy and the other two as backups."

"So you followed the two men who'd entered upstairs."

"My instincts were right." Father Stanislaw gripped a table for support. "Of the two men I followed, one made himself a further decoy and eventually joined his confederate at the kitchen. But the third man remained behind, to protect his associates if they were surprised. As they were. He shot at you. But I shot him." The priest closed his eyes, swallowing hard.

"You're sure you're okay?"

"Quite the contrary. I'm not okay." Father Stanislaw's face was the color of chalk. "It occurs to me that this is the third time I've saved your life. Back at the retreat house when I hid in the chapel's confessional. At Satan's Horn. Now here."

"I'm in your debt," Drew said.

"Three times," the priest reminded him.

"Yes." Drew looked at his friend. "No matter the cost, even my life, I promise to return the favor."

"In kind."

"I don't understand."

"In kind," the priest insisted.

"All right. Whatever that means. In kind."

"Make sure you remember that promise. Because"—Father

Stanislaw breathed painfully again, his face white—"when we finish this, I intend to demand . . . on your honor that you fulfill your word." He coughed. "Right now, we have business to attend to."

Drew understood. He stalked toward the men he'd shot. Grabbing the one who was still alive, he shook him hard. "Where's your boss?"

The man groaned.

"You think you hurt now?" Drew said. "You don't know what 'hurt' can mean." He reached back his hand, preparing to strike him.

"No!" Father Stanislaw said.

Drew barely heard him. *Where's your boss, you bastard? You'll tell me or—"*

"No!" The priest grabbed Drew's hand.

Drew glared at him. "I get it now. You don't mind the killing. But you don't like seeing your victims suffer. What's the matter? You're not prepared to go the limit for your faith? You'd better watch out. You've got a soft spot, Father."

"No." Despite his pain, the priest straightened fully. "For my faith, I've gone what you call 'the limit.' Many times. More than you can imagine." His ruby ring—its sword and cross intersecting—glinted. "But never unless it was necessary. Torture? Certainly. Unless there were chemicals available. But *only* when it was necessary to make someone talk. I know where Ray is. The location of the final number you were given. Now put that man down!"

Drew stared at the man he was holding, feeling his heart contract in disgust at what he'd almost been forced to do, reminded again of how far he'd come from the monastery. Gently, almost with reverence, he set the man down. "All right. We'll call your people and get him medical help. He's just a drone. He deserves the chance to live. But I have to say, that's a chance the bastard wouldn't give *me*."

"Of course," Father Stanislaw said. "And that's what distinguishes us from them. Our motives aren't based on money. Or the need for power. Or political theories, which by definition are fleeting and shallow. No, our motives are ultimate. And our mercy, if suitable, is that of the Lord."

Drew felt a sudden rush of sorrow. "Too much, too long," he said. "I'm tired of running. I want this to end."

"And it will. Tonight, if God wills it." Wincing, Father Stanislaw reached in his suit pocket. "I have the address. I can take you to Uncle Ray."

18

But despite his anxiousness, Drew had something to do first. Like the ancient Greek paradox that to travel a mile you first had to travel a half mile and before that a quarter mile and before that an eighth of a mile, and thus by subdividing your journey you could never reach its end, so Drew felt there was always something more to do, yet another interruption, always another risk. Perhaps his ordeal would never end. Perhaps he was dead, and this was Hell.

He turned to the wounded man. "Can you hear me?"

The man nodded.

"If you want a doctor, you'll do what I tell you."

The man peered up, helpless.

"But I've told you we already have the address," Father Stanislaw said. "There's no need to—"

"Isn't there?" Drew's voice was urgent. "We've forgotten something." He explained what had to be done.

The priest looked distressed. "You're right. And he has to be made to do it soon."

Drew knelt beside the wounded man, giving him orders. "You understand?"

The man nodded, sweating, in pain.

"And then we'll get you a doctor. All you have to do is show us how tough you are. There's nothing to it." Drew dragged him toward the kitchen. "To stay alive, just talk without groaning."

In the kitchen, Drew sat him on the floor against a cupboard and lifted the cardboard box off the unhooked phone. Crouching, he held the receiver near the wounded man's face, leaning close so that he himself could hear what was said on the other end of the line.

He pointed his Mauser toward the wounded man's temple, silently ordering him to talk. The man's eyes glazed, out of focus. For a moment, Drew was afraid he would faint.

"We've got him." The man sounded hoarse as he spoke to the phone.

"Just a moment," a gruff voice replied.

In fifteen seconds, Uncle Ray's voice came on the line. "Is he dead?"

"That's right."

"What took you so long? You had me worried."

"We couldn't find him at first."

"He's alone?"

"Yes."

"Bring the body back here. I want to make sure it's disposed of."

"We're on our way." The wounded man's eyes flickered. He sagged toward the floor.

Drew set the phone down onto its receiver, breaking the connection, then eased the man flat on the floor. "You chose the wrong profession, my friend. You should have been an actor."

"You promised." The man groaned.

"I'll keep it. How did you get here? What kind of car?"

"A dark blue van. A Ford." The man's lips looked parched. "It's in the parking lot behind this hall."

Turning, Drew saw Father Stanislaw watching from the open kitchen door. "You can use this phone to get him a doctor now. And you'd better tell your people to remove the bodies." He searched the wounded man, finding what he wanted—the keys to the van. "By the way," he told the priest, "I'll need some help when we get there. Did Arlene explain?"

"I'll make the arrangements."

"And while you're doing that, I'd better let Arlene know we're okay. She'll have heard the shots. She'll be worried."

"She's beside the church." The priest picked up the phone. "I'll hurry."

"Please. There's a lot to be done."

Drew rushed from the kitchen. As he ran up the stairs, he remembered the powerful, unfamiliar emotion he'd felt when Arlene had gone up these same stairs two hours ago, his unexpected loneliness when she'd left and shut the door. Again he ached with longing. It seemed a betrayal of his years in the monastery that he wanted so badly to see her again, to hold her. And yet if it was a betrayal, he no longer cared. He stepped outside, saw her waiting near the church, and started toward her. Despite the dark, her eyes shone, relieved that he was safe, eager. In a moment, she was in his arms.

19

Fighting the impulse to press his foot harder onto the van's accelerator, knowing he'd be foolish to risk being stopped for speeding, he drove steadily north out of Boston. The city's glow filled his rear-view mirror; his headlights blazed toward nightcloaked trees and fields.

Knuckles stiff from the pressure of his grip on the steering wheel, Drew followed Father Stanislaw's instructions. At first, he hadn't recognized the address on the slip of paper the priest had given him. Then, with growing excitement, he had, no longer surprised that the priest knew how to get there. Because the priest had been at that address before—two days ago. It was Uncle Ray's country estate, north of Boston, on the Bay.

Drew had to admire his enemy's cleverness. Ray, appearing to have fled his estate on the Bay because of Drew's threat, had now reversed his tactic and gone back, apparently assuming that the estate was the last place Drew would look. But in gaining the advantage of the unexpected, Ray had chosen a site that was difficult to defend. Father Stanislaw had described the estate as remote and sprawling, too large, with too much cover to be adequately protected. "Getting onto the grounds will be easy," the priest had said. "Getting into the house, though, that's another matter. He'll concentrate his men there. To go in and grab him, you'd need a small army."

That won't be necessary, Drew thought, as he headed relentlessly toward the Bay. All we need is the three men I asked for.

And three untraceable cars.

Shortly after seven, he reached the Bay, its white-tipped waves distinct in the dark. Rolling down his window, he smelled a cold salt breeze and stopped at the side of the road where his headlights revealed a historical marker about the Revolutionary War.

He waited. Five minutes later, headlights appeared in his rearview mirror, stopping behind him. The headlights at once went out. He stepped from the van, noting with fondness Arlene's silhouette behind the steering wheel of the Oldsmobile, the priest slumping beside her as if asleep.

He saw three other pairs of headlights coming toward him. They slowed and stopped in a row behind the Oldsmobile. They too went dark. Three men got out of the cars. As Arlene left the Oldsmobile, Drew joined them on the gravel road.

"The Lord be with you," he said to the men.

"And with your spirit," they answered as one.

"Deo Gratias." He studied the men. They were in their middle thirties. Their outdoor clothes were dark, their haircuts conservative, almost military, their eyes direct, disturbingly serene. "I appreciate your help. Father Stanislaw says you've had experience."

They nodded.

"For what it's worth, if everything goes as planned, if there aren't any accidents, I don't think your lives are in danger."

"It doesn't matter," one said. "Our lives don't matter. The Church does."

The Oldsmobile's passenger door came open. Father Stanislaw stepped from the car. "The equipment's in the trunk."

Arlene had the key. When she opened it, a light went on. Drew blinked in surprise at automatic weapons, magazines filled with ammunition, grenades, even a miniature rocket launcher.

"You've had this stuff in the trunk all the time?" Drew asked, astonished. "You could start a war."

"We *are* at war." Father Stanislaw's face was as pale as the sling supporting his arm.

They reached inside the trunk, taking up assault rifles, inspecting and loading them. The light inside the trunk glinted off a large red ring on the middle finger of each left hand. The rings had the same insignia—an intersecting sword and cross.

The fraternity of the stone.

Drew felt a chill.

"What do you want us to do?" the first man asked, holding the barrel of his weapon toward the dark sky.

Hiding his increasing astonishment, Drew matched their professional tone. "Adjust the carburetor on each car." He turned to Father Stanislaw. "How far is the estate?"

"A mile down the road."

"Good enough. The timing shouldn't be a problem."

He finished explaining. They thought about it.

"Could be," one said. "As long as he does what you expect."

"I know him. Besides, does he have a choice?" Drew asked.

"If you're wrong . . ."

"Yes?"

"Nothing. Our part's easy. You're the one taking the risk."

20

The van approached the estate's closed metal gate. Two armed sentries stood beyond it, one on each side, but when the headlights came close enough for the guards to recognize the van, they snapped into motion and opened the gate. *"Bring the body back here. I want to make sure it's disposed of,"* Uncle Ray had told his man on the phone. As Drew had anticipated, these sentries were under orders to expect the retrieval team and to let the van through at once. Not stopping, the driver waved in thanks and drove quickly through the opening in the wall, proceeding down a blacktop lane past shadowy trees and bushes toward the large three-story Tudor house in the distance.

The carburetor on the van had been adjusted, its idling mechanism turned up so high that the engine would race even if the accelerator weren't pressed. Because the van had an automatic transmission, a driver could leave the gear shift in drive, leap out of the van, and know that the van would follow the direction in which it had been aimed: in this case, down the lane toward the mansion.

As the driver, clutching a weapon, tumbled smoothly onto the lawn and disappeared into the dark, the van continued surging forward. It bumped up onto a sidewalk and jolted to a stop halfway up the mansion's front steps. The driver had lit a fuse before leaping out, a fuse that blazed back to dynamite above the van's gas tank. Now the vehicle abruptly, stunningly, exploded. Its massive roaring fireball, chunks of metal flying, ripped apart the mansion's entrance.

The guards at the gate had not yet fully closed it. Spinning, startled, toward the deafening roar, they raised their weapons, rushing toward the blaze in front of the house. At that moment, three other vehicles, their headlights extinguished, crashed through the partly closed gate. Each of these vehicles too had an automatic transmission, each carburetor adjusted to give the engines maximum idle, so that when these drivers also lit fuses and leaped from their vehicles, the cars continued on course, one to the left and two to the right of the blazing van on the steps of the mansion.

In rapid sequence, the vehicles struck the building's facade, erupting in a fiery wallop. Windows shattered. Flames roared up the front of the building.

As the drivers scurried back to shadowy cover, they fired their automatic weapons, strafing the blaze that obscured the house. They riddled parked cars, rupturing tires, shattering the grill of a Rolls Royce and a Mercedes. Tracer bullets made gas tanks explode. Burning gasoline spewed across the pavement. The assailants threw grenades at the guards who raced down the lane from the gate. The guards flew backward, landing motionless on the road. More grenades followed, this time aimed at the mansion.

Arlene, who'd leaped from one of the vehicles, used a portable rocket launcher. The model, an RPG-7, was a favorite of terrorists because it was only slightly longer than a yardstick; and because it weighed only fifteen pounds, she could carry it easily when she leaped from her moving vehicle. Its projectiles were 3.3 inches wide, capable of piercing 12-

inch-thick metal armor. One by one, they blasted impressively into the mansion, blowing out one entire corner.

Now guards raced from the building, some of them screaming in horror, flailing at their fiery clothes. The reflection of the blaze off night clouds could be seen, it was later reported, fifteen miles away. The powerful blasts rattled windows in the nearby town. The entire front of the mansion began to sag. Defensive automatic weapons rattled from adjacent buildings to which the guards had raced. Throughout, the attackers kept shifting their position, firing, reloading, shooting, throwing grenades, making the assault force seem huge, gradually pulling back.

Two minutes had passed.

21

Drew wasn't with them. On foot, he stalked toward the estate through the dark, along the rocky shore of the Bay. Two days ago, Father Stanislaw had studied the perimeter of the grounds, noting the small yacht moored at a dock. As soon as the fireballs erupted from the house at the top of the slope, the three guards who patrolled the beach swung toward the startling brilliance and charged up the wooden steps toward the rattle of gunfire. His dark clothes indistinct against the black water, Drew raced along the rocks of the shore. He rushed down the dock and onto the boat.

There he hunched below deck. Thirty seconds later, he saw figures scurry down the wooden steps from the house. Waves lapped the hull of the yacht. It tilted slightly starboard, then port.

Though he hadn't seen Uncle Ray for six years, he recognized the elegant, well-dressed silhouette hurrying down the steps. He also recognized the silhouette of a second man, distinctive because he wore a cowboy hat. And *that* man Drew hadn't seen since 1968. My, my, Drew thought. You must be in your sixties, Hank Dalton. I've got to give you credit. You ought to be retired by now. But I guess it's in your blood. You can't give up the game.

Ray and Hank reached the beach before the others. They paused on the dock. "All right," Ray told the guards who'd come with him, sounding as smooth as ever. "You know where to go. Use the dark and disappear. Don't try to fight them. They've won. But our turn will come. Just remember, I appreciate your loyalty. Good luck to each of you."

The guards spun toward the automatic gunfire at the burning mansion on the hill. They hesitated only a moment before they separated, disappearing into the dark. Ray and Hank rushed down the dock, their footsteps rumbling hollowly, and hurriedly cast off the mooring lines, climbing onto the yacht. Behind them, on the bluff, another explosion shook the night. Ray darted forward to start the engines. The stern sank slightly as the screws gained traction. Then the yacht evened out, gaining speed, cutting through waves, roaring toward the dark of the Bay.

Standing at the rear of the yacht, surveying the battle zone, Hank braced his hands on his hips, his cowboy hat profiled against the rising flames on the hill. "Shitfire. Who'd have figured?" he muttered. "I taught him too good."

In all the years since '68, Drew had thought of Hank as eternal. This sudden realization of how students could one day outmatch their teachers was shocking. Is that what it means to get old? There's always someone better coming along, because that person is younger?

And it felt so easy. All Drew did was creep forward from the below-deck hatch and nudge Hank. That's all. Nudge him. A gentle tap on Hank's shoulder, and Drew discovered that his former master . . .

(In those days, I thought you were God. I went to sleep in fear of you. I trembled when you spoke.)

. . . was only human. Hank tumbled gracefully into the Bay. His cowboy hat floated. Splashing, coughing, he came up.

"I never asked you, Hank! Can you swim?"

"You son of a bitch!" Hank sputtered.

At the wheel, Ray spun in alarm. Drew pointed the Mauser at him. "Be very careful, Uncle. Keep your hands on that wheel. I wouldn't want to have to kill you. We still need to talk."

In the churning water, Hank kept sputtering, yelling obscenities.

"That's the stuff, Hank. Keep up your spirits. You're close enough to shore—you can make it. Remember what you taught us? Get a fire going—find dry clothes. You don't want to die from hypothermia!"

As Hank's wave-tossed body receded in the distance, Drew—his Mauser steady—never took his eyes from Ray.

"That's right, Uncle, keep your hands where they are. On that wheel. Because, believe me, I'm out of patience. For a moment there, I almost hoped you'd give me an excuse to shoot. But you didn't. So. What I think"—Drew stalked angrily forward—"is, *now we talk.*"

At the house on top of the bluff, one last explosion shook the night, its flames reflecting eerily off the clouds. The rattle of automatic weapons dwindled as the yacht continued into the dark of the bay. A few seconds later, the rumble of the engine obscured the shots completely. But the shots would soon be stopping anyhow, Drew thought. Arlene and the three men would be pulling back. They'd forced Ray out of the house, and now they'd have to disappear before the police arrived.

Ray glanced from Drew toward the burning mansion on the bluff, its aura receding into the distance. Night enveloped the yacht.

Drew reached inside his coat and pulled out a packet of

C-4 explosive, holding its Play-Dough shape in front of the control panel's lights so Ray could see it. "I assume you recognize my incentive for conversation."

Ray's pupils widened.

Drew set the plastique on top of the control panel, removed a timer and detonator from his coat, and attached them to the explosive. He twisted the crank on the timer. Eight minutes. It began to tick.

"So," Drew said, "that ought to give us plenty of time for a chat. If not . . ." He shrugged.

"You'd be blowing yourself up, too."

"At the moment, as tired as I am, as sick of running"— Drew exhaled—"I don't really care."

"I don't believe you."

Drew studied Ray—tall and slender, with a lean, handsome face and deep blue eyes that glinted from the control lights. He'd be in his late fifties now, but he looked fit and youthful. His short, sandy hair had hints of silver through it, but these only made him seem more distinguished. Beneath his open topcoat, he wore an impeccably tailored gray suit, an immaculate white shirt, a striped club tie. His shoes were custom-made, Italian. His topcoat, Drew realized with anger, was brown camel's hair, the same type of coat that Ray had worn the Saturday morning in October in 1960 when he had come to the playground in Boston where Drew had mourned for his parents, for his ruined life.

Now it was October again. Boston again.

Drew's jaw muscles hardened.

"Oh, I believe you'd kill me," Ray said. "What you did to my house—or what your *friends* did to my house—is thoroughly convincing. You'd shoot me, yes. But blow us both up? Take your life with mine?"

Drew's voice was thick. "You still don't understand." The

timer kept ticking. Drew glanced at it. Less than seven min-utes. "You need to ask yourself *why* I would want to live. Give me a reason."

Ray frowned, unsettled. "Well, that's obvious. Everybody wants to live."

"For what? Why do you think I entered that monastery? From the time I was ten, I hated my life. The last happy mo-ment I knew was the second before I saw my parents blown to pieces. Everything after that was desperation."

"But you got even for what happened to them. I *helped* you get revenge!"

"It sure as Hell didn't bring me peace. There was always an-other terrorist to kill, another fanatic to punish. But others showed up to take their place. There'd never be an end. And what did I accomplish?"

Ray looked baffled. The timer kept clicking. He swallowed.

"I thought I was right to get even for my parents. The ter-rorists think *they're* right to attack governments they feel are corrupt. How many rights can there be, Ray? In the name of what I thought was right, I did the same thing I condemned them for. I murdered innocent people. I became the enemy I was hunting."

"The timer," Ray said.

"We'll come to that. Relax. For now, I want to explain about the monastery. I'm sure you're anxious to know about it. As soon as I realized what I'd become, I wanted to leave the world and its horrors, to let the madness go on without me. Let the world blow itself to Hell for all I cared. The monastery gave me refuge. But you destroyed it. You forced me back to the horrors. And for that, I can't forgive you."

Six minutes.

"What I am, Ray, is a sinner. But you're a sinner, too. You made me what I am."

"Now just a second. Nobody forced you. You *wanted* my help!"

"You manipulated me into joining Scalpel. You know what I think? Sometimes, in the blackest part of my mind, I think it was *you* who ordered the death of my parents."

"I loved your parents!"

"So you say. But isn't it interesting how many different motives there might have been for killing them? A fanatical Japanese might have decided to blow up my parents in revenge for the atomic bombs we dropped on Japan, as a way of showing us how much we weren't wanted there. Or the Soviets might have killed my parents to increase the tension between Japan and America, to jeopardize the new defense treaty and keep America away from Southeast Asia. Or maybe someone like you had the bright idea to blow up my parents and blame it on the Japanese, as a way of shaming the Japanese into stopping their demonstrations."

"That isn't true! I never—!"

"Someone, for one of those twisted motives, did! Maybe it wasn't you. But you were ready enough to have me kill that boy and his parents in France. To me, you're no different than the self-righteous bastard who did kill my parents. If I'm a sinner, *you're* a sinner. And I think it's time we atoned for our sins, don't you?"

Ray stared again at the timer. Less than five minutes now.

"Drew. For Christ's sake . . ."

"Yes, that's right. Now you're getting it. For Christ's sake."

Suddenly exhausted, he felt himself tremble. The yacht rumbled farther into the blackness of the Bay. Behind, the blaze of the house had diminished to a glow.

"You don't think I'd blow myself up with you?" Drew asked. "The way I feel right now, I can't think of a reason not to."

"No." Ray's eyes flickered with sudden hope. "You can't. You don't dare. It's suicide. You'd automatically damn your soul to Hell."

"Of course. But I deserve to go to Hell. Certainly *you* do. Because of the hit on the monastery. Because of Janus and the attacks on the Church."

"But wait a minute, Drew. There isn't *really* a Hell. What are you talking about?"

Drew's exhaustion intensified. He could hardly listen.

"There's no God, Drew. You've got your mind confused by superstition. Shut off that timer. Please. Let's talk."

"We *are* talking. No God? No Hell? Do you feel like gambling, Ray? What do you say we find out?"

"*No!*"

"That's too bad. Because I'm in a gambling mood. I have to be honest, though. You're right. I don't intend to commit suicide."

"Then you'll shut off the timer?"

"No. I've got something else in mind. A test. Just before the yacht explodes, you and I are going over the side."

"We're miles from shore! That water's freezing! We'd never be able to swim to—"

"Maybe. That's what I mean by gambling. There was a time, back in the Middle Ages, when they tested to see if someone was a sinner by throwing that person into freezing water and forcing him to stay there for hours. He passed the test if God allowed him to live. What I'm thinking is, if we die in the water, God wasn't happy with us. But it wouldn't be suicide. Because God's in control now. If He allows us to survive, if He lets us make our way to shore, it'll be a sign that He isn't angry. He'll be giving us the chance to save our souls."

Ray trembled. "You've gone crazy." He stared at the cold, dark water. At the timer. Almost three minutes. "What do you want to know? Just turn off the—!"

Aiming the Mauser, Drew shook his head. "It depends on what you've got to say. I'll even be generous and help you get started. Scalpel, Ray. In 1980, because you'd exceeded your authority, because the program was dangerously out of control, you were forced to resign from the government. Scalpel was disbanded. So you founded the Risk Analysis Corporation."

"How did you learn—?" Ray stared at the timer. "All right, yes, a private intelligence service."

Drew blazed. "A private *assassination* service."

"We work for major corporations. Sometimes for other intelligence networks. We helped organize the rebels in Nicaragua, for example. That way, there's less criticism about the U.S. interfering with foreign governments. Because the Agency isn't officially involved, it keeps Congress from complaining but still fights the Communists in—"

"I don't *care* about Nicaragua! Janus, get to Janus!"

Ray took a hand off the wheel to gesture impatiently. "Give me time! I'm—!"

Drew tensed his finger on the Mauser's trigger. "Put your hand back on that wheel or you won't be alive when that bomb explodes."

Ray grasped the wheel again. His eyes darted toward the clicking timer. Two minutes, forty-five seconds.

"Janus!" Drew said again. "*Why?*"

Ray's chest heaved. "We have another contract. In Iran. To take out the Ayatollah."

"Yes." Drew bitterly smiled. "Our old friend, the Ayatollah. Isn't it amazing how things keep leading back to him? Who gave you the contract against him?"

"I was never told. A freelance negotiator came to us with the offer. But I always assumed it was Iraq." Ray became more agitated as the timer clicked. "What difference does it make who hired us? I gladly accepted the contract. The Ayatollah's a maniac. Something has to be done about him."

Two minutes, twenty seconds.

"You'd better hurry, Ray."

"We haven't been able to get near him. Five attempts. Whatever we do, he seems to know about it. So we tried another tactic. Oh, please, shut off . . . We wanted to force the West to decide he was so insane he had to be stopped. Something so outrageous that the U.S. and Europe would side with Iraq against him."

"Janus. What about Janus?"

The timer kept clicking.

"You'd bungled a hit against the Ayatollah. It looked as if you'd become a rogue—that you'd sold out to him. Even if you hadn't, you'd become too unstable to be trusted with what you knew. I hated to do it."

"But you tried to have me killed."

"*Tried?* I was *sure* you were dead. Later, after Risk Analysis was formed, after we had the contract against the Ayatollah, I realized a way to use you even in death."

One minute, forty seconds.

Ray shuddered. "I invented Janus. The two-faced. You. The turncoat, working for the Ayatollah. Since you didn't exist anymore, the authorities would be chasing a ghost. To keep them on the trail, I used Mike to make an appearance once in a while. Not for anything dangerous. A blurred photograph taken near the site of a job. A conversation with a hotel clerk who'd remember him later when the authorities asked about strangers in the area. Once we'd established Janus, Mike went to ground. He put on a little weight. Changed his haircut. Kept to himself, but maintained a regular schedule. He had alibis. No one could link him with Janus. Then my people did the actual jobs. Drew, *the timer.*"

"Jobs against the Catholic Church?" Drew burned with such outrage he wanted to crash the butt of his pistol across his uncle's face. *"You killed priests to create a smokescreen?"*

"A holy war. We wanted it to look as if the Ayatollah was fighting a *jihad* against the heathen, against the Church. He's fanatical enough to do that. A new crusade. But in the reverse. This time not in the Mideast but in Europe."

Fifty-five seconds.

"Shut it off!"

Drew touched the knob on the dial. "Then you'd publish proof of what the Ayatollah was supposed to be doing. The West would react with outrage and crush him. When the dust settled, Iraq would have gained what it wanted."

"The *world* would have gained! I don't care about the money. What I did was necessary!"

Drew repeated the word, almost spitting it out with contempt. "*Necessary?*"

"Yes! Now shut it off!"

Instead, Drew shrugged and let the timer click off its final seconds. He smiled. "Goodbye, Uncle Ray."

Ray gasped. "No! Wait! You're really going to do it?"

"You'd better start believing in God. If I were you, I'd make an Act of Contrition. Remember how it goes? 'Oh, my God, I am heartily sorry . . .' "

With a scream, Ray lunged toward the stern. A wave buffeted the yacht, adding force to his dive. He went over, plunging into blackness.

The timer stopped. A cold wind stung Drew's face. Waves, splashing the yacht, sent an icy mist over him. He shut off the engine. The night became silent—except for the hiss of the wind and the whump of waves against the hull. He grabbed a rubber flashlight off the control panel and walked to the stern, peering toward Ray, who was struggling to keep afloat in the churning water.

Panicked, Ray squinted at the flashlight's glare.

"I'd take that overcoat off, if I were you," Drew said. "It'll drag you down."

"The bomb." Ray thrashed in the water.

"An oversight. I forgot to attach the timer to the detonator. As I said, I didn't intend to commit suicide."

"You son of a bitch!"

"Here. Take this life preserver." Drew tossed it to him.

Ray clutched it, spitting water. "Cold." His voice shook. "So cold. You can't imagine."

Drew studied him.

"Please. Pull me in."

"Sorry. I gave you the life preserver so you wouldn't drown. That doesn't mean I won't let you die from exposure. Drowning's too quick, and they say it's even pleasant. But this way . . ."

"You bastard, I did what you asked! I told you what you wanted to know!" Ray's face was shockingly white. His teeth chattered. *"Please!"*

"But you didn't tell me everything. Those priests Janus murdered. How could you bring yourself to order it? How could you think that good could ever come out of the murder of innocent priests?"

His voice quivering, Ray thrashed in the water. "If those priests were strong in their faith, they went to Heaven. They were martyrs. They gave up their lives to stop the Ayatollah. *Anything's* justified to stop him."

"You claim those priests went to Heaven? But a while ago, you said you didn't believe in an afterlife. You'll say anything, *do* anything, for what you think is right." Drew paused; certainty filled his soul. "You did kill my parents. For the sake of a principle." Bile rose bitterly in his throat. He was afraid he was going to be sick.

"But I didn't! Please . . . so cold. Get me out of here!"

"We'll see. It all depends on how you answer my next few questions. Then I'll decide what to do with you. The monastery. I need to know about the hit on the monastery.

How did you find out I wasn't dead? How did you learn where I was?" Though Drew suspected the answer, close to vomiting because of it, he needed to know for sure.

"Jake." A wave struck Ray's open mouth, making him gag.

"What about him? What happened to him?"

His teeth chattering, Ray struggled in the cold, black water. "I caught him investigating Janus. My men picked him up. Under amytal, he confessed he hadn't killed you. He told me about the monastery."

"You had him killed?"

"He knew too much. He couldn't be trusted. It had to be done."

"No!" Drew shivered in revulsion. He screamed out his grief.

How could he tell Arlene?

"My arms." Ray sank, then struggled to the surface. "Cramps. Help me. Cold . . . In the name of . . . Please! So cold!"

Jake was dead? All along, Drew had realized that possibility. He thought he'd prepared himself to accept it. Now he felt so stunned that he almost didn't hear Ray beg. But a wave sloshed across the yacht, stinging Drew's face, shocking him into awareness.

Again Ray sank beneath the water.

Vengeance insisted. It would feel so good to let Ray die. And yet Ray's death wouldn't bring Jake back.

Ray didn't come up. Tensing, Drew understood. God was testing him. And the consequence would be ultimate. I can't hope for God to show mercy if I don't show mercy to someone else.

Drew pulled the rope on the life preserver frantically. But when he tugged Ray to the surface, the body was motionless, mouth hanging open, draining water.

No!

Drew strained on the line. Desperate, he dragged Ray over the side, slumping with him onto the deck.

Ray moaned. Alive!

I have to make him warm!

In search of blankets, hot tea, dry clothes, Drew scrambled toward the hatch that led below deck. No! he realized, appalled. *I should take him with me. It's too cold up here. The mist from the waves will make the blankets wet!*

He spun, rushing back toward Ray.

And dove to the deck as his uncle fired.

Ray's hand shook from the icy water he'd been in. His bullet missed Drew, walloping into the cabin. Ray gripped the gun with both hands, cursing as he steadied his aim.

Drew shot him three times in the face.

And screamed. In rage, in frustration, almost in despair. Too much death. Everywhere. But this time, he'd tried to prevent it.

Pointless. Useless.

And the worst part was, he knew what was coming. He'd have to tell Arlene her brother was dead. He knew what Father Stanislaw would ask of him now. His ordeal wasn't over yet.

Waves crashed icy mist across his face. The dark closed in.

22

The god of beginnings.

Drew stood in the cemetery in Boston, once more staring down at the graves of his parents, a ritual he hadn't been able to obey since leaving the monastery. Robert and Susan MacLane. Their birth dates were different, the date of death the same. June 25, 1960. With a flinch, he remembered the segments of his father's body strewn across the Japanese garden. And the shards of broken glass projecting from his mother's bloody cheeks.

In my beginning is my end.

It was one day after Uncle Ray's death. Saying prayers for the dead, Drew had dumped the body overboard and guided the yacht south along the coastline, finding a private dock where after removing his fingerprints he left the yacht unmoored, letting it drift back out to the Bay. In the dark, he headed into Boston.

Now the sun was setting again. As twilight gathered around him, he continued to stare at the gradually dimming names on the gravestones. A cold breeze ruffled his hair.

A figure approached, making no effort at stealth. In the thickening shadows, Drew wasn't sure who it was, but because the figure was taking care to be obvious, Drew subdued his alarm. He saw a swath of white against a black overcoat. A sling for an injured arm. Father Stanislaw.

The priest came up beside him, his voice respectful. "Am I intruding? If so, I can wait for you at my car."

"No. Stay if you like. I don't mind the company. But how did you know I'd be here?"

"I suppose I could pretend to understand you well enough to predict your patterns. The truth is, at the townhouse when you woke up this afternoon, you told Arlene where you'd be. I hope you don't think she violated your confidence by telling me."

"Not at all. I trust her judgment."

"It's peaceful here."

"Yes. Peaceful." Drew waited for the priest to say what was on his mind.

"When we first met"—Father Stanislaw's voice was resonant—"you asked me about my ring. I told you, one day when we knew each other, I'd explain."

"About the fraternity of the stone?" Drew's interest quickened.

"Yes."

Even in shadow, the ruby was so rich that a subtle fire seemed to glow within it. Father Stanislaw rubbed its insignia. The intersecting sword and cross. "This is a copy of a ring that dates back to the time of the Crusades. It represents history. Are you a student of history?"

"You have my attention, if that's what you mean."

Father Stanislaw chuckled. "Palestine," he said. "Eleven ninety-two. The Third Crusade. With the blessing of the Pope, armies from France and England invaded the Holy Land to capture it from the Muslims, the heathen. But at the victorious siege of Acre, a rift developed between the French and English forces. You see, the English claimed considerable territory in France, and the French king, Philip, grasping the chance to gain an advantage, decided to take his forces and leave the Holy Land, to go home. His purpose was to ensure control of those contested regions in France while the English king, Richard, and his army remained in the Holy Land, continuing the Crusade."

"Politics," Drew said with contempt.

"But shrewd. And good came out of it. Before the French returned to Europe, their intelligence officers met with their English equivalents. As a gesture of professional brotherhood, despite their political differences, the French proposed a solution to a growing dangerous problem that the English would now have to deal with alone. The assassins."

"Yes. The first of their kind. They originated terrorism," Drew said.

"The crusaders were certainly terrorized. As knights, they were used to a noble code of battle, in the open, face to face. They had no experience with an enemy who considered it equally noble to attack under cover of night, to enter an opponent's tent and kill him while he was helpless, unarmed, asleep. The assassins took particular delight in cutting off the head of a crusader and setting it on the altar where mass would take place the next morning. Such barbarism made the crusaders feel that the world had become unhinged."

"The purpose of terrorism."

"Precisely. To kill so as to demoralize. But the French intelligence officers, before they left the Holy Land, proposed a solution. Fight fire with fire. Use assassins to fight assassins. Demoralize as they themselves had been demoralized. This proposal met with serious objections from the English. 'Descend to the level of our enemy? Never.' But in the end, the English agreed. Because the Christian assassin would not be one of themselves but, instead, a former Muslim. A Palestinian who'd converted to the one true faith, Catholicism. A monk at the Benedictine monastery in Monte Cassino, Italy.

"This monk, because of his heritage, knew the traditions of the assassins. And because he was of their race, he could pass easily among them. An assassin attacking assassins, he would fight terror with terror. But *this* terror would be different. With the blessing of the Pope, this crusading assassin would be killing for God. His terror would be holy."

Drew listened with growing distress, the darkness seeming to smother him.

"The monk's Christian name was Father Jerome. His Muslim name has never been verified, though legend has it that he was called Hassan ibn al-Sabbah, by divine coincidence the same name as the founder of the original Muslim assassins. I take this to be apocryphal. But of his achievements, there is no doubt. He did strike terror into the terrorists, and at the close of his service for God, when the Third Crusade was over, he returned to the monastery at Monte Cassino, where he was given the honor and rewards he deserved."

"By 'rewards,' you mean the ring?"

"No, that came later. In fact, it was first given to someone else, though in time it was also given to Father Jerome."

The cold night air stung Drew's face. "If you expect me to play Twenty Questions . . ."

"Forgive me for being cryptic. The history is complicated. At the end of the Third Crusade, the English king, Richard—he was known as the Lion-Hearted—set out to return to England. Part of his motive for discontinuing the Crusade was his realization of the mistake he'd made in allowing the French to return before him. The French king, Philip, had negotiated a treasonous bargain with Richard's temporary replacement. Indeed, the acting head of state was Richard's brother, John. The bargain was intended to settle the dispute about the English lands in France. John agreed to give up England's claim to the lands in France. Philip in turn agreed to support John's claim to the English throne—against the rightful claim of Richard."

"So Richard decided he'd better head home," Drew said.

"But he was stopped. On his way through Europe from the Holy Land, he was captured by the Austrians and held for ransom. The problem was, how to pay it. Richard's brother, John, didn't want his brother released. John did everything possible to prevent the ransom from being paid. He sent agents pretending to be from Richard and had them collect valuables intended to be part of the ransom. But those valuables went into John's own treasury. Meanwhile Richard rotted in prison. At last, in desperation, Richard found a way to guarantee that his subjects would know which ransom collectors were truly from him and not from John."

"The ring? Am I right?"

"Yes. The ring. Almost identical to the one I wear." Father Stanislaw rubbed its insignia again. "Richard gave his ring to a trusted assistant. His subjects had learned to identify the ring with him. By showing it, the assistant could prove that the valuables he collected would help get Richard out of prison and not go into John's treasury."

Drew shook his head.

"You see a problem with that tactic?" Father Stanislaw asked.

"To stop his brother, all John had to do was order a jeweler to make a copy of the ring."

"John had mental limitations. He never thought of it. If he had, he might have gained the throne. Instead, with the aid of the ring, Richard's assistant collected the ransom, and Richard was released. He returned to England and crushed his brother. *Because of his ring.* With a slight distinction, *this* ring. It had importance. It was a password. It possessed a power."

Drew became more uneasy; he sensed a disturbing undertone to the story.

Father Stanislaw continued. "Richard refused to abide by John's agreement with the French. He took his army to the mainland and reclaimed his territories. But there, one of his new subjects, a French peasant, saw him walking outside the walls of a castle one day and shot him with an arrow. The wound was in the shoulder. It should not have been fatal, but unskilled treatment made it mortal. Dying, Richard insisted that his attacker be brought before him. 'Why did you kill me?' Richard asked. The peasant answered, 'Because you would have raped my wife and starved my children.' Richard objected, 'My subjects love me. All I wanted was the land. I would have let you live in peace.' But the peasant answered, 'No, your brother would have let us live in peace.' And Richard, understanding how this simple man had been used by his enemies, said, 'God help you. You know not what you've done. I forgive you. Let this man go away unhurt.' It is said that the priest who was present at Richard's deathbed exhorted him to repentance and restitution for his sins, but Richard drove the priest away and died without benefit of the sacraments."

"And the peasant?" Drew asked. "Was he allowed to go away unharmed?"

Father Stanislaw stepped closer to Drew in the darkness. "That's the point of my story. After Richard died, his angry associates debated what to do about their lord's final wish. They wanted to question the peasant to learn if anyone else had been involved in the assassination. But before they did, a priest went to hear the peasant's confession. The peasant died shortly after his confessor left. It seems he committed suicide by swallowing poison, though no one discovered how he got the poison."

"From the priest?" Drew asked.

"Would it help if I said that the priest who heard the peasant's confession was also the priest whose medical treatment failed to save Richard's life?"

Drew felt a chill. "The priest was Father Jerome?"

"No. His Mideastern features would have betrayed him. But the priest was *trained* by Father Jerome."

"And why did he kill . . ."

"To keep the peasant from revealing that King Philip had hired him. Only a priest would not be suspected of silencing Richard's assassin. In this way, a Franco-English war was averted."

"That's not what I meant. Why a priest? Why did Father Jerome let himself become involved?"

"In exchange for his service—and his assistant's service—Father Jerome gained some of England's land in France for the Church to which he'd converted."

Drew felt sick. "And the Church went along with it?"

"The Church, the Pope and his associates, never knew. They have *never* known. The fraternity of the stone is an order located on the Atlantic coast of France, in one of the regions once claimed by England. Its symbol is this ring. The intersecting sword and cross."

"Religion and violence?" Drew was appalled.

"The symbol of a warrior for God. Holy terror. Through the years, using the example of Father Jerome, the fraternity has intervened for the Church whenever the profane world has threatened it. Soldiers for Christ. Church militant. We fight Satan with Satan's tactics. In Richard's time. And even more today."

As he'd felt last night when Uncle Ray had died, Drew wanted to vomit. The revelation put him on guard. The priest was telling him things Drew shouldn't know.

"The three men who helped you last night—you noticed their rings—are members of the fraternity," Father Stanislaw said. "I emphasize that our order is distinct from the members of Opus Dei who've been assisting us. Opus Dei is the intelligence branch of the Church. We are—"

"The Church's assassins." Drew was outraged. "Except the Church doesn't know about it."

"Though we do have the Church's sanction."

"That doesn't make sense. Sanction? How? If the Church doesn't know."

"By tradition. Just as each Pope inherits the mandate given by Christ to Peter, so we inherit the absolution given to Father Jerome by the Pope at the time of the Third Crusade. A Pope is infallible. If it was justifiable to kill for the Church at *that* time, it must be equally justifiable to kill for the Church at other times."

"I don't want to hear any more."

"But I thought you'd find it interesting." Father Stanislaw rubbed his ring. "After all, you did ask for an explanation of the stone. Given your reaction, you realize now why I waited."

"Till we knew each other better."

"Yes."

The cemetery was silent in the deepening night. Drew sensed what was coming.

"Join us," Father Stanislaw said.

In spite of his premonition, Drew wasn't able to prepare himself. He reacted automatically—with disgust. "Become an assassin for God?"

"To some degree, you already are. Since you left the monastery, you've killed several men. To protect the Church."

"I had a different motive."

"What, to stay alive? To get even with those who'd attacked you? You're a complex man. Those reasons aren't sufficient. A Carthusian, who once was a killer but for the wrong reasons, you could use your skills now for the *right* reasons. To safeguard the Holy See. To defend Christ's mission on earth."

"To defend Christ's mission?" Drew couldn't contain his anger any longer. "Maybe I read a different New Testament than you did. Didn't Christ say something about turning the other cheek, about the *peaceful* inheriting the earth?"

"But that was before his Crucifixion. The world, my friend, is a desperate place. Without the fraternity, the Church would long ago have failed. History, which is the record of God's will, has justified our cause."

"I pass," Drew said.

"But you can't."

"Killing? I want nothing more to do with it. What I want is peace."

"But in *this* world, peace isn't possible. Only a long hard fight. Till Judgment Day."

"You're wrong. But I'll pray for your soul."

Father Stanislaw inhaled sharply. "Three times I saved your life."

"I know that. I promised I'd do anything to save your life in return."

"You aren't remembering correctly. Last night, you promised you'd return the favors in kind. Remember how I phrased the demand? Return the favors *in kind*! And now I'm asking you to fulfill your promise. To keep your word. Join us. Not to save my life—to save the life of the Church. Use your talents for the good of the Lord."

"I wonder," Drew said bitterly. "Which Lord is that?"

"God. I'm asking you to serve God!"

"But how many Gods can there be? The Ayatollah thinks his God is the one and only. The Hindus think theirs is. The Buddhists. The Jews. The Muslims. The Catholics. The Protestants. The aborigines who pray to the moon. God sure gets around. And He sure seems to want a lot of killing. How many millions have died for Him? You say history's the record of God's will? To me, it's an uninterrupted sequence of holy wars. And each side was absolutely certain it was right! Totally confident that if they died for their faith they saved their souls! Well, how many true causes can there be? How many heavens? Last night, Uncle Ray told me that to stop the Ayatollah, he considered it justifiable to make the Ayatollah seem to be attacking the Catholic Church. The priests who died, he said, would achieve salvation because of their unknowing sacrifice. Ray didn't even believe in God, yet he used religion to defend his actions. Madness. Religion? Save us from the sins we commit in the name of religion."

Father Stanislaw shuddered. "Then you vindicate the Ayatollah?"

"No more than I vindicate you. Or Ray. To kill in self-defense I can understand. I've done it myself in the last two weeks. But to kill for the sake of a principle? That's inexcusable."

"Then we don't disagree."

Drew felt his heart pounding. "How can you say that?"

"Because we protect the Church," Father Stanislaw said, "it *is* self-defense."

"The Church shouldn't need protecting. If God stands behind it—or any other religion—He'll make sure it survives.

Without violence. He sent you a test. You failed. I told you, I'll pray for your soul."

Drew walked away.

"I'm not finished yet!" Father Stanislaw said.

Drew kept walking.

Father Stanislaw followed. "You can't refuse my offer!"

"I did." In the shadows, gravestone led to gravestone.

Father Stanislaw kept after him. "There's something I haven't told you."

"It won't make a difference."

"Remember, I said this ring was *almost* identical to Richard's? The ruby's the same. The gold band and setting. The insignia. The intersecting sword and cross."

Drew passed a mausoleum.

"But there's a crucial difference." Father Stanislaw walked close behind him. "The stone tilts up. And beneath the stone, there's a tiny compartment. Within, there's a capsule. The poison is instantaneous. Because if one of the order should ever be captured, he must guarantee that no outsider can threaten us. Our secret must be kept. I can think of no other instance in which suicide would be justified. Surely you understand what I'm telling you. If we're prepared to kill ourselves to protect the order's secret, we're prepared to go to other extremes."

Drew continued through the dark.

"My friend, if you don't stop right now and agree to join us, I'll be forced to kill you. No outsider can ever know about us."

Drew didn't turn. "You want me to make it easy for you? I'm supposed to try to fight? So you'll feel justified? Like hell. In the back—that's how you'll have to kill me. And you'll be doing me a favor. Because if I die refusing you, I'll have a good chance of saving my soul."

"Don't force me to do this," Father Stanislaw said. "I've grown to like you. Even to admire you."

Drew didn't stop.

"Your choice is final?"

Walking, Drew studied murky tombstones.

"Very well then." Father Stanislaw sighed.

"You know I'm not a threat to you. I'd never tell."

"Oh, certainly. I have no doubt. You'll never tell."

Drew felt an icy tickle between his shoulderblades, where the knife or the bullet would strike. Self-defense, he thought. It's not a sin if I protect myself.

The spit of a silenced pistol was terribly close behind him. He dove to the right, scrambling around a marble angel of death, drawing his Mauser.

Instead of another spit, he heard a groan. He reversed his direction, spinning the opposite way around the angel, risking exposure to fire.

The risk was needless.

Father Stanislaw sagged toward the grassy mound of a grave. His silenced pistol went off. With a muffled report, it tore up grass on top of the grave. He fell across the grass, his head toward the gravestone. Trembled. And lay still.

Drew tensed, scanning the darkness.

A shadow moved. He held his breath, crouching.

The shadow emerged, coming closer.

Jake.

EPILOGUE

"AND FOR YOUR PENANCE . . ."

THE WANDERERS

※

1

An hour later, Drew entered the townhouse in Beacon Hill. "We'd better get going," he told Arlene.

She seemed surprised. "Right now?"

"Our business is finished. It's safer not to stay in town."

The woman who'd taken care of Father Stanislaw asked if the priest would be returning.

"No. He's been called away on an urgent matter. He asked me to thank you for all your kindness. He thanks your friends and the man who lent us this house. I've put the sports car in the garage." Drew gave her the keys to the car and the house. "May God be with you."

"And with your spirit."

"*Deo gratias.*"

2

"What's going on?" Arlene demanded. "Why the rush?"

In the night, Drew walked with her around the corner.

She stopped, confused, when she saw where the Oldsmobile was parked. "But you said Father Stanislaw had been called away."

"In an ultimate sense, he was. He's dead."

"He's *what*?"

"Someone shot him." Drew gestured toward the Oldsmobile's trunk. "The body's in there."

"Shot him?"

"Saved my life."

"But *who*?"

Drew opened the passenger door.

Jake grinned. "Sis, how about a hug?"

She burst into tears.

3

Jake had changed little. His mustache was as red as ever, his hair thick, crinkly, and red, his forehead high, handsome. He wore outdoor clothes. Hiking boots. A nylon pack sat beside him.

"They wanted my death to look like an accident—to keep you from asking questions, Sis. I was supposed to take a fall while I was climbing. They forgot how good I am." Jake grinned. "I made the idiots with me take the fall and got my ass away from there."

"I wish you'd told me. You could have sent a message to me somehow and let me know where you were, so I wouldn't worry."

"But suppose they questioned *you*? If they gave you amytal, even though you're my sister, you'd have had to tell them where I was the same as they used amytal to make me tell them Drew was still alive and in the monastery. I couldn't risk contacting you. I kept checking for news about a hit on the monastery. Nothing in the papers or on television. I started to wonder. Had something gone wrong with the hit? Had Drew survived? I couldn't go to you, Sis, but I knew there was one place Drew would go if he was out. Maybe not right away, but eventually. The same place I found him in seventy-nine."

"My parents' graves," Drew said.

"And now we're together," Arlene added.

But for how long? Drew wondered.

4

Leaving Boston, they drove the Oldsmobile back to Pennsylvania, to Bethlehem, to Arlene's Firebird where they'd left it at a long-term parking garage. The journey, three hundred miles, took most of the night. Along the way they stopped near the grave of Stuart Little to bury Father Stanislaw in the dark on a cold, high, wooded slope.

Before they covered the body, they removed his priest's clothes, a St. Christopher medal around his neck, and his ring. As Drew had done when he'd lowered Uncle Ray's body into the Bay, he silently recited the prayers for the dead. Maybe God is truly forgiving, he thought. Maybe He makes allowance for those who worship Him too fervently. As a gentle rain began to fall—possibly in blessing—Drew turned away.

In Bethlehem, at 4 A.M., Arlene roused a sleepy garage attendant, redeemed her Firebird, and followed Drew and Jake in the Oldsmobile to a secluded bank of the Lehigh River. In the rain and dark, they pushed the priest's car and its weapons down a steep embankment into a deep part of the river. With its windows open, the car sank quickly.

Drew pulled Father Stanislaw's ring from his pocket, traced his finger along the intersecting cross and sword on the ruby, and hurled it far out into the river. In the gloom, he never saw where it disappeared.

The rain fell harder, obscuring dawn. They headed east, crossing the Delaware River into New Jersey, where finally exhaustion forced them to pull in at a roadside rest area. Drew slept fitfully, squirming from nightmares, until the blaring horn of a passing semi-truck startled the three of them fully awake, upright, just after 11 A.M. Weary, anxious, they continued eastward.

Throughout the afternoon, the news on the radio repeated the details about the attack on Uncle Ray's mansion, and his mysterious disappearance. A former intelligence official, committed to fighting terrorism, he was rumored to have been kidnapped, killed by terrorists in reprisal for his lifelong vendetta.

A separate story from State College, Pennsylvania, announced that the body of a man found four days ago in the cellar of a student rental complex resembled photographs of an international assassin known as Janus. Preliminary reports revealed that this mercenary had been using various cover identities, including that of Andrew MacLane, a member of a disbanded government antiterrorist group, who'd disappeared in 1979. MacLane, it was theorized, had been killed by Janus because their coincidental resemblance allowed Janus to assume MacLane's identity. Hunting MacLane, a dead man, the authorities would thus be misled from the actual target of their search.

Taking turns driving, Drew, Arlene, and Jake reached New York and waited until night before scouting Twelfth Street. The brownstone was not being watched. Drew wasn't surprised; with Uncle Ray gone, Risk Analysis destroyed, and Janus exposed, there'd be no reason for anyone to stake out the house. Neither Drew nor Arlene had given their names to Opus Dei. The fraternity didn't know that Father Stanislaw was dead. Arlene could not be linked to Risk Analysis. Nor to Drew. Nor Drew to her. Going in seemed safe.

But cautious by nature, they entered the brownstone through a building on Eleventh Street, leaving that building's rear, crossing a narrow garden in a walkway where Arlene had once tried unsuccessfully to grow flowers.

The kitchen smelled musty. Arlene opened windows, checked the refrigerator—she'd thrown out anything that would spoil before she'd left to go to Satan's Horn, at the start of her search for Jake—and opened several cans of tuna that she kept in the cupboard.

"You still won't eat meat, huh?" she kidded Drew.

He didn't smile at the tease. "It's the last habit I kept from the monastery."

Not quite.

Jake seemed to understand. "I'd better leave you two alone."

5

Drew glanced across the table toward Arlene.

"What's wrong?" she asked.

He didn't answer.

"Do I make you nervous?" she asked.

"How could you possibly make me nervous?" He smiled and took her hand.

"Because I made you promise when this was over we'd talk."

He remembered the promise and sobered. "Yes, we'd talk."

"About the future. Us. I don't want you to feel any pressure," she said. "I know you need to make a lot of adjustments. After six years in a monastery. But there's something we used to have. To share. It was special. Maybe one day we can have it again."

"One day," he echoed dismally.

"Do you want to go back to the monastery? Is that what you're trying to tell me?"

"No. I won't go back. I can't."

"Can't?"

He couldn't bring himself to explain. He'd promised they'd talk when this was over. But he couldn't subdue his apprehension that this wasn't over. Explain? Ruin what might be their last peaceful moments together? Instead, he walked over, embracing her.

Without a word, they went upstairs to her bedroom.

And at last made love.

He felt no guilt. What Arlene had once said was true: His vow was really one of celibacy, not chastity. Given the Church's attitude toward communal property, a member of a religious order wasn't so much forbidden to have sex as not to marry. The restriction was legal, not moral, to prevent a wife from wanting to share what her husband worked for, the Church's assets.

Otherwise, the restriction was only one of self-denial. And at the moment, weary, heartsick, Drew didn't care about self-denial. It occurred to him that two human beings who chose to give comfort to each other, to ease each other's pain, couldn't possibly be committing wrong.

Naked, his body against hers, feeling her warmth, her lean, lithe, muscular response to his thrusts, her body returning his thrusts, hard yet soft, demanding yet giving, he felt a completeness in himself.

The feeling was sensual, yes. Erotic, yes. But it was more. For beyond the physical pleasure, this sharing of each other cast away his loneliness, his anguish, his sense of imminent doom. In this long eternal instant, he no longer felt damned.

But eternity was shattered. The present cruelly insisted as Drew heard the phone ring.

He pivoted from Arlene's body, staring toward the phone on the bedside table.

No, not yet! I had things I wanted to say! I wanted to—!

The phone rang again. He felt Arlene's body stiffen next to him.

But I'm not ready! Couldn't they have given us a few more hours together?

The phone rang a third time. Its jangle seemed extra harsh in the gathering silence.

"I'd better answer it," she said. "Maybe a neighbor saw the lights and decided to make sure I'm back. We don't want the cops to show up looking for a burglar."

He nodded in agony.

She picked up the phone. "Hello?" Her eyes darkened. "Who? I'm sorry. I don't know anyone with that name . . . Oh, yes, I see. I understand. Since you put it that way." She pressed a hand across the mouthpiece.

Drew didn't need to ask who it was.

"A man wants to speak to you. I don't understand how he knew you were here. He says he offers you a choice. The easy way, or—"

"I get the point." Straining to quell his apprehension, Drew took the phone. "Hello?"

"Brother MacLane"—the voice was deep but smooth; Drew imagined it intoning a mass—"we'd like to know what happened to Father Stanislaw. He didn't check in with us as scheduled. We know he went to recruit you. We want you to tell us what you did with him. *And with his ring.*"

The room seemed to tilt. "I can't discuss this over the phone."

"Of course. Shall we meet in fifteen minutes? At the arch in Washington Square? It's just a few blocks away."

"I'll be there."

"We know you will. We're sure you're as anxious as we are to settle any misunderstanding."

"That's what it is. A misunderstanding." Swallowing, Drew hung up.

He reached for his clothes.

"Who *was* that?" Arlene asked.

He put on his shirt and pants.

"*Who?*"

"The fraternity."

She shivered.

"They want to know what happened to Father Stanislaw. They want me to meet them. In Washington Square."

"But you can't take the risk!"

"I know." He hugged her, long and hard, feeling her naked body against him. "If I let them get their hands on me, no matter how I resist, I'll be forced to tell them who killed Father Stanislaw. Jake, not me. And after they've finished with me, they'll come after Jake, maybe even after you. I can't let that happen. Christ, I love you."

She held him so tightly his injured shoulder throbbed. "But where will you go?"

"I don't dare answer. In case they use drugs to question you."

"I'll go with you."

"And prove you're involved?" Drew shook his head. "They'd kill you."

"I don't care!"

"But I do!"

"I'd go *anywhere* for you."

"To Hell? I'm giving you your life. Next to your soul, that's the greatest gift. Please take it."

She kissed him, sobbing. "But when will . . ."

Drew understood. "We see each other again? One day during Lent."

"What year?"

He didn't know. As a drowning man clutches his saviour, he clung to her.

Then released his grip.

And was gone.

EXILE

Egypt. South of Cairo, west of the Nile.

He wandered into the Nitrian Desert, where in A.D. 381 the first Christian hermits, fleeing Rome, had begun monasticism. It hadn't been easy for him to reach this wilderness. Without money or a passport, pursued by the fraternity, he'd needed every trick and wile, every ounce of strength and scrap of determination. His torturous journey had lasted six months, and now as he walked across the sun-parched sand, squinting toward the rocky bluff in the distance where he meant to establish his cell, he felt a great relief, a burden falling away from him. Safe now, away from people, the horrors of civilization, he no longer had to fear for Arlene's safety. All he had to fear for was his soul.

Finding a cave among the rocks, a tiny waterhole nearby, a village a day's walk away where he could buy provisions, he reestablished his routine from the monastery, silently reciting the vespers prayers, recalling the matins service, providing responses to an imaginary celebrant of mass. He meditated.

Rarely he saw another person passing by in the distance. He always hid. But every six weeks—he waited as long as possible—he had to encounter the world when he went to the village for more provisions. On those traumatic occasions, he spoke only as much as was necessary to conduct his business, and the tradesmen, normally fond of haggling, didn't invite conversation. This tall, lean, sunburned man with haunted eyes, his hair grown past his shoulders, his beard hanging down his chest, his robe in rags, was obviously a holy one. They gave him distance and respect.

His days were filled with solitude. But not with peace. As hard as he meditated, he still was often struck by thoughts of Arlene. One day in Lent, he'd vowed, I'll go back to her.

He thought about Jake. And Uncle Ray. And Father Stanislaw. The fraternity. Would they ever stop hunting him? Or was
that part of his penance, constantly to be hunted?

Sometimes he remembered his parents. Their deaths. Their
graves. Beginnings and ends.

He gazed to the west toward Libya, the madman who ruled
it, the terrorists being trained there.

He gazed to the east toward Iraq and Iran, toward Israel
and its enemies, toward the Holy Land and the birthplace of
assassins and terrorism.

His heart filled with gall.

He had much to think about.

HEARING VOICES

by

David Morrell

Readers often ask me which of my books I like the best. I usually answer that I need to choose four instead of one: my debut novel, *First Blood* (which introduced Rambo); the memoir I wrote about my dead son, *Fireflies; The Brotherhood of the Rose;* and whatever book I'm currently working on. But if someone asks me which of my books has my favorite beginning, I can easily pick a single title: *The Fraternity of the Stone*. The remote monastery, the penitential spy, the dead mouse, the poisoned monks, the spy's escape to the outside world, which he hasn't seen in six years—these elements made me smile when I first imagined them, and all these years later, they still do.

The idea for the book came to me because I grieved for a character I'd killed in my previous novel, *The Brotherhood of the Rose*. There, two boys grow up in a military-style orphanage, where a middle-aged man visits them frequently and becomes their surrogate father. Only as adults do they realize that he's a powerful member of the CIA and that he trained them to be his private operatives. Because they love him, they'll do anything for him, including kill. He doesn't love them in return, however, and when he fears they know too much about him, he arranges to have them eliminated. Unfortunately for him, only one is killed, and the survivor goes after the man he once thought of as a father, chasing him around the world to get revenge.

At the time, I wasn't sure which orphan to kill. One was Chris, an Irish Catholic who felt racked by guilt about the terrible things he'd done for his surrogate father. For a while, his turmoil drove him to a monastery. When that didn't help, he tried to starve himself to death. By comparison, the other orphan, Saul—outgoing and Jewish—was a model of mental health. To some degree, that made him less interesting to me, and in an early draft, Saul was the one who died.

The book froze. Whenever I tried to write a scene in which Chris confronted his surrogate father, I couldn't make it work. Finally, after repeated frustrating attempts, I saw a hand waving at me from a corner of my imagination. Turning my mind's eye in that direction, I discovered Saul.

"You killed the wrong guy," he told me.

I'm not exaggerating. Most novelists admit that their characters talk to them. For us, it's normal to hear voices, although a clinical psychologist I once sat next to on a crowded airplane didn't think it was normal when she asked about my creative process and I made the mistake of telling her that my characters talked to me. Despite our cramped seating arrangements, she strained to put as much distance between us as possible, clearly concerned that I was a serial killer.

"Chris tried to commit suicide, remember?" Saul told me. "He isn't emotionally strong enough to go after the son of a bitch we thought of as our father. Put Chris out of his misery. I'm the one who can get the job done."

Saul was absolutely correct, and after I rewrote the death scene so that Chris was the victim and Saul survived, *The Brotherhood of the Rose* pepped right along. Still, I continued to feel that Chris was the more interesting character, and I so missed writing about him that I decided to create a version of him in another novel. This new character, Drew MacLane, would be an orphan like Chris. He, too, would be a spy and racked by guilt for the sins he'd committed in response to orders. He would do penance in a monastery, but by no means would he be suicidal, and he wouldn't have a "brother" as a companion. Instead he would live alone in a monastic cell for six years, and when he was forced to rejoin the world, he would be absolutely bewildered by the changes that had occurred.

At that point, my imagination stopped. I had no idea what would happen next. Normally, before I start a book, I have a sense of how it will end, but in this case, all I had was the notion for a long first act that I couldn't wait to put on paper. I have seldom felt more creative excitement than when I wrote those initial hundred pages. Then I took a long breath and realized that Drew and I were going to discover the strange new outside world together.

What I'm about to tell you may seem as strange as my claim that characters speak to me. In this case, it was the *story*, not a character, that spoke to me. Yes, I know that reinforces the clinical psychologist's suspicions about my faulty grasp of reality, but actually the process is a lot less weird than it sounds. Many actors, if asked to state their primary goal, will answer something like, "To serve the story." I give similar advice to my writing students. "Listen to the story. Open yourself to it. Let it tell you what it wants to do."

With *The Fraternity of the Stone,* I literally did that. At the end of each day's writing session, I shut off my word processor and gave my imagination a rest. But truly a writer's imagination never rests. It just goes off-line for a while, and when it comes back, the writer discovers that the imagination's been working all along. Each morning, I looked at my keyboard, wondering what was going to happen next, and all I needed to do was pretend that the story had a personality and that I could speak to it, asking, "Where do you want to go now?"

Inevitably an answer came to me. As Drew made his way to Boston and Manhattan and the rock-climbing area I called Satan's Horn, I didn't feel that I created those scenes as much as I followed Drew while the story guided both of us. Somewhere along the line, the organization I called the Fraternity of the Stone announced itself, and the theme of the connection between religion and violence controlled the book. Using a complex form of role playing, I felt like Drew when he discovered that he was in a totally dark room, using all his senses to learn about the unseen person across from him. The story emerged in that fashion, from darkness to shadows to light. If I stood still and waited, the story came to me.

That scene in the totally dark room acquired a reputation as an innovative set piece in thriller literature. But it wasn't the only element that made the book distinctive. *The Fraternity of the Stone* pioneered a genre that now seems ubiquitous—the religious thriller, the most well-known examples of which are Dan Brown's *Angels & Demons* and *The Da Vinci Code*. To the best of my knowledge, it's the first novel that features Opus Dei, the Catholic Church's secretive lay organization, which I call the intelligence branch of the Vatican.

Further, although *The Fraternity of the Stone* was published in 1985, its discussion of terrorism feels extremely contemporary. It may be the first novel to identify 1966 as the year that modern terrorism was created. As *Fraternity* makes clear, that was when Fidel Castro invited revolutionaries from eighty-two countries to come to Cuba for an intensive guerrilla-warfare training session, known as the Tricontinental Conference. In turn, Muammar Qaddafi organized similar deadly training schools in Libya, later incarnations of which now train Muslim zealots in remote areas of Afghanistan and Pakistan.

"How many Gods can there be?" Drew asks a religious assassin in a speech that feels as if it were written today and not several decades ago. "The Ayatollah thinks his god is the one and only. The Hindus think theirs is. The Buddhists. The Jews. The Muslims. The Catholics. The Protestants. God sure gets around. And He sure seems to want a lot of killing. How many millions have died for Him? You say history's the record of God's will? To me, it's an uninterrupted sequence of holy wars. And each side was absolutely certain it was right. Totally confident that if they died for their faith, they saved their souls. . . . Madness. Religion? Save us from the sins we commit in the name of religion."

The Fraternity of the Stone is the middle novel in what came to be known as *The Brotherhood of the Rose* series. I say "came to be known" because when I wrote it, I had no idea that it was part of a group. *Fraternity*'s plot and characters are independent of *The Brotherhood of the Rose,* after all, and yet as I explained, *Fraternity* does have a relationship to that prior novel because Drew was inspired as a replacement for Chris, the character I did my best not to kill.

Shortly after *Fraternity* was published, I went for a five-mile jog, and again Saul spoke from a corner of my imagination. But this time, he wasn't alone. Drew was with him.

"Bring the brotherhood back," Saul told me.

"Can't," my imagination answered. "Chris is dead."

"But *I'm* not," Drew reminded me. "I'm a substitute for him. Bring Saul and me together. When he meets me, he'll feel that Chris has rejoined him."

Thus, I was moved to start *The League of Night and Fog,* in which Saul finds a new "brother." That subsequent novel turned out to be a rarity—a double sequel that was also the conclusion of a trilogy. It wouldn't have happened if I hadn't listened.

DAVID MORRELL holds a Ph.D. from the Pennsylvania State University and for many years was a professor of American literature at the University of Iowa. His numerous *New York Times* bestselling novels include *The League of Night and Fog* in which the main characters of *The Brotherhood of the Rose* and *The Fraternity of the Stone* join forces in a double sequel that ends the Brotherhood trilogy. Co-founder of the International Thriller Writers organization, Morrell is considered by many to be the father of the modern action novel. He resides in Santa Fe, New Mexico, with his wife, Donna. His website is www.davidmorrell.net.

Printed in the United States
by Baker & Taylor Publisher Services